Troublesome CREEK

JAN WATSON

Troublesome
CREEK

Tyndale House Publishers, Inc., Wheaton, Illinois

C

Visit Tyndale's exciting Web site at www.tyndale.com

TYNDALE is a registered trademark of Tyndale House Publishers, Inc.

Tyndale's quill logo is a trademark of Tyndale House Publishers, Inc.

Troublesome Creek

Copyright © 2005 by Jan Watson. All rights reserved.

Cover photo copyright © by Getty Images. All rights reserved.

Cover photo of woman copyright © by Getty Images. All rights reserved.

Author photo copyright © 2005 byBrenda Metzler/Hart Studio. All rights reserved.

Designed by Jessie McGrath

Scripture quotations are taken from the *Holy Bible,* King James Version.

Library of Congress Cataloging-in-Publication Data

Watson, Jan.
  Troublesome Creek / Jan Watson.
    p. cm.
  ISBN-13: 978-1-4143-0447-2 (pbk.)
  ISBN-10: 1-4143-0447-1 (pbk.)
  1. Rural families–Fiction. 2. Kentucky–Fiction. I. Title.
  PS3623.A8724T76 2005
  813'.6–dc22   2005017422

Printed in the United States of America

11 10 09 08 07 06 05
 7   6   5   4   3   2   1

For my son Stephen C. Watson.

Truly, I could not have written this without your help.

And to the memory of my husband,

Charles C. Watson (1940–2005). You were precious to me.

❧ FOREWORD ❧

Jan Watson's *Troublesome Creek* rose quickly to number one from more than 280 submissions in our Christian Writers Guild First Novel contest for unpublished authors. Having just completed my part in the editing of this stellar work, I'm reminded anew what a masterpiece Jan has wrought.

This is a settle-in-and-savor type of a read, set in the exotic mountains of the South and evoking a period decades ago. With rich texture and detail and unforgettable characters that lodge themselves in your heart, Jan transports us to a world without modern convenience where we live with the people of the land.

Danger, tragedy, faith, romance—it's all here in spades.

Though I was working on it, still I found it a great, great read and know you're in for a treat. I look forward to seeing more from this talented author.

Prepare to be captured by the denizens of *Troublesome Creek*. . . .

Jerry B. Jenkins

❦ ACKNOWLEDGMENTS ❧

Lord, dost Thou show a cornerstone for us to build our hopes upon,
That the fair edifice may rise sublime in light beyond the skies?
—"Cornerstone" by Philip Doddridge (1702–1751)

I wish to acknowledge the many people, these mentioned and those behind the scenes, who helped in the building of this book. My deepest gratitude to Jerry B. Jenkins. Your generous offering of time and talent humbles me. ✳ Mark Taylor, Ron Beers, Becky Nesbitt, and Jan Stob at Tyndale House. You've given me a precious gift and I appreciate you. ✳ My editors, Anne Goldsmith and Lorie Popp. You were always patient and kind. Thanks for seeing me through. ✳ Rick Anderson and all the folks at the Christian Writers Guild. You've become family. ✳ My amazing-grace place, Southern Acres Christian Church. You renew my spirit. ✳ My first readers: Julie Ashcraft, Terry Taylor, and Peggy Miller. Your belief in this book sustained me. ✳ Bob Taylor for giving me the character of Willy. ✳ Fellow writers from the Grassroots Writers Group. You are a blessing in my life. ✳ Friends and coworkers on the mother-baby unit at Central Baptist Hospital. Thanks for caring. ✳ The staff of 108B at Oakwood in Somerset, Kentucky. Your tender care of my son Drew gives me peace of mind. ✳ My dear children: Stephen, Charles, and Catherine Prather Watson. What would I do without you? Your encouragement keeps me going. ✳ And always to Drew. You teach me daily to live in the valley with grace and dignity.

CHAPTER I

1881

"Girl! You'd better get to the house. If your mam catches you in that creek again she'll skin you alive!"

Copper Brown jumped. The jar slicked through her hands and fell into the swiftly flowing water of Troublesome Creek. "Caught again," she muttered under her breath. "I'm sorry, Daddy. I'll be home directly."

"You'd best be!" he boomed from the ridge above.

She shaded her eyes from the hot summer sun and saw him stride away, his tall shadow bumping along behind. She should have seined farther upstream where the willows wept upon the bank, the perfect hiding place; her father wouldn't have found her.

Then again, she shouldn't have left the breakfast dishes

soaking in the pan, and she should have scrubbed the floor like she was supposed to, but the day had called to her from beyond the kitchen door and she couldn't resist. Without a moment's thought to Mam's wrath she was out the door and into the creek, assuming that Mam was too busy ironing to notice her missing anyway.

Now, from her perch on the footbridge, she watched a dozen bug-eyed tadpoles dart out of the canning jar and into the riffle beneath her dangling feet. The creek was as clear as the window glass she'd polished just this morning. She dipped her big toe in the cool water. A minnow-sized, muddy-green newt slid out from under a ledge and cautiously nibbled the offering then flitted away, disappointed.

Copper had meant to keep the tadpoles on her windowsill and watch as they turned into long-legged jumpers. Last spring she'd garnered eight frogs from her collections. The secret was creek water. You couldn't use well water or water from the rain barrel: only creek water, adding a little fresh each day. It had been such fun to watch the tadpoles develop—fun until they got loose and hopped all over Mam's clean kitchen. Copper liked to have never heard the end of the one that got in the lard bucket. Mam screamed and dashed at the poor thing with a broom until it jumped out the door and slid right off the porch. Copper hoped he made it back to the creek. Maybe these were some of his children. . . .

It seemed to Copper that everything fun last year was just confusing now. She used to play in the creek every day, once she finished her chores. It was her favorite place. But things had changed somehow, and she didn't know why. It seemed Mam was always watching her, just like the red-tailed hawk circling the chicken yard, ever vigilant. "Laura Grace, act like a lady" was her constant refrain. Copper didn't like being called such a stuffy name. It asked too much somehow, like she was supposed to act all straitlaced and buttoned-up.

Mam didn't understand that a lady was the last thing Copper wanted to be. Ladies didn't have any fun. Ladies wore their hair up and never lost their ribbons. They wore confining under-garments and shoes. Shoes even in the summertime!

Daddy was on her side, though. She'd been about to open the screen door just yesterday, coming in with a basket of sun-dried laundry on her hip, when she heard him tell Mam that Copper did not need to grow up so fast, that Mam was too strict with her. But then, as she snuck a peek through the fly-specked screen, she also heard Mam's stern reply: "Will Brown—" she'd shaken her long-handled, wooden spoon in his frowning face— "my sister was a lady, and if it takes the last breath in my body, I will raise her daughter to be a lady too."

Copper nearly dropped her basket. She'd learned not to ask about her long-dead natural mother, because when she did Mam got all pinch-faced and turned away, and Daddy looked funny and talked about something else. Most times she didn't even remember that Mam was not her real mother, for she was the only one Copper had ever known.

She gathered her supplies—a dented tin dipper, three green Mason jars, four zinc lids she'd punched air holes in, and the seine she had fashioned from an old window screen—then placed them in the woven willow basket Mam had given her for her fif-teenth birthday a few months before. She grabbed a dead sycamore limb, snagged the jar she'd dropped in the creek, and dragged it to the bank. She dried it with the hem of her faded feed-sack dress, nearly dropping it again when two little boys suddenly appeared in front of her.

Usually she heard the five-year-old twins well before she saw them, for they were rarely quiet. If they weren't talking or singing they were whistling, a trick Copper was sorry she had encouraged them to learn. It wouldn't be so bad if either of them could actually pucker up to a tune, but generally they just made loud blowing noises. Then it was, "Sissy, Sissy, we forgot how to whistle. Show us again."

And that's another thing: I've got way too many names. The boys call me Sissy; Mam calls me Laura Grace; Daddy calls me Copper; and John Pelfrey calls me Pest. . . . How could anyone keep it all straight?

"Guess what, Sissy," Willy demanded, right in her face. "We tracked you here! We're better'n Mr. Lincoln's soldiers. Don't you reckon so?"

"I expect Mr. Lincoln would have been in a heap of trouble if he'd had you two jabbering jays in his army," she replied, grinning.

"Mam's getting mad, Sissy," Willy said, his smile turned upside down.

"Yeah, Mam's getting real mad," Daniel echoed, pulling his face into a frown, trying to match his brother's. "She sent us to find you and bring you home lickety-split. An' I think Daddy's gone to cut a switch."

She hung her basket on her arm. "Then we'd best get started, boys."

"But I don't want Daddy to whip you." Daniel grabbed a

fistful of Copper's dress as tears welled up in his big green eyes. "Let's just stay here tonight."

"Yeah, great idea!" Willy agreed. "We can make camp just like soldiers, and we'll have a bonfire and go hunting. Sissy, you can fry us up some squirrel for supper. But first we'll have to go see if Daddy will let us have his gun."

Daniel looked thoughtful. "We could get the slingshot, Willy."

"Boy howdy, Daniel," Willy responded as he hitched up his britches. "Don't you know soldiers don't use slingshots?"

Copper pulled both little boys into an embrace. "Boys, you know you're way too young to use the gun or the slingshot. We'll make camp another time. Right now it's time for me to face the music."

"Music? We sure like music. Don't we, Daniel? Let's go see if Daddy will play his fiddle after supper."

"Oh yeah," Daniel replied, "then Mam will forget to be mad at Sissy. Hey, Willy! Race you to the barn. . . . Last one in's a rotten egg!"

Copper slowly trailed them, wondering if this whipping would be like all the others. And wondering too why Mam was so hard on her all of a sudden.

⊹

Will Brown folded his muscular arms and leaned against the rough wooden siding of the barn. A fit of coughing had left him suddenly tired. He stirred the dust at his feet with the switch he'd cut to please his wife. She and his daughter were always at odds lately. He knew Grace was a good wife and a good mother to Copper and the twins, but she was way too strict, bent on citifying country children. It was just her way. Once a schoolmarm always a schoolmarm.

Will himself was not much of a disciplinarian. He dreaded the whipping Grace deemed appropriate punishment for Copper's misdeed. His problem was that he didn't want to see his little girl grow up. He had been shocked when Grace told him of Copper's recent physical development, shocked even more to learn of her desire to send Copper away to boarding school.

"Oh, Will," she'd pleaded the day before. "Do you want Laura Grace to live here forever? Do you want her to marry some coal miner and spend the rest of her life scrubbing floors and having babies?"

He still lamented his stern reply. "Would that be so terrible, Grace?" He had caught her arms in his calloused hands and pulled her to him so he could look into her eyes. "Do you regret the day I took you away from the life you so want for Copper and made you a coal miner's wife?"

She had turned away, and he'd seen her back stiffen. She'd fiddled in her apron pocket for the starched and ironed handkerchief she always kept there. He could tell she was dabbing tears.

He'd touched her shoulder. "Ah, Grace, I'm sorry. Don't cry."

She'd folded and refolded the handkerchief. "I just want Laura Grace to get the education I can't give her here. How can you deny her that?"

How indeed? he wondered now on this hot, humid day as he waited for his daughter. *How indeed?*

Over the crest of a hill, two dust devils raced toward him, whirling this way and that until the minitornadoes became instead his mischievous sons.

"Whoa, boys." Will laughed as he caught one twin under each arm and let them dangle there. "You'll scare Molly into making buttermilk. You'll make the hens lay green eggs. Why, with all your noise, you'll turn Paw-paw into a cat."

Wiggling, Willy cried out, "Let us down, Daddy. Let us down! Come on, Daniel. Let's go find Paw-paw and see if he can meow."

As the boys tore around the side of the barn to find the dog, Will spied his daughter coming slowly over the wooded ridge that separated their cabin from the creek. Her hair flared as bright as fire in the sunlight. His heart caught. Grace was right–Copper was growing up.

"Hello, Daddy," she said. "I'm here to claim my punishment."

"Copper, you know Mam just wants what's best for you. You need to be more responsible. Let's get this over with."

Copper turned her back to her father. Her shoulders shook.

"Be quiet," he cautioned as he raised the supple willow branch over his head. "It wouldn't do for your mother to hear you laughing." Forcefully, he brought the switch down once, twice, and then again–three smacks to the barn door, then one more for good measure.

"Do you want me to cry?" Copper teased.

"No, I want you to stay out of the creek. Now go apologize to your mother."

Will watched his daughter cross the barnyard and step up onto the porch. The main part of the cabin was the original log structure built by his grandfather for his young family on their arrival from Maryland in the late 1700s. Many a night of Will's young life was spent listening to his father tell of the arduous journey through the Cumberland Gap and the hardship endured by his grandparents' homesteading the dark and bloody ground of Kentucky.

His ancestors were of English, Scotch, and Irish descent—a stoic, courageous, dark-humored bunch of renegades seeking freedom from the tyranny of their governments. They didn't want or need much—a rough-hewn cabin, a pipe of homegrown tobacco, sweet clean water. Rather, they sought a place of tolerance, where folks not unlike themselves could worship unopposed and live as they chose, unfettered by the rules of other men. They found that place on the banks of the creek they called Troublesome for its unpredictable nature.

Will had done well with the land inherited from his father. She centered him, helping him to focus his energy on the needs of his growing family. He rarely thought of that other time, that other wife, unless Grace herself caused him to. She seemed to cling to the memories of her sister, while he just wanted to forget. He had loved Julie fiercely, but the pain of her untimely death made him disremember the joyous times he had had with her.

Unbidden, his mind sought recollections that caused his gut to clench and a heaviness to settle in his heart. While a rapidly forming storm stirred the humid air and a sudden gust of wind stripped leaves from the sugar maple, Will's attention drifted. Memories long stifled became as real as the warm rain that dampened his shirt.

As he stepped into the shelter of the barn, he closed his eyes and gave in to what he could no longer keep at bay. Julie came to him then, as young and beautiful as ever. His mind's eye reflected

on the first time he ever saw her, a yellow-haired girl with flashing eyes who had captured his heart with a rooster's crow. *Julie
. . . Julie . . . Julie.* The August heat faded away. Twenty years dis-
solved as if they had never been, and Will was transported to a
time gone by. A smile tugged at the corners of his mouth as he
became the man he used to be. . . .

CHAPTER 2

Young Will Brown met his intended, Julia Anne Taylor, in the city of Lexington, a much gentler clime than his mountain home. Named for the first glorious blow struck for independence, the Battle of Lexington, the city was not quite Southern, but certainly not Northern. Established on the Town Fork of Elkhorn Creek, Lexington proudly sported numerous churches and public buildings, paved streets, and lush green landscaping. The city most believed to be the handsomest in Kentucky never failed to impress.

Will had kin in town, his mother's second cousin Sarah, and he'd come to Lexington that fall to stay with her family during court days, a time for bartering and selling goods. The streets, lined with booths and wagons from which people displayed their wares, had a festive air. Will was an excellent hunter and trapper and brought hides to trade as well as tins of molasses and the occasional hound puppy.

One evening he accompanied Sarah to a hymn sing at the Baptist church down the street from her house. The big brick building had floor-to-ceiling windows made of brightly colored pieces of glass held together with what looked like lines of lead. Each of the eight windows told a different story. Will wondered who had made such beautiful things. He thought he'd like to put one of those windows in his church at home, maybe like the one where Jesus knelt in the garden. That would be something to see. He'd have to study on it some more.

He hung back as Sarah made her way to a front pew in the crowded sanctuary. He had never been to a church like this before. It seemed everyone was dressed like a king. At home you didn't have to wear finery to praise the Lord. He felt uncharacteristically shy, his homespun shirt not quite right, his overalls too short, his rough leather boots unpolished. He took a seat against the wall in the last row, folding his long arms across his chest and tucking his feet under the bench, trying to make his tall frame as inconspicuous as possible. He was sorry he'd let Sarah talk him into coming.

He took a hymnal from the wooden rack in front of his knees and stood when the song leader addressed the congregation. He wasn't used to singing from books. At home everybody knew the words. Sometimes they'd be singing up a storm on one song when someone would start midverse on another. Then they'd all sing that one 'til they got tired or the preacher started to preach. His favorite hymn had eleven verses. He wondered if they'd sing it: "Before the sun, the font of light, a single round had run; God's church was present in His sight, as chosen in His Son."

"Bringing in the Sheaves," he heard instead. He fumbled through the pages to find the proper place.

Two young men on one side of him looked his way and laughed, poking each other in the ribs. "Hillbilly," one said under his breath. "Won't do you any good to hold a songbook when you don't know how to read."

The pianist pounded away. "'Bringing in the sheaves, bringing in the sheaves,'" rang through the sanctuary, nearly but not quite, drowning out the other feller's stage-whispered taunt.

"Hey, Slick, why don't you crawl back up the hollow you came from? We don't need your kind here."

Will's temper flared. Nobody talked to him that-a-way. Back home he wouldn't put up with bullies. About two years before, Calvin Huff had pushed him just one time too many and come up with a mouthful of mud. Will didn't like to fight, but he could. His big hands shook as he set the hymnal back in the rack. He thought about the knife in his pocket. He could gut a buck with that knife quick as any man. Maybe he'd take it out just to scare the loudmouths. He could tell by their doughy hands they'd never used a knife.

"'We shall come rejoicing,'" the song continued, "'bringing in the sheaves.'"

And he remembered where he was. No call for his temper. No call to bring disrespect to the Lord in His own house. He kept his eyes straight ahead. He couldn't bring himself to take the songbook back out of the rack, but he'd stay there and wait out the service.

"You deaf as well as dumb?" the first one started in again.

"You hush up, Oscar Thornton," a quiet voice said. At the end of the pew a yellow-haired girl near his age pushed her way past the fellows to his other side. "Here," she said, handing Will her songbook. "You can turn the pages for me."

Will was struck dumb. He couldn't get his tongue unstuck from the roof of his mouth. The girl was the prettiest thing he had ever seen. Prettier even than the top of Pine Mountain when the sun first came up—prettier than a rainbow trout flashing on the end of a line. She even smelled pretty.

It was bad enough before she started to sing, but when she did, his knees got weak. Surely, the angels' chorus wouldn't sound this good.

He was sorry when the service ended. He couldn't get his long legs untangled fast enough, and so she was out the door, his tormentors in hot pursuit, well before he was. Once outside he eyed the crowd, not sure what he'd do if he did see her. She was too fine for the likes of him—like a rare mountain canary in a raucous blue jay's nest.

Will was about to give up and head out to Sarah's house when there she was right in front of him. He opened his mouth, but nothing came out.

"You may walk me home," she said.

Then the one she called Oscar staked his claim. "Hold on just a minute," he said. "You told me at Sunday school this morning that *I* could take you home tonight."

"That was before I learned that you have no manners, Oscar Thornton."

"Come on, Julie Anne."

"Apologize," she replied.

He stuck his hand out to Will. "Sorry. No hard feelings?"

Will squeezed until he saw Oscar flinch. Apology or not, Will was the one to escort Julie Anne.

They walked a piece before she spoke again. "Well, can you talk?"

He opened his mouth and what came out sounded like a screen door rusted upon its hinges after a long wet spell. He was glad they were in the shadows between gaslights because her tinkling laugh brought the blood rushing to his face. He'd never felt so embarrassed. He wished he was anywhere but standing here with her.

She clapped her little hands together. "Do it again," she begged. "Do it again."

And so he did; then he did it once more just to please her.

"I can do a rooster." She tucked her hands under her arms, flapped her elbows, and crowed loud enough to raise Lazarus.

Before he knew it, he was laughing with her, and much too soon she was taking her leave.

"We have to stop here," she said. "I don't want my sister to know you walked me home. I'm only allowed to walk alone to church—not socialize." She glanced up at him, and her face looked so sad he felt his heart reach out to her. "But," she continued, "I get so lonely sometimes . . . if I don't talk to someone I might burst."

They stood at the edge of a well-trimmed lawn. A winding brick path led to a two-story house fronted by white columns. The porch lights were on, but the windows were dark and uninviting.

"We don't talk much in my house, for Father is ill and my sister, Grace, does not want him disturbed." She touched his arm. "Come to revival again tomorrow night, and save me a seat."

Then she was gone, and he realized he'd never said a word.

And so, the romance of Julie and Will began with the innocent flirtation of youth. Will was smitten. He couldn't seem to leave her so he lay over in Lexington for several weeks, the longest he'd ever been away from the mountains. He knew his friend Daniel would see to things for him.

Julie told him about the death of her mother from pneumonia the year before. She said her father had taken to his bed, and her older sister didn't allow talking above a whisper in the house. Grace was twenty-eight, ten years Julie's senior. Julie said Grace taught music and deportment at the same finishing school Julie had just graduated from. When her sister was working, Julie sat in her father's darkened room and read to him. But she didn't think he heard.

Will was in that house only once, on the night he was to return to the mountains. Will and Julie had met after dark in their trysting spot in the side yard by the apple tree. Julie still didn't want her sister to find out. She sat in a rope swing, and he pushed her ever higher. She started to laugh, then caught herself and cried instead, but quietly with little choking sounds. He caught the swing, and she turned in his arms and he kissed her.

"Please," she begged just like the first time they'd met, "do it again."

Their nest under the tree smelled of summer apples and fallen leaves. The warm autumn night lay soft as a blanket upon their young bodies. He tried to stop. He was a farm boy; he knew where their passion might take them, but she was so beautiful . . . and then it was too late.

Afterward she pulled him along behind her into the kitchen. Funny, it was in the cellar, underneath the house. She said the cook and the other servants wouldn't be about at that hour. She wanted him to sit with her at the table. She wanted to feed him. He guessed she wanted to play house.

She got out bread and cheese and poured goblets of cider. "Please don't leave me," she said.

He choked down a little piece of cheese and a crust of dry bread. "Now, Julie, we already talked about this. I'll be back come spring."

"But you can't just go! Not now. Not after–" She jumped up from the table and started sobbing.

He went to her and gathered her in his arms. He kissed her tear-streaked face with tender longing kisses. "Honey, I'm so sorry. I shouldn't have let that happen."

"But what will I do without you?" She twisted his shirtfront in her hands and leaned against his chest. "Please, please don't leave me."

Her pleading broke his heart, but there were things he had to do at home. He had led her into sin. He had to make it right. "I'll be back. I promise you I will. I want to meet your sister and ask your father for your hand. We'll wed, and then I'll take you home with me."

And so he left that very same night, saddling his horse in the dark, his heart in turmoil from a newfound love and a shame so stalwart it lodged in his soul like a living thing. How could he have taken something so pure and beautiful and tarnished it for his own selfish need? He would never forgive himself. The memory of Julie's tears was fresh as he guided his mount eastward back to Troublesome Creek.

Before Will knew it, the guilt of autumn had turned into the chilly remorse of winter. Deep snows alternated with ice storms and kept him quarantined for a long spell. Julie's tear-streaked face haunted his dreams, and every time the rooster crowed he remembered the night they'd met, and his heart seized with longing. He kept a few leaves from the apple tree in her side yard in his pocket until one day he reached for them and felt nothing but the dust of his promise to her.

He didn't wait for the spring thaw but led his horse down the treacherous mountain, then rode out across the rolling hills toward Lexington.

At last he stood on Julie's front porch, his heart slamming in his chest. Will wore the new leather jacket he'd sewn from hides he'd cured himself. He'd shined his boots with stove blacking. He was fresh from the barber, and in his hand a bouquet of roses trembled, an offering for Julie's sister, Grace. He knocked and knocked.

Finally the door opened. An older, bespectacled version of Julie stood there, except for the hair. Julie's was the color of the center of a daisy, but Grace's was bright red and sprang out around her face in spite of her trying to slick it behind her ears.

"I-I'm Will Brown," he stammered. "I've come to marry Julie." He thrust the flowers toward her. "These here are for you."

"I know who you are," she said, her voice as hard as the ice on the mountain he'd slid down to get here. "Don't you think every gossip in town told me about your little summer romance with my sister?" She flung the flowers across the porch. "Go away. I've got trouble enough without your sort coming around."

Grace started back through the door but paused and turned toward him. Her green eyes flashed like those of the wildcat he'd once cornered in the henhouse. "Mind my words," she hissed. "Or I'll have the law on you."

Grace Taylor stepped inside and leaned against the closed door. What was she to do? Everything had gone wrong since her mother's death. Life had been so good, so full of God's blessings. Grace taught music and deportment at the Finishing School for Young Ladies, a vocation she loved. She'd had a suitor and plans to marry, but she'd given up everything to care for her father and her sister, and this was the thanks she got? Julie sneaking around like a thief in the night with an ill-dressed young man who probably couldn't even read.

The only thing that kept her going during this time of despair were the letters she received from Philadelphia, letters from her closest friend Millicent Dunaway. Millicent had married well, moved to Pennsylvania and, along with her husband, David, established a boarding school for children of the wealthy. What joy it must be to have a life like Millicent's.

She shook her head to think of that man standing on her doorstep with his flowers. His presence threatened the careful plans she'd laid to save her sister. She wouldn't let him ruin Julie's life. If he came back, she'd send for the sheriff. A few days in jail would send him packing. Nobody would be the wiser about her sister's predicament if he stayed away.

She paused and stared at the hall mirror. A red-haired reflection looked back at her. She leaned closer. Were those crow's feet at the corners of her eyes? Was that a strand of gray springing like a corkscrew from her head? What had happened to the Grace she wanted to be? Wasn't she once as vibrant as Julie? Didn't she have her share of suitors?

Grace hadn't slept a night through since her father had taken to his bed. A night nurse was out of the question, for it was her duty to care for him. Her sacrifice was taking its toll, but tired as she was, she'd have to be extra vigilant until she was sure Will Brown had slunk back to the mountains.

She spotted a film of dust on the table in the front hall. She'd have to speak to the housekeeper. And she needed to talk with the cook. They had to come up with something her father would eat. She smoothed the front of her dress and adjusted her spectacles. She felt better. There was work to do.

Will stood under the apple tree that night for hours, just waiting. A cold wind whipped around him. He wished he'd brought something warmer than the jacket that had failed to impress Julie's sister.

But finally, toward morning, his longing brought Julie to him. She carried a pillowcase stuffed with necessities. When he pulled her up behind him on the horse, the swell of her belly pressed against his back. He didn't stop to question her then but reined in the horse after they'd gone far enough to escape her wild-eyed sister, tethered the animal in a grove of trees, made camp, and lit a fire.

He sat beside her and held his hands out to the fire. "Do you have something to tell me?" he asked.

She wouldn't look at him, but he heard the anguish in her voice. "Will, I'm sorry."

"Julie, honey, tell me."

Loud, wailing sobs broke the stillness of the night. "Oh," she cried. "Oh, please don't take me back. I don't care if you don't want me anymore, but take me someplace safe, somewhere I can raise my baby." She jumped up from her place by the fire and ran a short distance before he caught her and lifted her face to his own.

"What have I done to you?" he said.

She leaned against him, no longer crying. "I was so afraid, Will. Grace said you wouldn't come back and that you wouldn't want me if you did. She planned to send me to a home where they would keep my baby." Her long, shuddering sigh spoke to his heart of her weeks of fear and suffering, but she looked at him directly as she asked, "Am I just damaged goods to you now? Do you hate me?"

The fire popped and crackled its song of warmth as he circled her with his arms. He would have laughed had he not been afraid of hurting her feelings, making light of her fears. "Julie," he said, "I'm so sorry for what I've caused, but it was all out of love. I can't fault your sister for her anger, but nobody is taking our baby."

"She wouldn't let me leave the house since . . . since she found out. She stopped going out to teach, and I had to stay upstairs . . . I couldn't even see Father."

"Honey, how did you know I'd come? How did you know to meet me by the apple tree?"

"I believed your promise." She settled into his embrace. "I've been watching from an upstairs window for weeks. I prayed you'd come before Grace sent me away."

He made her a pallet from the blanket roll he carried on the back of his saddle, but she wouldn't leave his side, just sat snuggled up beside him as if he were her savior instead of the man who'd caused such pain. She didn't want to talk anymore, and as the minutes passed he could hear her even breathing as she slept. She seemed fragile as a skim of ice on the creek to him, like one wrong move might make her shatter.

He couldn't sleep, which was just as well, because he needed the whole night to pray for guidance and forgiveness.

Toward morning he felt at peace, and he dared move his arm from around her. "Julie, honey, wake up. We need to get going."

She woke with a start, then stood and stretched. "You're still here," she said, sounding genuinely surprised.

"I'll never leave you again," he said, his promise as good as any proposal on bended knee. "We'll wed as soon as we get home. Troublesome Creek is as good a place to raise a young'un as you'll ever find."

She stood in front of the dying fire as the sun began its climb. Tucking her hands underneath her arms, she flapped her elbows and belted out a loud crow of joy and triumph.

He thought he'd never stop laughing as he fixed them a bite of breakfast and then broke camp. And as far as he could tell, Julie never looked back during the long journey.

Before the sun set on the day they arrived in Troublesome Creek, the young sweethearts were married by Will's uncle in the church in the shadow of the mountains. Will's kin and friends accepted Julie and her condition with open arms.

The couple set up housekeeping in the cabin Will's father had left him, within walking distance across Troublesome from Will's friend Daniel and his wife, Emilee. Emilee became Julie's teacher and complimented Will on marrying such an avid pupil, so eager to learn homemaking skills. After choking down many skillets of burned corn bread, dozens of plates of half-raw fried potatoes, and too-many-to-count, flat-as-a-pancake biscuits, Will could have kissed Emilee when his bride finally set an edible meal on their wobbly kitchen table.

Their baby boy was stillborn on a warm spring morning. Two daughters followed during the next few years—one born too early and one who died in her father's arms after a time of struggle. Her little heart was too weak to give her color. Three small graves, all in a row, rested at the foot of Will's parents' plot in the Brown family section of the cemetery.

Despite their tragedies, Will and Julie's passion never wavered. Julie obviously loved her new home and the mountain people. And though usually wary of strangers and obsessively clannish, the folks on Troublesome Creek loved her right back.

Sunday morning became their favorite time. Will and Julie would get up early and carry mugs of strong black coffee outside, regardless of the weather. Will added a fine tin roof to cover the porch, and they would sit in matching rockers with their coffee to watch the sun come up or the rain come down. Some mornings Julie was already out there when he rose, as if she couldn't get enough of their mountain paradise.

When Will had finished his first cup, he'd refill hers and then bring out the Bible that had belonged to his father and read to her. Julie told him she'd gone to church every Sunday, but the Scripture never came to life for her until she heard it from his rich baritone.

"Will," she'd said one morning after he read, "you make me feel as if I can just wrap God's Word around me and wear it like a suit of clothes."

One Sunday morning it was pouring. The rain ran off the corners of the roof in little rivers and splashed like a waterfall down the stone steps that led to the yard. A cool wind blew the damp their way, so he covered them with the quilt from their bed and read to her from their cozy tent.

The sweet smell of her breath mixed with the heady aroma of coffee that day as he read from Isaiah. "'Fear not: for I have redeemed thee, I have called thee by thy name; thou art mine. When thou passest through the waters, I will be with thee; and through the rivers, they shall not overflow thee: when thou walkest through the fire, thou shalt not be burned; neither shall the flame kindle upon thee.'"

Nearly every Sunday she requested that Scripture again. She said it was her favorite.

Over the years Julie received many packages from Grace. Will would carry them in from the post office and watch Julie open lavender-scented toilet water, luxurious silk hair ribbons, expensive fabrics, and fashionable dress patterns. Julie never sewed dresses from those patterns though. Instead, Emilee helped her make the easy-fitting print shirtwaists and skirts favored by the women who lived on Troublesome Creek. As far as Will knew, every gift Grace had sent was tucked away in a trunk under their bed.

Will carried their letters back and forth for years—Julie's to the post office and Grace's back to Julie. He never asked her what was in those letters, but he often wondered if Grace was softening toward him. When their father finally died after a long, lingering illness, Julie was pregnant again so Will could not take her to the funeral or to visit her sister. Julie cried herself to sleep many nights. He knew her tears were filled with longing to see her sister. He swallowed his pride and wrote to Grace himself, begging her to come to Troublesome Creek to stay for a while with Julie. He waited and waited for her reply.

One day, toward the end of Julie's fourth confinement, a fine, four-wheeled, leather-topped surrey was delivered to their door. Julie was delighted. She told Will it had been her father's Sunday carriage. Inside, fastened to the horsehair seat, was Grace's latest missive: *"Come home, both of you. Come home and bring the baby."*

That, of course, was impossible, for the mountains were in Will's blood. He could not have lived any other place, and Julie could not live without her Will.

The baby had been easily born considering Julie's small stature. Will had paced the yard with his best friend, Daniel, until he'd nearly worn it down to bedrock, he was so anxious. Daniel's wife, Emilee, and Granny Pelfrey attended Julie.

When the cabin door opened, Will turned, hoping for good news.

Emilee handed her own squalling six-month-old son to his father. "Take him, Daniel. He cain't be hungry. He nursed just an hour ago. I swan, he's going to be as big an eater as his pa." With her hand on the door latch, she flashed a reassuring smile. "Don't look so worried, Will. It's near over."

A scream rent the air, and she rushed back inside.

Will hastened to follow but was restrained by Daniel. "My friend, birthing is women's work. Best leave them alone with it. You know Granny will take good care of Julie."

True, Will's wife could not have been in better hands. Granny Pelfrey was Daniel's grandmother, and she lived with Daniel and his family. Stooped from the thinning of her bones, hands gnarled from rheumatism, her eyesight fading, she was still the best baby catcher on Troublesome Creek. Truth be told, she was the best for a hundred miles in any direction. The first thought that crossed the mind of a newly carrying woman was, *I've got to talk to Granny.* Chances were better than good that Granny's hands had also guided that woman into the world.

Years of midwifery had honed her skill, but she was a natural healer with a sixth sense when it came to the unborn. She could cast one look at a pregnant belly and discern the sex of the baby. She would watch the woman's waddling, splay-legged walk and predict whether the delivery would be difficult or easy.

Granny was a little woman, not even five feet tall and eighty-seven pounds, but powerfully strong for her eighty years. Her black shoe-button eyes looked out kindly from a round face, spiderwebbed with wrinkles. She liked a good laugh, and she was most proud that she still had her teeth. A long puckered scar trailed down the right side of her face from her eyebrow to the corner of her mouth. When she was still, which was rare, you could catch her tracing that scar, rubbing it like a talisman, over and over. She kept her sparse gray hair in a long braid that she twisted and fastened to the back of her head with anything handy—a blue jay's wing feather, a broken comb, the branch from a rambling rose stripped of thorns. In daylight she kept her head covered with an old silk bonnet, but at night she took her hair down so it fanned across her pillow.

She'd been born again as a girl and baptized when the creek was so cold her daddy had to skim the ice before she waded in. She didn't believe God was just for Sundays. She saw evidence of His power and presence everywhere she cast her gaze, even in the unpredictable waters of Troublesome Creek. But most of all there was a quiet knowing deep in her heart that kept her centered in her faith.

Granny had learned the power of herbs from her mother, who had learned from her mother. Every passable morning she'd take up her walking stick and strike out up the mountain. She liked the early morning best when the first and weakest rays from the sun cut through the dense gray fog. Even the infirmity of age did nothing to dilute the pleasure she got from those treasure hunts. With her stick she'd poke among the weeds and brush looking for the familiar sprigs of comfrey, boneset, calendula, and other potent medicinal plants. She was particularly pleased if she found the greenish cluster of flowers that signaled the aromatic forked root of the ginseng plant. Ginseng fetched a pretty price at the market.

Some herbs she cultivated tenderly in her garden, much the same as she cared for the newly born. She delighted in the lavender, meadowsweet, and velvet dock that thrived with each dipper of water from her granite bucket and each gentle scratching from her child-size hoe. Her special delight was the yellow-flowered sassafras tree her husband had planted just inside the garden gate when they were first married. Most mornings the thought of a cup of tea made from its shaved root was what brought Granny back from her wandering.

Will praised the Lord for Granny Pelfrey that momentous spring evening when she laid his daughter in his arms. When the baby clutched his finger, his heart swelled to bursting. No one could have prepared him for the rush of emotion this tiny creature brought forth.

Though Emilee fussed at him to keep the baby warm, he laid her on the bed and loosened the swaddling cloths and the bellyband. He smiled to see the little legs, fat as baking hens; the surprisingly long, narrow feet; his mother's full mouth and button nose; Julie's long, fair lashes framing almond-shaped eyes; and, a source of particular pride, his own fingers in diminutive, capped with nails like the tiniest of pink shells. As he stroked her plump cheek, she turned to root at his hand.

"Give her to me, love," Julie said. "I think our daughter is ready for her first meal."

It nearly stopped his heart to see his beautiful wife holding their baby close, and he felt filled to the brim with praise to the Lord for the healthy infant they'd finally been given.

"Yes, Will," Emilee replied, "Granny and I have lots to do for Julie and your young'un. You all go on over to our place for the night, for we don't need no men in the way. You can come back in the morning."

Reluctantly, Will agreed. He knew that Granny always spent the night with her new mothers. Emilee and her babe would stay as well. Granny might need her help.

"Emilee, you come get me if you need me," he said. Then with a last kiss for Julie and a look of longing at his daughter, he went out into the night.

As soon as Will was out of the way, Granny and Emilee set about the evening's tasks. Emilee put the soiled bed linen to soak in a washtub full of cold water while Granny massaged Julie's belly. She noted the firmness of the womb and the amount and color of her flow. She assisted Julie with the baby's feeding, though the baby didn't need much guidance—she was a hearty eater.

"Nursing will cause your womb to shrink and cut your bleeding. I've heard of city women near flooding to death for lack of feeding their own young. I've heard they suckle with glass bottles. Law, the Lord's way is best, I reckon."

When the infant had her fill, Emilee bathed Julie, then took down her braids and dressed her hair. "I swan, Julie, if you don't have the purtiest hair in the county," came the familiar refrain as Emilee carefully pulled a comb through the long blonde tresses, hair soft as a little girl's but thick as a horse's mane.

CHAPTER 3

Granny watched as Julie nursed and cuddled her new baby that night.

"Granny, does she look all right? Her feet are purple."

"Julie, this 'un's not a blue baby like yore last 'un. She's full of vim and vigor–just note how hard she sucks."

"Oh, Granny, I'm so afraid. I think God is punishing me for what Will and I did before we married. That's why He took my babies back." Julie began to sob. She clutched her little daughter to her chest as tears streamed down her face.

Granny sat down on the bed. Her old, thin bones barely made a dent on the corn-shuck mattress. She took Julie's hand. "Have ye asked Him to forgive ye, Julie?"

"I have, Granny, but I don't think He heard me."

"'Behold, the Lord's hand is not shortened, that it cannot save; neither his ear heavy, that it cannot hear,'" Granny quoted from Scripture. "God forgives ye, honey. He surely does."

"How can He forgive my selfishness when I can't forgive myself?" She turned her face away. "I hurt my family," she continued, her voice a strangled cry around a clot of tears. "I left my sister to care for my father on his deathbed with never a thought for anyone but myself."

Granny put her arms around the distraught young mother. "How much do ye love this wee one, Julie?"

"Oh, you know how much. With all my heart. I'd die for her."

"What if she grows up to disappoint ye? What if she ever needs your forgiveness?"

Julie sat up straight. She gazed at the infant and stroked her rounded cheek. "She could never do anything to lessen my love for her."

"Nor can ye lessen God's love, Julie. It says in Jeremiah: 'Yea, I have loved thee with an everlasting love.' If there ain't no forgiveness in yore heart for yoreself, how could ye forgive anyone else?"

Julie squeezed the old woman's hand. Her voice came out as a strangled plea. "Pray for me, Granny."

Granny eased up off the bed and placed her hand on Julie's bowed head. "Lord, we come to Ye today to ask for the light of Yore mercy to shine upon Yore servant Julie. Fill her heart with the spirit of forgiveness and Yore never-ending eternal love. For this we petition Thee in Jesus' name. Amen."

Julie wiped her tears with the palm of one hand. She gave a

long, shuddering sigh. "Thank you, Granny. I feel at peace.
I think I can rest now, finally."

The baby sucked one finger.

"Look here," Granny said. "This little rascal wants to eat all
the time, even in her sleep. I believe this 'un's going to be a
match for Emilee's son."

Julie twirled a strand of the baby's hair around her finger.
"She has the same color of hair as my sister, the color of a sunset,
and it curls just the same. I'm going to name her for my sister:
Laura Grace. Isn't that pretty?"

Granny took the baby from Julie's arms. "Ye done yore sister
proud, I reckon. Sleep now. I'll watch out for yore wee one."

Granny commenced to rocking the baby. Emilee was already
asleep, curled around baby John on a pallet at Julie's side. A log
in the fireplace burned through and sent a shower of sparks up
the chimney as it fell against the grate. Granny snuggled the
infant under her chin, so close she could feel her milky-sweet
breath against her neck. She shifted in the chair. A sense of foreboding settled in the old woman's bones. The air around her
stirred as the wings of dark angels brushed past her—Lucifer and
his host, forever nibbling at the edges of her faith.

"Get away, Old Scratch, you sly devil." She shooed the air
with one bony hand. "There ain't no gone geese here, less'n it's
me you're after." She tightened her hold on the baby. "Ye shore
ain't taking this little soul."

Emilee barely had time to make coffee, let alone fry the fatback for
breakfast, before Will burst through the door the next morning.

"Where're my girls? Where're the beautiful blonde Julie and her fetching red-haired daughter?"

"Law, Will," Emilee replied, "you'll wake the dead. Seeing as there's only one room here, I reckon you can find them without any help."

Will grabbed her plump waist and danced her around his kitchen-dining-sitting-sleeping room. He planted a noisy kiss on her dimpled cheek. "Emilee Pelfrey, it's a good thing you're married to my closest friend, or I would sure enough have to add you to my harem."

"Save your charm for your wife, Will Brown." A blush covered Emilee's cheeks, and a grin deepened the just-kissed dimple. "Where is my Daniel this morning? He always wakes hungry as a hibernated bear."

"Don't fret. He just stopped to feed the animals."

With all the commotion, both babies began to cry.

Will scooped his daughter from the cradle. Holding the baby in his arms, he bent his long body to the bed and kissed Julie awake.

⁂

Baby John overcame the newborn's squalls with hunger-fueled wails of his own. As usual, a few quiet words from Granny brought everything back under control. She sent Will to gather eggs for their breakfast, then tended to her patient's needs. Everything was going as expected. Julie was recovering nicely.

After Julie fed the baby again, Emilee would help her out of bed. Granny didn't believe in lying in bed for weeks after childbirth. Her patients couldn't afford the luxury of lazing around–

most had more than one hungry mouth to feed. Besides, she had observed, new mothers didn't stay weak for long if they got out of bed as soon as they were steady on their feet.

She was not surprised to learn that citified women would be puny for weeks after childbirth and couldn't care for their own households. It made sense, all that pizen blood backing up in there with nowhere to go—no wonder they had so many female complaints. Granny's mothers were up and seeing to their families merely days after delivery.

Julie was up in the rocker. The men had eaten breakfast and were having a smoke on the porch. Emilee had finished scrubbing the floor with bleach water and was packing baby John on her hip, making ready to leave. Granny was pulverizing egg shells she had burned in the iron skillet to mix with a little sweet milk for Julie.

"Here, honey, drink this down," she instructed. "Don't want ye getting sickly. This is a remedy my mommy taught me. I was weak as a kitten after Daniel's daddy was borned. 'This'll keep yore strength up,' Mommy said." Granny lifted a small queer-shaped rock from the counter. "This here's Mommy's pestle. It's the onliest thing I've got of hers, save one grease lamp."

Julie swallowed the chalky-tasting drink. She caught Granny's hand and drew it to her cheek. "Thank you for helping me through this. What would I have done without you?"

"I just do what the good Lord set about for me. He gives us all a talent. Yours is your purty voice; mine is birthing babies."

"Wonder what mine is," Emilee said. "Taking care of Daniel?"

"I believe yours to be having the babies for me to birth." Granny tee-heed.

"How many, Granny?" Julie asked, smiling at her friend. "How many babies will Emilee have?"

"A tribe, I reckon. A baker's dozen."

"And me? Will I have more healthy babies?"

"Don't fret yourself, Julie. Enjoy this'n 'fore you worry about more. Now I have in mind to talk straight to Will before I leave ye."

Granny found Will in the side yard, still patting himself on the back, proud as a peacock. "Now, Will," she started. "I got a right smart to learn ye. I don't want to leave Julie less'n yore up to it."

"Don't you trust me?" Will huffed.

"Don't get all toucheous, Will. Ye need to know things ye never needed to know before. Just listen."

Will hung his head. "You're right, Granny. I'm sorry."

"Julie's pert near back to normal, but ye need to watch after her and the baby." She pulled a passel of linen cloths from her deep apron pocket. "These are clean rags for her. If she floods and it don't seem to stop, send for me." She kicked up a little trace of red-clay dirt with her booted toe. "It should be 'bout this color, brownish red. If it's bright, like a sliced beet, that ain't good."

Will took the rags and listened intently as Granny continued. "Make her eggnog with fresh eggs and warm milk." She walked a little ways to the springhouse door, and he followed. "The afterbirth is in here, wrapped in oilcloth." Her eyes, deep as a well and black as pitch, pierced his. "Ye must bury it tonight in the north corner of the yard." He shivered when she gripped his arm. "Ye must line the little grave with willow branches and set a heavy stone atop it. When that is done, take a handful of the fresh-dug dirt and throw it over yore right shoulder. Make sure it scatters over the grave. That'll keep the haints away. Yore other wee ones were not meant to live, but this 'un's born strong. Ye have to protect her."

Will didn't believe as Granny did, that the devil was busy playing tricks on people and that sometimes you could trick him back. She still held to some old mountain ways, and the weight of her concern rested heavily on his shoulders. He knew that nothing but the grace of God would protect his wife and family, but Granny stood like a little sentry between him and the cabin until he agreed.

"All right, Granny," he said. "I won't forget. I won't let you down."

It was unusually warm for a March day in eastern Kentucky, and the dank, dark smell of coal smoke permeated the air held close in the valley by rain-weighted clouds, obscuring the tops of the mountains. A jagged bolt of lightning ushered in the thunder boomer Will Brown had been predicting all day.

Will was as happy as he had ever been while he dashed across the barnyard with a pail full of milk, still warm from the cow, and half a dozen brown eggs, stolen from the chickens, in his jacket pocket. He was thinking of the story he would tell Julie, of how mad the hens had gotten when he lifted them from their nests and helped himself to the products of their labor.

"Hey, girls," he'd said. "Share a few eggs with me. Remember who supplies the corn you like so much. And you have to admit, I'm much better looking than that other thief, old Mr. Possum."

The hens had squawked and ruffled their feathers, pecking indignantly at Will's arms before settling back on their nests.

He needed the eggs and milk to make eggnog for Julie like Granny Pelfrey had told him to do. He was so grateful to the old midwife that he would do anything she asked of him, most anything. A pang of guilt tickled his mind when he remembered the other instructions she had given after the birth of his daughter forty-eight hours earlier. *Well,* he consoled himself, *I did near everything. A man can never do all a woman asks.* He figured he'd done the best he could.

He mounted the porch steps and set the bucket of milk on the rough plank floor. He reached into his pocket and pulled out his pipe and a pouch of tobacco. He would have a quick smoke and watch the storm for a minute before he went inside.

Will remembered being glad that evening when Daniel had ferried Granny and Emilee across the creek, swollen from the rain that fell steadily from leaden skies. "Our good-luck sign," Julie had dubbed it, for it had also rained on their wedding day.

Thunder rolled, startling Will from his reverie. The shower that started two days ago, right after the baby's birth, continued and was turning into a serious storm as night approached. Suddenly, hail began to fall and bounce as loud as gunshots against the tin roof. He hastened inside with the milk pail as the wind gusted in around him.

Closing the door, he entered the spacious one-room haven that was his family's home. He picked up the heavy iron poker that had belonged to his father and stoked the fire in the cookstove, then added a chunk of coal. Stirring sugar into the saucepan of warmed milk and beaten eggs, he carefully added a pinch of Julie's precious nutmeg. He poured the drink into a heavy white mug and carried it to the bedside.

The baby had burrowed under the blanket, and he pulled it back from her face. He noted a smudge of white at the corner of her mouth. So Julie's milk was in; praise the Lord. That would make them all happy. Laura Grace had been fussy all day, demanding to be fed almost hourly. She would suck with fury for a few seconds, then pull away, red-faced and screaming like a banshee. Granny had prepared them for this possibility. She'd left sugar soothers—pieces of twisted linen, which he dipped in boiled sweetened water—for the baby to suck on. That worked for a little while, but the infant was hungry and ready for the real thing. So she slept at last, sated on her mother's milk.

Will had proudly accomplished all of Granny's tasks. Well, almost all. Only one thing pricked his conscience like a blackbird on an ear of corn. As Granny had instructed, he carefully kept track of the number and heaviness of Julie's pads, fixed her meals, and cared for the fussy baby so Julie could rest. Why, he even changed the soiled nappies and wiped her tiny bottom. He told Julie the only thing that saved him was that the nappies didn't stink. He thought he might save them to tar the roof. She had laughed and laughed.

What nagged him was the burying of the afterbirth. As Granny directed, on the evening of the birth, he had taken a shovel and a lantern to the springhouse and retrieved the little bundle. He carried it to the northernmost part of the yard and dug a deep, round hole. Satisfied, he paused to wipe rainwater from his eyes, then placed the wrapped package into the depression and quickly covered it. He tamped the dirt firmly into place with the back of the shovel and looked around for a stone big enough to cover the small mound. The lantern he had placed on the ground sputtered and cast an eerie green glow over the scene. He turned his back and pitched a handful of soil over his shoulder. It didn't scatter—too wet—but sat there in a lump, like a reproachful frog. He jabbed at it with his shovel.

It was then he remembered the willow branches. He had forgotten the grave's special lining. Shivering in the damp wind, he drew the collar of his coat tightly around his throat. *Well,* he thought, *I'm cold and I'm tired. I'll fix it in the morning. Maybe the rain will stop by then.* He laid the bowl of the shovel across the grave and hurried into the house.

What made him a little uneasy was the condition of the grave when he went to check it this morning. The shovel had been cast aside. The grave was open and empty, strewn with shreds of bloody oilcloth. *Dug up by wild dogs,* he reasoned as he had smoothed the dirt back into place. *No harm done.*

Will heard Julie moan in her sleep. She never complained but suffered the aches and pains with her usual good nature. She'd told him the bodily discomfort from having this baby was easy after having endured the heartache of losing their other three. She awoke easily when Will caressed her shoulder. She leaned forward as he positioned a pillow to her back, then slowly sipped the warm eggnog.

"How do you feel, sweetheart? You were moaning in your sleep."

"I'm all right. Just a little sore. Did you notice our little

chipmunk's finally sleeping? She nursed for the longest time."
Julie leaned back against the pillow and handed him the cup. "I
need to get up," she said, slowly raising a hand to him. "Help me
please, Will."

Will proffered a steady hand as she swung her legs over the
side of the bed and stood. "Oh, the room's spinning," she gasped.
"I feel sick." Will could feel her panic as she clutched his shoulders. "Something's not right. I think I'm flooding!"

Forcing himself to stay calm, Will eased Julie back against
the bed. An ominous red circle spread on the sheet beneath her.
Granny had warned of this, but he had expected it would happen earlier if at all, and not this much. Struggling to remember all
Granny had told him, Will placed his hand on Julie's belly and
began to rub.

"Will," she cried, "you're hurting me! Stop, please stop."

"I have to do something!" Will replied as his mind spun nearly
out of control. "You're bleeding too much! Oh, Lord, please help us."

Julie grabbed his hand, forcing him to stop. "You need to take
me to Granny." Her voice steadied as if the very thought of
Granny calmed her fear. "She'll know what to do."

"It's pouring outside. You'll get soaked." His mind cast about
for a solution; he couldn't take his wife out into this weather in
her condition. "I'll go fetch her."

"No, Will. I'm so afraid. It's just a short way. Please don't
leave me." He could see the terror on her face, and hadn't he
promised years ago to never leave her?

"All right, sweetheart," he said finally. "I'll go get the horse
and buggy. Can you sit up a little so you can nurse the baby?
That will make your womb clamp down."

Famished after her long nap, the baby suckled greedily.

Will wiped his bloody hands on his shirtfront, grabbed his slicker, and ran out into the storm, praying, pleading all the way to the barn. He fumbled with the leather gear as he harnessed the male of his pair of workhorses to the light carriage. Fleetly, he considered the sturdier wagon, but the surrey that Grace had sent would keep Julie and the baby dry.

He pulled the suddenly balky Samson to the barn door. The big horse neighed as he faced the thunder and lightning. Delilah, shut up in her stall, whinnied. She was always restive when Samson wasn't in his stall next to hers. The barn cat stretched, came out to meet Will, and wound herself around his ankle. Her kittens mewled frantically from their gunnysack bed in the corner. Will shook his leg. The cat stalked off, her tail in the air. She and her new kittens would have to be company enough for Delilah until Samson came back.

He led the horse to the porch, speaking softly in spite of his urgency, stroking the animal's long nose. Looping the reins loosely over the porch rail, he rushed back inside.

Julie stood by the bed, pale and shaky, her eyes closed. Her lips moved in silent prayer. She'd managed to put on a clean gown, and he knelt to help with her shoes. He handed her the only medicine they had—a little glass of whiskey—and she shuddered as she drank it in one gulp. Stripping off his oilcloth jacket and wrapping the baby in it, he pulled a quilt around them both and carried them to the buggy.

Will took up the reins and urged Samson forward. Within minutes they were at the banks of Troublesome Creek. They'd have to cross here to reach Daniel's cabin. The creek was usually not much more than knee-high on this side of the footbridge, while farther downstream calm pools lay deep enough for swimming and fishing. This night, however, two days' steady rain had given over to a deluge, causing muddy water to surge down the bed and overflow its banks.

The great horse balked at the water's edge. Will flicked the reins sharply, then flicked them again. Samson was resistant, but as always he followed Will's commands, pulling the carriage into the swollen creek. A tree limb swept past as they were caught in a torrent. Too late Will realized his mistake. There was nothing to do but go on. He shouted to Samson above the storm, "Gee! Gee!"

Thunder rolled. Samson did not respond. The stream they'd crossed a thousand times was suddenly no longer familiar. Water crashed against the horse and buggy. In a flash of lightning Will saw the horse falter. Samson flung his big head around as if he needed reassurance from his master. Then a tremendous bolt of lightning struck an ancient cottonwood on the far bank. Sparks flew as a large limb fell flaming to the ground.

Samson reared, neighing.

Will slacked the reins and called out, "Steady. Steady." Darkness overtook them. The buggy tipped and swayed, then overturned, dumping its passengers into the roiling black water.

Will went under twice before his feet found purchase on the slick, moss-covered rocks. The frigid water swirled around him as he fought to stay upright. He sputtered and coughed and flailed, feeling for Julie and the baby beneath the surface before the buggy finally slammed against his chest. He inched to the other side of the vehicle, praying to find them.

Another bolt, and for seconds the scene was bright as day. Relief flooded through him when he caught sight of his wife clinging to a wheel that jutted incongruously from the water.

He circled her with one arm and tugged.

But she resisted. "My baby! My baby! I lost hold of her!"

"Let me get you to the bank!" he yelled against the howling wind, her words barely registering as he worked to get her to safety.

"Noooo!" she wailed in anguish. "The baby!"

He had forgotten all about Laura Grace, so anxious was he to find Julie. How could a little baby be found in this? Against his better judgment, knowing there'd be no hope for Julie if he didn't find her baby girl, he left her holding securely to the carriage.

He ducked under the water and scrabbled along the bottom of the creek, scraping his hands raw on the rough rock that held the other wheel lodged under the water. Lungs bursting, he came up for air and found himself back where he had started. He inhaled deeply, ready to try again when the newborn's lusty cry came from inside the overturned buggy! Reaching blindly, he felt the seat lying on its side. He leaned in, frantically feeling about, the infant's bawl more distinct. Miraculously, his jacket had caught on a brace and held her inches above the surging muddy flood. Ever so thankful for his daughter's loud cry, Will jerked the fabric loose and pulled the baby out.

Darkness black as a witch's heart surrounded him; a roaring, pounding flood assaulted him as he fought his way back to Julie. Faint with relief, Will grabbed the wheel where he'd left her and pressed himself against a cold and empty space.

Julie was gone! His mind couldn't grasp it. He'd left her clinging to the wheel only minutes before. She couldn't be gone. The baby squirmed against his chest. Fighting rising panic, he gulped in ragged breaths. "Julie! God, please . . . Julie!" His head cleared. *She's on the bank,* he told himself. *Somehow she's made her way to safety.*

The carriage provided him some protection on the downstream side, its bulk diverting the angry floodwater. Using it as a guide, Will made his way to the now docile Samson. The horse trembled in fear and exhaustion beneath Will's hands. He grabbed the halter and called, "Gee! Gee, now!"

Samson shook himself, like a dog caught in the rain, and heaved forward. With a screech and a groan, the buggy dislodged from the creek bed and floated up as Samson strained toward the bank. Will feared it would drag the horse off. Struggling to hold the baby out of the water, he unhitched the carriage and held to Samson's thick mane as, now free, the animal pulled them back to the opposite shore.

A monstrous rupture split the eastern sky and sent a jagged finger of fire to strike a rotted stump and reveal a surreal scene: a horse, too weary for fear; a whimpering baby wrapped tightly in a brown slicker; and a tall, disheveled man screaming his wife's name over and over. The buggy rode a wash of water downstream, one wheel spinning wildly as it went. There was no woman waiting on the shore.

Julie had vanished.

CHAPTER 4

Granny sat in a bent-willow rocker close to the fire, a cup of sassafras tea cooling on her knee. A tattered quilt, faded from many washings, covered her thin shoulders. Her Bible lay open in her lap. She loved this quietest part of the day, after everyone had gone to bed. The need for less sleep was one of the blessings of old age. Nothing made her feel cozier than listening to a good thunder boomer while she rocked by the fire.

She was not enjoying the storm that raged this night, however. The vague sense of unease that had started with the birth of Julie's baby had been replaced by the sure knowledge that someone she cherished would be passing this turbulent night.

The signs could not be denied. Just last week, while walking up the mountain in the woods above the cabin, she'd spied a cluster of honeybees swarming from a hollow log. It was an early spring, so the apple trees were releasing their fragrant blossoms, enticing the bees from their dormant state. The air was soft and clear, the sunlight slanted just right to reveal to her clouded vision the color of the bees–black, solid black. She couldn't remember the last time she'd seen black bees. . . . Maybe that time just before they found Lost-Lum Sizemore swinging from the black walnut tree up Crook-Neck Holler. *God rest his soul. Poor Lum, he couldn't bear the burden of hisself no longer.*

And then, the morning after the birth, when Will had burst jubilantly into the house, a little brown wren followed through the door. In the clamor that followed, she'd quietly guided the bird outside with a broom. The foretelling signs continued that very morning when Emilee showed her tea leaves forming the shape of a coffin in the bottom of her cup.

Granny leaned her tired old head back against the chair. Her own mommy had taught her the signs, way back before Jesus came into her heart. Her daddy liked to say, "A wicked and adulterous generation seeketh after a sign." He'd try to persuade her mother that "the only real sign is the cross." They were all happy when at last her mommy was saved. And even though Granny was a born-again believer, she couldn't help remembering the signs her mommy had taught her and believing that somehow they were God's way of using His creation to warn of things to come.

Granny had not shared her foreboding with Emilee. She'd grieve soon enough. Young folks had such a hard time with loss. The older a body got, the sweeter the beckoning of heaven's gates. Granny was readying to enter that land. She just couldn't figure out why the chariot was coming for one of the young'uns and not for her.

She closed her eyes, too old for tears, and bowed her head. "Lord, help me to get a holt of this," she whispered as the rain drummed on the roof and the wind rattled the windowpane. "I put my trust in Ye."

The death knell sounded. The veil would part before midnight.

Will felt himself floating above the riverbank, as if he could look down and observe himself, a stranger. Surely that was not him clutching a baby and screaming his wife's name while his heart splintered in his chest.

He could hear himself shouting for help . . . feel his hand caught tight in Samson's bridle as the horse galloped through the night. But it couldn't be real . . . for he was warm and safe at home with Julie. This was only a dream, a nightmare! He would scare himself awake soon. He watched the man with the baby slide from the horse, scramble–staggering–onto the porch of Daniel's cabin, and pound on the door.

Granny, still wrapped in the quilt, opened the door to the frantic knocking. Will burst in and thrust the baby into her arms. Nearly incoherent, he babbled about the creek, the storm . . . Julie! Julie!

Looking startled, Daniel stumbled from the small back bedroom, Emilee close behind, and stepped into Will's nightmare. Will stood just inside the door. Water streaming from his clothes formed dirty puddles on the floor. Granny held Laura Grace, the infant nearly smothered in Will's coat. Then Will sprang forward and grabbed Daniel's arm, as if clutching a lifeline, while relating his desperate plight.

Emilee rushed to get Daniel's boots while he pulled pants on over his nightshirt. Shoving his arms into his jacket, he took the slicker from Granny as she unwrapped the baby.

"No time! No time for that!" Will cried out as Daniel placed the garment around his shoulders. He would have them both run naked into the night in his panic to find Julie.

"We'll find her, buddy," Daniel consoled. "Just give me a minute. Emilee, light the lantern."

Will followed as Daniel led Samson to the barn, where they quickly saddled riding horses. Mounting, they rode off into the night. The storm had abated. The torrential rain was now a steady cold drizzle. Daniel took the lead. Holding the lantern high, he guided his horse toward the roiling, muddy water of Troublesome.

Inside the cabin, Emilee rocked the newborn girl, wrapped in Granny's quilt, still warm from the fire. Granny steeped a pot of chamomile tea for Emilee to sip while she nursed poor Julie's wee one. Chamomile would keep the baby from getting colic caused by being so cold and wet. She drifted off to sleep, her tiny hand, fingers splayed, resting on Emilee's arm.

Granny pulled a straight-back chair close to the rocker. She and Emilee clasped hands while they prayed for Julie. Tears flowed from Emilee's eyes as she prayed that Daniel and Will would find her precious friend. She cried to Granny that she couldn't bear to think of Julie afraid and cold, out in the night alone.

Granny prayed for Julie's soul and for the peace that passes understanding. In the morning she would boil some dried asparagus root and make a potion for Emilee to drink to keep her milk up. . . . Now she'd be nursing two, her own John and Will's motherless daughter.

Emilee wouldn't go back to bed. She dragged her quilt and bolster across the floor and slept at Granny's feet, baby John nestled in the crook of her arm. Granny held the infant Laura Grace and settled in for a long night in the rocking chair. There wasn't anything quite as sweet as rocking a baby. Granny's fingers found the long-mended scar on her face and traced it over and over. Traced the history it told; traced it from eyebrow to upper lip. She let her mind wander to earlier times, to a baby of her own. One she'd lost many years before. . . .

She was a young woman with two little boys and a headstrong husband when first she came to Kentucky. Oh, it was a wild and beautiful place back then. The mountains shot up around the little lean-to they'd scurried to build that first fall before the freezing rains of winter set in. They'd played house is what they'd done. Finally off to themselves with their love and their babies. The winter was so cold she'd barely gone outside for weeks. Ben took care of them. He brought in sides of deer meat to roast in the fireplace that seemed to take up half the little shack, and the cornmeal and taters they'd carried from Virginia finished out their meals.

Two years they'd lived there on that willful creek in that

place of peace and beauty. She'd carried her daughter that second summer. The Spicers were their neighbors on the ridge over yonder, and sometimes Millie Spicer would visit with her children, or Granny and Ben would go over to the Spicer place on a Sunday afternoon. Both little families would have church together, and sometimes another couple or two would join them. Jack Spicer was a good hand at preaching. Millie had been the one to help her birth Leah. She was a kind and gentle woman.

Then came that dreadful day when she and Ben had seen the flames shoot up and smelled the smoke that drifted through the trees. She'd started to run in that direction, baby Leah in her arms. But Ben had stopped her, made her go back inside the sturdy cabin Jack Spicer had helped him build. He'd pushed her and the children in, then closed the door and bid her to stay inside. She remembered his warning as if it were yesterday. It still chilled her blood. She sat against the inside of the door all afternoon–her little boys close beside, baby Leah in her arms–and waited for the whooping sound of Indians that never came. Not to her door anyway. But her friend was dead. Scalped. And Jack, the good preacher, had an arrow through his heart.

Ben found one of Millie's children hidden in the rain barrel. He was half drowned. It was solace to Granny's soul to have Millie's boy to raise.

Granny had prepared to leave then. She was packing up her bedding and her pots, but Ben wouldn't go. "It will be all right," he'd said. "Chances are they won't be back."

And so she'd stayed. She loved Ben, didn't she? There wasn't anything else she could do, was there?

It was nearly a year later before the Indians came again.

She'd set little Leah under the clothesline, a rock on the tail of her gown to keep her from crawling off. Her two boys and Millie's one were off with Ben hunting game for supper.

She had turned her back for less than a minute. Just long enough to walk to the porch for more wet laundry. The baby's scream froze her in her tracks. She couldn't turn around at first, but when she did, a half-naked red man had her baby, her little Leah, by the heels. She rushed at him, hit at him with something—the laundry paddle? a handful of clothespins? One swipe at her with his hatchet and she was down, her baby's fractured skull a puddle of loss she saw with her one good eye.

Ben would have taken her back to Virginia then—she and her two boys and Millie's one. But he loved it here on that Troublesome Creek, loved the little plot of ground that was their own. And so she stayed. She loved Ben, didn't she?

Granny laid Julie's little one on the quilt beside baby John and went to stir the fire. She settled a hickory log on the embers and swung the teakettle over the hot coals. Her scar flared as sharp as a toothache, as if it had happened yesterday. And the eyes that were too old for tears spilled over, as wild as the water that washed Julie down Troublesome Creek.

It was late the next morning before Daniel returned to find Emilee pacing up and down the narrow split-rail porch that ran the length of their cabin.

He shook his head as he dismounted and joined Emilee on the porch. "Nothing. We found nothing but the busted-up buggy." He folded her into his arms. "And Will is a crazy man. I couldn't get him to come with me. I brought his horse and left him there on the creek bank. At least he stopped yelling her name." He patted Emilee's back and then released her. "I've been by Nathan's. He's going to send his boys around to rally a search party."

Daniel took off his old felt hat and slapped it against the porch rail, then splashed his face with a dipper of cold water from the bucket on the wash shelf. "Emilee, you won't believe the creek this morning. It's back down, but there're brush and tree limbs all over the place. It was a flash flood that caught Will unawares. She could be miles down the bed. . . ." He faltered, seeing Emilee flinch. "I know, honey. We've got to pray to God for a miracle, or we'll have to bury Will alongside her." Daniel stepped inside for dry clothes and for some of the breakfast Granny had waiting for him. He could not rest until Julie was found.

Emilee pestered him with her fears and her prayers. "Miracles happen," she kept saying. "Miracles happen."

And he reckoned she could be right. A mother would fight to stay alive for her young'un.

Granny stuck a sack of fried ham and biscuits in Daniel's pocket as he got up from the table, then handed him a jar of black coffee. "See if ye can get Will to eat a bite," she called as he left, this time on foot, carrying Granny's walking stick, his hound trotting along by his side.

Daniel aimed to traverse the twisting hollows that issued off Troublesome like limbs from a gnarled tree and filled with floodwater whenever the creek overflowed its banks. A man on foot could climb the cliffs, which were tangled with briars and vines–Devil's Shoestring–so thick a horse couldn't put a hoof down. And he was the man for the job, for he knew its paths as dead sure as he knew Emilee's face. Scarcely a day passed that he and Old Blue didn't hunt for their supper in that wild place, and on nights when the moon was full they tracked possum there just for fun. He wished with all his might that he and his dog were setting out on such a jaunt now.

Daniel picked up his pace. He needed to find Julie soon.

Several men on horseback and more on foot spent the long spring day, dawn to dusk, searching for Julie Brown without result. They assembled in the early evening at the site of her disappearance, the banks of Troublesome Creek, only a few feet below where the footbridge–now splintered into kindling–just yesterday had straddled the water. They stood or squatted stoically, looking sideways at Will without so much as moving their heads, as if seeing his grief full on might blind them.

The men shared this tragedy as they had shared others, accepting God's will. For as much as they revered their mountain home, they were well aware that it was often at great cost that they dwelt in such a beauteous place. Occasionally, one or another would break the silence to point out, yet again, the stump charred by lightning, the deep gouges in the earth caused by Samson's struggle, the huge limb from the cottonwood that lay half in, half out of the now gently flowing stream. It was as if they needed evidence that the calamity had actually occurred, for it was difficult to take in, impossible to believe that Will's young wife could disappear without a trace.

Will stood apart from the others, exhausted and in shock. He appeared emotionless. There were no tears, no further shouts of rage or terror. He was spent.

Daniel dispersed the men. They would meet again at first light, but for now they needed food and rest, and Daniel was certain in his heart that there was no longer a need for haste in the hunt for Julie. Will stumbled numbly when Daniel took his arm and led him away. Will stopped only once for a long searching look at Troublesome Creek, then turned and followed his friend.

While his family slept and Will lay bedded on a pallet in front of the fireplace, poleaxed from one of Granny's potions, Daniel sat on the porch and contemplated the events of the past twenty-four hours. He was keyed up with a kind of angry energy that made it impossible to rest. He had lain with Emilee while she cried herself to sleep, and then, easing his bulky body from the bed, he dressed in silence and sought the solace of the night and a pipe of tobacco.

Old Blue crept on padded feet, quiet as a rabbit in its lair, to the chair and dropped his head to Daniel's lap. Absentmindedly, Daniel stroked the dog's silky ears and scratched his bony back. A soft woof and a cock of his head informed Daniel that the dog was not ready to give up the hunt. "All right, Old Blue." He stood and knocked his pipe against the porch rail, spilling hot ash on the ground. Master and dog set off to search for Julie.

The night sky was mostly clear, and Daniel's hunter's eyes adjusted quickly, making the footpath easy to follow. They forded the creek and reached Will's cabin minutes later. Daniel bade the dog to stay while he entered the empty house.

It was odd to be in Will's house alone. For a second he fancied he heard Julie's voice. His heart leaped with joy, and he turned quickly in the direction of the bed, where he'd last seen her wrapped up in a quilt with her new baby. He knew there was no one here, but the sound was as real to him as the empty chair that sat in a little square of moonlight near the cold fireplace. It seemed she called out for him to find her.

He searched for an article of clothing that held her scent. No easy task, for while the men of the community were hunting for her, he knew the women had been busy as well, scrubbing and washing everything they could lay their hands on, preparing the dwelling for Julie's return. Groping in the darkness, Daniel felt the brim of a bonnet hanging from a peg inside the door. *This is good*, he thought as he stepped outside and held the bonnet under Blue's nose. The dog could track a rabbit or a possum for miles by following its scent; Daniel hoped he could do the same with Julie's.

He led the dog to the far bank where he figured Julie might have been. He knew that Blue couldn't trace a body in water, but if she had washed up somewhere along the way, his keen sense of smell might alert him to it.

They had traveled several miles—the dog snuffling along the ground, sometimes whining and running ahead only to return and push his long nose into the bonnet in Daniel's hand—when suddenly Blue froze in his tracks. Ears up and nose sniffing the cold night air, the dog pulled away from his master and broke into a run.

Daniel let him take the lead and watched as the night swallowed Blue. A cloud obscured the moon. It was as dark as the inside of a cave. The skittering sound of a small varmint running away caught him off guard, and the once-familiar landscape now seemed threatening. Huge twisted grapevines hanging from towering oaks and water maples caught at his clothing like monstrous arms. The soft *whoo-whoo* of an owl was interrupted when he stepped on a loose rock and fell heavily, sliding down a steep incline and nearly rolling into the creek before he caught himself. Daniel stood, brushed at his clothing, released a shaky laugh, and shook his head to clear his mind. The familiarity of the place restored, he proceeded with caution.

He had just about decided to call the dog back in when an eerie bay in the distance caused the hair on the back of his neck to rise. He had never heard such a mournful sound. Rushing to see what Blue had found and wishing at the same time that he would never have to see it, he approached the scene with dread. He closed his eyes tightly, not trusting his own vision, when moonlight glinted as if reflected from marble and revealed a small white arm lying before him on the bank of Troublesome Creek. Tasting bile, his legs buckling, Daniel sank to his knees before the object of his quest.

The hunt was over.

Julie's body floated serenely in a deep, dark pool, her left arm tangled in a blackberry bramble, her long blonde hair streaming out around her still face, her green eyes staring into eternity. The full moon reflected the perfect backdrop, as if she swam upon its golden surface.

As carefully as if she could feel his ministration, Daniel

loosened her arm from the thorns and pulled her body, cold and slick as glass, from the frigid water. He dried her as best he could before wrapping her in his own long, homespun shirt. Kneeling there, he thought of Will and the heartbreak this find would bring. The whimpering of the dog mingled with the common sounds of a forest at night: animals seeking refuge or comfort or food, water tumbling over rock, pines sighing lonesome songs in the breeze.

Daniel stood, hearing none of it, and cradled the lifeless form in his arms. "Come, Blue," he commanded, as once again that long night they began a journey that could only end in sorrow.

CHAPTER 5

A pickax grated against rock and disturbed the early morning hush in the old cemetery. Daniel leaned on the handle of his shovel and watched Nathan's youngest son flail about with the ax. Isaac was not strong enough to break rock, but he'd wanted to help, so Daniel had brought him and his brother Jeremiah up the mountain to the boneyard near daybreak. A flock of doves, startled into flight, sought new shelter in a wild cherry tree. They fretted and cooed and looked down on the gravediggers with beady, frightened eyes. Isaac swung the pickax so hard sparks flew off the rock.

"Easy, boy," Daniel said. "You'll break the handle off that way. Here, let me show you."

Daniel took the tool and *tap, tap, tapp*ed against the rock before he gave it a solid hit. The rock broke into several small pieces.

Isaac flung the pieces into a pile of brush, then grabbed the shovel and started digging. His thin shoulders shook with the effort.

He'll have to be a preacher like his pa, Daniel thought. *He's too puny for real work.* Not that Daniel had anything against preachers, especially Brother Nathan—that man could talk the stink off a skunk—but they weren't much hand at anything but preaching and eating, as far as Daniel could see. Isaac was built like his father, not much bigger than a banty rooster and him nearly fourteen. Now Jeremiah, on the other hand, was already big as a man.

"Let me have that shovel," Jeremiah said. "You ain't even made a dent in the ground."

"Leave me be," Isaac replied. "I want to do this for Julie."

Daniel knew that Isaac had a strong attachment to Will's wife, like everyone else on Troublesome Creek. Isaac was attracted to her easy familiarity and teasing ways. He often showed up at the bank where Daniel and Will mined coal. He'd scurry back into the holes and retrieve slivers of coal that broke off when they chunked out the big lumps. He'd gather a gunny-sack full to take home to his mother. Will's house was closest to the coal bank, and so at noon they'd take dinner there. While they ate, Julie read stories from the newspapers her sister sent from Lexington. She read of bank robberies, house fires, weddings, births and deaths, funny things and sad things. And things they'd never heard of, like the brightly painted circus train with animals from India and Africa: monkeys with curled tails, striped cats as big as a calf, and a huge animal with floppy ears and a short tail who carried its own trunk.

Isaac would sit, forgetting to eat, listening to her read those papers. Many days when they went back to work, he'd stay at Julie's kitchen table, struggling to write his name on a piece of lined paper with a fat red pencil.

One day he'd come to the bank with a Bible in his hand. He'd run all the way from Will's house. "Listen," he'd said to Daniel and Will, and then, just like that, he read: "'For God so loved the world, that he gave his only begotten Son, that whosoever believeth in him should not perish, but have everlasting life.'"

In the fall, Isaac would be leaving the confines of his mountain home. Julie had arranged through her sister for him to attend boarding school in Lexington. He hoped to get his teaching certificate and then return to Troublesome Creek and share the gift Julie had given to him.

Daniel's thoughts returned to the job at hand. Before too long, they had a good-size hole dug. They'd fallen into a pattern. Daniel slung the pickax to break the ledge rock, Jeremiah hauled it out, and Isaac shoveled the dirt. They dug the grave in three vaults, the first two feet wider than the next two, and the last one just wide enough to hold a casket. They smoothed the sides of the grave with a broadax and the last vault in the six-foot hole was lined with wooden planks.

It was well past noon when they finished their task. They sat around the opening with their feet hanging in. They passed around a jar of cold springwater and spoke of the next day's burying, knowing that the grave they dug would be admired by the men of the community as a job well done.

Daniel was the first to stand. He gathered the shovels, the axes, the maul, and the hammer. "You done her proud, boys." He gripped Isaac's shoulder. "We'll come back in the morning to get things ready for the mourners."

Halfway down the mountain, Jeremiah stopped to remove his boots. Tying the laces together, he slung them over his shoulder. "Nothing feels better than green grass between your toes after a cold winter."

Daniel looked back at the graveyard, a dark foreboding place, deep in the shadow of overgrown trees and vines.

Isaac turned also. "I'm going to bring a hatchet up here soon. I'm going to clean out the hyacinth bean vine and the thistle weed and chop down that raggedy cedar that blocks the sun. Then I'll plant some day-eye blossoms so she'll have something warm and pretty to keep her company." He choked up and wiped his nose on the sleeve of his shirt.

"That would make her happy, boy," Daniel replied, feeling a little sting in his own eyes. "Julie liked purty things."

Emilee stood, hand on her hip, in the doorway. She had just finished nursing her baby and was resting. She sipped asparagus-root tea Granny had fixed for her. She shuddered. "It's bitter, Granny."

Granny dipped a spoon into the jar of molasses on the kitchen table and stirred some sweetness into the potion. "Ye need to drink it straight down. Nursing two babies and crying all night has got ye all dried up."

"I want to go with you to dress Julie's body." Emilee took off her apron and hung it behind the door. "Brother Nathan's wife can watch the babies."

"She can sit with you whilst Ellen Combs and I ready the body. Her two girls'll be there to help out, I reckon."

"Please, Granny?" Emilee pleaded.

"Yore place is here with these young'uns," Granny told her. "Ye got to build up yore milk." She tucked her sparse hair up under her old bonnet.

Emilee sobbed anew.

Granny gathered the grieving young woman in her arms. "Honey," she consoled, "I know that Julie named you her closest friend, and I know how ye ache to do for her, but don't ye reckon that nursing her wee one is the thing that would mean the most? There's nary another person that kin do that for her but you, Emilee, nary a soul but you."

Emilee pulled the rocker beside the open window. The newborn, Laura Grace, nestled in her arms. Little John sat at her feet on a bright rag rug gnawing on the end of a baked potato.

"Pray with me before you go, Granny," Emilee said, finally giving in to Granny's will.

A puff of cool air blew through the open window. In the distance they could see the mountain where Daniel was digging the grave.

Granny laid a little flannel blanket over the baby, then bowed her head and prayed. "Thank Ye, Lord, for saving this baby from the darkness of the water. Be with us all tomorrow, especially Will. It will be hard, putting Julie in the ground. Yore will, not ours, be done."

Granny drew back the sheet that covered Julie. Her body was whole and unscarred. She hadn't been in the creek long enough to do much damage, and thankfully the water was cold. Daniel had placed her on a board that rested on two sawhorses. He'd managed to close her eyes, and now two silver coins rested there. Granny blessed the corpse before bathing it with cool soda water. Then Ellen Combs plaited the long hair into ornate ropes of gold that she arranged like a crown on top of Julie's head. When that was finished, they dressed her in clean undergarments and a simple shroud of black cotton, cut up the back, which Mrs. Combs had sewed.

"When I am yet dead, I shall wear black," Granny repeated the old refrain, "but when I walk in heaven, I shall wear white."

They laid Julie's cold hands across her chest, and Granny called for a saucer of salt to set under the shroud on the still-rounded belly. She explained each task to Mrs. Combs's daughters so they would know what to do when it was their turn to ready the dead for the grave. The salt was to keep the body from swelling by absorbing fluids, the little cheesecloth bags of soda tucked here and there cut the odor, washing the face with a rag dipped in soda water helped preserve the color, and placing a small pillow under the head made the body look more lifelike. "The face just don't look natural if it ain't propped up a little."

When all the careful tasks were completed, the girls helped lift the body and lay it in the coffin that was padded with cotton batting and lined with cream-colored silk.

The carefully constructed, highly polished rosewood casket

was Granny's own, fashioned by her grandson Daniel during long winter evenings and tucked away in the hayloft against the time of her need. When Daniel had come to fetch her early in the morning after he had found Julie's body, she had requested, over his protest, that he give it to Will for Julie's internment.

"Daniel, I don't need nary a thing so fine to lay these old bones in," she told him. "But it'll do us all good to view Julie laid out in such a purty box."

"Well, Granny, I reckon I got years yet to make you another." That said, he'd hauled it over here to Will's place.

The ladies stood in silence to admire their handiwork. "Why, she looks just like a princess," said Mrs. Combs's eldest.

Julie's hair shone. They had opened a jar of pickled beets and dabbed her cheeks with the juice so there was a touch of pink on her cold blue face. Her garment lay gently upon her small frame.

Mrs. Combs's youngest daughter placed a bouquet of white service berries in Julie's folded hands. "I gathered them just for her," she said shyly as she picked a stray petal from the front of the shroud.

"Ye done her proud." Granny praised the girls before she went to the porch and hung a wreath fashioned from cedar to the outside of the Browns' cabin door. The cedar wreath, along with the tolling of the church bell, would alert the community that the viewing could commence.

The day of the burial dawned warm and beautiful. Spring in all its glory had come to the mountains. Every flowering plant was bursting with color and fragrance, birds seemed to be in contest to see whose song was sweetest, and the gentlest of warm breezes stirred the soul and warmed the spirit.

Daniel waited with Isaac at the graveyard for the mourners. They had assembled rough-hewn benches near the gravesite. A gray granite bucket filled with cold water from a nearby spring and a matching dipper sat on a hastily constructed table. It was a long walk up the mountain, and people would need to quench their thirst. Daniel removed the boards that covered the deep hole, grateful it was still dry, and placed them beside the grave for the casket to rest on during the service. He did not mind missing the service held at the church—although he loved to hear Brother Nathan's stirring funeral exhortations—because he wanted to do this last small task for Julie.

He'd sat up all night at the wake with Granny and several others. They'd pulled straight chairs to face the coffin, which rested on sawhorses hidden under a white quilt. It seemed like everyone in the valley had come to view the body and to express sympathy to Will. But strangely, unaccountably, Will was nowhere to be found.

He'd disappeared after seeing the lifeless form of his wife laid out in the very place where they had known such joy. Will had stood over the small form for several minutes, staring down at the shell of his beloved Julie. He'd not shed a tear, just touched her once, gently stroking her cheek, then leaned down and whispered in her ear. His breath stirred a strand of her hair. "I found your baby" was all he said, just that one thing. "I found your baby." Then he had turned on his heel and walked out into the dense early morning fog, leaving Daniel and Granny to care for the body. He'd not even told them how to reach Julie's sister, who surely would have wanted to know what had happened.

They could hear the funeral procession long before it came into view.

> *"Shall we gather at the river,*
> *Where bright angel feet have trod;*
> *With its crystal tide forever*
> *Flowing by the throne of God?"*

The familiar refrain mingled with birdsong as it echoed up the mountain.

They watched as six stalwart men labored up the hillside carrying the coffin suspended from two hickory rails by heavy rope. The pallbearers walked three on each side, the rails resting on their shoulders. One of the biggest boys in the procession walked behind the wooden box, a hand stretched to steady it and keep it from sliding from its bonds. Occasionally, the men would pause to catch their breath and wipe salty sweat from their eyes; and then they would fall into the measured, respectful step that carried the body to the grave. The coffin was followed by family and friends in order of importance, with a space left for the conspicuously absent Will.

On reaching the graveyard, the pallbearers let down the ropes and set the casket on the grave boards.

Brother Nathan offered a final prayer for the soul of the departed and for solace for her loved ones. "Brothers and sisters, I know your hearts are troubled. I know God's ways are sometimes hard to fathom. As Jeremiah cried out to the Lord, 'When

I would comfort myself against sorrow, my heart is faint in
me. . . . Is there no balm in Gilead; is there no physician there?'"
Pausing, he wiped a tear from the corner of his eye.

"We need but to petition God, and He will supply our every
need. He will surely comfort us in this dark and dreadful time.
Brothers and sisters, let us recite the Twenty-third Psalm, David's
gift of solace to us. 'The Lord is my shepherd; I shall not want.
He maketh me to lie down in green pastures: he leadeth me
beside the still waters. He restoreth my soul: he leadeth me in
the paths of righteousness for his name's sake. Yea, though I walk
through the valley of the shadow of death, I will fear no evil: for
thou art with me; thy rod and thy staff they comfort me. Thou
preparest a table before me in the presence of mine enemies:
thou anointest my head with oil; my cup runneth over. Surely
goodness and mercy shall follow me all the days of my life: and
I will dwell in the house of the Lord for ever.' Amen and amen."

In conclusion, the preacher stooped to gather a handful of
grave dirt, nodding for the pallbearers to lower the casket into
the vault.

The men held tight to the rope—Daniel could hear the *whir*
as it slid through their hands—and let the weight of the coffin aid
its descent until it reached bottom, six feet down.

Brother Nathan stepped forward. "Ashes to ashes. Dust to
dust." He released a stream of red-clay soil from his hand. It was
so quiet the mourners could hear the pebbly dirt ping off the
nailheads that secured the top of the casket. It seemed even the
squirrels and jays had stopped their raucous chatter in honor of
the dead.

"Ashes to ashes, dust to dust. Sleep here all night, sister," each person intoned as they, in turn, sprinkled dirt into the dark hole and bade their sister in Christ a last good-bye.

Every eye followed Emilee as she carried the baby to the edge of her mother's grave. She'd dressed the infant in a long yellow gown with fanciful embroidery around its hem and a little knit bonnet. Dipping her free hand into a small reed basket, Emilee scattered its contents around the grave's opening. Tiny white blossoms fell like snow onto the raw red earth, emphasizing the gaping wound.

The baby began to cry, a mournful long-noted wail that brought tears to the eyes of each assembled there.

Suddenly Will appeared out of the shadows. Some ladies gasped at the sight of him, for his shoulder-length dark hair and bushy brown beard had turned white in the course of one night. He held out his arms to Emilee, and she cautiously handed Laura Grace over. Then he did the oddest thing. Holding the baby in one arm, he began to unbutton his shirt. Emilee stepped forward, but Granny put out a hand to hold her back. Will tucked the infant next to his skin, then buttoned the shirt around her. As he placed his hand against the bundle of his daughter, she quieted and cried no more. Will stopped before Daniel and grasped his shoulder before vanishing again, swallowed up by the anonymous forest, baby and all.

Turning his attention back to his task, Daniel picked up his shovel and began to pitch dirt into the grave.

The people murmured among themselves as they gathered up their Bibles and church fans and began to straggle off down the mountain. They would gather at Daniel's for a noonday meal prepared by the women of the church. He knew the past couple of days had taxed their spirits. The fellowship of breaking bread would help to salve their sorrow.

Snatches of comments drifted to Daniel as he worked— "Strangest thing I ever seen. . . . Poor little young'un. . . . Did you see Will's hair? White as snow. . . . I've heard of it. . . . It were the shock. . . . Brother Nathan done a good. . . ."

Finally, after what seemed like hours, Daniel finished, and all that was left in this world of Julie Brown was the little hump of dirt at his feet.

CHAPTER 6

"Daniel, you have got to say something to him," Emilee fretted. "This just can't go on."

Man, Daniel thought, *am I between the bull and the barn door.* On the one hand, he understood Emilee's concerns; he had some of his own. On the other, he couldn't bring himself to chastise Will for his bizarre behavior. It had been two weeks since the burial, and Will still spent his days roaming around the woods with the baby tucked inside his shirt. At intervals when Will could no longer ignore her mewling cry of hunger, he would show up at their door and hand the infant over for a feeding. Each evening at dusk he'd leave the baby for Emilee to bed down with little John, then go sleep by the creek, alone.

Daniel knew Emilee was near exhaustion. Laura Grace

wanted to nurse constantly during the night to make up for what she missed during the day. Also, to add to Emilee's indignation, the baby had a bad rash. Even Granny's special paste of borax and honey didn't clear up her sore bottom, and she cried every time Emilee washed her.

"Emilee," Daniel replied, "I swear I'd druther be in hell with my back broke than to interfere with Will that-a-way."

"If you don't remedy this situation soon, you won't have to go to hell to get your back broke. I'm near dry as a lizard on a hot rock now. And this little girl don't need to suffer because her pa's gone quare."

Daniel's tone turned sharp. "To think you'd say that after what Will's been—"

"I know. I'm sorry. But he ain't the only one to suffer a loss," Emilee said, a trace of anger in her voice. "I miss Julie too, and I love her baby like my own. Will needs to let me have her, Daniel. I want to raise her up with little John."

Granny commenced stirring the bubbling thick oatmeal she was fixing for their breakfast. She could stand in the middle of the week and see both ways to Sunday on this one. Daniel was right to allow Will to heal in the only way he knew how, but Emilee was also right in her desire to protect the baby. Granny had thought Will's treks would stop of their own accord, that he would come to terms with his loss, but so far there seemed to be no lessening of his pain.

She portioned the cereal into white ironstone bowls, topping them off with a dollop of blackberry jam. She set the bowls on the table beside the platters of fried ham and biscuits. *Food will help,* she reckoned. *A full belly don't grumble.*

The baby was newly fed and freshly bathed when Will came for her later that morning. She'd had her first dipping bath, for her navel cord had finally shriveled and come off. Daniel met Will at the door and took him to the barn for a "little talk."

Granny and Emilee tarried on the porch. Granny picked over pintos, flinging the pebbles and broken beans out into the yard. Emilee busied herself by untangling a morning-glory vine and trailing it up the string she had fastened with a tack to the eave of the cabin.

"Granny, this will be purty when it blossoms," she said. A fat red hen scratched around her feet. "It'll make a nice shade where I can set my rocker and feed my babies." The hen cocked its head and pecked at Emilee's bare toes. "Shoo, now. Shoo!" Emilee flapped her apron. "There's corn in the chicken yard. I don't want you messin' on my clean porch."

They watched Daniel put his arm around Will's shoulders and heard Will say, "Never, Daniel! I'll never give my baby up!" Will stalked away from Daniel and stood, arms dangling at his sides, shoulders slumped, looking out across the valley for the longest time.

He's got so thin, Granny worried. *It'd take two of him to make a shadow.*

She could see his resolve from where she sat. First his spine stiffened; then he stood straight as a sourwood sprout and put his hands on his hips. He turned back around and spoke in a voice so soft Emilee cupped her hand to her ear. "It's not that

I don't appreciate all that you and Emilee have done for us, but my baby keeps me sane. Having her with me stills the anguish in my heart. Sometimes, up in the hills, I just hold her and look at her, and she looks right back with eyes so full of wisdom. . . . It's like Julie is telling me how to survive through our daughter."

Having reached some sort of agreement, the men joined Granny and Emilee on the porch.

"You're right, Daniel," Will said. "I've been thoughtless. I can't raise Laura Grace inside my shirt. I'll go back to my house. I'll make myself go in, and I'll start taking care of the baby the way I should." He took Emilee's hand. "I hope you can forgive me, for I'll need a heap of learning about babies from you and Granny."

"It's all right, Will." Emilee kissed his cheek. "You know I'd do anything for you and for Julie's baby."

Over the next few weeks, Will's odd behavior was on everyone's minds up and down Troublesome. This or that one would stop by Daniel's front porch and puzzle over Will's attachment to his daughter.

Daniel wouldn't talk about it, but Emilee agreed with the others. It was much more common to see a man turn against a child if his wife died during or soon after childbirth. Why Sam Heller, over in Quicksand, left his twins with his sister not two days after his wife died of childbed fever. Not only that, Emilee told Daniel, but Lucinda Mark had told her that his other three were farmed out to anyone who would take them. Talk was that he had moved a sixteen–year-old in to take poor Anna's place. Sam, with that sneaking look on his face, like a sheep-killing dog.

Of course, Will couldn't have taken care of Laura Grace if Granny hadn't moved in with him; that's what turned the trick— that and Emilee's milk. You had to hand it to Will, though. He sure wasn't like other men.

The first night the baby was gone, Daniel found Emilee sobbing when he came in from the fields with a fat, young rabbit for their supper. He couldn't bear to see her cry, so he pulled her onto his lap and kissed the tears from her round face. "Sweetheart," he said, "we'll have more young'uns."

Emilee laughed through her tears. "Chances are they'll all be boys. Matthew, Mark, and Luke to go with little John."

What no one could have predicted was Will's long-term solution to his dilemma. He rode off that summer, in the year of Julie's death, and came back with a new mother for the baby he'd dubbed Copper because her hair shone in the sunlight like a newly minted penny. Nobody could have figured that Will would bring a stranger into their midst. But he did. He went all the way to Lexington and fetched Julie's sister, Grace.

CHAPTER 7

Years of memories came and went for Will Brown this stormy August afternoon. Days long gone were still as clear as yesterday in his mind. He struck out blindly with the willow switch he'd cut just hours before and called his dead wife's name as if he were still on the banks of the flooding Troublesome, not in his barn more than fifteen years later. His heart seized violently, and emotion as raw as the night Julie had been swept away threatened to overwhelm him.

He couldn't help but blame himself. *What if I had encouraged Granny to stay longer? What if I'd listened to my own intuition and taken the wagon instead of that flimsy buggy? What if I hadn't forced Samson into that raging creek?* Even his horse had had more sense than he did that awful night.

"Will!" He heard a call from far away. *Grace,* he thought. Another reason to feel guilty. He'd practically forced her to leave the place she loved to come and help him raise Copper. Every time he looked in her eyes he could see that she hadn't forgiven him for that. It didn't matter that he had fallen in love with her.

"What are you doing?" Grace asked as she stepped into the barn.

"Nothing," he said, fighting to keep his voice steady.

"Who are you talking to?"

"No one," he said, his back a barrier to her worried voice.

"You missed your dinner," she said as if it mattered.

"Save it for supper." He was suddenly weary. It was all too much.

"Will . . ." She touched his arm.

"Leave me be, Grace!" He shrugged off her hand and fled. He had to get to the cemetery. Maybe there he could find forgiveness.

Grace stood alone in the barn, her hands clenched. The storm was nearly over, but a drip of rain still fell through a hole in the roof. A dirty puddle at her feet received each drop that fell. *Plop. Plop. Plop.* Her heart beat in cadence with the leak, the drops like a broken strand of pearls, reminding her of her inability to comfort her husband.

As much as she had come to love Will, secrets from the past kept their hold on her heart. Things had gone terribly wrong somehow, for even though he showed his love in countless ways, she couldn't bring herself to freely love him back. She'd hardened her heart, made a shield against him out of cold guilt and hot anger.

Grace had her own memories from days gone by. . . .

Will had shown up on her front porch months after Julie's death, with a proposition for her. He wanted her to come back with him to Troublesome Creek to help him raise her sister's daughter. He had been honest in his intent; she had to give him that. But she was not. Oh, she certainly was not.

Her life in Lexington was not as she pretended it to be, not at all as she had portrayed it in her letters to Julie. She would sit at the window with her pen and paper and spin fanciful tales of a full and exciting life. The ink flowed with colorful words while the world outside her window was cold and as gray as ash. She wrote of days too short for everything she needed to accomplish while the clock in the parlor ticked out minutes of loneliness, hours of despair.

All of her friends had husbands and children. When she was invited to their homes for luncheons or dinner parties, she was always the odd one out. Even at church she sat alone, the pew marked *Taylor* a sad reminder of happier times. The suitor she had planned to marry before her mother died–before her duty to her father and her sister claimed her life–now had a wife, a son, and a daughter. She knew people felt sorry for her, and she chafed under their pity. She could see her life unfolding as the spinster schoolteacher caring for everyone's children but her own. Sometimes her arms ached for a child. There seemed no hope, no love anywhere for Grace.

Will had come to her house every day for a week, asking the same thing. He was persistent—none of her arguments against his plan deterred him.

One morning he had come early, much too early. She was in her wrapper, drinking tea and looking at the morning mail. The maid answered his knock at the door, and he strode, unannounced, right past her to where Grace was sitting. Grace hadn't even dressed her hair yet, and it hung in a long, messy braid halfway down her back. Her hands flew up, arranging pins, twisting the braid into a knot.

"For heaven's sake," she exclaimed, shifting in her chair and clutching her dressing gown at her throat. "Give a body a moment's notice!"

"I figured you'd been up since daylight milking cows and gathering eggs." His smile was quick and warm and dimpled his cheeks.

She saw the twinkle in his eyes. "Do I look like I milk cows?"

"No, ma'am, you surely don't. But wouldn't you like to?"

He took a chair and turned it around. He straddled it and sat facing her, his dark brown eyes taking her measure. Despite her misgivings, she enjoyed his visits. He was a spark of excitement, and she found herself responding to his warmth. It had been a long time since anyone had looked at her like she was needed.

"It's like this," Will said. "The baby needs you. You're the nearest to a mother she could have now. You're her kin. You owe it to us."

He'd struck a nerve. He was much too close to the truth as Grace knew it. She covered her face with her hands. When he'd written and told her of the circumstances surrounding Julie's death, she nearly died herself, for she was guilty in a way she would never admit. Her mind ticked off all the gifts she'd posted, all the letters she had written, none offering the love and forgiveness she knew her sister longed for. When she had discovered her sister's shameful condition, she had made plans to send her away to a home for unwed mothers. Julie had cried and pleaded to keep her baby, but Grace was not moved by her histrionics. Julie would not be allowed to bring shame into their house. They would say that Julie was away at school; then she could come back and no one would be the wiser.

These were things Will didn't need to know. He was right about her debt, but she owed *him* nothing. Her balance due was to her sister and the baby, Laura Grace. For, after all, Grace had sent her sister to her grave. She'd given Julie no choice but to run away.

She'd cocked her head and considered the man in front of her. Will Brown was not the stammering boy she'd banned from her property five years ago when he'd shown up to claim Julie. He was a man—determined and persuasive. She couldn't help but notice his face was handsome, even in ragged grief. And he was charming. He was a man on fire, and his love for his daughter consumed him.

"Give us a year of your time," he had pleaded, "and then if you can stand to leave Laura Grace, so be it. You're the nearest person to her mother, and she needs a woman's touch. I don't know what I'll do if you won't help me."

Her mind churned with thoughts of what she'd lose if she did his bidding. She was a single woman—how could she leave town in the company of a man? She could never come back to Lexington once her reputation was ruined, and she fully intended to come back.

After some thought, she devised a plan, a mock wedding. They would marry in name only; she would give him his year, just long enough for her to persuade him to let her leave with the baby. Then she could raise her niece as she saw fit, in the proper way and in the proper place. It made perfect sense. She would keep her father's house, and with her inheritance she would turn it into a girls' school. It mightn't be perfectly proper–she would be a woman who'd left her husband after all–but as long as there was no divorce she could function once again in polite society.

She'd told him her terms, if not all her plans, and he agreed. He'd not even given her time to buy a new hat. They married at the Fayette County courthouse on their way out of town; the janitor and his wife were their only witnesses. Then he'd whisked her away to a place where people lived without libraries, without concerts and plays, without education, and–to her mind–without the hope of anything better.

Oh, that was a dreadful time. One day she was teaching music at the Finishing School for Young Ladies, the next she was no better than a servant living in a run-down cabin, surrounded by the boxes of books she'd had shipped, her piano, and a baby to raise. She lived on hope–the hope of escape.

It didn't turn out the way she'd planned, of course. When did things ever turn out right for her? Will was so good to her, so respectful and kind, and she had never known a man so tender toward his child. It was as if her heart had a mind of its own.

Against her dearest wish to leave and take the baby with her, she stayed. How could she have been so weak?

Grace knew Will would never love her the way he had loved Julie. She wished that it were different, but every time she looked at Laura Grace she remembered Julie and she knew it would never be. How could she compete with a ghost? She never meant to fall in love with him, but she did. And in the dark of night, she would think about her sin against her sister. Out of pride she'd turned her back on Julie when she needed her most, and then out of weakness Grace had fallen in love with the man who would always love her sister best.

Often Grace would take out Julie's letters. One she had written soon after she ran away still broke Grace's heart.

> *Dear Grace,*
> *I am so sorry for leaving you and Father the way I did. You know why I had to do this. Just know and accept that it is for the best. I am happy, and Will is good to me. Please be happy for me, and, dearest sister, please forgive me.*

Grace had answered her sister's letters, but Julie never received her forgiveness. Julie went to her watery grave without knowing how much Grace loved her.

Grace had kept her resolve against Will for nearly a year. To the outside world they lived as man and wife, but behind closed doors he had his bed and she had hers. He never forced the issue.

But that one time . . . he'd found her in the springhouse. . . . It was so cool there, a relief from the summer heat, and the fresh clean smell of mint from her herb garden drifted in from the open door. She'd glanced up from her work and caught his look of need. She could have left; he wouldn't have stopped her. Instead she welcomed his embrace.

He'd murmured, "Ah, Grace . . ." against her neck. . . . Then there was no turning back.

The thin gold ring on her finger gave him rights, but she still held herself apart. To do otherwise would be to betray the sister who looked over her shoulder every time Will held her close.

And so the years passed, and she found herself settled on the creek with little hope of ever leaving. If she had thought Will might let her take Laura Grace, that hope was dashed when their twins were born. He loved them to distraction, and they adored their father.

And now, fifteen years after she first came to Troublesome Creek, sometimes the work was enough. Sometimes she was almost happy: well, content anyway—content to be in the same room as Will, content to be his wife, even if by default. Until memories of Julie lodged in her heart and made her feel like the substitute she knew she was. She'd never be better than hand-me-down clothes to him, never more than second best. Her stomach churned, and her head began to pound in its familiar rhythm of resentment.

Her anger pulled her back from her memories, back to the barn. She smacked her arms against her sides, then walked to the window and watched as Will climbed the mountain beyond the meadow. *He's going to the cemetery,* she thought. *Julie claims him even from the grave.* A taste as bitter as green persimmons puckered her mouth. *I never stood a chance.* She stood there trapped in guilt, a martyr to her own cause.

The next morning dawned hot and muggy. The brief respite from the heat generated by yesterday's rain dissipated rapidly as the sun rose into the hazy August sky.

Copper ran her hand beneath her thick red hair and cooled her neck with a church fan. She stood on the porch and watched the twins play beside a mud hole, shaded by the leafy branches of a runty apple tree. Later she'd have the boys gather the knotty green apples that lay scattered on the ground; then they could feed the fruit to the pigs. That was all it was good for anyway. That tree could never hold its fruit until harvesttime.

Copper longed to join in their fun as Willy patted out mud pies and Daniel decorated them with bits of leaves and small twigs.

"Sissy, Sissy," Daniel called, "come and play! You can make a chocolate cake in this old pan."

"Yeah," Willy replied, "then Daniel will eat it!" He laughed so hard at his joke that he tumbled into the water.

Daniel giggled and splashed Willy.

"I sure wish I could," Copper said, "but I'd best finish the breakfast dishes. I'll save the rinse water for you little pigs. Mam will whip us all if she catches you covered with mud."

Leaving the door open, she entered the large front room of the cabin. Colorful and spacious, decorated with finery seldom seen in mountain homes, it served as both kitchen and parlor. One wall held two large bookcases separated by an upright piano, and the polished wood floor was covered by a worn Turkish carpet, its once bright red faded to a rusty brown. Starched white curtains crisscrossed the sunny windows.

Copper poured hot water from the heavy iron teakettle over the dishes in a large white enamel pan. Daddy had bought it off a gypsy tinker just last week. It had one little rust spot up near the rim that the tinker had repaired. No telling where he'd gotten it. Folks all said gypsies were thieves, but Daddy had simply declared, "There but for the grace of God . . ."

Her fingers traced the cheery-red rim of the pan. *It's too pretty for such an ugly job.* Dried egg clung stubbornly to the plates and forks, and coffee stained the cups. "Ouch," she said under her breath as a splash of boiling rinse water hit her hand. She hopped in place, a quiet little dance of pain, and reached for the butter to soothe her burn.

Without a pang of guilt, Copper stacked the dishes to dry on one of Mam's monogrammed tea towels. She'd have plenty of time to put them in the cupboard before Mam discovered that they weren't dried by hand. Mam didn't cotton to shortcuts.

Once Copper sized the inside of the cast-iron skillet with a dollop of lard from the yellow lard pail, she hung it on a nail by the stove. Copper saved the dirty dishwater in the slop bucket for the hog, but she left the rinse pan on the table.

She checked on the boys. They were laughing and flinging mud at each other. Crossing the room, she eased the bedroom door open, holding her breath against its creak. Mam lay with her eyes closed, enduring one of her sick headaches, a rag across her forehead. Copper peeled off the warm rag and soaked it in the bowl of water that sat on the bedside table. The sharp tang of vinegar stung her nostrils as she wrung the rag out with her good hand. She massaged Mam's temples and whispered, "Are you feeling any better?"

Mam drew the rag over her eyes. She waved Copper away. "Too loud. Keep them quiet."

Copper carried the little basin Mam had retched in outside and emptied it by the fence row. She rinsed the basin and carried it back to the bedside, then fanned Mam for a few minutes, barely stirring the humid air that drifted in from the only window in the room.

A single sheet of stationery fell from the nightstand to the floor. Retrieving it, Copper shook her head. She should have known. Mam often took to her bed after receiving a letter from her friend Millicent. Reading about that woman's *wonderful* life in faraway Philadelphia always stirred up trouble. A shriek from Willy sailed in through the screen. Mam moaned and turned to the wall.

Copper straightened the sheet around her shoulders. "Should I take them for a walk?"

Only Mam's soft grunt acknowledged her, so she slipped from the room.

She pushed the screen door open with her hip and carried the heavy pan of rinse water out. The boys stood on one end of the porch, their clothes in a soggy pile. They shivered as she poured cups of water over their heads and washed them clean with a bar of lye soap. Willy giggled when she rinsed them with dippers full of warm water from the rain barrel. They stood in the sun to dry as she scraped mud from their overalls with an old butter knife. Once that was done, she draped the overalls over the porch rail. It was two days 'til washday. Copper knew the clothes would sour if left in a wet heap. She'd put them with the rest of the laundry when they dried.

"Boys, would you like to scout for locust shells?" she asked softly. She grabbed at Willy, who hopped wildly across the porch, one leg in, one leg out of his clean overalls. He was impulsive, strong-willed, and always busy—a little whirlwind with his blond hair sticking straight up and his eyes dancing. He stood a head taller than his twin and was built like Daddy with broad shoulders and wiry muscles.

Daniel was a dreamer. He puzzled over things, taking his time, thinking before he acted. He was so slight he looked younger than Willy. With his white-gold hair and his sleepy green eyes, he didn't favor his twin. He took off to the cellar and came back with a canning jar.

"Stand still, Willy," Copper whispered harshly. She combed their hair, slicking Daniel's behind his ears and pulling Willy's into bangs across his forehead. "You'll have to be as quiet as Indian scouts. Any noise could make the locusts fly away."

Copper tied the strings of her brown-and-blue-gingham sunbonnet under her chin, tucked a spool of black sewing thread in the pocket of her matching dress, and proceeded down the limestone walk that split the front yard. The two little boys, lips tightly sealed, faces drawn in concentration, waddled like ducklings behind her, scuffling only once as Willy tried to wrest the jar from Daniel.

Copper stopped. Willy was so preoccupied with the jar that he smacked into Copper's backside. She turned to face them and arched her right eyebrow, a perfect mimic of Mam. Willy

released his hold on the jar, leaving Daniel to carry it importantly, clutched to his little round belly.

They approached the creek several yards upstream from
the family's favorite picnic spot. They were hidden from
view because the brook twisted in upon itself there and
formed steep banks covered with tall weeds and blackberry
brambles.

Copper led the boys to a stately sycamore. Chances
were, she knew, locusts had picked that tree on which to shed
their skins. The tree probably reminded the insects of a giant
locust, seeing how it was also shedding. Long strips of gray-
white bark lay scattered along the ground and crackled when
they stepped on them. Sure enough, several empty shells
clung to the tree. They made fine playthings and were
surprisingly sturdy. The boys would have a good time with
them.

"All right, scouts," she said to her big-eyed brothers. "I am
going to leave you here to collect these rare specimens while
I commence on up the creek to see if I might come upon a
snakeskin to add to our collection. Can you handle this job
alone?"

Two heads nodded in unison, and two little mouths
remained clamped shut.

Copper hurried up the creek to the point where her father's
farm was separated from Daniel Pelfrey's by only a narrow crook
of water. She hoped to see Daniel's son John working in the
cornfield there. She needed to talk to him. Oh, she was so tired.
She stopped and stretched and rubbed her eyes, thinking of the
night before. . . .

They'd eaten a cold supper without Daddy, and he didn't come in for the Bible reading. Mam sent them to bed early, and Copper tried to sleep despite the loud creaking of Mam's chair.

She'd roused as the mantel clock bonged eleven times and the screen door slapped shut.

"What do you want from me, Grace?" Copper heard through the walls of her bedroom.

A heavy silence.

Footsteps sounded across the floor. The rocker stopped.

Copper wished for sleep; she pulled her pillow over her ears against their angry voices. Mam's accusations about his traipsing around all night. Daddy's rejoinder. But then her own name perked her ears. She might as well listen if they were going to fight about her.

"Why are you so set on sending her off somewhere strange?" Daddy's voice. "There's nothing she needs to learn that you can't teach her right here."

"Will, she needs to experience other things, other places. You're being selfish. . . ." Mam's voice trailed off.

"How do you know you're right? She's happy here." His voice was exasperated.

"For how long? She's not your little girl anymore. Can't you see that?"

"Grace, give me time. I don't know if I can send her away." He sounded so sad it made Copper want to weep.

Mam's silence spoke volumes. Copper could picture

Mam turning away from Daddy, how she'd present her straight back and rigid shoulders to him, the way she often did to Copper. Mam closed you off like she lived behind a screen door. And she'd rarely let you slip the latch.

Her father sighed. "I'm going to take a smoke."

Two sets of footsteps sounded in opposite directions. Their bedroom door opened and closed. The screen door slapped again.

Copper had knelt, her featherbed mattress sinking under her knees, and stared out the window at the big yellow moon floating over the tall pines in the backyard. *Mam won't send me away,* she'd vowed. *I'll leave this house before I leave this mountain....*

Now Copper stood hidden behind a tree on her side of the creek. She clutched a handful of green acorns, their little caps stuck tight to their shells, and bided her time. She watched John Pelfrey shuck an ear of corn. He tested its hardness with his thumbnail. "Not quite ready," she heard. "Another week or two." His hound sat at his feet and gazed up at him as if she understood. John popped a few kernels into his mouth, then handed the ear to Faithful, who wrestled it along the ground.

"Oh!" He rubbed his arm and jerked around. "Ouch!" He stood on one foot and rubbed his ankle against his leg.

His dog dropped the corn and wagged her tail, looking off across the creek.

Copper flashed a smile and took off running. She laughed when John yelled threats and followed her, splashing across Troublesome Creek. She'd have to be fast, for John was much taller and could cover ground quickly. He was also stronger, though she would never admit it.

He caught her before she ran twenty feet and locked her head in the crook of his arm. "Drop it!"

She clenched her fist and looked up at him. He wasn't smiling, and his green eyes had a serious look. He scrubbed her scalp with his knuckles until she opened her hand and let several acorns fall to the ground.

"Uncle!" she yelled.

"I've a mind to keep you here 'til the sun sets." John scrubbed her head again.

Copper pinched his arm hard and danced away, laughing.

"You're not being very ladylike, Pest."

"I don't want to be a lady, John Pelfrey."

"Well, you ain't. That's for certain sure. What're you doin' here?" He pushed his thick wheat-colored hair off his forehead, his face softening as he looked at her.

"Just came to aggravate you."

"Well, you did." John turned to cross the creek again. "I got work to do."

"Wait—please—I need to talk to you. Can you meet me down by the creek tomorrow night?"

"Sure," he replied. "But cain't you tell me what's wrong?"

"Not now, John. I've got to get back. See you tomorrow night."

When Copper got back, the boys were right where she left them. They each had three locust shells clinging to their denim overalls, and several live ones thrummed inside the Mason jar.

"Did you find any sheds?" Daniel asked.

"Just one." She unwrapped a long, dry skin from her wrist. "But it's a good one. Must be four feet. Probably a blacksnake's."

Willy took the shed. "Nope," he said. "This here's from a king cobra from India, like Mam showed us in that picture book."

"Huh." Daniel stroked it with one finger. "Wonder how it got here."

"Swum clean across the ocean." Willy draped it across his shoulders. "They're fine swimmers once they get out of them baskets."

Copper carried the jar and let the boys run ahead to the shade of the porch. She took the spool from her pocket and tied a length of heavy thread to a back leg of two of the buzzing bugs. She handed a thread to each of the twins. "Hold tight." The tethered insects flew in circles above their heads. "Play quietly now. I'm going in to check on Mam and start supper."

CHAPTER 8

Washday dawned, and muddleheaded Copper stared sleepily into her oatmeal. She'd sneaked out of the house the night before, just after the clock struck midnight, to meet John Pelfrey down by the swinging bridge. He was her best friend and the only boy she liked. Sometimes it seemed like they were kin they were so close. She even called his ma and pa Aunt and Uncle, even though they were no relation.

Aunt Emilee liked to tell stories about when Copper and John were little. Copper's favorite was of when they were babies, and though John was older by a good six months, she learned to walk first. Aunt Emilee said he would sit like a fat king and hold out his hand for Copper to help him up as she toddled by. If she didn't do what he wanted, he would grab her ankle and drag her down beside him.

Now Copper loved to go to Aunt Emilee's to help with the Pelfrey's latest babies, twins like Willy and Daniel. There were twelve boys, counting John, in their family, and their house was full of fun. Unlike her own house, she thought, which was full of work, work, work.

As if to prove her point, Mam called from the front porch, "Laura Grace, please finish your breakfast and come help with the wash."

The big, steaming copper kettle sat over a fire Willy was stoking, fueled by small twigs and hickory logs. Mam was stirring the first load of dirty clothing with a long-handled laundry paddle. Nearby, the washboard sat in a smaller tub of water. Copper took over stirring while Mam used the board. Mam rubbed a pair of Willy's pants up and down its ribbed front, applied lye soap to a stubborn grass stain, then doused the pants under water before scrubbing them again. Finally she placed them on a steadily growing mound of laundry waiting to be placed in the boiling wash water.

The sun was beginning to warm the day, and Copper paused to take in the beauty of the moment. *God is good.* She wished she could be up in the mountains in the distance, where the same sun that warmed her shoulders was burning off the fog that rose like gauzy gray ribbons of smoke.

"Mam," Copper said, "look how pretty the mountains are this morning."

Mam stayed hunched over the washboard. "Stop daydreaming." Stung, Copper fished whites from the kettle with the wooden paddle and dropped them into a galvanized tub of clean rinse water. As Mam dumped shirts, church pants, skirts, and aprons into the wash, Copper rinsed the whites, wrung them out, and hung them to dry on the clothesline in the sunny side yard. Forgetting Mam's rebuke, she hummed a tune as she worked.

Soon the line was full of shirt—tails up, seam to seam—pegged to the sagging cord with wooden pins that Daddy had whittled. Copper folded sheets in half and hung them with matching pillowcases. Towels, tea towels, and a tablecloth merrily embroidered with butterflies and daisies stretched to meet nightgowns that danced in the breeze beside bashful pantalets and camisoles. She laid sturdier articles on the grass, artfully arranging Daddy's work shirts and overalls with his long brown socks until the yard looked like an army of resting headless men.

While Mam and Copper were busy with the wash, Willy and Daniel were charged with keeping the dog and chickens out of the yard until the clothes dried. They stood like soldiers, wooden play guns poised, ready to chase any creature foolish enough to venture into their territory. Copper thought washday must be their favorite day of the week. They loved to pester the chickens.

Quietly, Willy waited while a hapless hen came close, pecking and scratching at the ground. Then, screaming like a banshee, he charged the poor thing, causing her to spread her wings, trying to fly as she ran awkwardly back to the barnyard.

"I got one, Daniel," he crowed. "I sure scared that Johnny Reb back where he belongs."

"Willy," Mam said, "for heaven's sake, just shoo the chickens. Don't frighten them to death. And where did you get the term *Johnny Reb*? I don't think that was in last week's history lesson."

Copper listened to Mam admonish her little brother. She knew Willy had picked up more than one expression Mam wouldn't like while playing after church. It seemed the men and boys of the community would never let that terrible war die. It had been years since the last battle, yet still the boys chose sides as Yankees or Rebels and fought it all over again. And grown men still argued which side was wrong and which was right.

"Mam, those two are busy making next Monday's wash," Copper said. "Maybe we should just let them run naked."

"Is that an appropriate thing for a young lady to say?" Mam arched an eyebrow. "Though the thought does have merit. Let's sit on the porch in the shade for a minute and catch our breath. I'll get some tea."

Copper sat on the plank floor, letting her legs dangle off the side, watching the wash flap in the summer breeze. Mam was being nice; it made her feel guilty about sneaking out of the house last night.

Lord, Copper prayed silently, selfishly, *please don't let Mam find out.*

"Laura Grace," Mam said through the screen door, "have you seen the blackberry jam? I thought I put out a new jar this morning."

"No, ma'am. I had honey on my biscuit."

"I don't understand what is happening around here lately." Mam handed Copper a glass of tea. "Things keep disappearing. Last week it was the sugar bowl. The week before, my tortoise-shell comb. I've got to keep a better eye on the boys, though they deny any wrongdoing."

"Maybe it's a raccoon. Remember a couple of years ago when one stole all of Daddy's quarters?"

"But a sugar bowl, Laura Grace?" Mam took off her spectacles and pinched the bridge of her nose. "That doesn't seem possible."

"I don't know, Mam. They have hands just like a man. Maybe they pair up and one holds the door open while the other one pilfers from our kitchen."

Mam shook her head. "Your imagination. I sure miss my comb. I'll have to order another. . . . If it is coons we'll have to keep the windows down at night. They'll tear up the screens."

Copper fanned her face with her hand and sipped her tea. "Oh, that would be miserable hot, Mam. We should just let Pawpaw sleep in the kitchen. He'd scare the varmints away."

"Yes, and eat everything in the house at the same time," Mam declared. "That dog would be worse than the raccoons."

After a few minutes of resting from the morning's labor, Copper stood and stretched, rubbing the sore spot on her lower back—the one that appeared like clockwork every Monday, following hours of stirring a pot of heavy laundry.

By afternoon, Mam went inside to start supper, saying she had a mess of pole beans to snap.

Copper gathered the sun-dried, sweet-smelling laundry, then folded towels, dishrags, and the boys' everyday clothes. She piled them in a basket to put away directly. After supper, she'd sprinkle clean water over the starched whites and Sunday clothes. Then she'd roll them up, tuck them into the woven laundry basket, and cover it with a damp towel ready for ironing. She'd help Mam with that tomorrow.

She'd saved her least favorite job for last—scrubbing down the outhouse. She poured a bucket of soapy water from the cooling copper kettle and carried it to the two-seater. They kept an old, nubby straw broom in the corner, and she used its handle to knock down a fresh mud dauber's nest, closing her eyes against the dust, hoping the wasp wouldn't fly in and take revenge.

Just who, she wondered, *would scrub the outhouse if Mam sent me away? And who would milk the cow? Who would mind the boys?* It seemed like she did enough work to warrant her place in the household. She felt certain that if she left for a few days Mam would see that she couldn't get along without her.

Sticking her broom in the bucket of water, she scrubbed the bench seat, then sluiced water out and washed the floor. She used the damp broom to swipe spiderwebs out of the corners and sprinkled lye down the toilet hole. It left a fresh, clean smell.

Pleased with a job well done, Copper finished the task by placing sheets of torn newsprint in the basket kept for that purpose. She put the broom back in the corner. It would be handy in case there was a lizard lurking about. One good whack against the bench would send the beady-eyed, nosy little creature scurrying away. Lastly, she propped the door open so the sun and breeze could freshen and dry the toilet.

She dreaded the thought of more work waiting for her back at the house. The porch needed mopping; the steps needed scouring. And the rinse water needed emptying into the barrel kept to store water clean enough to use again for baths or to clean the house. Nothing was wasted.

As she worked, Copper pondered things she'd heard Mam and Daddy say. She'd caught snippets of conversation before—

"finishing school," "old enough," "better for her," and the dreadful "young lady"–but she'd always thought Daddy's will would prevail. She'd never fretted about it. But since her fifteenth birthday, things had subtly shifted. She was afraid Mam was wearing Daddy down.

She was glad she'd met with John last night. He would help her find a place to hide out when she needed it. One thing was sure and it grew surer as each day passed: Copper Brown was not going to boarding school. She was not leaving Troublesome Creek.

A hint of fall tinted the air the next day when Copper went out to milk. She was sure she could smell burning leaves, though they were just beginning to turn, and the early morning air had a crispness about it, but that wouldn't last much past sunup. It was so quiet she could hear the creek burbling down its bed, and the mountains that surrounded their cabin stood like noble sentries, guarding her day. Oh, she loved this place.

Her favorite Scripture played like a familiar melody in her mind: *"Even them will I bring to my holy mountain, and make them joyful in my house of prayer."* She couldn't wait to get up there where the morning's hush would surround her with peace so palpable you could wear it like a shawl.

She found her cow at the stable door waiting for breakfast. "Come on, Molly." She pestered the fat cow, holding her feed bucket just out of reach, making the lazy animal enter the stall before she got a bite. "That's a good girl. Have some."

Molly licked the corners of the grain box with her big rough tongue, enjoying every morsel of her breakfast, then nibbled at the hay sticking out of the manger before leaning her head against it and falling asleep. The cow snored like a man. There was something hypnotic about the pull and swish of milking: the same movements over and over 'til all four teats were stripped, Molly's udder was empty, and the bucket was full.

Copper patted the cow's round, fawn-colored side. She remembered the malicious Beulah who would wait until the milking was nearly done, then shift her weight and stick one manure-clotted foot right in the bucket or swing her tail hatefully, catching Copper upside her face. She'd take Molly over Beulah anytime, especially today, when she was in a hurry to finish her morning chores. She had to act as if she wasn't, though, as if it were any other Tuesday.

She carried her full bucket to the springhouse. Daddy's daddy had built it out of thick blocks of limestone over a spring that bubbled up icy cold from the ground; it was always cool. There were square openings in the stone floor through which you could lower the milk or whatever else needed to be kept cold into the water below.

She poured the milk through a strainer into another bucket, tapped the lid on, hung the bucket on a rope, then gently lowered it into the water. They always had fresh milk, plenty of butter and cheese, and every third day, Mam gave the milk to whoever came to the door for it. Aggravated as she was with Mam, Copper had to admit that she was awfully good to people. She kept a little purse tucked away in the chiffonier and every so often, when Brother Isaac—who had taken over the pulpit when his father, Nathan, died not long after he had returned from

Lexington with this teaching certificate–told her of a need, she'd take it out and press bills into his hand. Her only request was that he not tell where the money came from. Sometimes Copper wondered what Mam's life had been like before she came to live with them. Daddy told her a little bit, but Mam didn't want to talk about it.

Copper liked the springhouse and usually lingered there looking through the holes to spy frogs or turtles. But she hurried now, scouring the milk bucket and the strainer, anxious to be off.

She carried a crock of fresh cream to the house, where Mam was ironing, then sat at the table and ate her breakfast. The heavy sadiron hissed when Mam took it from the stove and pressed it across the damp starched fabric of Daddy's Sunday shirt.

"I never found that jar of jam," Mam fussed as if the missing fruit were a personal affront. "And it was the final jar of blackberry from last year too." She sprinkled water from her hand across the yoke of the shirt.

"That's okay, Mam. This marmalade's fine with me. I like how we wait 'til the first snowfall before we open the summer's canning. Seems that makes it all the sweeter."

"I should be finished with the whites by noon." Mam finished the shirt, then folded a sheet in quarters and smoothed it across the ironing board. "Then you can get to the rest of the ironing. I'll save the pillowcases for you."

"Thanks." Copper loved to do the pillowcases. They were so easy, and she liked the embroidered edges. "I'll be really careful not to scorch them today."

"Everyone has to learn. I burned my share of linens," Mam admitted.

Copper nearly choked on her biscuit. Mam burned linens? Copper was sure that never happened but once.

"I was married to your father before I ever hefted an iron. At home we had a woman who came in and did the wash." Mam's voice was wistful.

She was making Copper feel guilty, being so nice. Copper could almost forget that Mam was plotting to send her to boarding school. Almost.

❧❀☙

After breakfast, Copper sneaked off to meet with John Pelfrey, but Paw-paw wouldn't stay behind. "All right, but you'll have to keep my secret. No telling the barn cats!"

Paw-paw snuffled at her hand, then trotted to keep up. He was Copper's pet—a gift for her fourth birthday. Eleven years later, his muzzle was gray, and one leg didn't bend anymore. Daddy said he had rheumatism and let him sleep in the house by the fireplace on cold nights.

John was waiting for her at the edge of the cow pasture. "I was thinking we'd look there." He pointed up the mountain. "Yonder, past the graveyard. I remember some caves from once when I was fox hunting."

"How did you get away today?"

"I just laid down my shovel and walked off. Ain't like nobody watches me work, Pest."

"You're so lucky to be a boy." Copper kicked the dirt, frowning. "Every move I make is minded."

They climbed steadily—she trying to match his long stride, he pausing occasionally to let her catch up.

"Have you been here 'fore today?" he asked, stopping at the entrance to the cemetery.

"Only when Granny Pelfrey died. I was maybe five. Why do you think our folks are all buried in the same place?"

"Probably because we're close as kin. You want to go in?" He tore a length of Virginia creeper vine from the iron gate and forced it open.

"I don't think so," Copper replied but took his hand as he led the way inside the graveyard. "It's creepy in here, John."

"Nah, it ain't. There's nobody in here that's not family. Mind the poison ivy." He gestured to a thicket not six inches from her foot. "Hold your skirts up. The poison will climb right up you."

"Look, here's Granny Pelfrey's grave. Do you remember her?"

"'Course I do. Don't you recollect she lived with us 'til she died?"

"She used to take me up the mountain to look for herbs and mushrooms." Copper brushed some twigs from the grave. "I still remember lots of things Granny taught me. She knew how to fix about anything that ails a body."

John looked at her, his green eyes, as always, honest and direct. "You make me think of her sometimes, the way you're so strong-minded. Granny was like that."

"Why do people get buried up the mountain, all catty-wampus?" Copper asked. "Why not down where it's flatter and easier to get to?"

"Closer to heaven, I reckon. Our kinfolk were all highlanders. If they'd wanted to lay flat, we'd be living in Kansas. Watch yourself there. . . ." John reached around her as she leaned against the monument marked *Pelfrey* and flung a yard-long blacksnake clean over the fence.

She shivered. "I hate it when they sneak up on a body like that."

"I think it's tuther way round, Pest. We snuck up on him."

"See why I don't like graveyards?" She wrinkled her nose. "Let's go. . . . What's this, then? Julie Brown?" She knelt. "That's my mother's name."

"Sure, 'cause that's your mother's grave. I used to come up here with my ma to visit her."

"Why has no one told me about her? Everything's such a secret. What do you know, John?"

"No more'n you, really . . . just that Ma loved her."

"Look." Wilted daisies hung over the small stone marker. "Where do you reckon those came from?"

"Somebody's visited, seems like. This grave's cleaner than the rest, and it looks like somebody with long legs has been stepping over the fence there." He shaded his eyes and looked at the sun. "Come on—it's getting toward noon. We ain't got much time."

"Paw-paw," she called. "Come!"

The old black hound tore out of the brush like a pup, the far-flung snake hanging from his mouth.

"Leave it," she commanded, pointing.

He whined but dropped his prize and followed her in his lopsided, three-legged gait, his crippled leg stuck out like a stick.

Three-quarters of a mile later, John figured they'd best head back down mountain. "It's farther than I recollected, Pest. We'll be found out if you don't get back soon. How about tomorrow?"

"Can't—we're canning tomatoes. Maybe Thursday?"

"Okay by me. Let's meet at the cemetery. That'll save time."

"Don't let it slip to anyone that we were up here. Nobody must know what I'm planning. If Mam finds out she'll put stamps on my head and mail me to Philadelphia."

John chuckled. "You come up with the strangest ideas."

"I'm serious," she replied. "We must be careful."

By the time Copper returned to the house, most of the ironing was finished and put away. She sighed in relief. Nobody seemed to have missed her. She heated up the iron and did the work clothes, saving the pillowcases last for pure pleasure. There were five, one for each pillow, starched slick and stiff as the ironing board. When they were first put on the pillows, your head would slide right off onto the feather bed and you'd wake with a crick in your neck. You had to pound them a little to break them in.

She carried the finished stack to the press and placed them beside the sheets Mam had done. They had to be in a certain order so the embroidery of the cases matched the embroidery of the sheets. That way when they pulled them out Monday morning to make up the beds, the job would go faster. One washday, she remembered, she didn't get out of bed fast enough so Mam rolled her right out onto the floor when she pulled her sheet off the bed. It didn't take but once for Mam to teach you a lesson.

Supper was already cooked that night when Daddy came in from the fields. A plate of sliced tomatoes sat beside a platter of fried chicken, and a skillet of corn bread, cut in pie-shaped wedges, cooled on a teaberry plate. Mam was just dishing up the shelly beans. Copper poured cold buttermilk into a pretty glass for him.

"Where's my Mason jar?" Daddy asked.

"I don't know," Mam replied. "I couldn't find it."

"Well, fiddlesticks. I can't drink out of this frill."

"Will," Mam cautioned, as four little ears perked up, "please. Where did you leave it?"

"Let's see . . . hmm . . . by the rocker on the porch. I had a cool drink of springwater before bed last night."

"I don't see how I could have missed it," Mam said. "Willy, go look."

"Fiddle–," Willy started to say before Daddy reached across the table and thumped him on the top of the head with the middle knuckle of his right hand.

"I'll fetch it," Daniel called over his shoulder as he scooted off his chair and slammed out the screen door, leaving Mam to shake her head at Daddy.

"But I was supposed to," Willy whined.

"It ain't no place out here," Daniel called through the door.

Mam sighed. "Oh, Daniel, your language."

"Sorry, Mam. I forgot. It's not no place out here."

Mam sank into her chair, a look of resignation on her face, as Daniel took his place at the table, giggling behind his hand when Willy slurped a long drink of milk, then belched.

"Let's say grace," Daddy said, restoring order as they clasped hands. "Lord, thank You for our food. May it nourish our bodies, the temple of our souls, and thank You for laughter and belches and boys."

Thursday morning found Copper and Paw-paw waiting for John Pelfrey at the cemetery gate. She had rushed poor Molly through the milking with a promise of extra feed and hurried away before Mam could find her another task. Her willow basket hung on her arm.

"Hey," John called. "You ready? I hope you got something to eat in that tote."

"I brought some leftover potatoes and some corn bread. Are you hungry now?" She eyed his uncombed hair. "Your head looks like a just-mowed field. Stand still." She stretched on tiptoe to smooth his hair. She trailed her fingers down his cheek. "What's this?" she teased. "You're growing whiskers."

"That's what men do, Pest." John squared his shoulders as she watched his eyes take her in. "Looks like I ain't the only one changing."

She crossed her arms over her chest and frowned. "I don't want us to change. I like things as they are."

"Some changes are good," he replied, looking at her with eyes as green as her own.

"Not if they get me sent away, John. Growing up's going to get me sent to boarding school."

"Not if I can help it." He took her basket. "Let's go find that cave. You could hide up there for days and no one would ever find you."

The cave they sought was one of many connected by tunnels that twisted like a rabbit's warren back into the mountain. Set way back under a rocky cliff, the mouth of the caves was shadowed by an outcropping of dark gray shale like the unbroken brow of a brooding face.

"It's just as I remembered," John said. "This entrance leads to a room that has a little tunnel off to the side, just big enough to squeeze through. Kind of reminds me of the igloos in your mam's geography book, 'cause once you get through that, you come into a round space with a hole that lets in light. I could never figure where the light comes from, seeing as how this whole place is inside the mountain."

"I want to see, John. Let's go."

"Let me light this." He pulled a small tin box from his overall pocket and extracted a sulfur match, then swiped it against a rock. He stuck it to a pine torch he found inside the cave. It flared quickly before settling to a steady flame. "I can't remember exactly where the little tunnel is. Hold this." Thrusting the torch into her hands, he dropped to the ground and crawled around the perimeter of the cave. "Here it is, but it's smaller than I remembered. I used to crawl through easy. Now I think we'll have to stretch out and wiggle through." Sitting back on his heels, he pointed at her dress. "You'll tear your skirts on the rough walls, Pest. You should have worn britches."

"Mam won't let me anymore. I have to wear all this." Copper kicked out her skirts. "But, wait . . . here, take this torch. I'll just–" She dropped her skirt and stood in the damp cave in her shirtwaist, petticoat, and long drawers. "There. Now I'm ready."

John looked at her as if she'd taken leave of her senses, then blurted, "I'm hungry. Let's go eat." He started out.

"Well, wait, John. I can't see to put my skirt back on without the light. Why didn't you say you wanted to eat before we came in? Hold up!" Feet tangling in her skirt, she nearly tripped in her haste to follow him.

He had the basket open and was drinking buttermilk from the jar when she came out of the cave, fussing with the buttons at her waist.

"John Pelfrey, that was just rude! What's wrong with you, anyway? I could have broken my neck in there in the dark."

"Sorry," he said. "I'll bring some pants for you next time. You can't be dropping your clothes just anywhere, Copper."

"You're just like Mam." She sighed. "I don't understand why you've all changed so much. Didn't we used to go swimming in our underwear? Didn't Aunt Emilee bathe us in the same tub when we were babies? Whatever is the matter with you?"

"I said I was sorry," he said shortly. "Let it be. Do you want some of this corn bread?"

"Just don't boss me around," she answered, breaking off a piece of the bread. "I get enough of that at home. Here, Pawpaw, good boy. Are you a hungry dog?"

She turned her head and fed the dog a chunk of bread. Angry tears slid down her cheeks, and she wiped them on her sleeve.

"Ah, don't be doing that, Pest. I didn't aim to hurt your feelings." John patted her back awkwardly.

She shrugged him off. "My feelings are fine! I'm mad is all. If I'm so much trouble, I'll borrow Daddy's slingshot and come by myself next time."

"No! Promise me you won't do that!" John took her shoulders and made her face him. "It can be dangerous up here.

Wampus cats and bears use caves for their lairs. You never know what you might find tucked back in here."

"Can we come back tomorrow? Can you bring me some overalls?"

"Me and Henry Thomas are hired out to old man Smithers to grub sassafras roots tomorrow. It'll be a while 'fore I can get back up here." He picked up a chip of wood and threw it hard. "He's paying me twenty-five cents a day, so I want to find a lot of roots." He fixed a firm gaze on Copper. "Promise you'll not come back alone."

"All right, bossy, I promise," she demurred, her hand behind her back, fingers crossed in a broken vow.

"I mean it." He grabbed her hand and untwisted her fingers.

"Ow!" she yelped and shook her hand. "You're mean, John Pelfrey."

"Here, you're not hurt." He took her hand in his and stroked her fingers, then surprised her by bending his head and kissing her palm. "There. All better?"

"You do that just like Aunt Emilee," she said, oblivious to the turmoil on his face. "Well, let's not waste our picnic. You sit there—" she pointed to a big flat rock—"and I'll serve your dinner. Isn't this nice? It feels so peaceful."

"Yeah," he replied around a mouthful of cold potatoes. "Sure a lot quieter than my house anyway. Someday I'll build us a cabin over there. That's a good place . . . right by the creek."

"Us?"

"Think about it, Pest. If we was to marry, couldn't nobody send you away."

She choked on her corn bread. "Marry? Why'd we want to do something stupid like that?"

He looked at her as if she didn't know up from down. "Folks cain't just take up housekeeping without a license. It ain't fitting."

"Hmm, I never thought about marrying." She stood and shook the crumbs from her lap. She walked over to the creek. "Whoever built here wouldn't have to haul water."

The sun fell in a slant across her shoulder. It was nearly noon—the day was wasting.

"We've got to go," Copper insisted. "Mam will be looking, and I've still got to find a hedge-apple tree. I told her I was going to hunt for some to keep the spiders out from under the beds. Here, Paw-paw!"

The dog trotted back on all threes, a wood chip in his mouth.

John poured the last of the buttermilk out in a little depression in the flat rock so Paw-paw could lap it up. Then he took Copper's basket. "There's a hedge-apple tree off the side of the boneyard. Come on. I'll show you."

They filled her basket full of the knobby green fruit. John stuffed some into his pockets and down his shirtfront to take to his mother.

Copper hoped Mam wouldn't question why she'd been gone so long. The full basket would help explain her absence. They would have enough hedge apples to put under all the beds and in each corner of the house. *That's good. Mam hates spiders.*

CHAPTER 9

Gully-washing rains kept Copper from exploring the caves for weeks. When the sun finally came out, it was mid-September and time to finish preparations for winter. All of a sudden the mountains were on fire with color. Brilliant red, gold, purple, and ·orange leaves swirled like cascading jewels when the wind blew, ushering in cooler days and cold nights.

Copper loved the fall. There was a sense of urgency in the air. Mam took the heavy quilts and woolen blankets from the trunk, scattering smelly mothballs across the floor, and hung them on the line to air out. Daddy stayed busy harvesting crops and laying by a store of coal and wood for heating and cooking. Copper and the twins gathered potatoes, onions, turnips, and yams and sandwiched them between layers of clean, sweet-smelling straw on the dirt floor of the cellar.

Even last Sunday's preaching spoke of the harvest: "'Go to the ant, thou sluggard; consider her ways, and be wise,'" Brother Isaac had admonished as he read from Proverbs, "'which having no guide, overseer, or ruler, provideth her meat in the summer, and gathereth her food in the harvest.'"

My family has gone to the ants for sure, Copper thought. For the harvest was at hand—apple-butter time. Willy and Daniel carried basket after basket of red apples from the trees behind the house and dumped them on the porch at Copper's feet. Her job was to peel each one, a burdensome task that nearly suffocated her with boredom. She hated paring the apples as much as she loved eating the butter.

"You have to pay the fiddler if you want sweets this winter," Mam reminded Copper as she peeled and peeled and peeled.

The fiddler's paid so one can dance. Copper bit back the tart reply. *Mam would never let me dance anyway, although sometimes my feet just itch.* She distracted herself with thoughts of the cave and how she'd fix it up with gingham curtains, never mind the lack of windows, and then she'd dance if she had a mind to—dance and sing the day away and nobody would boss her again.

Splut, splut. The peelings hitting the weathered porch entertained a blue jay as he strutted and pecked at the ripe fruit.

"Shoo, shoo!" Copper stood and waved her arms. "How can I see which letter I've made if you eat the parings?"

The jay hopped a few feet away, cocked his head, and waited for Copper to take her seat before he returned to forage the long curls of apple skin, his beak making a soft *thud, thud, thud* against the floor behind her.

"What an endless, thankless duty," Copper grouched to no

one in particular as she settled back, knife in hand, to her chore. She had been working since early afternoon with only a short supper break. Her fingers were stiff and sore, and a blister had popped on her right index finger, but ten five-gallon buckets of sliced apples sat on the floor beside her. She figured she had two buckets to go.

"Remember to cut out the bruises," Mam admonished, covering a bucket of sliced fruit with a clean linen cloth. "We'll have lumps in the butter if you don't."

"I'm being careful," Copper replied and slung a peel over her shoulder. She glanced behind her. "*Q?* How surprising. So far, I'm supposed to have sweethearts whose names begin with *L, C, P,* and now *Q.* Do you know any *Q*s, Mam?"

"You'll have to leave these mountains to find a Quincy, Laura Grace. Now please stop playing and finish the apples. We need to get up early in the morning."

He'll probably be a lawyer, Copper daydreamed. *Quincy Adams, like the president–John. Hmm, but I'll never marry Cletus Curtis, no matter what the peelings say.* Why, the very thought made her shudder. *P* might be all right. She'd caught Silas Parker peeking at her during the benediction at church. But then again, she wasn't sure if you could trust a person who didn't keep his eyes closed during prayer . . . like she did.

She thought about John Pelfrey's suggestion. If they married she wouldn't have to listen to Mam, and Mam couldn't send her away. If he would promise not to try any more of that kissing stuff, she just might take him up on his proposal. They'd have a sweet little cabin up mountain by the stream that ended in a waterfall. She daydreamed until she held the last apple in her hands.

One more apple, one more sling—"*S*? Who could that be?"—and she was nearly finished. She lugged the buckets into the kitchen. She didn't aim to work all day only to feed the possums and raccoons. Lazy things. She went back out and swept the porch before she was off to bed, where she dreamed delicious dreams of boys standing all in a row, each holding a shiny red apple . . . hers for the picking.

At 6 a.m. Copper glanced at the mirror over the washstand. Red tendrils sprung in all directions from the blue bandanna she'd tied around her hair. "Some big floppy shoes and I'd look just like a clown." She sighed as she retied the scarf and went outside.

A fire already roared under the big copper kettle in the side yard. Mam was waiting for the small measure of water to boil. The twins danced and whooped around the fire, giving themselves Indian names like Running Deer and Crow Flies.

Daniel stumbled, nearly falling into the fire.

Copper caught his arm. "I name you Sitting Bear," she stated. "Sit here and measure this. And, Daniel, warriors don't eat sugar."

He sucked the finger he had stuck into the sack and started portioning the sugar into a glass measuring cup.

Copper knew which boy to trust with which task, for they'd been in her charge since the first day they toddled across the sitting-room floor. Mam had been more than glad to turn them over to Copper once they started showing independence and getting into things. Copper cherished the job. She knew the boys inside out.

She kept Willy close beside her but allowed him to poke at

the fire to keep it burning evenly as she stirred the boiling water and Mam poured the first two buckets of fruit into the kettle.

As the apples cooked down, more were added, a bucket at a time, until the pot was half full. Copper and Mam took turns wielding the heavy wooden paddle, stirring continuously to keep the apples from sticking to the bottom of the pan.

Copper watched Mam carefully, learning from her precise ways. She liked being outdoors working beside Mam, even though the work was hard. Mam wasn't as fractious as when she was inside, where the walls seemed to close in around them. Besides, if Copper managed to keep herself out of boarding school, she'd need to know how to make her own butter soon enough. Dreaming, she could see herself standing in front of her own cabin, stirring her own apples, from her own trees, in her own pot. Then she'd be free to do as she pleased. She wouldn't have to listen to Mam or anybody else.

By noon the cooked fruit began to change color. Careful stirring continued until Mam judged the butter dark enough. Daniel was allowed to pour his cups of sugar into the pot, while Willy added the expensive oil of cloves and the powdered cinnamon.

"Sissy," Willy sang out, "this cinnamon's the same color as your hair. If we run out we can just stick your head in."

Copper reached for the bandanna that had slipped down over her eyes. "Oh, fudge!"

"Daughter!" Mam admonished, one eyebrow raised, the paddle, dripping fruit, pointed in Copper's direction.

Copper ripped off the kerchief and flung it toward the faded summer rosebush, where it caught and fluttered on a thorn. She should have known that the day wouldn't pass without Mam getting after her about something. *"Fudge* is not a swearword. It's not even in the Bible."

"'Let your speech be alway with grace,'" Mam cautioned, "Colossians 4:6."

"And 'seasoned with salt,'" Copper replied saucily, taking her turn at the paddle and stirring vigorously.

Copper saw it coming when Mam squared her shoulders and looked her way with eyes that stung like a bee. *Why*, she wondered, *can't I ever keep my mouth shut? Why must I always stir the hornets' nest?*

"You may copy Luke chapter 6 verse 45 twenty-five times before you go to bed tonight, Laura Grace," Mam said, her voice as sharp as her eyes. "And be prepared to recite it to me at the breakfast table."

"Yes, Mam," Copper replied, head hung. *Mam's so old-fashioned. Stir . . . fudge! Stir . . . fudge! It's just a word . . . just a word.* Her anger against Mam bubbled up as hot as the mixture she stirred.

"Mam?" Willy whined. "Can I have the first taste? I did the hardest work. Daniel just sat around measuring while I stoked this hot ol' fire and carried heavy buckets of water." He wiped imaginary sweat from his brow.

"Young man, the word is *old*, not *ol'*. Daniel's work is no less important because he used his brain instead of his brawn."

Copper couldn't help but notice Mam's voice was considerably softer than when she had chastised her.

Mam peered into the pot, then let hot sauce drip from the end of the paddle. "This is not thick enough yet."

Copper suppressed a groan. Her back and shoulders ached,

and her eyes stung from the smoke, but she knew better than to complain, for a sermon was sure to follow. Besides, she loved apple butter. Just the thought of hot biscuits dripping with the fruit added vigor to her work.

By midafternoon they were ready for the first taste. Copper put a small amount into a tin cup and handed it to Willy. "Now, King William of Troublesome," she intoned, "you are the keeper of the cup. You must find a willing subject to taste this potion for you."

As befitted his royal status, Willy handed the cup of the tasty mixture to his brother.

"Yup," Daniel stated importantly after his first bite, "this butter's ready for biscuits."

There was much work to do, however, before the biscuits could be baked. Copper began filling the washed and sterilized jars. She ladled hot butter to nearly the top of each jar, then ran a kitchen knife around the inside to remove air pockets before she carefully wiped each rim with a clean feed-sack towel.

Last winter, during the first snow, she had gone to the cellar to fetch a jar of fruit for breakfast, only to discover a fine fur of green mold on the surface. Twelve jars were ruined. Mam said it was because a speck of fruit had broken the seal. *That won't happen this year,* Copper determined, eyeing her work one last time before she snapped the glass lids on with the metal bail.

The boys helped her lug the jars to the kitchen, where Mam took each jar, turned it upside down to help the seal, and nestled them all on the windowsills. They'd sit there and cool until morning, when Copper would carry them to the cellar.

Forty jars of apple butter glinted like amber in the fading

evening light before Copper finished her day's work. She leaned headfirst into the deep copper kettle, scrubbing away at some butter that had stuck and burned on the very bottom despite their careful stirring. "Willy," she called out, "bring me a corncob. I need it straightaway."

"Whatcha going to do, Sissy?" Willy teased, putting the cob behind his back. "Make corncob jelly?"

"I will scrub the bottom of this pot with your head if you don't give that to me right now!" she snapped. "And it's 'What are you going to do?' not 'whatcha,' for heaven's sake!"

Willy handed over the corncob, beating a hasty retreat as Copper huffed and puffed.

I sound just like Mam, she reflected. *I'll be a spinster school-teacher wasting away up some holler waiting for my* Q, S, *or* P *to come carry me away, while I beat backward mountain boys over the head with grammar.*

Words, just words. There were so many much more important things to learn in order to survive on Troublesome Creek. Mam just didn't understand. She had begun to despair of Mam ever understanding. Mam wanted a fine lady for a daughter, and Copper didn't see the point.

Oh, well. That's fodder for another day. Pushing the tangled hair from her eyes, she realized she must look a sight. "I can't go milk like this," she muttered. "I'll scare Molly to death!"

The least she could do was tame her hair. Where was her scarf? The rosebush where she'd tossed it earlier in the day gave off a musty perfume when she shook its brown and drooping blossoms. Copper scratched her head. "Willy? Daniel? Have you seen my blue bandanna?"

"No, Sissy, but since you're looking for things, have you seen Mam's biscuit cutter? Me and Daniel's in trouble 'til we find it. What I want to know is, why does everyone think we're always the guilty ones?"

"I can't imagine," Copper answered, rolling her eyes. "What's that behind your back?"

"Apple butter. I snuck some," Willy confessed boldly. "Do you want a bite?"

Copper turned toward the barn, calling back, "No, I'll wait for supper. I've got to go milk. Want to help?"

Grace watched Copper and Willy walk toward the barn and then went about her business, retrieving her wooden bread bowl from the curtained-off pantry. She kept flour sifted with baking powder and salt ever ready so all she had to add was an egg-size dollop of lard and a splash of milk. She stirred the mixture until dough formed, then sprinkled a circle of flour on the kitchen table. Dumping the dough out, Grace kneaded it with the heel of her hand. She patted it until it was about half an inch thick and reached for her biscuit cutter, only then remembering it was gone. Flour smudged her brow as she wearily rubbed a hand across her eyes and rummaged in the pantry for a small tin can to make a new cutter.

What was to become of the girl she'd raised and had such high hopes for? Laura Grace was already taking on a womanly figure, and the young men were beginning to notice. Just last Sunday there'd been a scuffle in the churchyard between John Pelfrey and Henry Thomas, both wanting to walk her home.

Next, Laura Grace would be in trouble like her mother had
been. Oh, that had been a terrible time. Their father so sick and
Julie sneaking around, pleasing herself instead of helping Grace
take care of him. And then, of course, Julie left with Will with
never a thought of what she left Grace to bear alone. The neighbors all talking—first about Julie, then about her father. They said
he killed himself, but she knew better. He died of a broken heart;
he'd quit living when her mother passed on, though it had taken
him years to die.

But there was still hope for Laura Grace. She simply had to
think of a way to get her off the mountain.

"Lord," she talked to God as she worked, "sometimes I
despair for my children. The boys take things and then deny it.
Laura Grace sasses and has no repentance. Give me strength."

After cutting the biscuits and putting them in the oven, Grace
went to the mirror over the washstand and wiped flour from her
face with the hem of her apron. Her eyes stared back through
eyeglasses as round and thick as nickels, the bridge of her nose
eternally red from where they rested. Sometimes she didn't even
recognize herself anymore. A familiar despair wrapped around
her and blocked the light as effectively as the brooding mountain
outside the door. She needed air. She wrenched up a window and
propped it open with a folding screen.

Will had installed windows all along the front-room wall
when she carried the twins. No easy task, for he'd had to saw
through logs put in place nearly a hundred years before. But she
hadn't been able to stand the oppressive darkness in the low-
ceilinged room . . . the feeling of weight. She washed those windows with vinegar water every Friday and polished them with

newsprint. When he finished the windows, he'd added two bed-
rooms for he knew she needed privacy.

Suddenly Grace wrinkled her nose at the smell of something
burning. *The biscuits!* She rushed to the kitchen and pulled them
from the oven. She'd have to scrape the bottoms when they
cooled. Sighing, Grace shook herself as if flinging off her cares
and finished her family's supper—biscuits with fresh apple butter
and glasses of milk for her and the children, plus leftover fried
chicken for Will. Men had to have meat.

Moments later, Will opened the screen door; the boys followed close on his heels. "My, something smells good," he said.
"I'm so hungry I could eat a horse."

"If I was a horse, I'd be wild so's you couldn't eat me, Daddy."
Willy neighed and pranced around.

"Then I'll take this old plow horse." Will scooped up Daniel
and nuzzled his belly. "Mrs. Brown, what would you take for this
give-down horse? I'd like to have him for supper."

She pasted on a smile and played the game. Her husband
and children deserved better than the mood she was in. "Oh,
kind sir, he's not for sale. He lives in my house and eats apple
butter on biscuits." She turned her back and tucked her handkerchief back into her pocket.

After supper, after the dishes, and after the boys were tucked
in bed, Grace had a moment to herself. She stared out the dark
window, although she could see nothing outside. The jars of
apple butter she'd canned stood as straight as soldiers along the
windowsill. The cellar held food enough to feed her family all
winter, and she knew Will would keep them supplied with fresh
meat when they needed it. Through the reflection in the glass,

she watched as he slowly rocked in his chair in front of the fire. The Bible that had belonged to his father lay open on his lap. She was embarrassed to remember how she'd once supposed he couldn't read.

She took her dishrag and wiped the already spotless kitchen table, gazing at Will from the corner of her eye. He was a good man, she knew, kind to his children and considerate to her, and every Sunday without fail he saw that his family was in church. *So what's wrong?* she wondered. *What's wrong with me?* Why couldn't she be happy with him and with the life God had given her? She had so much more than many women, but hard as she fought it, she couldn't keep her own guilt and resentment at bay.

Laura Grace entered the room, her braided hair tucked for sleep under her nightcap, and leaned over Will's shoulder to look at a Scripture he underlined for her with his finger.

Grace felt her emotions roil at the sight. Try as Grace did, Laura Grace never approached her with the same ease. She gave him a peck on the cheek. "Good night, Daddy," Grace heard her say before she came across the room to lay a piece of paper with Luke 6:45 printed in a tidy script twenty-five times on the table.

"Well done," Grace said as she appraised the work. "Now, what do you say?"

"I'm sorry, Mam. Good night." Laura Grace kissed her on the cheek as she had her father.

Grace's fingers traced the little kiss when her daughter left the room. A sudden sadness brought tears to her eyes. How close she was to losing Laura Grace in one way or another. She tapped the paper against her chin. What could she do to make things right? Boarding school was the answer, she knew, but how was she to change Will's mind and how was she to make Laura Grace believe?

She pressed both hands into the small of her aching back. Maybe she'd get a letter from her friend Millicent soon. It seemed like a lifetime ago when they attended teachers' training school together. Now Millicent and her husband owned a school in Philadelphia that catered to the finest families. Grace had been anxiously waiting to hear if they would take Laura Grace as a boarder. She cleaned her spectacles with her handkerchief. There would be more time to worry about that on the morrow. Will was banking the fire. It was time to get to bed.

Later that week, Copper was sweeping the porch when she heard the distinctive *clip-clop, clip-clop* of the postman's mule, Sweetie. She hung her broom on a nail by the screen door and called inside, "Here comes Mr. Bramble!"

Mam bustled out with her embroidery scissors and took her seat in her rocker, while Willy and Daniel ran to the road with water and an apple for Sweetie. "Don't dally, boys," Mam called. "I'm anxious to see the post."

Mr. Bramble didn't hand the mail to the twins, however. Instead, he handed Sweetie's reins to Willy and walked toward the porch. "How do?" he said. "Mind if I sit a spell?"

"Please do, Mr. Bramble," Mam replied as he handed her a stack of mail and newspapers wrapped in brown paper and tied with string. When Mam cut the string, the paper dropped to the floor, a puff of wind sailing it across the porch like a boat. "Laura Grace," Mam ordered, "fetch Mr. Bramble a glass of water."

He drank the cold well water straight down. "Miz Brown, c-can I beg a favor?" he stammered, eyes downcast.

"Of course," she answered, handing the opened packet of mail to Copper. "How can I help you?"

Copper took the mail inside and dropped it on the kitchen table, one ear cocked toward the screen door, trying to keep a peg on the conversation. She could see Mr. Bramble take a battered envelope from his pocket and slowly withdraw a paper as thin as onionskin from it.

"It's this here missive, Miz Brown. I can read print real good, but this is some kind of foreigner writing, I suspect. You, being educated and all, are the onliest person I figure could decipher it—besides the postmaster, that is—and I didn't hardly want to bother him." He leaned toward Mam. "See, he marks my parcels before Sweetie and I set out. Will's number, 23, never changes." He underlined it with a dirty fingernail. "Will Brown, 23. I got my route stuck in my head."

Copper kept out of sight. It wouldn't do for Mam to catch her eavesdropping. She watched as Mam adjusted her rimless glasses and took the piece of stationery from Mr. Bramble.

"Why, Mr. Bramble," Mam said, "it seems this is from your cousin Maynard in Oklahoma. He writes in a beautiful cursive."

"Well, that proves me right," Mr. Bramble replied. "I knew it was foreign. Otherwise I could have read it."

Stifling a giggle, Copper bumped the table, knocking the letters and newspapers to the floor. She picked them up as Mam read of dust and grasshoppers and dry wells. A slim brochure illustrating a school caught Copper's eye. A school in Philadelphia . . . a boarding school. Anger flushed her cheeks as she scanned the pamphlet. *Mam's already decided. She's going to send me away!*

Mr. Bramble took his leave while Copper neatly stacked the scattered mail. Seething, she secreted the brochure in her apron pocket.

"Beholden, Miz Brown," she heard him say over the ringing in her ears. "If I can ever do anything for you, just holler."

"Would you like me to reply to your cousin for you, Mr. Bramble?"

"I'll need to study on it awhile, ma'am. Once you get a government job everybody thinks you got the funds to nurse 'em. I need to see what I got extra 'fore I send cash money to a body I ain't heerd from in nigh on twenty years."

The next day Copper stood, her back to the open cellar door, and admired her handiwork. She'd spent the morning organizing the summer's canning, making sure what remained of last year's foodstuff was placed in front so as to be used first. Really, there wasn't much left—just a few cans of parsnips, no one's favorite. Mam would use them in vegetable soup, though, so nothing would be wasted.

It was a balmy, Indian-summer day, and sunshine spilled through the open door, bringing warmth to the chilly cellar. She felt a little stir of pride as she looked around. Forty quarts of apple butter lined a freshly whitewashed shelf. Jars of whole blackberries, blackberry jelly, blackberry jam, pear butter, pear preserves, and jewel-colored rhubarb crowded quarts of green beans, canned whole tomatoes and tomato juice, carrots, beets, corn, and kale. Under the shelves sat crocks of sauerkraut, pick-led pigs' feet, and a whole hog's head cleaned and packed in salt.

A large brown crock sat covered by a wooden disk weighted down with a rock. Copper's mouth watered with desire. She could feel the crunch of Mam's bread-and-butter pickles against her teeth, taste the sweet-sour flavor on her tongue, the vision so real she wiped nonexistent juice from her chin.

Why not take a pickle? She was so mad she took the crumpled boarding-school brochure from her apron pocket and shoved it behind the crock of sauerkraut. Anger at Mam turned to self-pity as Copper stood in the cellar remembering the day before. "They're going to send me away without even asking what I want," she told a small gray mouse who scurried in through the open door, hoping to make a tidy home in the onion bin.

She cornered him behind a stack of pumpkins and held him up by his long, hairless tail. "Well," she continued as the mouse swung before her eyes, "I won't let that happen. I'm going back to the cave, John or no John. And as for you, you'd be smart to find a home in the barn before Daddy sets his traps."

CHAPTER 10

The mouth of the cave was harder to locate than Copper imagined, set back in the mountain as it was. Paw-paw actually found it, his excellent nose tracking the way. The cave seemed damper and darker than when John was with her. She removed her skirt and petticoats, folded them neatly, and laid them on a rock shelf. She'd swiped Daddy's old overalls this morning; when she put them on the legs spread like puddles around her feet.

"I should have cut these off," she told Paw-paw as she rolled the hem several times. "There now, that's better. Paw-paw, we're on our way. If this cave turns out the way I expect, you and I will live up here for a while until Mam drops her plans for boarding school." She patted his head and scratched him behind the ears. "Now, where did John leave that torch?"

After finding the tightly bound bundle of reeds, she nearly set herself afire when she stuck a match to it. The bundle caught in a bright *whoosh*, then subsided to the steady flame of a dozen candles.

A flutter of wings above her head made her skin crawl, and she looked up to see a soft furred fruit bat hanging upside down on the low ceiling. Slowly, he unfurled his leathery wings. She fancied she could hear the clicking of his sharp teeth as he suddenly swooped toward the light she held. Covering her head with one arm, she struggled to hold the torch steady as she cowered from the bat's attack. Just as he was about to fly straight into the flame, she watched him pull back, surprised by the heat, and fall like a small gray stone to the floor.

Boy, she wished she'd waited for John or remembered to bring the slingshot. Her knees felt weak as she searched about for the bat, afraid he might make his way up her pant leg. At least he wasn't in her hair. Folks said bats would land right on your head and make a nest so tight you'd never get them out. Bats in the belfry for sure. But never fear—there was Paw-paw, growling a warning of alarm and nosing the bat around the floor.

Trusting her dog to keep the bat busy, Copper dropped to her knees and, with the help of the torch, searched for the entrance to the tunnel. There it was, a dark passage just big enough to admit her. She stuck the torch in a crevice. Did she really want to go in? What if a hundred bats nested on the other side? What was worse, bats or boarding school? She slithered on her belly into the narrow tunnel that should lead her to a hidden room.

Paw-paw whined and barked behind her as she twisted and turned along the tunnel. He would have to wait for her on the other side, for she was sure his crippled leg would prohibit his entrance. She crawled about ten feet before she came to the end and pulled herself into the cave John had described to her. Her eyes popped wide with wonder as she broke through. *Why, it's beautiful!*

Sunlight streamed through an opening in the ceiling and lit a waterfall that burbled out of the wall about twelve feet above. It fell with a splash into a small basin of stone. *It must be very deep,* she reckoned as she cupped her hands and drank the icy water. Strange lacy ferns, a sort she had never seen before, grew along the basin's edge and trembled from the water's spatter. The cavern was maybe triple the size of their cabin's front room, and the ceiling soared. Copper stood, head thrown back, but she could not guess the ceiling's height. Something about the absolute hush of the place, broken only by the music of the falling water and the golden light pouring in from its great pinnacle, seemed holy to her. She felt she had entered a sacred place. Closing her eyes, she breathed in the centuries-old scent of rock and water and earth, God's building blocks.

She knelt beside the basin for several minutes, absorbing the beauty of the place, before she began to explore. Keeping the waterfall in sight, she backed into the center of the room, then flung out her arms and twirled around, drunk with pleasure.

Suddenly she saw something her eyes would not believe. She stopped and stared, blinked several times, then reached out to touch Mam's tortoiseshell comb stuck like the stem of a flower in their sugar bowl, which balanced precariously on the mouth of Daddy's Mason jar, which held the missing biscuit cutter. The items were placed ceremoniously on her blue bandanna spread neatly on a table-shaped rock. She stooped to look closer at the kerchief. A bright feather was tied to each edge—one jay, one bluebird, one cardinal, one wild canary. A silver tablespoon they hadn't even missed held traces from the blackberry-jam jar Mam couldn't find.

Swift as a flash flood, a fearful presence filled the cave.

Copper's heart knocked against her ribs in a jerky dance of dread. Her head swam and she felt sick. The dense, moist air of the cave turned as thick as clay as she bent at the waist and forced several ragged breaths into her lungs. Scared as she was, she took no notice that Paw-paw had indeed followed her into the cavern and was busy licking a fresh wound on his old, stiff leg.

The rough walls of the tunnel scraped her arms as she scrambled out of the cavern. Copper flew from the mouth of the cave and collapsed on the grass, wheezing and coughing. *Calm down,* she commanded herself. *Calm down!*

Soon her heartbeat slowed as curiosity overtook fear. She stretched out in the warm sunlight, leaning back on her elbows, and pondered what she had seen. *John has to have done it for a joke,* she thought, *but that doesn't make sense. Then again, how else could our things have gotten into that cave? Willy? Daniel?* Copper frowned. *No, they'd never keep still about something like this cave. . . .*

The sun thawed her fear. She'd lost a comb or two in the tunnel, and her hair, glinting copper and gold, tumbled into her eyes. She shook it out and let it fall loose across her shoulders. It would be good to rest a moment longer, until her knees stopped shaking and Paw-paw showed up.

A crow called out a raucous song, and a fat bumblebee

buzzed a stalk of goldenrod near her arm. Copper was lulled
by the familiar sounds. She dozed a minute, tired from her morning's work in the cellar at home and her sudden fright in the
cave. A fleeting breeze riffled the branches in a grove of ash trees
and showered her in red and gold. She felt a leaf catch in her
hair and reached back lazily to remove it.

A tingle shot up her spine as a chilling whisper filled her ear,
"Purty . . . purty."

Her fingers met with those of another, tangled in her hair.
The cold squeeze of her heart gripped her again, and she gasped
and flung herself away from whatever was behind her.

"Paw-paw!" she screamed as she bolted up and raced down
the mountain. She took a chance and glanced over her shoulder to see a curious creature crouched on the hillside, lacking
in color save for a single splash of red. Then Copper ran
pell-mell, as if chased by the devil himself, until the old cemetery was in sight. Its familiarity was a comfort, and she felt
a little safer until, without warning, the ground gave way
beneath her pounding feet and swallowed her whole, leaving
only the trace of her scream, as temporary as a whisper of
smoke.

"What in the world?" Will said as he rounded the corner of the
barn. There stood Molly, her pitiful bawls loud enough to raise
the dead. He didn't have to wonder why she cried so as he spied
her full udder. Will led her into the barn and opened the door to
the stall, then poured a measure of feed into her box. She rolled

her big brown eyes when he patted her flank. "We'll get you milked directly," he said, turning back toward the house.

"Where's Copper?" Will asked as he entered the kitchen. "Molly's not been milked."

"I don't know," Grace replied. "I thought she was in the barn. She hasn't set the table either."

"This is odd, Grace." Will took off his old felt hat and ran his fingers through his bushy white hair. "Much as she rambles around, Copper's never missed a milking. She'd never leave Molly to suffer that way. Boys!" He called Willy and Daniel in from the porch, where they were shucking dried beans. "Where's your sister?"

"I don't know, Daddy," Willy answered.

"Daniel?"

"Last time I saw Sissy was after she did the cellar. She was taking a mouse to the barn."

"A mouse?" Willy groaned. "Why didn't you tell me? We could have made a cage and a little trap in case he got out."

"Seems like if we built a cage good enough, Willy, he couldn't get out," Daniel responded, looking thoughtful.

"Well, that don't matter, does it, 'cause we don't have a mouse," Willy said, exasperated.

"Boys, stop that chatter," Will interrupted. "This is important. Your sister's missing, and we've got only a couple of hours to find her before dark. Daniel, go look in the cellar and the barn. Willy, you walk around the pasture. Grace, you'll need to milk Molly. I'm going over to the Pelfreys' in case she's visiting Emilee and forgot the time. Ring the dinner bell if Copper comes back before I do."

CHAPTER II

Copper lay on a ledge of rock, fifteen feet down an old sinkhole. She'd knocked herself silly when she fell and now lay dumb as a fence post while her head whirled and tiny sparks of light shimmered before her eyes.

She came to herself gradually. At first she thought she was still in the cave, for she was in a cold, damp place and a small shaft of light poured down as it had in the cavern. But this was a narrow space, about six feet across, and it didn't seem to have a floor.

Her nose felt swollen, and she tasted blood when she licked her upper lip. Gingerly, she pulled herself to a sitting position, testing her arms and legs, grateful for no broken bones. Glad for the waning light, Copper peered cautiously over the edge of the rock ledge. Her heart stopped at what she saw . . . water, just a short distance below. It was not clean and pure like the water in the cave but smelled of mold and decay. A small grayish animal, unidentifiable in death, floated on the pool's greasy surface. She watched in horrid fascination as an odd S-shaped thing glided across the dark water and bumped against the lumpy remains, sending them careening into the wall.

"Snakes!" Her scream bounced off the walls as if she'd shouted down a well. Crablike, she scurried backward on the ledge and hid her face behind her hands. She sobbed, near hysteria, until she was exhausted. Woozy, Copper gathered her hair in her hand, leaned carefully over the side of the rock, and vomited into the rank water below.

"Copper, stop it." She gave herself a little shake that set her head to pounding. "You're not even afraid of snakes." She wiped her mouth on her sleeve and laughed a shaky little laugh to hear her own chastising voice echoing until it slowly waned. She was left in stillness so profound she could hear the ripples in the water as the snake swam away.

Leaving the Pelfreys' house with no news of Copper, Will hurried home. There was Grace pacing the porch as Will mounted the steps. "She's not here?" he blurted out. "I thought surely–"

"No. Where could she be?" Grace frowned, wringing her hands. "I'm getting worried."

"Try not to upset yourself," he said as fear gnawed like a rat at his gut. "I'm sure she'll be fine." Will steadied himself. He had to believe the words he'd just spoken to Grace, though his alarm grew with each passing moment. *God,* he thought in silent, urgent prayer, *You've got to keep her safe. I can't go through losing her like I lost Julie.*

As the hours passed, darkness seeped into the sinkhole like a mist rising from the water. Copper could see light at the opening above her even as her feet . . . her knees . . . then her hands disappeared in the darkness below. She kept her head back, her eyes focused upward, until even that last pale solace faded.

She wrapped her arms around her legs, leaned her head against her knees, and dozed fitfully. Every time she woke, she'd pat the rock around her, finding her place, fearful she'd moved too close to the edge. Thirst and cold gripped her. She wanted her old quilt and a cup of chamomile tea, but what she longed for most of all was light. Just the tiniest candle flame to ease the fearsome night. If she angled her body just so and cocked her head to the right, she could see a star shining ever so brightly above her.

Bits of Bible verses, sweet as honey on her tongue, caroled in her mind and gave great comfort: *"I am the light of the world." "My light I give to you." "The Lord is my light and my salvation." "Thy word is a lamp . . . and a light." "When I sit in darkness, the Lord shall be a light unto me."*

Words have such power, she thought—and she had plenty of time for thinking—to hurt or comfort, even to give light in the darkness. Then something she'd said earlier came back to her. *"Words, just words . . ."* Her biting reply to Mam's correction the day they'd made apple butter. *If I ever get out of here, I promise to think before I speak. I promise to listen to the words of others and not be so quick with my own.*

Copper was freezing and thirsty, and her mouth tasted like

vomit. Her neck ached from a crick, but she dared not move for fear of losing sight of the star: her light . . . her promise.

Grace, her open Bible in her lap, prayed fervently for the safe return of the girl she loved as much as if Laura Grace were her daughter by birth. She put her head back and rested her eyes. Visions too horrific to give voice to skittered behind her closed eyelids: Laura Grace had fallen down the mountain and lay help-lessly, her leg broken, waiting for rescue; she'd drowned in the forbidden swimming hole; that catamount Grace hated and feared stalked Laura Grace as she clung desperately to the branch of a tree. . . .

It had to be that mountain lion she sometimes saw in the early morning patrolling the high ridge behind their cabin. Grace had begged Will to shoot it, but he refused. "No sense hurting something that ain't hurting us," he'd said.

Oh, she hated this place sometimes, this place and its stub-born people.

Grace bowed her head again and folded her hands upon her Bible. *I'm sorry. Forgive me, Lord. You know I don't hate the people here. And, oh—never Will, Father. You know I love him, but he's a product of this place, and sometimes this is a dreadful place to be. Keep Laura Grace safe. Please . . . please keep her safe.*

Sick with fear, Grace was thankful the twins were asleep—at least she didn't have to deal with them. They'd pestered her to no end, begging to go with Will and Daniel Pelfrey, especially when they discovered Daniel's big boys were also looking. . . .

All the boys but John. He was away, hired out to someone.

It's too bad, she thought. John would know better than anyone where Laura Grace might be. Those two had wandered every nook and hollow of the mountain together. Grace knew they'd have to fetch John if they didn't find Laura Grace soon.

Grace stood abruptly, dropping her Bible to the floor. She picked it up, wiped its cover with her apron, and placed it on the table beside her sewing basket. Moving to the window, she drew back the curtain, but it was so dark she couldn't see a thing. Tears gathered, threatening to overflow as she wrung her hands. *Something terrible has happened. I just know it.* She knelt then, there by her chair, and put out a fleece. *Lord, my help in times of need, bring her back to us. It's my fault she's gone, I know. She's trying to escape from me. Bring her back and I'll give up my notion of sending her away.*

She had a pot of coffee on the stove and was making biscuits when Will came in an hour later. He looked haggard and old. Worry creased his handsome face, and his eyes were rimmed with red.

Her heart ached. *He's been here before,* she thought. *This is not the first night he has spent searching for someone he loves. At least it's not storming like that night. At least if Laura Grace is in the creek she won't be lost to us.* Her stomach lurched at the thought of Julie's precious body being swept away, like worthless flotsam, by the violent waters of Troublesome Creek.

Will sat heavily and took the mug Grace offered. "Ah, Grace—" he stood back up—"don't cry." He rubbed his eyes as he gathered what strength he had left. "Daniel took his boys home. We're not doing any good in the dark. I'll start again at first light."

"I can't abide this, Will," Grace said, turning her back to him, her voice rising in panic. "I simply cannot abide this."

He moved toward Grace to comfort her. When he touched her shoulder, she whirled around so quickly that she knocked the cup from his hand. It crashed to the floor and shattered, sending shards of glass and splashes of hot coffee everywhere. He could see the desperation in her eyes.

"But what do you think?" she demanded. "A wild animal? That catamount we keep seeing up on the ridge? I'm sure I heard its scream just past midnight." Her voice gave way, and she began sobbing.

"Grace, Grace." He patted her back. "You're letting your worry shadow your faith. God will provide for Copper. " He spoke with certainty, but his confidence had been hard earned. He'd had to decide to trust in the Lord after he lost Julie. It was that or become a raving madman. He had struggled then, the faith he'd found so easily in his youth turning brittle as shale with his loss. But God had reached down and comforted him all those years ago when he'd rambled the woods carrying his baby girl against his chest.

At first he had been so angry when Julie had been found, drowned in the place he'd always loved so much. Those days were bleak, soul-stealing days. Shaking his fist at the heavens, he'd railed at God and blamed Him for his loss.

But one day in the early morning hush as he'd climbed and clawed his way to the very top of Pine Mountain, the baby safely bound close to his heart, God had sent a glorious sunrise that lit the mountain like flames of fire and tipped the leaves of the trees in shimmering gold. Even in his sorrow he had to acknowledge its beauty. He'd stood stock-still atop the highest point of all the mountains and relished the scene.

Suddenly a murmuring, low and melodious, had filled the air around him. A breeze stirred the gold-tipped leaves, and he thought a summer storm must be approaching. He stood there on that high peak as, against all reason, the rustling trees sang to him of hope. *"I have called thee by thy name; thou art mine. When thou passest through the waters, I will be with thee."* Julie's favorite Scripture pierced his soul like arrows shot from angels' bows. A strange sensation sent goose bumps up and down his arms, and he took the baby from underneath his shirt to see if she was cold. He tightened the little white knit blanket Emilee had wrapped her in, and she snuggled into his arms.

Then it had come to him, the knowing that would see him through his terrible loss: *God is all-present.* It was so simple it took him to his knees. God is all-present, whether in good times or bad. He is the author and commander of every moment of life present and life past and all life that is yet to come. Will gained a sure and present faith that day before he took his daughter back down the mountain to Emilee, and it had stood the test of time.

Now all he had to do to remind himself of that certain knowledge, that unshakable faith, was to step outside this cabin. The mountains he loved so much were like God's own arms surrounding him. No matter what the outcome, God was in charge of this night, he reckoned.

Will embraced his wife, and she didn't resist. It felt so good to rest his body against hers for a moment.

Daniel stumbled into the room. Rubbing his eyes, he plucked at Will's shirtsleeve. "Daddy?"

Will pulled Daniel into the circle of their embrace. "What is it, Son?"

"Daddy . . . I'm not supposed to tell." Daniel leaned against his leg. "Willy said we'd get a whipping for going up there, but that's where Sissy is."

"What are you talking about?" Will cupped Daniel's chin. "You'd best tell me what you know."

"It's that old graveyard. Me and Willy tracked Sissy there once. She had a picnic basket, and we wanted to go on a picnic too, but she went too far and Willy got thirsty and we went to the spring that's up there by that big old oak tree, and when we went back to the graveyard she was gone, so we–"

"Whoa, boy, slow down." He turned Daniel's face up toward his own. "What makes you think Copper might be there now?"

"Because before I went to sleep, Daddy, I said, 'Please, heavenly Father, please tell me where Sissy is.' And so in my dream He showed me a big, dark place in the ground, and it was by the graveyard. So that's where Sissy is."

⁂

Copper stirred. She was stiff and sore, hungry and incredibly thirsty, but soft rays of morning's first light spilled down the shaft and cheered her. She was tired of being trapped, giving in. *I have to get out of here.* Her legs cramped from the long night on the ledge. Slowly she stood, using her hands to steady herself against the damp dirt wall. *There has to be a way.*

She took stock of her surroundings. Gnarled tree roots and pieces of rock protruded from the walls of the sinkhole. *It's like a ladder,* she thought. *If the rocks and roots are secure, I should be able to climb out.*

She stepped cautiously onto a jagged rock and grasped a twisted root above her head. She pulled herself up inch by inch, groping blindly for each handhold, cautiously testing each foot-rest before releasing her weight to it. Halfway up, she was gasping for breath. Straining, she grabbed a solid loop of root and then felt the rock beneath her foot give way. It tumbled down the wall, bounced off the ledge that had sheltered her during the long night, and hit the water with a sickening plop.

Copper hung by one hand, dangling in midair. Her feet scrambled to find purchase as her fingers tightened like claws around the root. Finally, in seconds that seemed like hours, one foot wedged in a fissure.

Desperate for a stronger hold, she forced herself to take deep, calming breaths and eased her head back to look up at the opening. A tangle of wild grapevines hung above her, and a curious wooden box jutted out from its midst. After finding a new foothold, she made her way up. Scrabbling, her fingers closed over the side of the box. For a minute it held her weight, but just as she was about to heft herself up, it shifted dangerously. Then with a groan and a screech, it gave way and broke apart, showering Copper with dust and dirt, old wood, and ancient bones.

Bones! A skeleton, yellow as horses' teeth, slid as slowly as a waltz past Copper's face. In spite of herself, she reached to stop it and gripped one bony hand. The skeleton hung there, twisting . . . bones clattering dryly . . . until, strained from its own weight, the hand separated from the wrist with a dull *pop* and sent the rest of the skeleton crashing to the ledge below.

Copper stared, horrified, at the skeletal fingers intertwined with her own. Then, unable to cast the hand to the rank pool below—it had belonged to a living person, after all—she shoved the bones into the pocket of her dirty overalls. She was almost there. With one foot perched on what remained of the old coffin, she groaned mightily and pulled herself out of the sinkhole.

She lay for several minutes, hugging the earth, sobbing a prayer of thanksgiving before finally she stood, knees wobbling, and made her way toward home.

⤛⤜

Copper seemed like an angel to Will there at the old graveyard. Backlit with sunlight filtered through a dense early morning fog, her hair flared copper red and wild as she staggered toward him. Daniel had been right. Praise the Lord.

"Daddy! Daddy!" was all she said before she collapsed into his arms.

The joy of holding his daughter safe brought tears to his eyes as he gently lowered her to the ground. He came close to losing all composure when he kissed her fevered brow. She seemed all right, though her face was battered and so swollen he'd never have recognized her except for her hair. *I never doubted You, Lord,* he prayed. *I trusted You'd keep her safe.*

He rose, his step light despite her weight as he carried her home.

⤛⤜

Copper was abed for days with a fearsome sickness. She vomited every teaspoon of broth Grace managed to get down her and shivered with a raging fever. Bedclothes, wet with perspiration, collected in the corner as Grace soothed her with cool cloths and fresh sheets.

The twins were banished from the room they shared with their sister and so slept with Will instead. And every morning they huddled together on the porch, uncharacteristically subdued, running to fetch Will whenever Grace called for him.

Grace kept a big pot of pinto beans simmering on the stove and baked dozens of rounds of corn bread, for they had a constant stream of visitors. Several ladies brought sweets: stack cakes and fried-apple pies, and Mrs. Oriander Wilson brought her specialty—a cake a foot high with pink icing so sweet it made your teeth hurt.

Everyone wanted to see Copper—Grace told Will it reminded her of a wake. They'd just stand in the doorway, shake their heads, and *tsk, tsk, tsk*. Then they had to be fed. Emilee Pelfrey came to help, though pregnant again, her ankles swollen over her shoes. She parked her youngest twins, Matthew and Mark, in a clothes basket under the table and kept the kitchen humming.

John, home from his hired job, did the milking and would have sat by Copper's bed but Grace wouldn't allow it, so he busied himself with her chores. One morning as he went about his work he fretted to Will that somehow he'd been the cause of all this. He hung his head and confessed his part in the accident that had nearly killed Copper. Will could see the boy was truly contrite, for guilt was firmly stamped across his face.

"W-why was I so foolish as to ever take her to that cave?" John stammered like a little boy. "I might have known she wouldn't wait on me to take her back."

"You've got that right," Will replied. "I know better than anyone that you can't stop Copper once she sets her mind to something. Your only shame was in sneaking around with my daughter, John." He rested his hand on the boy's shoulder, surprised it was nearly even with his own, and gave it a squeeze. "I've always trusted you to guard and protect her like a brother."

"I promise you," John said, his eyes meeting Will's without flinching, "I'll not lead her astray again."

"That's all I ask. Now finish the milking so's you can go in for some breakfast." Will stuck a pitchfork into a stack of hay and forked a rasher over the horse's stall.

"Will?" he heard John say, his one word filled with need.

Will's lips twitched with a suppressed grin as he turned back toward John. "What is it, boy?"

"When this is done, when she's herself again, can I . . . that is, could I maybe . . . if it's all right with you and Miss Grace—can I call on Copper?"

"Well, I reckon that'd be up to Copper, but I don't expect either Miss Grace or I would stand in your way."

John's smile stretched ear-to-ear as he wiped his hand on the leg of his britches and stuck it out to Will. "Whew," he said. "I'm glad that's over. I been wanting to ask you for the longest time."

Will laughed and pumped John's hand. "You got your work cut out for you, Son. That's all I can say."

The deacons came that first evening after Laura Grace was home. They pulled her bed away from the wall and clasped hands to form an unbroken circle around her. They prayed aloud, then anointed her with oil. Brother Isaac was very faithful—morning and evening he sat by her bed and read from the Scriptures.

"She's taken leave of her senses," Grace told Will after the second long night. "She tosses and turns, crying about skeletons and ghosts, and this morning when I bathed her she pointed out the window and said, 'Look, there's a spirit that's taken the form of a silver fox with a red tail.'"

"It's just the fever talking," Will responded. "She'll be herself again when it breaks."

And indeed she was. On the morning of the fourth day, Laura Grace woke clearheaded and hungry. After a breakfast of milk and toast, Grace let her sit on the porch, wrapped in a wool blanket, though the October day was warm. Willy and Daniel sat at her feet, and Will drank an extra cup of coffee while keeping her company.

"I'm going in to sort the laundry," Grace announced from the open doorway. She raised her shoulders and let them drop. She was weary, so weary after four nights in a straight-backed chair. But strangely, she hated for the vigil to stop. Seemed it was the only way she could get close to her daughter, who'd turned so difficult.

It reminded her of her early days on Troublesome Creek. . . .

Upon returning home after they married in Lexington, Will had left her in the gloomy cabin to freshen up from their arduous journey while he went to fetch the baby from Emilee Pelfrey. As soon as he'd left her alone she knew she couldn't stay. She'd nearly screamed in despair when she realized what a monumental mistake she had made.

The entire cabin was one room. Just one room, and it was so dark and depressing she immediately went in search of a window that would open. She had to have air. Stepping out onto the rough, split-log porch, she took a deep breath, but she found no solace, for the very air was like the hulking mountains that surrounded her–damp, heavy, tasting of rock and clay. She'd never be able to take a full breath again.

Sinking to the floor, she'd covered her face with her hands. "What have I done?" she cried. "Oh, what have I done?"

"Grace?" She heard Will's voice, felt his hand upon her shoulder. "Look'ee here." He knelt before her and placed the baby in her arms.

She stiffened with the burden of the little body. "I can't," she remembered saying. "I don't think I can do this."

He stood and turned from her when she tried to thrust the baby back to him. "Well, you're here and you're her mother now, and I reckon you don't have much choice." Then he walked toward the barn and left her alone, alone with her dead sister's baby.

Grace wasn't a natural at child care and felt awkward around Laura Grace, as if the baby knew she played a charade. Laura Grace was a good, easily satisfied child as long as it was Will who satisfied her. She rejected Grace at every turn. Grace had the devil's own time trying to get her to nurse from the bottle. Usually she just gave up and trekked her across the creek to Emilee Pelfrey's or waited for Will to come in from the fields.

Until one night way after midnight while Will slept up in the loft and Grace lay awake in her bed. Every time she drifted off, Laura Grace woke her with her crying. Tossing and turning, she prayed for rest, and then the baby woke again and began to fret. Wearily, she scooped blankets and all from the cradle and carried the baby to the rocking chair. She dragged it under a small square window, where a light so brilliant it looked like mercury spilled in and splashed across the floor.

Grace rocked and patted and soothed and even offered another feeding, but Laura Grace would have none of it. She wasn't crying really, just fussing and nuzzling the front of Grace's cotton nightdress.

She thinks I'm her mother, Grace thought, surprised. The baby squirmed in her arms. "What is it, baby? Whatever do you want?"

Laura Grace answered by throwing back her little red-haired head and opening her mouth in a full-blown fit of temper.

I'm going to have to give her something besides plain milk if she's ever going to eat for me, Grace surmised. She bundled the baby into the seat of the rocking chair and left her there while she went to the stove and stirred a tiny bit of thick molasses into a cup of warmed milk. Some she poured into the baby's bottle, and some she left in the cup. The baby cried on as loud as thunder to Grace's ears. How could Will sleep through it?

Grace's heart turned over when she picked the baby up. The little thing was in such distress. Sitting, she cuddled the baby against her chest. Holding the cup between her knees, she dipped one finger into the sweetened milk, then stuck it into the baby's mouth. Laura Grace stopped mid-scream and sucked greedily. After several finger-feeds, Grace substituted the bottle nipple. Wonder of wonders, Laura Grace nursed without one whimper.

Satisfied at last, the baby grinned so broadly that Grace could see the nub of a tiny new tooth in her lower gum. Laura Grace sighed a long baby sigh and reached up and patted her aunt's face with one tiny, dimpled hand. Grace leaned over and kissed her fat cheeks. Laura Grace laughed from deep in her belly.

"I'm here," Grace said. "You don't have to worry anymore, sweet baby. I loved your mama and I love you. I'll always be your mother."

Grace fell in love that night, utterly and completely in love with Laura Grace. And she vowed there in the silver light of the moon that she would give her sister's daughter everything she had and all the strength she'd need to get the baby and herself away from that dreadful place, that despised Troublesome Creek.

Now Grace came back to herself as if waking from a dream and found her face wet with the tears of self-recrimination and sorrow. Things had not turned out as she had hoped. The place she herself hated, these mind-numbing mountains, delighted Laura Grace.

She pulled the sheets and quilts from the floor where she'd tossed them. Underneath the pile lay the clothes she'd stripped from Laura Grace the morning Will carried her in. She'd barely noticed the raggedy overalls then, but now she turned them right-side out, puzzling at her daughter's strange attire.

She gasped when she stuck her hand in a pocket and pulled the spectral fingers out. "Will, come in here!"

Will frowned as he turned the bones over and over in his hands. "It's from a dead body."

"Well, I know that!" she cried. "But where did Laura Grace get it?"

Copper rested that day, and by the next morning she felt restored, except when she thought of the cave . . . the foxlike creature . . . the dark prison of the sinkhole. Then her heart sank, and she felt half drowned. She hoped it was a nightmare, that she'd dreamed it all when she fell asleep outside the cave.

She was rinsing dishes when Daniel opened the screen door. He held the dog's dish, a battered tin pie pan. "Where has Paw-paw got to?" Daniel asked. "Ever' morning and ever' night I put out scraps for him, and nothing eats them but the chickens."

"Oh no." Copper dropped a cup into the water. "Paw-paw!"

She was sick at heart as she went to find Daddy. How could she have left Paw-paw? He must have followed her into the cave and gotten stuck or hurt or– She couldn't let her thoughts wander further down that path. Oh, what had happened to her Paw-paw?

She told her father nearly everything as they made their way up the mountain on horseback–how she'd read Mam's mail and discovered the brochure for the boarding school, her plans to run away, how she'd dressed in his overalls and explored the cave, her night in the sinkhole. But for some reason, she kept to herself what she'd found inside the cave and the strange being that scared her silly.

Daddy reined the horse in and swung Copper down when they reached the graveyard. "Copper, you've filled your head with foolishness. We wouldn't send you off to school unless you agreed, but I'm beginning to see the wisdom of your mam's desire. You've learned a valuable lesson, I hope."

Copper hung her head. "What if Paw-paw's dead, Daddy? I don't think I could bear it."

"He's a tough old hound." Will glanced down the mountain before chuckling to himself. "I figure he's been off courtin'."

They searched the tall grasses and weeds for the sinkhole. "Careful!" Will grabbed her hand as a small stone she'd kicked dropped away before their eyes.

"This gives me the willies," Copper said with a shiver.

Daddy knelt by the hole. "It's sure well hidden." He peered in. "I'll need to mark this or fill it lest someone else falls in." He leaned over as far as he could without falling in himself and let out a long, low whistle. "Well, that answers that."

"What?" Copper said, shrinking back a little, afraid of what he'd seen.

"There's half a coffin sticking out of the wall, and it looks like a heap of bones on a ledge at the bottom. That's where the bones Mam found in your pocket came from."

She shuddered. "I remember now. I grabbed the skeleton when the casket broke, and the hand stayed with me." She pulled at his shoulder. "Let's go, Daddy."

"Just let me–" He wrenched out of Copper's grasp and rolled a large rock to the edge of the hole. "The skeleton will have to be buried proper." Slapping his hat against his leg, he turned back to Copper. "Here." Making a step of his hands, he hefted her up onto the horse's back. "I'll tend to this later."

They found the tunnel easily once they were inside the cave. Daddy tried every which way to shove his wide shoulders through the tunnel entrance. Finally he gave up and shook his head. "I can't let you go in there alone, Copper. No telling what's on the other side."

At that very moment they heard a joyous bark, music to Copper's ears.

"He's trapped in there, Daddy," she cried. "I'm going in to get him."

Copper quickly snaked her way through the narrow tunnel once again, her heart fluttering like a bird in cupped hands. When her head finally poked out the other side, a slurping wet tongue kissed her cheeks. "Paw-paw!" she blurted out in relief. "You old, sweet thing. You're alive!"

Paw-paw danced lopsidedly around Copper, his stiff leg bound with strips of the skirt she'd discarded days before.

"I don't understand," she said, kneeling to examine the neatly dressed leg. "Who could have done this?"

Suddenly, quick as a sneeze, a strange colorless creature darted into her vision. "I done it, Purty," the apparition spoke, its voice low and thick. "I done took keer of your dog here."

"Who? . . . What?" Copper gasped.

"Don't be feered, Purty," the being whispered, face close to Copper's, its lashless eyes a watery skim-milk blue.

"Copper!" Daddy called through the tunnel. "Are you okay in there? Can you get Paw-paw out?"

"I'm all right," she yelled, never taking her eyes from the creature crouching before her, "but I'll need the rope."

"I'll go fetch it," Daddy answered, his voice fading into the distance even as he spoke. "Be right back."

"Okay!" she hollered, then reached out and grasped a small

brown-stained hand that jerked away and hid itself behind its owner's back.

"That be from walnut hulls," the slow voice announced.

"Why, you're just a girl," Copper mused. "What are you doing here all alone?"

"I'm waiting 'til my ma sends for me," the girl said, as if she talked to Copper every day, as if it was not unusual for her to be living in a cave alone. "I cain't go home yet."

"Well, you can't stay here. It's going to be cold soon," Copper said, taking charge.

"Copper?" Daddy yelled down the tunnel. "Here's the rope. You'll have to come get it."

Copper turned toward the sound. "Daddy, there's–"

"Don't tell, Purty!" the girl beseeched, eyes wide, her skinny body trembling. "My pap mustn't know where I am. Promise?"

"Okay, okay . . . it will be all right," Copper soothed. Reaching out to stroke the girl's thin shoulder, she felt the jutting bones, but the girl quickly ducked and turned away. A bushy, bright red foxtail fixed to the back of her dress swept the ground when she moved. Copper knew she couldn't keep this girl a secret. She'd have to tell Daddy.

"Don't never come back here," the girl growled suddenly, startling Copper with her venom.

"Copper?" Daddy called again, his voice taking on a questioning edge.

Copper glanced at the tunnel and looked back at the girl. She chewed her bottom lip in frustration. "I'm coming, Daddy!" She retrieved the rope and tied it around the dog's neck, then shimmied back through the tunnel with the free end. Handing the rope to her father, she explained her plan. "When I get ready, Daddy, you pull—but not too hard. It's tied around Paw-paw's neck." She clambered back into the tunnel, wondering if somehow the girl had disappeared. Maybe she had just imagined her. "I'll go back and push."

She went back for Paw-paw and was startled to find the girl's face staring at her at the end of the tunnel, watching for her return.

"There, there, Purty," the girl said as Copper tumbled out. "Can I trust ye not to get in my business?"

Copper shook her head, perplexed. What a strange situation. But something about the girl gave her pause. Obviously she needed a friend, and Copper sensed if she betrayed her in the slightest, the girl would steal away as quickly as she'd come.

Paw-paw whined, and his tail thumped against Copper's leg. He was ready to leave. Copper heaved him into the tunnel, then paused and studied the girl. "I'll find a way to help you."

The girl squinted. "Keep to your own self," she hissed. "Ain't nobody said I needed minding." Her crestfallen look belied the malice of her words.

Copper ignored the thinly veiled threat. She couldn't abandon the girl—somehow she'd have to earn her trust. "Come to me if you ever need help." Her eyes took in the table that held her family's missing things. "Obviously you know where I live."

Without waiting for a reply, Copper turned onto her belly, following Paw-paw into the darkness of the tunnel. She prodded his rear end and kept him squirming along the passage until he was finally free.

"Hey, old man." Daddy patted Paw-paw's head. "Let's get you home."

John had come calling while they were off searching for Paw-paw. Copper knew something was amiss when she saw him standing by the screen door with his shirttail tucked in and his hair slicked back. He had his hands behind his back, and when she stepped up on the porch he brought out a little bunch of wildflowers.

"These here are for you, Pest," he said, thrusting them in her face.

"But I'm not sick anymore."

"Well, that's good, but I brung you flowers anyway. Would you like to sit a spell?" He motioned toward two rockers placed close together.

"Uh, John, this is my house. I don't have to be invited to sit on my own porch," she replied, confused.

"R-reckon not," he stammered, looking at his feet, color creeping up his neck. "Do you want to go to my porch?"

Daddy brushed past them and went inside the house. Copper was sure she could hear him guffawing as he edged the door closed.

"Would you mind telling me what's going on?" she asked. "Why are you acting so silly?"

"Um, well, I . . . it's like this, Pest . . ." He stood on one foot and polished his shoe on the back of his pant leg.

Paw-paw crammed himself between them, and every time he wagged his tail it thumped against the back of her knees, nearly buckling them. Men and dogs—she'd just about had enough.

Putting her hands on her hips she leaned toward John, tapping one foot. "Forevermore, John, chew it slow and spit it out."

"We're courtin'," he replied. "You and me–your daddy said we could."

"I should think I would be the one to decide!" She turned her back and poured a little water from the bucket into an old fruit jar before arranging the wilted posies in it. They were right pretty. "What if I don't want to be courted?"

"I reckon I didn't think on that, Pest. Do you?"

"What, John?" she teased, turning back to him, her nose pressed deep in the flowers. "Do I what?"

He blushed again, red as a rooster's comb. "You're plaguing me now."

Taking pity, she sat demurely in one rocker and batted her eyelashes as she asked, "Would you like to sit a spell?"

"Don't mind if I do, Pest," he answered, sitting beside her and rocking up a storm. "Don't mind if I do."

CHAPTER 12

Grace watched from the screen door as the children played. The evening was cool. Soon they'd have to leave the door closed all the time. She hated winter. It gave no peace. Sometimes in the summer she could steal a whole afternoon with her books . . . transported to another place by the poems of Dickinson, Shelley, Browning, and Keats. Will would be gone working; the children would be out chasing this thing or that. She never had to worry about the boys–their sister would watch over them.

A pressure behind her eyes caused her head to thrum a familiar steady beat. She dipped a drink of water from the bucket on the washstand and caught an unwanted glimpse of her face, pulled in a frown, into the wavy mirror. She tried a smile. It looked false, her teeth too full for her mouth. When had she forgotten how to smile? She took out her combs and shook her hair loose. Gray-streaked red curls tumbled to her shoulders. A faded imitation of her youthful self stared back at her, unforgiving.

No wonder Will was always gone. It had gotten worse since Laura Grace's accident. He blamed her, she knew . . . blamed her that Laura Grace had tried to run away. Now he made the trek up the mountain to the cemetery to Julie's grave nearly every evening.

Footsteps pounded across the porch. Jerking away from the mirror, she twisted up her hair. She and Will had to talk, come to some resolution. She couldn't stand it anymore.

"Move, Paw-paw!" She shoved against the old dog's rump with the door. He rarely left the porch since his escapade in the cave and now spent all his nights indoors, much to Grace's dismay.

"Daniel, take three baby steps," she heard Laura Grace say as she stepped out onto the porch.

"Mother, may I?" Daniel asked, nearly standing on his sister's toes.

"No fair!" Willy cried from his stance near the porch. "He always wins."

Grace didn't correct his unwarranted judgment of his brother, just tightened her shawl against the coolness of the evening. There wouldn't be many more days of outside play. "Laura Grace, get the boys ready for bed, please," she said, her voice a sigh of resignation. Even her books couldn't take her away from this suffocating place for long. She always had to come back. "Be sure they wash their feet." She started down the walkway, then paused. "You may read two chapters from your book about pirates tonight."

"Oh, boy," Daniel replied. "I love pirates. Don't you, Willy?"

"Yeah, I'm going to be a pirate when I grow up an' have a parrot an' lots of gold dub . . . dub . . . what are them things called, Sissy? Oh yeah, double loons. But no wooden leg."

His voice faded away as Grace entered the barn. Her eyes adjusted to the dim light, but she could find no sign of Will. She went to the little window beside the rickety ladder that led to the hayloft and saw him then, faintly, the white of his shirt visible as he crossed the meadow.

Her heart twisted with bitterness as he stepped into the barn. She stayed at the window, her back to him, her eyes fixed on the shadowed mountain. The strength of his presence cast an aura around her.

"Grace?" was all he said. As usual, he left all the unsaid words to her.

She didn't mean to. She'd steeled her heart against it, but as soon as she opened her mouth to speak, tears came instead– great racking sobs that doubled her over and felt for all the world like the hard contractions of childbirth.

He reached for her shoulder, but she shook off his hand. "What's wrong?" he asked, his voice worried. "Is it the children?"

"They're fine," she spat. "It's me! Do you ever wonder how *I* am?"

"What's got your dander up? You never used to carry on like this."

A wash of color bright as blood clouded her vision. She wanted to break something. She wanted to push him straight through the barn siding. Instead she grabbed the milk bucket that hung on a peg near Molly's stall and flung it out the little window. They could hear its metallic ring bouncing off one rock after another.

"That bucket'll be ruined," he said as if the bucket was what mattered. "It'll be full of dents."

She rushed him then, catching him full in the chest and knocking him onto his rear.

He struggled to a standing position as she beat at his head with closed fists. Catching her hands, Will pulled her into a firm embrace. "Grace, honey, stop." She struggled against him, but he wouldn't let her go.

His strength overpowered her, and she sagged against his chest. "Why must you go up there to her grave every night? Why don't you talk to me?"

Will shook his head, holding her away from him so she could see the disbelief on his face. "You can't be jealous of your own dead sister."

Suddenly she was as cold as ice. Her shoulders slumped. "You're right," she said, resigning herself to the situation. "I know I can never take her place. I don't even want to try anymore."

He tightened his arms around her again. She could hear his heartbeat against her ear, and it muffled his reply. "Listen to me carefully, Grace. I loved Julie. She was my heart, but you are my soul. I love you none the less because you are second." He traced the track of her tears with his thumb. His words were a balm to her aching heart.

"I always felt that you were too good for me, that you held yourself apart because you could never love the man who caused your sister's death." He rested his chin on the top of her head. "I've felt so guilty for loving you as I do."

Emotions she'd long kept at bay threatened to overwhelm her. Why had she always turned away from such powerful love? What could be wrong with loving the man who so obviously loved her?

Will's next words nearly broke her heart. "Seems I should suffer every day of my life. Instead God has blessed me with you and our children."

The pride that had sheltered her nearly all her life shattered; like a broken crystal vase it lay in pieces at her feet. She would take a chance and open her true self to him. The sound of a sob clutched her heart, and she felt his tears drip down her own face. A man's tears—so much heavier than a woman's.

"I've been so stupid, so wrong," she confessed. "Will, I always felt that if I gave in to your love then I was betraying Julie somehow. I think it was because I never got to make my peace with her."

He bent his head to hers and murmured against her ear, "I'm so sorry. . . ."

A gentle rain began to tap its music on the barn's tin roof. Twilight deepened to dusk, and dusk ushered in the night as they grieved their terrible loss together. He put his arm around her shoulders and drew her close as they sat on a stack of newly mown hay.

Their tears mixed together as he told her of the guilt and anger he carried with him daily. "I didn't take proper care of Julie. I was so full of myself, so sure I could handle everything. I couldn't wait for Granny and Emilee to leave so I could take care of my family myself." He bowed his head as if in prayer. "God forgive me, but it was my own negligence that killed Julie. Granny warned me to be careful, but in my haste, I took the buggy instead of the wagon. If we'd been in the wagon it wouldn't have turned over in the creek."

"But that was my fault, Will."

He looked at her. "I don't see how you figure that."

Grace leaned her head against her bent knees. Her voice was hushed, contrite. "When you took Julie away, I was so angry. I meant to make you pay. If I hadn't sent the buggy to Julie after father died, the accident would not have happened. I sent it to entice her back to me. I sent it to show her what she was missing."

Grace fished in her pocket for her handkerchief. She wiped her tears and turned her face away from him. "And then, Will," she said, her voice hoarse from crying, "I betrayed her even more when I fell in love with you. I've harbored such anger toward you . . . as if it were your fault that I love you."

He stood and lit the lantern that hung by the barn door, turning the flame down low so just a little yellow glow protected them against the darkness of the night. He settled down beside her and tenderly plucked a piece of hay from her hair before he took her hand. She felt his fingers trace her own and hoped he didn't notice how rough hers had become over the years at Troublesome Creek. For a moment she wished she could turn back the clock and give him her youthful self once again.

"When did you come to love me, Grace?" His voice was husky. "How was it that I didn't know?"

"That's the part that gives my heart such grief, Will. I came here for the baby, for Laura Grace, but I stayed for you. I stepped into my sister's life, and I fell in love with my sister's husband." She paused, afraid to reveal too much, yet her heart told her she couldn't turn back now. "I think I loved you from the time you came to Lexington to get me, but I wouldn't admit it . . . even to myself."

He stood and helped her to her feet. "Julie was so gentle and so kind, and she loved you, Grace. She wouldn't deny us happiness." The night outside their little circle of light was as dark as the inside of a well. He put his hands upon her shoulders, and she let them stay, warmed by his touch. "No more hiding. No more secrets. It's time we truly buried the past." His face was set with determination and tenderness. "I do love you."

"And I love you," she replied, tasting the unfamiliar words on her tongue. "I love you, Will Brown."

Their kisses were tender, tentative, as if they were new lovers, and in a sense they were.

Much later, they returned to the house to find the children asleep in the same bed–Copper in the middle with a twin curled on each side, an open storybook tangled in the covers.

Will put his arm around his wife's shoulder, and she let him hold her. "Should we tell Copper?" he asked, gazing at his sleeping daughter. "Should she know about the night her mother died?"

"Oh, Will," Grace said, "let's give it a while. That's a heavy weight to put upon such young shoulders."

CHAPTER 13

Copper and Daniel were churning butter when Willy dropped a dead hen at their feet. "Daddy said for you to clean this, Sissy. Something got in the henhouse last night and drug off two other chickens."

"Probably a possum," Copper replied, eyeing the plump bird.

Willy poked the dead hen with his bare toe. "This'n got left behind. Daddy says we might as well have chicken and dumplings for supper."

"Mam?" Copper yelled through the screen door. "Do you want me to finish this butter or pluck this hen?"

"There's no need to raise your voice, Daughter." Mam stepped out, pulled the dasher from the churn, and looked at the clots of butter hanging on the wooden rod. "It's nearly ready. I'll finish. You go ahead and dress the chicken."

Copper went to the side yard and started a fire under a cook pot filled with water. She chopped off the chicken's head and hung the body by its feet from the clothesline. Blood dripped onto the grass. *Still fresh. It will be all right to eat.* She gathered her skirts beneath her and settled down to rest for a minute. *Wonder what varmint got into them. I need to patch that fence.*

She stuck a chunk of wood onto the fire, letting her mind wander. There was something different about Mam today. She kept looking at herself in the mirror, and she'd put on one of her nice dresses, but they weren't going to church. Maybe she'd received a letter from her friend Millicent–that always made her smile. But Copper didn't remember seeing one in the post yesterday. Mam always let Copper read the letters before she put them in the little dresser drawer that held her few pieces of jewelry. Millicent lived in Philadelphia, where she and her husband ran a school. Millicent was always after Mam to come to Philadelphia for a visit.

Bubbles rolled and popped in the kettle, catching Copper's attention. Turning her focus back to her work, Copper took the hen off the line and dunked it in the roiling water. Up and down, then up and down some more. The black-and-white feathers loosened, and she easily plucked the chicken bald, except for a few tenacious pinfeathers.

Copper had done this task a hundred times. As she worked, she wondered why Mam's friend never came to visit. Millicent ought to know after all her times of asking that Mam wasn't going there, Copper mused as she hung the pitiful-looking bird back on the line. She rolled an old piece of newsprint into a tight cone and stuck the end of it into the fire.

As expected, Willy came running. He liked anything to do with fire. "Can I do it, Sissy? Can I fire the bird?"

"It's called *singeing*, Willy." She guided the burning paper around the hen. "We want to scorch off all the little pinfeathers."

Willy held his nose. "Boy howdy, that stinks."

"Yes it does," Copper agreed, ruffling Willy's hair. "Let's keep our minds on how good the dumplings will taste."

Supper was especially good tonight. Mam made fine dumplings, and the chicken was fork tender.

"Do you think it was a possum that made off with the other two hens, Daddy?" Copper asked.

"Seems like something bigger," he replied between mouthfuls, forking up another helping of dumplings. "A possum or a coon would likely get just one. Something rode one side of the fence around the henhouse down to the ground. I shored it back up."

"Maybe it was a bear," Willy added.

Mam looked startled. "Will, surely not."

"Don't fret," Daddy replied. "Bears don't much like chicken."

"Shucks," Willy said. "I wish chickens had four legs. Are you going to eat your drumstick, Daniel?"

Mam stood and put the kettle on the stove. "Willy, leave your brother's food alone. Daniel, eat your supper or you're going straight to bed."

"I can't eat all this, Mam," he said and turned his head away as if his plate held a shovelful of food.

Daddy pushed back his chair and went to the tall cupboard in the corner of the room. He took down his slingshot–Copper's favorite weapon–and headed for the door. "You kids finish up and we'll have a little target practice."

Copper quickly started scraping the plates. Mam turned her back, and Daniel slid his drumstick onto Willy's plate. Lickety-split, Daniel was finished with his supper.

"May we be excused, Mam?" Willy asked.

"Yes, go on," Mam said. "And you too, Laura Grace. I'll do the dishes tonight."

Something strange has happened to Mam, Copper thought. But she didn't give Mam time to change her mind. She was out the door on the heels of the twins. She couldn't wait to get her hands on that sling.

Whir, whir, whir, round and round over her head, then release. The little pebble she slung hit the barn door with a rewarding *thunk.*

"That's good, Daughter." Her father's voice was proud. "Now loosen your grip just a little and aim higher."

Copper did as Daddy instructed and hit the bull's-eye midcenter. "I could do this all night," she exclaimed. She loved the feel of the smooth leather in her hand and the power released from the sling's pouch.

After taking their own turns, Willy and Daniel drifted away to do other things. Daddy retreated to the porch with his pipe. It was getting dark. Mam lit the coal-oil lamp in the kitchen window. But Copper stayed out, flinging stone after stone until she could hit the bull's-eye every time.

Copper and the boys were all alone when the varmint came back to raid the henhouse once again.

A "hello to the house" woke them near midnight when John Pelfrey came to fetch Mam to help with the birthing of his mother's latest baby. Daddy and Mam left with John, leaving Copper in charge.

While they were gone, Copper tossed and turned in her bed, twisting the bedclothes in a knot. She dreamed a large blackbird was pecking and cawing on the roof, trying to get into the house.

Sometime in the night, Willy climbed into her bed and placed his cold feet against the small of her back. "Sissy, wake up! Wake up! I've done something really bad." Fat tears rolled down his cheeks and dripped onto Copper's face.

"Whatever is the matter?" She scrubbed her face, trying to wake up, and looked at Willy through scrunched-up eyes.

"Sissy, promise you won't tell Daddy. Swear on a stack of Bibles." He leaned into his sister and sniffled against her chest.

"I promise," she answered. "Now what is it?"

"Swear, Sissy. Swear on a stack of Bibles!"

Copper yawned mightily, wishing to sink back under the bedclothes. "Oh, Willy, we don't have a stack of Bibles. Besides, it's a sin to swear. Just tell me."

"I've done the biggest sin. . . ." He ducked his head, twisting the front of his nightshirt into a wad. "Well, okay, here it is . . . I left the henhouse door open, and something is eating all Mam's chickens!"

Suddenly the squawking she was hearing made sense.

"Be very quiet so we don't wake Daniel, and I'll go and see what's wrong." She stepped out of bed and forced her feet into her shoes. That aggravating possum—she'd finally put an end to him.

"Good idea," Willy said, his tears forgotten. "Daniel never could keep a secret." He crept behind her as close as a shadow.

"It would behoove you to worry about the chickens rather than yourself," she fussed as she cracked the kitchen door, admitting a bar of moonlight.

"I can do that. I can sure do that. I'm worried if some old rat-tailed possum eats them hens Daddy's gonna behoove me good. Yes, siree, I'm real worried about them hens." He placed a hand on his rear end as if he could already feel the sting of the paddle.

"I'll take care of it, Willy. Here, stay on the porch and hold the lantern." Taking pity on her brother, she paused to squeeze his shoulder.

Copper had nearly reached the rollicking chicken coop, a three-quarter moon lighting her way, when a frightening scene stopped her in her tracks. Between her and the henhouse stood a bobcat. A fine specimen—she judged him to be forty pounds at least. His back to her, his ears pricked, he stalked the boys' pet rooster. Cock-a-Doodle was trapped against the fence, jumping about in an odd pirouette and flapping his wings.

Copper backtracked quickly, never taking her eyes from the varmint. Backing all the way into the kitchen, she pulled Willy and the lantern along with her. She dragged a straight-backed chair to the corner cupboard and stood on it to retrieve the leather sling. Placing the lantern on the washstand, she directed the dumbstruck Willy to stay in the house and shut the door behind her.

Searching the moonlit path, Copper chose a smooth, round stone, about the size of a marble, and seated it snugly into the leather pouch. Poor Cock-a-Doodle had exhausted himself in his futile attempt to escape and now lay flopping on the ground as his predator closed in. Copper took aim at the back of the bob-cat's head.

Wham! The rock missed its mark and slammed instead against the wildcat's rump. He turned on her, a warning growl releasing from deep in his throat.

This wasn't as easy as the bull's-eye on the barn door. Her mouth went dry, but she stood her ground. She wouldn't let the hateful thing eat Cock-a-Doodle.

"Please, Jesus, help me finish this!" she prayed as she seated another stone. Her eyes and hands steady, she whirled the sling round and round, faster and faster, and let fly the missile that found its mark with lethal accuracy. The wildcat dropped with-out a sound, dead as four o'clock on a Sunday afternoon.

Just then, Willy flung open the cabin door and burst out with the lantern. Cock-a-Doodle perked right up and made a beeline for the light on the porch. Willy stood, mouth agape, the lamp dangling at his feet, as a dozen squawking, feather-ruffled hens, following the rooster's lead, rushed into the house, through the open bedroom door, and straight under Mam's bed.

"Now you've done it, Sissy," he chided as Copper came in. "How will we explain feathers and chicken pats under Mam's bed?"

"Well, Willy, what a fair-weather friend you've turned out to be." Copper stood with her hands on her hips and narrowed her eyes at her brother. "Here I've saved your hide, and you have the audacity to blame me for letting the chickens into the house! Didn't I tell you to keep the door closed?"

Tears returned to his sad little face. "I can't be a fine-feathered friend, 'cause I ain't got no feathers. And I don't know what *aubacity* means, and you're supposed to help me 'cause you're my sister."

"Fair-weather, Willy," Copper corrected sharply. "It means . . . oh, never mind. Stop crying and I'll let you see the wildcat."

Once outside, Willy let out a long whistle and touched the dead cat's body with one bare toe. He begged the sling from her and lobbed a couple of rock chips toward the barn door. "Know what this reminds me of, Sissy?" he asked finally. "David and the giant."

She smoothed the hair back from his forehead. "Let's see if the chickens have calmed down. We've got to get them out of the house somehow."

They were calm all right. Copper couldn't help but laugh when she pulled up the corner of the bedspread. In the light from the lamp she saw a mass of feathers under the bed. All the chickens, heads tucked under their wings, nested, fast asleep. The only one missing was Cock-a-Doodle. She sat back on her heels and held the lantern high. Finally she spotted him perched on the headboard of Mam and Daddy's bed, proud as a peacock. Copper laughed until tears streamed down her cheeks.

Willy tapped Copper's shoulder with one balled fist. "This ain't one bit funny. I'm going to get a whipping if you don't move them chickens before Mam comes home."

Laughing all the way, Copper took Willy to the chicken house and positioned him at the door. He held the lantern high while she returned to the house and swept the feckless birds out from under the bed and through the kitchen with a broom. Once the chickens were safe and Cock-a-Doodle preening as if he alone had saved their lives, sister and brother climbed into bed with the softly snoring Daniel.

When they awoke the next morning, Mam and Daddy were back to tell of Aunt Emilee's latest baby, a single after two sets of twins, and best of all a girl, after twelve boys. Copper was as proud as Cock-a-Doodle to hear about the baby girl named Julie Grace. She couldn't wait to visit.

And even though Mam made Willy scrub the floor with lye soap, he still strutted like the rooster each time he told the story of his sister and the cat as big as Goliath.

CHAPTER 14

The first time Copper went back to the cave, she carried the sling she'd used to kill the wildcat and her basket on her arm. A passel of smooth, round stones jostled in the pocket of the borrowed overalls she'd finally shortened, bumping against her leg as she walked. She climbed steadily up the mountain alone. The twins were off playing with some of the Pelfrey boys, and she'd shut Paw-paw up in a stall in the stable. She didn't want to lose him again. Besides, the cold weather made his old bones ache.

The days were turning cold and the nights colder still, and she knew animals would be seeking shelter in the caves. Bears were a special danger as they sought dens in which to sleep away the winter. The tunnel to her cave was too small to give passage to a bear, but there were many other caves branching off the mouth of the one she was headed for.

She was glad to be out for the day, away from the cabin that suddenly seemed too small to contain both her and Mam. Although Mam had stopped watching her every move, she still fussed about boarding school. Seemed like every meal now centered on conversation about Mam's friend Millicent and Copper's need for an education.

Millicent had even sent a letter to Copper, the first mail Copper had ever received. Millicent had tried to charm her with descriptions of dances and parties where she could meet other young people. And, she'd written, Copper could live with her and be a day student; she wouldn't have to be a boarder.

Daddy said it was Copper's decision. But Mam wouldn't give up. The air in the house was as tight as a cotton dress washed in hot water when Mam started in on her. Copper had kept the vow she'd made that night in the sinkhole: she was never rude to Mam. But the effort made her cranky, and she sorely needed this day away.

When she reached the cemetery, she set the basket down by the gate. It was full of things for the runaway girl, and Copper's arm was sore from the weight of it. The gate didn't creak when she pushed it open, and the poison ivy John had warned her about had been burned off. The stones that had toppled with age had been righted, and weeds no longer choked the day-eye blossoms that flourished among the graves. It was sad to think frost would soon kill the pretty wildflowers. Daddy and Daniel Pelfrey and some others had seen to the graveyard after Copper found the skeleton in the casket. Nobody knew whom the old bones belonged to, but at least the body's resting place was restored.

Copper was glad they'd spruced the cemetery up. She felt most at peace these days when she visited the grave of her mother, Julie Brown. She never told anyone about her treks to the cemetery; this place was hers alone. She didn't want to share the time spent with her natural mother.

She couldn't tarry, for it was a long way to the cave, but she took a moment to kneel and lay a few perfectly shaped pinecones on her mother's grave. The mound was covered with leaves, but she didn't brush them off. It cheered her to think of Julie sleeping under a quilt of red and gold and orange.

When she stood, a crow called from a tree above her head, "Caw! Caw! Caw!" She shaded her eyes and looked his way. His wings flashed like black gold as he flew away.

"I'll come back soon," Copper said as if her mother could hear. "I'll bring you something pretty."

She wondered about her mother. Did she know Copper visited her? Would she want her to go away to school? Did it hurt when she died? It must have happened when Copper herself was born. She guessed it was her fault—that was probably why Mam wanted to get rid of her. The older Copper got, the more she must remind Mam of the sister she lost.

Copper retrieved her basket and walked on up the hill. A little wind sent puffy gray clouds scurrying across the sun. She'd have to pick up her pace if it was going to rain.

The mouth of the cave was familiar now, and she found it easily enough. "Hello?" she called as she lit a torch inside and secured it in a crevice by the tunnel. "Is anyone in there?"

Nothing answered save the sharp wind that whistled out. She pushed the basket ahead of her as she wrestled through the rough-walled passage. There was no trace of anyone in the cave, and without the sunshine streaming from the vaulted ceiling, no trace of glory. The rock shaped like a table was just that—a rock. No bandanna covered it, no feathers, no biscuit cutter or jam jar. The cave was eerily silent, cold, and damp.

Tears trickled down Copper's cheeks. She had counted on finding the girl. She wanted to give her the clothes and food she'd brought, and the girl would need Copper's old boots to cover her bare feet against the coming winter. Rain now sluiced through the high opening at the top of the cave and ran in little rivulets down the walls to puddle on the floor.

Copper knew she'd better head for home. She put the basket on the rock table—she couldn't bear to take it back—and crawled back through the tunnel.

Molly was patiently waiting by the stable door, ready to be milked, when Copper got down the mountain, and Paw-paw jumped about joyfully and licked her hand after she let him out of the stall. He sat by her side while she milked and then followed her through the driving rain to the springhouse and then to the porch.

A fire roared in the fireplace, and Mam had supper on the table. The smell of hot corn bread made Copper's stomach growl. Paw-paw settled on the hearth, and Copper sat beside him to dry her hair. As soon as Daddy came in from the field, the boys tore in around him, their cheeks red from the hint of winter that swept toward them as sure as summer followed spring.

"Come and eat," Mam said, "before it gets cold."

They all took their accustomed seats and clasped hands for evening prayer. Daddy prayed aloud, but Copper didn't listen. She prayed silently for the lost girl, for warm clothes on her back and shoes on her feet. Copper's heart felt burdened, but her own problems felt light. As the twins chattered away about their day, Copper thought of the girl with each bite, with each swallow of cold buttermilk.

"Cat got your tongue?" Daddy asked, looking her way.

"I'm just thinking," she replied.

"Yeah," Willy teased, "thinking about John Pelfrey." He got up and danced around the table. "Copper and John up in a tree, K-I-S-S-I-N-G."

"Who knew you could spell, Willy?" Copper shot back.

"That spells *kissing*, Sissy," Daniel said seriously. "Is it fun to kiss?"

"How would I know?" Copper jumped from her chair and grabbed Willy. "This is what kissing feels like!" She held him down and planted kisses all over his squirming face.

"Yuck," he wailed. "Daniel, help!"

"For heaven's sake," Mam said. "Will?"

"You two won't get any sweets if you don't get up off the floor," he rebuked.

"Okay then," Willy said as he took his chair and scrubbed his face on his shirtsleeve. "That's enough of that."

Copper sat back down and watched Mam spoon up a serving of blackberry cobbler and set it aside before she dished up dessert for them. Funny, now that John Pelfrey had taken to coming around in the evenings, Mam treated him special.

Copper poured warm milk laced with nutmeg over her

cobbler. Mmm, it was delicious. She licked her spoon and looked at Mam from the corner of her eye. Mam's hand rested on Daddy's shoulder, and he reached up and patted it.

Mam was sure acting strange these days. She didn't want Copper courting–"sparking," Daddy called it–but she allowed it and always saved John a treat. Of course, nobody could be mean to John. He was always kind and treated Mam with courtesy. Sometimes Copper thought he was courting Mam instead of her. Mam was probably putting up with him because she was afraid of who else might come calling at their door. She sure hadn't liked it when Henry Thomas walked Copper home from church recently.

She thought of Henry later as she poured hot water over the supper dishes. He wasn't so bad. No, he didn't go to church, just hung around outside during service. Copper figured he could hear Brother Isaac's loud preaching just as well out under the trees, especially when the windows were open. Sometimes she longed to be out there herself. There was something about Henry she liked. Henry was short and wiry, and his hair was as black as wet coal. His brown eyes, when he looked at her, sparked with a hint of danger. Folks said he was "work brittle," but he worked enough to keep a jingle of coins in his pocket.

John didn't like him any better than Mam did. He said, "You'd better lock the smokehouse when Henry comes around." But she thought John was only jealous.

A knock at the door interrupted her reverie. She'd just dried the last pan and hung up her apron when John walked in. He brought the cold of the night in with him and went to warm his hands by the fire.

"Evening, John," Daddy said.

"Evening, Will. How do, Miss Grace?"

"There's some cobbler on the sideboard, John," Mam replied.

Daddy got out the checkerboard, and John settled down with his dish of cobbler in front of the fireplace to play their regular game. Copper sat with Mam, working on embroidery, although she hated any sort of sewing. She'd rather be playing checkers herself. Willy snuck out of bed and peeked around Daddy's chair as he crowned a checker. Daddy sent Willy packing before John jumped his game piece across the board.

"By doggies," Daddy said. "Whipped again!" He stood and stretched mightily. "Grace, let's give the young folks a little sparking time."

Mam laid down her embroidery hoop, her brightly colored skeins of floss, and her tiny scissors and followed Daddy. He left their door half open.

Copper was embarrassed to hear them settling into bed with John right there beside her. "Want to go to the well house with me?" she asked. "The bucket's nearly empty."

The rain had stopped. The night was cold and so clear it seemed you could reach right up and pluck a star. "Here, let me do that," John said when they reached the well. He lowered the heavy oak bucket they kept tied to a rope until he heard it splash below.

"I hope you don't start acting like I can't do anything." Copper frowned. "You know I draw water every day."

"I know." Hand over hand, he pulled the heavy bucket up from the depths below and emptied it into the granite pail she steadied on the rock lip of the shaft. "But I like to do it for you."

She took the tin cup they kept on a ledge in the well house

and dipped it into the pail. She offered it to him before taking a long drink herself. "Is there anything better than cold well water? Doesn't it seem like you can taste the mountains when you drink this?"

"I don't know about that," he answered.

"Close your eyes and try again, just a sip. See? Don't you recollect clay and rock and coal smoke all mixed up together?"

He closed his eyes like she asked and held the water in his mouth for a moment before swallowing. "Tastes like water to me."

"Oh, John, don't you have any imagination?"

He took her hand. "Here's what I imagine. You and me and our own house way on up the mountain. There's a stand of oak up past the cemetery that would make a fine cabin with more'n enough for a barn and the biggest well house you ever saw." There was a funny look in his eyes when he said that. As if they were already promised to each other, as if they were ready for a cabin of their own.

"Let's don't talk about that," she responded, busying herself with the bucket, unwilling to meet his eyes.

He took the full bucket from her, and they walked back to the house, his steps so steady he didn't slosh a drop. Their feet splashed through trifling puddles left by the rain. "Think on it, Pest. Just think on it."

The warmth of the house surrounded her when they opened the door. The fireplace was banked for the night, but she knew the water in the teakettle would still be hot. John set the bucket on the washstand. Daddy had shut his bedroom door, his sign that the courting was over.

"Good night," she said as John went out.

"Good night, Pest." Turning, he took her hand once again and gave it a squeeze. "Just think on it."

She fixed a cup of chamomile and stirred in the tip of a teaspoon of honey. Paw-paw snoozed on the hearth. She sat with her legs drawn under her and thought on it. It was time to make a decision. She had to tell Mam that she was not going to Philadelphia. It was not right to keep Millicent guessing. There was no way she was leaving Troublesome Creek. No way. Mam would be mad for a spell, but she'd get over it.

Her spoon went round and round clinking against the side of her mug. She'd yet to take a drink. She turned to face the fire. The smoke smelled of apple, her favorite tree. As to John's proposal, she just didn't know yet. He would be easy to live with, John would. But he had no imagination, no dreams. He could read—Mam had taught him when she taught Copper, like she taught all the Pelfrey boys—but he didn't like to. And he didn't much like to talk.

She took a sip of the tea she'd let grow cold. "What do you think, Paw-paw? Should I marry John?"

The old dog raised one rheumy eye, then scooted across the hearth to lay his head in Copper's lap. His heavy lids flapped closed again.

"Thanks for the advice," Copper murmured as she scratched his silky ears.

An image of Henry with his wicked smile and his dangerous ways glimmered in her mind. Life would never be dull with him. She squirmed on her seat. Thoughts of Henry made her feel guilty, but it wasn't her fault what happened when Daddy let him walk her home from church that Sunday. . . .

They'd strayed off the path they were supposed to walk. He'd asked her to go up the holler with him a little piece. He wanted to show her something, he'd said. She felt odd, like she was hiding. She could hear her folks' voices, filtered through the trees, as they walked along the lane below. "What could happen, Grace?" she heard Daddy say. "We're right behind them."

She couldn't stay with Henry but just a minute. Mam would be watching for her. He sat against the bank and asked her if she wanted to see something pretty.

"I don't have time for games," she replied curtly. "What do you have, Henry?"

There was a dead tree up the bank from where he sat, and he scurried up to it and stuck his hand into its hollow center. A minute later, he slid back down by the seat of his pants on a pile of fallen leaves, holding a quart canning jar full of water in his outstretched hand.

She turned to start for home. "I've seen water before," she said.

"This here's magic water. You'd better stay and have some." His voice was as slick as axle grease.

She walked back to him. "There's no such thing as magic."

He unscrewed the lid and took several long swigs. Wiping the lip of the jar with his shirttail, he stuck it out toward Copper. "Take a drink and find out. I promise you won't be sorry."

She held the jar with both hands. The water sparkled in the hazy shaft of sunlight that streamed in through the trees. It smelled like medicine. One little sip. What would it hurt? The chatter of a squirrel distracted her for a moment, and somewhere in the distance a cow bawled, calling for its calf. Hesitantly, she raised the jar to her mouth. A leaf sailed past her face, and she looked up to find Henry staring intently at her.

He licked his lips, and his eyes looked as hot as coals. "Try it," he egged her on.

She felt uneasy, and the smell of the drink made her queasy. "I don't think so." She handed him the jar.

"Then I'll drink by my lonesome," he slurred.

"Henry Thomas, is that liquor?"

"The best moonshine ever made." He took another drink and smacked his lips.

"Looks like you've already had more than enough," she said. "Aren't you afraid you'll go to hell?"

He held the jar overhead and sat against the bank. "If I do, I'll have plenty of good company."

"Well," she replied, "it won't be mine. I'm going home."

"Aw, come on, Copper," he wheedled. "Don't be so prissy."

She started down the ridge to the path that led home. "I'll pray for you, Henry," she tossed back over her shoulder.

"Alls I need is somebody to care about me," he cried down the ridge behind her.

She hurried down the path, anxious to get away from his voice. All of a sudden it looked to her like Mam had been right about Henry.

CHAPTER 15

Copper carried the milk bucket across the frozen barnyard. She tucked her chin into the collar of her coat as the biting wind whipped around her. Molly waited at the stable door, anxious for her breakfast and a respite from the cold.

A rainstorm that turned to hail and then to snow ushered in a record-cold December. Smoke poured from chimneys up and down the hollows of Troublesome Creek as families huddled before fireplaces, their front sides roasting while their backsides froze. John Pelfrey had brought news last night of a man from near Yancy's Branch who died when a foot-long icicle broke loose from his roof and impaled him just as he opened the door.

Copper took several items from her pockets and hid them in the haystack before pulling the milk stool up to Molly's flank.

She rubbed her hands vigorously and began to stroke the cow's teats. "Hope that helps a little. I don't want to freeze you."

Molly responded with a swish of her tail, clouds of steam rising from her body.

"Purty?" The low, thick voice that never failed to startle came from the empty stall next to Molly's. "You be doing all right? It's fearsome cold."

Remy had been visiting for weeks now, but her voice in the stillness caught Copper so off guard she nearly kicked over the milk bucket. "I'm fine, Remy. How about yourself?"

"Better'n you'd expect. I found these gloves, and I'm near toasty. Wish I could find me some bigger boots." She kicked the plank that separated her from Copper. "These here's got my toes stove up. If I was home, Ma'd cut the tops out so's I'd have growing room."

Copper nearly laughed but caught herself, sorry her cast-off boots didn't fit. Who would've expected a scrawny girl like Remy to have such big feet? Copper kept her face carefully composed so she wouldn't offend her friend's stubborn pride. For every time Copper tried to draw Remy in or anytime she mentioned taking the girl's problems to Daddy or Mam, Remy reacted like a feral cat, turning skittish and mean. And when Copper would press her to spend a night in the house, to have a warm meal, to let Copper tend to her frostbitten ears, Remy would accuse her of baiting a trap. She'd say, "Let it be, Purty, else I'll have to disappear into that rarefied air way on up the mountain."

She wouldn't let Copper give her anything outright, not the stalest biscuit or the sparest dress. So by leaving items about the barn–clothes and food–for her to "find," Copper pretended the situation was normal, like every fifteen-year-old girl had a wild friend such as Remy. It was the only way she could figure to help the girl who'd nudged into her heart, first with her desperate plight, then just because she was Remy.

She thought back to the day in October when she'd met Remy in the cave. At first she hadn't known what to make of the odd colorless being with the wild white hair, but then she'd discovered she was just a girl. Albeit a strange girl, one who wore a red foxtail affixed to the back of her dress.

Twelve years old and abandoned by her family—or so it seemed—Remy had taken to visiting on occasion, during Molly's early morning milking. Just like today, she'd pop up in the second stall. Copper never saw her come, and she never saw her go. Remy would stand with her back to the rough plank wall that separated them—she didn't like to be looked at—and tell stories. Copper surmised that some of the stories might even be true, but as much as Remy liked to tell tales, she was closemouthed about her family and where she'd come from.

Even her name was a secret to be guarded. But one morning she'd revealed her identity as if it were a precious gift, and Copper knew it was. Remy Riddle . . . the name fit like the missing piece of a jigsaw puzzle, as fey as the girl herself.

While Copper milked, she sneaked glances through the cracks in the wall, some wide enough to throw a cat through, and tried to judge if Remy was eating, if she was clean, if she had appropriate clothing for the weather.

"Purty—" she peeked at Copper now through a knothole— "air ye spoke for?"

"Spoke for?"

"Spoke for . . . I been spoke for. Quick Hopper's gonna give Pap six gold pieces for me. I seen 'em flashing in his hand when him and Pap was drinking shine one night. They liked to have caught fire they was so purty."

Copper wobbled on her T-shaped milking stool. "You can't mean you're to marry, Remy! You're much too young."

"That's what Ma said. She said not 'til I get my womanhood anyways. Air you a woman yet, Purty?"

Copper's face burned despite the chill in the barn. "You don't have to marry if you don't want to. I'm sure it's against the law to buy a person."

"Good thing is you can smell Quick long before you spy him. He's so old, he'll never catch me anyways."

Copper's temper flared. It was unbelievable to think anyone would be treated as Remy was. She'd like to thump Quick Hopper and Remy's dad too if she was given half a chance. She wished Daddy had heard. Why couldn't he have come into the barn for something? But her resolve to help her friend deepened. She'd never break Remy's trust. "I wish you'd let me help you, Remy. I wish you'd let me tell my father about you."

"You gave your word, Purty." One pale blue eye peered beseechingly at Copper through the knothole. "Pap says that's when real trouble starts—when folks start helping. Riddles take care of their own selves. Always have." Remy clutched the animal-skin cloak she wore and turned to leave.

Copper felt like a tightrope walker. How was she to deal with this burden alone? *Help me, Lord. Help me do the right thing.*

"Wait, Remy. Just a minute." She dipped a canning jar in the bucket and set a full glass of warm milk on the manger. Knowing the girl wouldn't touch it as long as she watched, Copper took the bucket and started toward the door. "Stay warm," she called over her shoulder.

"You too, Purty." Remy's voice followed her. "You stay warm too."

❦

Outside the small cabin on Troublesome Creek Christmas Eve, the mountains lay blanketed under the season's heaviest snowfall. Large wet flakes continued to drift gracefully from heavy, dark gray clouds.

Frosty air gusted in the open door as Will kicked his boots against the doorjamb, scattering big clods of dirty snow about, then dumped an armful of wood in the box by the cookstove. "Let's go sledding tomorrow," he said as he turned around. "We'd go fast as Snyder's hound down Turner's Hill on this packing snow."

Copper looked up from her mending near the hearth. "Oh, Daddy. Close the door."

Daniel laid aside the dried beans he was stringing. "But, Daddy, we don't have a sled." Leave it to Daniel to worry over the details.

"Why, I'll just pull a piece of tin off the barn roof, and we'll sled on that."

"That won't be near as much fun as a real sled." Daniel sighed, resigned.

"How would you know, Son? Far as I can tell, you've never been sledding." Will gave Grace a wink as she mopped up the melting snow.

"I can just imagine it," Daniel replied dreamily. "Going fast as the wind . . . but that's okay. I like tin sleds too."

"That's what I like about you, Daniel—you're easy to please. Not like some rascals I know." Will cast a glance toward Willy, who sat on the hearth, his lip poked out, clad in his new red hat, scarf, mittens, and kneesocks Grace had pulled up over his pant legs.

"Answer me this, Daddy," Willy said. "How can I sneak up on a squirrel if I'm wearing red socks?" He stuck his tongue through the space between his teeth. "You said when me and Daniel turned six you'd take us huntin'."

"Hmm, did I say six? As I recollect, I said fifty-six."

Willy collapsed in a heap, giggling. "Oh, Daddy, you did not."

Paw-paw, who'd practically taken up residence in front of the fireplace, yawned and huffed away from Willy's shenanigans.

Will slapped his hands against his thighs and headed for the door. "I say we wear our old gray toboggans and mufflers when we go hunting and keep these new red ones your mam knit us for church. Now is everyone ready? We don't want to be late for Christmas Eve service."

The little white church in the valley of the mountains was beautiful, its windows aglow with candlelight and its door adorned with an evergreen wreath. The place was packed. Brother Isaac always said there's nothing like the Birth and the Resurrection to draw a crowd of backsliders. He took his place behind the pulpit, then paused to look out over the people he loved so much.

There in the first row sat Will Brown and his family. Will, with his bushy white beard, had a twin on either side while his wife, Grace, beautifully attired as always, sat beside their daughter, Copper, who held Daniel Pelfrey's newest baby, Julie Grace. Daniel and Emilee, along with the rest of their brood, filled an entire back row. The rows between held various Millers, Hunts, Turners, Nevilles, Darnabys, Mullinses, and Fugates.

Such a blessing to minister to these rugged folk. He called himself "the preaching teacher." He could scarcely say which he liked best—each was an important ministry.

Isaac announced the reading from Luke and was rewarded with a whisper of pages as his flock thumbed to the place. Those who were able read along with him—and those who couldn't, recited—the beautiful story from memory: "'And it came to pass in those days, that there went out a decree from Caesar Augustus, that all the world should be taxed. And all went to be taxed, every one into his own city. And Joseph also went up from Galilee, out of the city of Nazareth, into Judaea, unto the city of David, which is called Bethlehem; (because he was of the house and lineage of David:) To be taxed with Mary his espoused wife, being great with child.'" He held up his hand, and the assembly paused.

The sweet, rich tones of a dulcimer came from the back row as John Pelfrey played "O Little Town of Bethlehem."

As the last note faded, Brother Isaac continued from the Scripture: "'And so it was, that, while they were there, the days were accomplished that she should be delivered. And she brought forth her firstborn son, and wrapped him in swaddling clothes, and laid him in a manger; because there was no room for them in the inn.'"

When Issac finished, Copper took her place on the small stage and, still holding the infant Julie, sang "Silent Night." Her angelic soprano wafted through the church and soared into the cold, clear night.

Isaac finished the reading of the Scripture, and each baptized believer filed to the altar to kneel and partake of Communion, the symbolic broken body and shed blood of Jesus.

"Merry Christmas! Merry Christmas!" rang out from family to family after the service. At the church door each child received a gift from Santy Claus—a little poke of hard candy, an orange, an apple, and a Brazil nut it'd take a hammer on an anvil to crack. In the churchyard, a few men fired their guns into the air. Firecrackers sputtered and banged, repeating like shotgun blasts up and down the valley as mothers captured children, and fathers unhitched horses and wagons.

Home from church, Willy and Daniel dressed in gray flannel nightshirts and lay wide-eyed in their feather bed. "You just don't understand, Sissy—me and Daniel have important things to do before Santy comes. We can't just go to bed like babies. You forget we're six now."

"Willy, Santy Claus will not come to our house if you're awake. He is very shy. Now please," Copper urged, more exasperated by the minute, "close your eyes and go to sleep. You too, Daniel."

"Huh," Willy retorted, her words clearly having no effect on him. "You think we would let old Santy see us? Me and Daniel want to trap him and see what's in that poke of his. Just think– we'd have enough toys and candy to last a year if we could just get that red sack."

"Yeah, Sissy," Daniel chimed in. "Just think."

"Scoot over, fellows," Copper said with a sigh. "I want to talk to you about Christmas." She eyed them both to make sure they were paying attention. "Were you listening in church tonight? Christmas is to honor the birth of Jesus. Many years ago He came to earth as a tiny newborn baby."

"Like baby Julie?"

"Yes, Daniel, like baby Julie, but Jesus had a great big job. He came as a newborn so He could live as we do, here on earth instead of with His Father in heaven. He gave us the greatest gift, eternal life, which means that if we believe and put our trust in Him, when we die we go to heaven, where it's like Christmas every day."

"I know that, Sissy," Willy snorted. "That's why you got baptized that time, right? Me and Daniel here are gonna get dunked soon as we can. Brother Isaac's been talking to us about it."

Daniel snuggled up under Copper's arm. "That's all good, Sissy, but what's it got to do with Santy Claus?"

Actually, not much, Copper thought. "Santy is to teach us about giving. He gives gifts to all good little boys and girls. What would happen to the other children if you took Santy's pack?"

Willy leaned toward his brother in alarm. "We didn't think about that, did we, Daniel? Daniel?" He kicked his feet up and down to shake the bed. "Oh, fiddle-faddle–he's gone to sleep and left me to do the figuring out of everything." Willy rubbed his eyes. "I'm not the least bit tired. I'll just listen for the reindeer."

When he glanced hopefully at Copper, she could see the wheels turning in his head. "I'll leave old Santy alone, but I'm gonna see them flying deer. Yes, siree, I'm gonna get me a reindeer. An' I'll be real good and share and let sleepyhead Daniel ride it even if he didn't stay awake to help me."

Willy yawned and snuggled under the covers until just his eyes peeped out. "Will Santy think I'm good," he mumbled around his thumb, "if I let Daniel ride that deer?"

Copper pried Daniel's arms from her waist and climbed over Willy. "I'm sure Santy will be pleased. You'll have to be real quiet to hear the sleigh bells when the reindeer come." She smoothed out the covers, making sure Willy didn't steal them all away from Daniel. "Good night, Willy. Sleep tight."

"Don't let the bedbugs bite," he muttered in return.

The soft breathy sounds of sleeping little boys followed Copper as she stepped from the room they shared. It was barely big enough for her bed under the window and theirs next to it. Not that the boys used their bed. Most mornings she woke to find one or the other—and sometimes both—wrapped around her. It was surely a blessing when Daniel had finally quit wetting the bed. Oh, that made for a cold night.

Mam was busy filling stockings with candy and toys when Copper came out.

"They're asleep at last. Willy's keen on catching one of Santy's reindeer. And he wants to take Santy's pack. He can be really selfish sometimes."

A smile tugged at Mam's lips. "They're just boys.

Understanding that it is more blessed to give than to receive comes with maturity, Daughter. Remember the bonbons?"

Copper did remember. . . .

She had been a feisty nine-year-old the Christmas of the bonbons. Mam had ordered candy from a department store in Philadelphia to distribute to the neighborhood children after church on Christmas Eve. It had been delivered in a pasteboard box. Copper's eyes widened as she and Mam carefully unwrapped the sweets—shiny peppermint canes, spicy ginger wafers, chocolate drops, red and green gumdrops, and the most entrancing of all: a packet of pink bonbons. Copper drooled while she removed the crinkled waxed paper that protected the delicate morsels. She imagined that anything that looked so lovely must taste like heaven.

She put a pair of green mittens, which she had helped knit, in the bottom of every small brown paper sack, then obeyed Mam and added two pieces of each candy.

"Why two pieces?" she had asked. "If we just put in one of each kind, then we'd have some left over for me . . . uh, us." Her face reddened as she glanced at Mam.

"The first piece is to eat quickly, as children will. The second is to savor," Mam replied. "Finish filling the bags while I nurse the babies. Then I'll help you tie the bags with ribbon."

It seemed like Mam was gone a long time. Copper could hear the twins mewling like new kittens from the bedroom. At least they were born with their eyes open, not closed tight like the barn cat's kittens, but they were still funny-looking, Copper thought as she'd set out the rest of the candy. She played with the treats, admiring their rich colors. Scanning the room to make sure no one was looking, she licked the bottom of one bonbon before she put it in one of the little sacks, then nibbled just the tiniest piece of pink coating from another. She held one to her nose, sure she could smell its sweetness.

"Laura Grace," Mam called from the bedroom, "have you finished?"

"Almost. I'm almost done, Mam." She put the last of the candies in the bags . . . except for every other pink bonbon, which she stuck in her pocket. *I should have some for filling the sacks. Nobody will even know they should have two.*

Not waiting for Mam, she tied a red ribbon around each sack, leaving a candy cane peeking from the top. Then, keeping an eye on Mam's bedroom door, she wrapped the stolen treats in paper and tiptoed to her room to slide them under her feather pillow.

When Mam stepped into the kitchen, fastening the top button of her shirtwaist, she said, "Why, your gifts are beautiful! I would never have thought to put the canes just so. Just think how the children will enjoy them." She gave Copper a hug. "I wish I could see their faces when you give them out, but the babies are much too small to take to church."

Indeed, Copper had enjoyed standing by her father's side, handing a bag of candy to each child as they departed the church after the Christmas Eve service. "A gift old Santy asked me to give to you," Daddy said each time.

Copper had a cane as colorful as a barber's pole deep inside her coat pocket. Mam had placed it there right before they left. She stuck the peppermint in her mouth as soon as they finished passing out the candy, and Daddy pulled her up behind him on the horse. It left a tingly clean feeling in her mouth, sort of like cleaning her teeth with salt and baking soda. It was good, but what she really wanted were the pretty pink bonbons under her pillow at home.

She feigned sleep after Mam tucked her into bed that evening. Eyes squeezed shut, she strained to hear the night sounds that would let her know her family was asleep: Mam's rustling as she turned in bed, Daddy's deep snores, and the absolute silence of the two babies who shared a cradle by Mam's side of the bed.

Copper groped under her pillow for the candy, propped the pillow behind her, pulled the quilt over her knees, and slowly unwrapped one lustrous piece. The waxed paper popped and crackled. She froze like a startled rabbit, not daring to make the slightest move.

Finally giving in to temptation, she licked the candy shell with the tip of her tongue. "Yummy, the very best," she whispered as she greedily popped the whole candy into her mouth. The hard pink sugar coating shattered, and she bit into the soft center.

"Yuck!" she gasped, covering her mouth to keep from blurting out her thoughts and being discovered. *What is this stuff? Oh no. Coconut.* She hated coconut! She spit the sweet out, then carried it to the fireplace and pitched it in. *How could anything so pretty on the outside be so ugly on the inside?* she wondered as she watched it sputter and melt.

Back in bed, she had asked herself what to do with the rest of the candy. *It won't be a very merry Christmas if Mam finds it. She probably won't even let me have a piece of the jam cake I helped her make this morning.* Her belly growled when she thought of the brown-sugar icing she'd stirred and stirred. *Well, nobody will be looking under the mattress tomorrow. I'll hide it there and pitch it down the outhouse hole when no one is looking.* Her mind at peace, Copper had drifted off to sleep, wondering what was in her stocking that hung so temptingly from the mantel.

She woke that Christmas morning, so many years ago, when Daddy placed a squirming baby on her bed. "Good morning, Willy," she said into the baby's sweet-smelling neck. "Merry Christmas, Daddy."

"Merry Christmas yourself, Copper. Come open your stocking before I go to milk."

She flung back the covers and rushed to the cozy kitchen. Buttermilk biscuits and a platter of fried ham sat on the sideboard, and Mam was breaking eggs into a cast-iron skillet. "Just a minute, Laura Grace. Let me turn these. There . . . now sit on the hearth and let's see what you have."

Copper had warmed her back as Mam handed her a bulging knee-length sock. Watercolors and artist's brushes spilled out, along with barrettes and beautiful plaid ribbons for her hair. A tiny wrapped box opened to reveal a small light green stone hanging from a fine gold chain.

"Oh, Mam . . . Daddy, it's so pretty." She held it to the fire and watched it glimmer. "The color looks wavy, like a piece of green glass underwater; don't you think? I hope there's a watercolor this shade," she chattered as she upended the stocking and shook two new pencils and a packet of pink bonbons onto the hearth. She felt herself blush as she stuck the candy back into her stocking.

"These are too pretty to eat right now. I'll save them for

later." She hugged first Mam, then Daddy. "This is the best Christmas I have ever had."

Just as in the Bible story of Rachel sitting on her father's stolen household idols, Copper slept on hers. Until one fine spring housecleaning morning when she helped turn the mattress on her bed and two packets of crushed pink bonbons fell at Mam's feet.

Copper learned valuable lessons that Christmas of her ninth year: things are not always as they seem, and pretty on the outside can be coconut-ugly on the inside.

"I still get embarrassed when I think of taking that candy," Copper said finally. "You're so generous, Mam, but do you ever wonder why we have so much when others have so little?" With a sweep of her arm she indicated the clean, warm kitchen, where three full stockings hung from the mantel.

Mam answered, "Remember, the Scripture tells us to whom much is given, much is required. You have to be careful to use wisely the gifts God gives you. He will hold us accountable if our neighbors want and we do nothing."

Copper nodded before taking her coat off a hook by the door. "I'm going to the barn. I want to hear the animals talk before I go to bed."

"Next year you'll have to tell Daniel and Willy the story about the animals," Mam said.

"They really do talk, you know," Copper said thoughtfully. "They tell of the night Jesus was born. You just have to know how to listen."

CHAPTER 16

Copper leaned against the stubborn stable door and pushed it open. She lit the lantern and turned the wick until it cast the palest yellow glow, illuminating the animals safely tucked in their stalls.

Molly raised her sleepy head and stuck out her sandpaper tongue. She mooed softly and was answered by the *bleat, bleat, bleat* of the woolly sheep and the horse's low neigh. Even Pawpaw, who had left his warm bed and shuffled along behind her, added a *woof* to the animal parley.

Copper settled down in the haystack. The rich smell of fodder dried in the hot sun of summer wafted around her. The barn cat, not to be ignored, meowed and stretched, then nested in Copper's lap. She scratched the cat behind the ears, setting off such luxurious purring that the other animals quieted to listen, then slept, adding their own night sounds, sweet as music to Copper's ears. She sighed and nearly slept herself until a soft pat on her shoulder caught her full attention.

"Remy! My goodness." Copper put her hand to her heart. "You always catch me by surprise. I was just listening to the animals."

Remy scooted around in the hay, a little ways behind. Copper turned her head. The lantern reflected only a pallid light, but she could see her little colorless friend and was no longer startled by her appearance. She reached out her hand, but Remy flinched and ducked, her tangle of white hair sticking out, wild as a thornbush.

"Remy, I won't hurt you."

"I know, Purty . . . but I don't like things coming at me. See my mantle?" She pulled the sky blue shawl Copper had left for her around her shoulders. "I found it up the ladder in the hayloft. And these here sweets–" she rummaged in her pockets and pulled out several hard candies–"ain't they purty? I'm saving them for my family."

Remy turned her unusual eyes, rimmed pink–the same pink as the inside of a rabbit's ear–on Copper. "And boots, I found me these here boots." She kicked her skinny legs out from the hay, the boots laced tightly to her ankles. "I ain't never been so warm."

Copper smiled to see her own Sunday boots on Remy. She wasn't sure how she'd explain their loss to Mam, or the shawl that had been her Christmas present last year. Copper loved the way Mam had knit cunning little gold stars all around its border, and it was ever so soft, but Remy needed it more than she did.

"I'm going away, Purty." Remy's gravelly voice was no louder than a sigh.

"Oh, Remy, where will you go?" Copper asked, suddenly frightened for her friend.

"Way on up yonder where the black shoemake vine grows in the ground. Home to my ma."

Copper held her breath, afraid the slightest noise would send Remy scurrying away.

Remy turned thoughtful. "Pap, he got took off by the law. The sheriff say Pap was stealing, but really Pap just finds things we need. My brother Riser come to tell me and fetch me home, but I say I got to tell Purty first. Riser, he's coming back tomorrow."

"You could stay with us," Copper pleaded. "We've got plenty of room."

"Ain't no Riddle ever took a handout! I ain't a charity case." She scooted away from Copper, nearly disappearing in the hay.

"Of course you're not," Copper soothed. "You could work and pay your way."

Remy sighed. "It's too soft here, too far down. 'Sides, my ma—she needs me." She paused as if weighing her next words. "They was two babies this last time, like yore brothers, Purty. Made Ma weak as a sore-eyed cat. But one of them was puny. Little thing never drew air. Pap, he flung it over the cliff, but I found it. It's buried in the cave where I keep my treasures." Remy's voice rose. "Pap say, 'Get out! You think you can go against me. Get out!'"

As if sharing her heavy burden had cleansed her anger, Remy continued wistfully, "Pap be gone awhile. Sheriff say four years. He be over his stew by then."

Copper sucked in her breath, sick at what she'd heard. There had to be a way to make this better. She took in the pitiful girl who was so slight she barely made a dent in the haystack. "Remy," she begged, "please tell me how I can help you. My daddy will build you a cabin, and Mam would help your mother. I know she would. Please—" tears ran in rivulets down Copper's face as she choked out her request—"let us help your family."

Remy looked at Copper straight on for the very first time, her pale eyes a window to her need. "Funny thing, Purty," she answered. "Folks like yourn always thinks ye got the only true way." Remy shrugged as if she searched for words. "See, most times me and mine are as peaceable as you and yourn. We just hit on a low spot is all. Riddles cain't be kept in a box like you cabin dwellers."

Copper felt like she'd just learned a valuable lesson. She wiped her eyes on her dress tail. "I'll miss you, Remy. I'll pray for you."

"What's *pray*?"

Copper's shoulders sagged. She was saddened far beyond anything she'd ever felt before. Her voice was gentle. "Prayer is talking to God."

"Oh, I know of Him," Remy replied quietly. "He lives in the sky with them purty things looks like butterflies."

Butterflies? Copper searched her mind. *Butterflies?* "Oh!" she exclaimed at last. "Angels—they're called angels."

"*Angels* . . . I like the sound of that. I'll name our new baby Angel, if it's still breathing. Ma say she run out of names." Remy hesitated. "Don't cry, Purty."

Copper couldn't help it. Tears turned to sobs as a rough little hand took her own for a moment. Copper put her head on her knees and wept for the girl who had already stolen away as quick as a blown candle flame, leaving Copper only a glimpse of the red foxtail bobbing on the back of her skirt.

It was as if she'd never been, as if Copper had made her up, except for the gift she'd pressed into Copper's hand. Copper turned it over and over before finally daring to look. Then she laughed out loud. "Oh, Remy, I will surely miss you."

Slipping the gift into her pocket for safekeeping, she rose, dashed the tears from her face, dusted hay from her skirt, and headed for the door. The snow had stopped. Everything was covered with a clean blanket so white it sparkled in the moonlight like sun-dappled water. Through a break in the clouds she could see the bright star of the east. Midnight. Christmas Eve gave way to Christmas morn. Behind her the animals woke and murmured among themselves, giving voice in their own way to the story that started in a stable in Bethlehem so many years before.

Copper yawned and stretched as she set the table Christmas morning. Willy and Daniel tumbled out of bed and into the kitchen, clamoring for candy and their stockings. Mam would have none of it until hair was combed, beds made, and breakfast eaten.

"Candy will make you sick on an empty stomach," she admonished sternly. "Your stockings aren't going to disappear while you eat. Willy, Daniel, sit down. Don't try my patience this morning."

"Sorry, Mam." Willy sighed. "It's just too hard to wait. Boy, I wish we'd stayed awake to see the reindeer. Next year we'll sleep in the barn. . . ."

A few minutes later, Willy scooted his empty plate across the table and said, "I'm finished, Mam. Now can we please, please open our stockings?"

"Wait, wait!" Daniel cried. "First I want to give you your presents—Mam's and Daddy's. Don't you want to do that first, Willy?"

"I guess so, but hurry up. Time's a-wastin'."

Both boys ran to get their gifts from the hiding place under their bed. Willy danced in place as Daniel handed out the presents.

"They're thumb cards, Daddy," Daniel explained, "to mark the place in your Bible, and for yours too, Mam." He helped Mam unwrap a piece of crinkly tissue paper and take out a rectangular piece of decorated cardboard. "Sissy helped, but we picked the Scripture ourselves. See, the one from me says, 'As ye would that men should do to you, do ye also to them likewise.'"

Willy leaned over Daddy's shoulder. "Mine says, 'Jesus wept.' Them long verses kept running off the end of my card."

"This is a fine gift, boys. Now I won't lose my place. Why, this makes me want to read a few chapters right now," Daddy teased. "Fetch me my Bible, Willy."

Willy's red face and wide eyes gave away his alarm as he wheeled toward Mam.

"Will Brown, don't make light of the Scriptures," Mam scolded. "Thank you for the lovely bookmarks, Daniel, Willy. Now let's see what Santy left."

Minutes later, candy, harmonicas, yo-yos, and picture books were strewn about the sitting area. Copper gathered the few pieces of gift wrap and ribbon and carefully folded them. She'd press them with a cool iron and use them again next year. It came to her that for the first time she had enjoyed the giving of gifts more than their receipt. *I think I'm growing up. Maybe being an adult won't be so bad after all.*

"Who's ready for a ride down Turner's Hill? Let's go before all the bountiful snow melts," Daddy said as he banked the fire.

Everyone pulled on coats, scarves, mittens, and boots.

"Boys, why don't you get that piece of tin from the barn?" Daddy suggested once they were outside. "We'll wait right here."

Squeals of delight drifted from the barn before Willy emerged, pulling Daniel on a bright red sled, its polished wooden runners gliding over the packed snow.

"You won't believe what Santy did!" Willy yelled. "You just won't believe it. He left this for Daniel and me, right there in the barn where Daddy keeps the burlap bags. We must have been awful good this year." He grabbed Copper around the waist. "Thanks, Sissy! Thanks for making me go to bed last night. This here sled is better than any old reindeer."

Daniel ran his mittens over the sled's smooth surface. "This is the best Christmas ever," he said with a smile. "The very best Christmas ever."

Everyone in the family was fast asleep, exhausted from an afternoon of sledding, bellies full from a quick supper of corn bread crumbled into glasses of cold buttermilk. Everyone save Copper, who tossed and turned in her bed and scrubbed at her cheek with the back of her hand. She was so angry. *That John Pelfrey. What right did he have to steal a kiss? He didn't even ask me.*

He'd jumped on the back of the sled with her and sent it careening down the hill. She'd laughed and laughed until they hit a rock and overturned. "Are you all right?" he'd asked as she sat up, dazed.

"Sure," she'd answered. "Just help me up."

And so he had, but when he took her hand, he pulled her to himself and kissed her right on the cheek.

Good thing Mam couldn't see. I'd never get out of the house again. And she'd already given him his Christmas gift—gloves she'd knit herself for his poor hands, all cracked and sore from hauling rock for Mr. Smithers in freezing weather. *If I'd known he was going to take advantage, I'd have kept them for myself, except John has such big hands they'd never fit me.*

Despite the buttermilk supper she'd eaten earlier, her belly rumbled. *I wonder if there's any more jam cake. . . .*

Seating herself in Mam's rocker, the last piece of cake on a saucer in her lap, she took her favorite Christmas gift from the table beside her. She'd been thrilled to receive her very own dictionary and vowed to read it every day. Actually, she was already into the *Al*'s. "Alb," she read silently, *"a white linen vestment. Albacore: a large pelagic . . ."*

She quickly flipped to the *P*'s. "Pelagic: *relating to, living or occurring in the open sea.*" Now back to the *Al*'s. . . . "Albacore: *a large pelagic tuna with large pectoral fins. Albeit: even though, all though it be. Albino: a human being or lower animal that is congenitally . . ."*

Um . . . She thumbed through *B* to *C. Here it is.* "Congenital: *being such by nature . . . Albino: a human being or lower animal that is congenitally deficient in pigment and usually has a milky or translucent skin, white or colorless hair, and eyes with pink or blue irises.*"

Remy—that's what's wrong with Remy! In her mind's eye

Copper saw the peaked face surrounded by clouds of tangled white hair and the pink-rimmed eyes. She took a bite of cake and licked the back of the fork. *The poor little thing.*

She fingered the little basket dangling from a thin leather cord around her neck and smiled to remember the night before when Remy placed the "gift" in her hand. Another of Remy's found treasures . . . found on Copper's very own bedside table.

Copper couldn't remember when she'd first missed the necklace, but it had been a while since she'd worn it. John had made it for her fourteenth birthday, a perfect basket made from a black walnut shell and threaded on a thin leather thong. Inside, he'd placed the tiniest brown pebbles he'd gathered from the creek. They looked just like eggs.

Her cheek tingled when she thought of John. Yawning, she wondered if he'd try to kiss her again. And she wondered if she would kiss him back.

She climbed into bed, then out again, sinking to her knees on the cold cabin floor to thank the Lord for her wonderful day and to pray for Remy, her little found friend.

CHAPTER 17

It was a perfect February day, bright and clear without threat of snow. John had saddled two horses, and he and Copper were off for a day of hunting. He wanted to scout for deer, but Copper couldn't bring herself to kill one of those soulful animals.

John made fun of her. "There's too many of them roaming the woods, Pest. Would you druther they starve? 'Sides, I've seen how you tuck into a mess of deer meat."

"I don't care if you take a buck. I just can't shoot one myself. They remind me too much of Molly. I'll be content with squirrels."

Daddy was sick with a winter cough, and he pined for fresh meat. He'd fussed about the house last night getting his gear together for a morning hunt, but she and Mam had conspired against him. And so he was toasting his feet in front of the fire and sipping from a cup of General Washington's Cure. Copper had made the tonic herself, and her hands still smelled of onion. Daddy's craving gave Copper the perfect excuse for another sort of hunt.

She'd broken her vow of secrecy to Remy and told John about the girl and her predicament. If Remy could be found, John was the one to do it. Copper had a good knowledge of the forest and mountains surrounding her home, but her roaming was often circumscribed by Mam's restraint, while John was free to explore at will.

Copper hadn't seen Remy since Christmas, and she couldn't help but worry. John had told her of some strange folks he'd come across up on Gobbler's Knob. Nobody much bothered going that far up, for the hunting was scarce. He said the knob was just a big old slick rock that jutted out into the air as sharp as Lincoln's nose. But on its back side there was a series of caves that would keep you dry or warm if need be. That's where he'd spied the people who might be Remy's kin.

He'd been coon hunting one night before Christmas when he lost his best dog, Faithful. She had run ahead, her nose pressed to the ground, and she didn't respond when he called her back. That had never happened before. John told Copper that her deep bay had sounded like it was coming from the top of the mountain, like it bounced off the sheer rock of the knob itself. He figured Faithful had trapped herself somehow.

He'd pulled himself up the rugged slope by vines and little bushes that poked out of the limestone. Faithful's bark was his compass, and the silver shine from the moon cut through the dark like the cold steel blade of a knife. Edging his way around the cliff, he found himself in a flat meadow bereft of trees. It was coming up daybreak by the time he finished his climb; he'd been out all night. Hearing a splash of water up ahead, he caught sight of a wet-weather spring gushing down a sheer rock cliff. Faithful's hoarse woof was coming from behind that spring. The dog had been yapping off and on for hours. He whistled loud and long, but she didn't come.

The rising sun surged over the top of Gobbler's Knob and revealed a great cleft, as clean as butchered meat, in the side of the mountain. John had been certain Faithful was hurt. He walked right into the fissure and made his way between damp rock walls that pressed like a vise against his shoulders. He kept his gun ready, afraid he'd find his dog mauled by a bear or a catamount. Strangely, his hunter's nose picked up woodsmoke mixed with the coal and packed-dirt odors of the mountain.

He rounded a corner, and there was Faithful. A ridge of hair rose on her back. Her long nose pointed straight ahead, her tail pointed straight behind. She stood on three feet, her left front paw curled close to her side.

"Quiet!" he commanded.

Faithful stopped barking, but her eyes never left her prey. He was right proud of his dog. He cocked his gun and peered around a corner into a cave as cozy as any lean-to he'd ever made. A hollow-cheeked woman sat hunched over a smoky fire. Her hair stood in disarray, a mass of black coils springing from her scalp. She stirred something in a large iron pot, then set it to the side to cool. A half-naked boy stood a few feet in front of Faithful, a piece of jerky in his hand. He didn't seem surprised to see John.

"Is this here yore dog, mister?" he asked. "Ma said I could keep it if'n I could ketch it."

At the sound of the boy's voice, the woman whirled to face John. "Riser!" she screamed. "It's the law come to git ye!"

The cave burst into action. Quick as doodlebugs from under a rock, half a dozen children, all with hair as dark as the woman's, darted out of a mound of ratty hides and dirty blankets heaped in the middle of the floor. A toddler tugged the corner of a blanket, and a sickly looking baby, wrapped as tight as a papoose, rolled toward the fire through no effort of its own. The woman plucked it up, and it opened its mouth like a baby bird, but no sound came out.

A tall, skinny fellow about John's age, dressed in buckskin, slept on a ledge rock. He never stirred when the woman screamed. A round tan-colored jug rested in the crook of his arm, and a long rifle lay close beside him.

The woman drew back with the only weapon she had at hand—the baby. Her eyes narrowed as she made a flinging motion. "Mister," she said, "what you want?"

"Ma," a girl said, "that's the baby."

The woman kept her eyes on John as she dropped her arm and slid the infant into the front of the greasy shift she wore. "Shorely," she pleaded, "you ain't aiming to take my boy Riser. You already got my man."

When John held out his hand, the small boy hung like a monkey on his outstretched arm. "I don't aim to make no trouble," John told the woman. "I was just looking for my dog."

"You swear you ain't the law?"

"I don't much care for the sheriff myself, ma'am," he replied.

"Then," she said, her furrowed brow relaxing, "stay fer vittles."

The cave was thick with the smell of unwashed bodies and rancid fat, but John hunched around the fire with the rest of them as the mother stuck a wooden spoon into the stewpot. He cupped his hands like the children and ate what she plopped in them.

"Sorry ye ain't got a bowl," the woman said, her coal black eyes on him. "We left out of our place in a right hurry, trying to keep ahead of the law."

John kept an eye on the fellow on the ledge she'd called Riser while he slurped the stew. It wasn't half bad. He'd always liked possum, especially cooked with onion, but if possum was all they had, then the passed-out drunk wasn't much of a hunter.

"What are you doing here, ma'am? Ain't you afraid these young'uns will freeze?"

"They's right sturdy, cept for this'n." She patted her dress, then reached around him and clunked the boy, who clung to John like a burr, up the side of his head with her spoon. "Rancy," she said, pausing to aim a spit of tobacco juice into the fire, "git off the man."

The fire popped and hissed, and the pungent smell of cured tobacco wafted up in a thin stream of steam. Rancy paid his mother no mind. John felt small hands going through his pockets.

"Huh," Rancy grunted when he came across John's knife. "Huh" again when he discovered the biscuit and sausage. Rancy let go of the knife and settled against John's side with the poke of food. Out of the corner of his eye, John could see a girl creeping up on them, but she stopped when the woman said, "Rilly, feed this'n. Leave what's in the bottom for Riser."

The girl took the baby and settled down by the stewpot. Every so often, she'd run her finger inside the rim and stick it in the baby's open mouth. The infant could barely suck, and its eyes had no color. The little thing was puny.

The woman's eyes met his across the fire. "I ain't making milk," she said, as if that explained the situation.

"The law took your man?" John asked.

"For a spell." She spit again. "Ain't no jail can keep Rastus Riddle fer long."

John stood and put his knife back in its sheath.

Rancy slid down John's side and scuttled across the floor, where he disappeared in the huddle of blankets with his biscuit and sausage.

"Ma'am," John said, "it'd be a right pleasure if you'd let me bring you some grub."

She looked through slanted eyes toward the sleeper on the ledge. "Ye'd have to leave it where Riser could stumble upon it," she whispered. "Riddles don't take handouts."

John paused in his story and shook his head. "It pained me, Pest, to see them living like that, broke as Job's turkey. Poor Miz Riddle left ever'thing to run from the law with her shiftless husband."

Copper reined in her horse and turned in the saddle. "That's them, John. Remy's family! Remy told me the same thing. 'Riddles don't take handouts.'"

"Sounds like they'd druther thieve. People like that'd steal the dimes off a dead man's eyes. It'd be best if you stayed clear of them."

"But you fed them for weeks." Copper's face flushed from the cold and from the anticipation she felt as they neared the cave John had found. Her horse ambled along beside his. They'd gone slowly, lost in conversation, content to be together.

"A feller don't like to see a bunch of starving kids," he answered. "It ain't their fault. I'd of liked to bring that one boy, that Rancy, home with me. He'd of fit right in." He flicked the reins, and his horse picked up its pace. "Come on, Pest. Let's get this over with."

She followed his lead until they came to the edge of the meadow he'd described. They secured the horses in a grove of trees and made their way to the sheer rock wall that she would swear was solid as a whetstone. But then he led her around the spring of clear water that flowed down the face of the mountain. They entered a passageway that was open to the sky.

"Hello!" John called. "Miz Riddle—it's John Pelfrey. I ain't bringing no law."

"John," Copper cautioned at his back, "you'll scare them away."

"Better than getting shot. Besides, this is the only way out."

Copper's heart beat fast, and she held her breath against her hope of finding Remy. Oh, she missed her friend. She reached up and put her hand on John's shoulder. He felt solid and safe beneath her touch.

They rounded a corner, and there was the cave. The passageway let in some light, and they could see remnants of a fire in the middle of the cave. John sifted ashes through his hand. He looked at Copper. "This has been cold for days."

"Maybe they're coming back," she said.

"Don't look like it." He scanned the room. "The cook pot's gone and so's the hides and blankets where they slept."

"We're too late." Her voice shook, and she couldn't stop the tears that welled up in her eyes.

He patted her back awkwardly. "At least they ate good before they took off." He kicked a pile of bones. "This is what's left of the deer I brung them." He stooped to pick up a withered potato. "They missed this'n."

"I wanted to see Remy, John, to make sure she was safe. How do I know she was even with them?"

"You cain't be certain, but it sounds like the girl knows how to take care of herself if need be."

Copper smiled through her tears. "That's for sure. Maybe she'll show up again one day when I least expect it." She walked to the shelf of rock that stuck out like an open drawer at the back of the cave. "Is this where you saw her brother Riser?"

"Yeah, sleeping off some corn liquor, I reckon. I never came back in here after that first time, just left stuff for him to find easy."

"There's something here, John." Copper leaned across the ledge where a tip of white stuck out of a little pile of rocks and earth. She pulled on the furry tip, and a red foxtail matted with dirt slipped out. "Remy. I'm sure this was hers."

"Reckon why she buried it? That seems kind of strange." He moved the smooth stones that protected a little mound of tamped-down earth. "Oh no. Don't look."

But of course she did. Her hands flew to her mouth and stifled a scream. A tiny, wizened face stared up at her from its makeshift grave. She turned into John's arms and hid her face against his chest. "Remy named her Angel," she said, her voice soft against his leather coat.

"Poor little thing starved," he said.

His words fueled a quick, hot anger. She turned away from him. "That stupid woman. Why in heaven's name didn't she feed her baby?"

"If you could have seen her, Pest, you would understand." He took the foxtail from her hand and placed it over the body. "She wasn't eating herself."

Copper wasn't mollified. She wanted to be mad, for anger flamed bright and quick but didn't last, unlike the sorrow that was sure to follow. Like the awful ache of missing Remy, sorrow took its own dread time, lingering in the heart like a high drift of dirty snow.

"How do you know that?" She sniffled and wiped her nose on the back of her mitten. "How do you know Remy's ma wasn't eating?"

"I seen it for myself. She was chewing tobacco to dull her hunger and giving what food she had to her children, not to mention me." He tamped the earth with his hands and put the stones back in place.

Copper blushed. "You're so good, John. I always rush to judgment."

"Think we should say a little something?"

She took his hand, and he followed her lead as she knelt before the ledge rock. "Dear Lord, please welcome this baby, Angel, into her eternal home. Be with Remy and her wandering family and grant them peace."

They walked back out into a day filled with sunshine so bright that Copper had to blink against the glare. They washed their hands in the splash of the spring, then drank their fill of sparkling cold water.

"Why aren't you wearing the gloves I knit you for Christmas?" she asked as she pulled on her own warm mittens.

"I don't want to mess them up."

"You sure you like them? I didn't do a very good job. They were kind of lumpy."

He looked at her straight on. "I cain't figure you ever doing anything that wasn't good, Pest."

"Why, John Pelfrey, you just paid me a compliment."

"I don't know about that—"

"That's a good thing," she interrupted.

"Well, all right then. I'm glad." He made a step of his hands and hoisted her up into her saddle. "I'll wear them gloves next time."

He rode ahead of her as they made their way home. He stopped once to shoot a couple of squirrels to take to her father. She didn't hurry to catch up as she usually did. She hung back so she could watch the way John moved in the saddle, so she could remember how it felt to hide her face against his chest.

Something had happened between them in the cave. She had some things to think about.

CHAPTER 18

Grace pulled her apron up over her arms and shivered in the early morning chill. She could hear Will banging about in the barn, preparing for a day of work, as she stood there on the porch. *Time is going too fast,* she fretted. *Laura Grace is sixteen now, and the boys are six. They'll be gone before I know it.*

What would become of her daughter? Will needed to talk to Laura Grace. . . . After all, the plans they had made affected her too. Following many long discussions, she and Will had decided to leave Troublesome Creek. Grace wanted in the worst way to give her boys an education, and Will agreed. Laura Grace would be all right if she never left the mountains—so would Willy for that matter—but it was no place for Daniel. He was so frail, and he lived inside his mind. How would he ever learn to cope with life if all he ever knew was Troublesome Creek's backward ways?

They wouldn't leave until Laura Grace came of age at eighteen, unless Will persuaded her otherwise. He was adamant that she be allowed to make her own decision. He said he'd tell Laura Grace when the time was right, but Grace wondered when that would ever be.

Grace still could hardly take in Will's acquiescence to her desires. They would come back to his home place, Will and she, once the children's educations were secured. She couldn't ask him to stay away from Troublesome Creek forever.

Grace scanned the mountains that surrounded her. How could they even contemplate leaving Laura Grace here? Of course, the girl had the skills to survive. She could kill and dress a squirrel as well as an eight-point buck, catch a mess of catfish with nothing more than a bent pin and a wiggle worm, and put up blackberry jelly so clear you could see through it. *But,* Grace thought, *I wanted so much more for my sister's daughter.*

Tightening her apron around her arms, Grace couldn't help but worry. *What a creature her father and I have wrought. What will become of her?* Her brow knit in frustration. *It's that young man, that oily Henry Thomas, sniffing around last evening with a flask of instant courage in his back pocket—that's what's upsetting me. His wanting Laura Grace to go to camp meeting with him tonight. Well, I sent him packing. I couldn't bear it . . . her with one of those Thomases. His poor mother, old at thirty-five, always pregnant, her teeth rotted out . . .*

Grace shook her head. *Why did I waste all that time teaching Laura Grace needlepoint and Shakespeare when I should have been*

*teaching her how to keep her sanity while having twelve babies in
twelve years?*

She let the apron fall. "I'm being an old mother hen this fine
July morning," she said aloud. "Here it is half-past five and I've
not started breakfast." She bent her head and closed her eyes.
"I leave it to You, Lord. You know what's best. But please make
a way to get Laura Grace off this mountain."

"Mam?" Laura Grace's voice cut across Mam's thoughts.
"Something wrong? It's not like you to talk to yourself. I've got
biscuits in the oven."

Grace turned as the screen door slapped behind her daughter. "I was thinking of you," she said, her voice soft, almost a
prayer still. "How proud I am of you. And I was praying for you.
I know the Lord will bless you."

"I was praying too, Miss Grace," Will teased as he swung a
full bucket of milk onto the porch. "I prayed for some fried eggs
and a rasher of bacon and some honey for my biscuits." He held
the door for her as she stepped in from the porch.

"You didn't have to milk, Daddy," Laura Grace said. "I was
coming."

"Molly came in early this morning," he replied. "She barely
had time to get to sleep over her feed before I was done."

Laura Grace lifted the milk bucket. "I'll take this to the
springhouse and get some honey from the cellar."

Copper swung open the heavy door and laughed at how frightened she had been of the gloomy cellar as a child, especially in

the early spring when the potatoes had long, white sprouts sticking out of their eyes and the apples were all withered like the dried heads of dead cannibals. Mam made her do it anyway, frightened as she was. She had to give Mam credit; she'd taught Copper a lot—like how to face her fears. Copper was sure that was a lot more important than anything she'd ever learn in boarding school. Thankfully, it seemed like Mam had given up on that idea. At least she wasn't pushing it anymore. She and Daddy always had their heads together these days, but they didn't seem to be plotting against her.

Kneeling on the packed-dirt floor, she pulled the heavy earthenware crock from under a shelf. The wooden lid was stuck tight with dried honey, so she pried it off with a butter knife. The crock was nearly empty. There was only a little piece of honeycomb left. Cutting off a pinch, she chewed the sweet while she puzzled over the changes in her parents. Lately they'd even started taking walks together after supper, and once Copper caught them holding hands. Sweet as the honeycomb, Copper thought, and it made her smile to think so.

She hoisted the crock to her hip and carried it to the porch, where she scraped the last of the honey into a saucepan and took it to the kitchen.

"This would be a good day to hunt for a bee tree," Daddy announced as he mopped honey from his plate with the last of his biscuit. "It's going to be hot as blue blazes, so the bees will be carrying water to their hives. They'll be easy to follow."

"I don't know, Will." Mam sounded worried. "You might get back too late for church service tonight."

"Where is it we're going tonight, Daddy?" Daniel asked, pushing his food around on his plate with his fork.

"Daniel," Mam cautioned, "you'll not be going anywhere if you don't finish your breakfast."

As Mam turned her back to pour more coffee into Daddy's mug, Copper watched a whole mouthful of Daniel's egg and half a biscuit disappear into Willy's mouth—Willy looking out for Daniel again.

"We're going to a brush-arbor meeting, Daniel," Daddy explained, sipping his coffee. "It's just church outdoors."

"Who's holding the service?" Mam asked.

"Some revival preacher from down in Tennessee," Daddy replied, standing and pushing his chair under the table. "I've heard he really stirs folks up. You kids hurry up if you're going bee hunting with me."

Bee hunting sounded like fun to Copper. It was one of her favorite things to do, maybe because she was so good at it. She secured her hair under Mam's black bonnet, turning this way and that as she looked at her reflection in the mirror over the washstand. She'd learned a lesson the previous summer when bees from a swarm had tangled in her bright red locks, having mistaken her for a beautiful flower. That's what Daddy said anyway, after he'd dunked her in the creek to dislodge the stinging insects.

"Now—" she tightened the strings under her chin—"there'll be no bees in my bonnet."

Willy and Daniel jumped up and down on the porch, excited that they could go along. Copper disagreed, afraid they would scare the bees away, but Daddy reminded her that she had learned to beeline when she was their age. So she had reluctantly dressed them in long-sleeved shirts and overalls, tying a string around each pant leg, then spent several minutes searching for their shoes.

Willy clomped around, protesting loudly that his shoes were too little and made his toes turn under. Mam said he could either wear his shoes or stay home with her.

"I'm sorry, Mam. Why, my toes are too numb to hurt," Willy backtracked. "I sure don't want to step on a bee and have my foot swole up like an old bullfrog. Come on, Daniel," he called. "Daddy's fixing to leave us."

Daddy led the way to the creek. Copper knew exactly where he was headed—a sandbar where bees liked to gather water. She'd seen them there herself just the day before.

"Why do bees need the water, Daddy?" Daniel asked.

"Bees keep their honey in wax combs. If it gets too hot the wax melts and the honey runs out, drowns the queen, and destroys the nursery full of larvae."

"What's larvae?"

"Baby bees," Willy answered knowingly.

"Why don't they put the baby bees on top of the comb?"

"Because, Daniel," Willy said, "then the babies would fall in the honey when the wax melted and they'd all be dead." He cupped his hands in the creek water and took a drink.

"That must be why bees are mad all the time," Daniel said, as if he'd finally puzzled out a mystery.

"They're not mad, Daniel—" Copper ruffled his hair—"just busy."

"Do dead baby bees go to heaven, Sissy?"

"Daniel," Willy answered his brother, "ain't it the land of milk and honey?"

"Boys, did you come to talk or to hunt?" Daddy warned.

"Hunt," the twins echoed.

"Then you'd best be still. You've scared off a passel of bees already. I think you need to watch an expert."

Copper stood still, one hand raised as if in salute, and watched as a buzzing bee landed lightly on the water at her feet. He drank his fill, then skimmed along the surface before he was aloft, flying toward a grove of thorny locust trees on the creek bank. Pivoting gracefully, she watched until the tiny creature was out of sight, then walked to the spot where he disappeared and stood quiet guard. There she waited until the next water-logged insect flew past. She marked its direction with her eyes and tiptoed there, her track straight as an arrow in flight.

Thus the hunt continued: bees buzzing, Copper watching and tracking, the twins and Daddy observing and following, until at last Copper waved the boys to her side. There in an old hollow sycamore, thousands of bees worked feverishly over their hive. The music of their labor was like that of an angry fiddle, and the rich smell of their nectar hung heavy in the air. Sporadically, dozens of bees would break away from the rest and dance drunkenly in the air, only to regroup and settle again with the mass on the tree.

The boys stared transfixed at the dangerous, undulating colony when all of a sudden a bumbling, stick-breaking, leaf-mashing ruckus signaled the entrance of another intruder into the closely choreographed world of the honeybees.

Daddy clamped his hand over Willy's open mouth. "Don't move. Don't even breathe," he whispered.

Everyone watched, mesmerized, as a half-grown black bear lumbered up to the tree. Snuffling and snorting his hunger, the bear stuck his paw into the hollow sycamore, not more than a foot below the angry swarm. He licked his fingers, then grubbed farther into the hole, his arm stuck up to his shoulder. He pulled out a hefty chunk of caramel-colored honeycomb and settled on his rump with a soft *woof* to chew on the waxy treat. Aggravated, he swatted at the bees who buzzed his ears, only to become trapped in his sticky paw.

It was a funny sight. The bees working incessantly above, making food for their winter stores, as the bear helped himself from below, plump and lazy, living off the industry of others, storing fat for his winter hibernation.

The family's chance for escape came after the bees had had enough of the nuisance and began to settle on the bruin's thick black pelt, landing painful stings on his shoulders and back, until he stood and trained his unblinking chocolate gaze on them for a long, frightening moment. Finally he loped off to content himself by wallowing in the cool creek, his long tongue savoring the honey on his chestnut-colored snout.

Not a word was spoken until, nearly a mile from the bee tree, Willy asked, "Daddy, why didn't you shoot that bear?"

"The bear just wanted some honey," Daniel chimed in. "You wouldn't ever shoot him, would you, Daddy?"

Daddy stopped, his rifle pointed at the ground. "Well, little Dan, I don't reckon so. My daddy taught me that God gave us the animals of the field and forest to sustain our bodies, so I kill only what I want to eat, and bear's a little too gamy for my taste. Now shake a leg. I'm hankering to get to that camp meeting. It's been a long time since I've seen anything like that."

Willy and Daniel talked about the bear all through the supper that Grace had waiting for her family when they got back. She hurried them along, so they would have time to change into the clean clothes she'd laid out on the bed for them. Her family wouldn't go to church looking like ragamuffins even if it was outdoors.

Grace was thankful camp meetings didn't happen often; she didn't really like them. Church should be orderly and respectful, not emotional like these tended to be. She didn't approve of all that hand waving and tongue talking, but maybe they'd get a good sermon out of it anyway.

CHAPTER 19

The smell of woodsmoke permeated the air as the buggy drew close to the field where the brush-arbor meeting was in progress. A large canvas tent, surrounded by slat-sided wagons and big-wheeled buggies, was staked in a newly mown meadow. A bonfire crackled and popped, enticing hungry mosquitoes away from the crowd and lighting up the darkening sky. Will helped the ladies from the buggy and reminded the boys to mind their p's and q's, then escorted his family to the service.

As they entered the open-air tent they could see at the far end a good-size platform with a roof constructed from fresh cedar boughs and heavy ropes of grapevine. It made a beautiful chapel, where the preacher and his deacons sat on horsehair chairs that had been provided from someone's parlor.

They found seating in the last row of backless split-log benches. Will and the twins moved to stand behind the long seat so there would be places for other latecomers. Many men and boys stood outside the tent, where the murmuring of the crowd mingled with the rough burr of cicadas and the shrill call of katydids.

Just as the edge of night deepened the shadow of the forest beyond the meadow, the six deacons lit the bull's-eye lanterns that hung from cords along the sides of the tent. A yellow glow lit the preacher when he took center stage. He was a tall, thin man whose rusty black suit drooped from his lanky frame as if he had survived a grave illness. A large black Bible hung from his bony hand, and he took a handkerchief from his breast pocket and mopped his brow as he surveyed the congregation.

He stood stock-still for long minutes until everyone was quiet. A hush as solemn and deep as the grave descended as his black eyes swiveled here and there. As if he were too weary for words, his head dropped to his chest, and he began to weave . . . swaying . . . swaying . . . as supple as a willow blown by a quick, hot wind. Every eye was on him when at last his head snapped up and a wail escaped his throat. With a loud moaning voice, he called for God to send down the Holy Spirit to anoint himself and the others gathered there.

"Send the cleansing fire, dear Lord, to burn away the stench of these sinners assembled here. For I know that the very sight of sin offends You as it offends me. They are not worthy—no, not one! We need the signs. Oh, Jesus, pray send the signs. As You revealed Your broken self to the eleven apostles, as You gave to them the signs of faith—demon driving, tongue talking. Glory!

Hallelujah! Poison drinking, sick healing, snake handling . . .
ain't that right, Brother Neace?"

Copper stared transfixed as one of the deacons behind the
preacher nodded. She dared to glance behind her. Willy stood
behind Daddy, peeping at the stage through the crook of
Daddy's arm. Daniel was on Daddy's other side, quietly taking
it all in. Mam's face looked disapproving, as if she'd stepped in
something.

Suddenly the preacher's black eyes swirled in their sockets
before he dropped to his knees and leaned backward, his body
a tortuous *V*, his black slicked-back hair sweeping the floor while
his head jerked back and forth. "As You revealed Yourself to the
eleven before You went to glory to sit at God's right hand, reveal
Yourself to these blasphemers. Save them from hellfire."

He shot to his feet in one fluid motion and looked intently
across the crowd. Unexpectedly, the sunken-cheeked preacher
man began a slow dance across the roughly constructed stage.
He took a little hop-step, hop-step, stroll . . . hop-step, hop-step,
stroll . . . his unpolished black boots beating out a rhythm until
all of a sudden he leaped from the raised platform to place his
hand upon the forehead of a sickly girl whose mother had thrust
her to the front of the gathering. The narrow-faced girl stood
trembling before the wild-eyed preacher.

"This here gal has a host of demons," he cried. "Lord God,
as You beheld Satan in the lightning falling from the sky, behold
this gal, a sinner, and cast out the evil from her heart."

Every person held his breath as the preacher and girl stood, locked in place, until the girl swooned and collapsed in the sawdust-covered ground at the minister's feet.

"Do you feel it?" the preacher called to the congregation. "The very air is a-swooshing and a-twirling around us. It's filled with the hot fire of hell as the devil and his henchmen flee this anointed place. Get thee behind me, Satan! Thank You, Jesus. Praise You, Lord."

The preacher began to hum and twirl in tight circles while several women shouted "Glory!" and others raised their arms, hands reaching for the sky, and swayed to the strange music of the night. A barefoot man dressed only in dirty bib overalls commenced to barking and running up and down the aisle before he crashed backward, thudding like a cut tree felled by the clergy's mighty hand.

In Copper's opinion, the crowning touch this hot summer night came at the very end of the service when the deacons carried a polished wooden box to the center of the stage. Kneeling, Deacon Neace pried open the lid, reached inside, and slowly withdrew a three-foot-long diamondback rattler. The lantern light glistened on the snake's rippling skin, revealing dark diamonds with light centers bordered by rows of yellow scales. Copper heard a sudden intake of breath as the audience gasped in surprise. She had seen rattlers before but never one this big.

Feeling a push from behind, she scooted over as much as she could on the packed bench so Willy could squirm his way in. He sat beside her and buried his head in Mam's lap. When Copper glanced around to see about Daniel, his eyes were glued to the stage.

Brother Neace, a look of rapture on his face, held the serpent aloft draped from his right hand. The snake writhed in the air, and its black forked tongue darted in and out. Its tail twitched rhythmically, making a sound like corncobs rubbed together, a dreaded sound they all recognized for its imminent danger. The deacon took no notice, just held the viper higher. He opened his mouth, and a mystifying musical language began to fill the tent.

"Tongue," a woman beside Copper murmured. "He's talking tongue."

The other deacons, one by one, also took up serpents from the box and formed a circle around Deacon Neace. Emboldened by the Spirit, they began to testify as they tossed the snakes back and forth. The congregation was on its feet–some singing, some shouting–awestruck at what they were witnessing . . . the awesome power of faith.

Packed shoulder to shoulder in the crowd, Copper could feel Mam stiffen. She saw Daddy place his hand on her shoulder as if to keep her from fleeing. For one thing, Mam despised snakes. Copper was always having to grab a hoe and chop one up if it dared to pick Mam's yard to sun itself in. For another, Copper knew Mam did not believe such goings-on as tongue talking had anything to do with worship. She could only imagine what Mam would say about taking up serpents. Copper tucked her hand into the bend of Mam's elbow and heard her sigh of relief when the benediction ended and the crowd was released into the muggy night.

Copper walked behind her parents, listening to them talk, trying to come to terms with what she'd witnessed. "Will," she heard Mam say, "surely you wouldn't have brought us if you'd known there'd be snakes."

"I had no idea, Grace. I didn't even know what was in that box until he pulled that rattler out. I've never in my life seen anything like that."

Willy clutched Mam's skirt tail. "I didn't like that scary preacher," he said. "Did you, Daniel? Daniel?"

Mam's heavy skirt fanned out as she twirled around, nearly sending Willy aloft. "Oh, my heavens," she cried in alarm. "We've lost Daniel!"

"Grace, calm down," Daddy soothed. "He can't have gotten far. Come on, Willy. We'll go find your brother."

"If it's all the same to you, Daddy," Willy replied breathlessly, "I'd druther not go back in there with them snakes. Whew—they just about scared me silly."

Copper could see by Willy's pale face that he wasn't kidding. He looked just as scared as Mam.

"Then you wait with your mother," Daddy told him. "Copper and I'll find Daniel and be back directly."

Copper followed her father as he shouldered his way through the crowd. "Copper, you go around this side of the tent, and I'll take the other."

Copper was already searching. She thought Daniel was probably hiding somewhere. If Willy had admitted his fear, then Daniel, the more sensitive of the two, must be terrified. She longed to find him and gather him in her arms. She made her way to the front, pausing to look under each bench and calling his name as she went. Finally as she approached the makeshift stage, she spied him standing before the platform in rapt attention, watching as the deacons packed the undulating, knotted reptiles back into the wooden box.

"Wait, Sissy." Daniel shrugged off Copper's hand. "I need to see this."

They were close enough to hear the warning *whir* of the big diamondback's tail as Deacon Neace held it aloft one more time before sliding it down the length of his arm and swinging it gently into the open box.

"Boy," the deacon called, "do you want to take a gander at these vipers?"

"Thank you, no." Copper grabbed Daniel's arm as he started up the rough-hewn steps. "Come on. There's Daddy."

The family was subdued as the horse pulled their buggy toward home. *Clip-clop, clip-clop*, the horse's hooves pounded the ground and accompanied Copper's thoughts of the brush-arbor meeting. She had never experienced such an exciting event. The sound of the preacher's exhortation, the smell of the sawdust-strewn floor, the sight of the snakes' skin glistening in the light from the lanterns, the feel of Mam's rigid body beside her, the fear that gripped her when Daniel was missing, her relief when he was found . . . it all tumbled through her mind causing her to feel keyed up, distressed, unable to contain her swirling emotions, and unsure of what to believe.

Was that preacher right? Did true believers have the gifts of the Holy Spirit? Could she speak in tongues? She couldn't wait to talk to Daddy about it in private. She pretty much knew what Mam's reaction would be. *It must be easier*, Copper thought, *to just believe what you believe, as Mam does, and not be pulled in different directions about things.*

Copper was comforted by her family as Daniel leaned

against her side yawning, almost asleep. Mam sat in front of her, shoulders squared, resolute, but Copper noticed that her hand rested on Daddy's thigh as if she also needed comfort. Daddy held the reins and sang the closing song: "'Through floods and flames, if Jesus lead, I'll follow where He goes. Hinder me not, shall be my cry, though earth and hell oppose.'"

Willy sat on the other side of Daniel, quiet for once. Copper could almost see the gears turning in his brain, trying to make sense of it all.

No one broke the silence until the horse turned toward the entrance to their farm. Then Willy said, "I don't know what anyone else thinks, but I think someone sewed them snakes' lips shut!" That said, he jumped down from the buggy to open the cattle gate and lead the horse through.

Tension drained from Copper's body as she joined her parents' laughter and lost herself in merriment. Daddy took off his hat and slapped it against his thigh, and Mam held her handkerchief to her mouth. Only Daniel remained quiet, as if he had his own answer to the mystery of the snakes.

CHAPTER 20

Several summer days later, things had settled back to normal. Daddy and Copper would have liked to attend more of the camp meetings, but after seeing the snakes Mam was adamant in her refusal to accompany them, and Daddy would not go without her.

Copper was sorely disappointed. The brush-arbor meeting was the most exciting event she'd ever witnessed, and it might be a very long time before another one was held. She'd tried to wheedle Daddy into taking her, but he said that wouldn't be fair to Mam. He might have been coaxed into letting her go with John, but as usual John was off working as a hired man. He said he needed to make money for a piece of land where they could set up housekeeping.

Copper spent most of the morning patching the fence that enclosed one side of the chicken house. The hens had become possessive of their eggs, signaling that there would soon be baby chicks to care for, tiny balls of fluff no bigger than the palm of her hand. All the while she cut and strung chicken wire and pounded stakes into the hard ground, she stewed. Why must everyone else decide what she could and couldn't do? Mam with her list of don'ts and Daddy always trying to please Mam, and now John determining they'd marry someday when last she knew she'd never even been asked! She crimped the last piece of patching wire in place and stomped into the henhouse, flinging her pliers onto the ground in frustration.

Her anger set the hens to murmuring and fidgeting on their nests. Discomfited, she stood in the middle of the small room and calmed herself. Chickens liked peace and quiet when they were brooding; she didn't want to scare them from their nests.

The chicken coop was just a little wooden shed with open boxes built along two walls. The boxes were several feet off the floor, so the hens would have a place to lay their eggs instead of dropping them willy-nilly under bushes and in clumps of grass. There was a small doorlike window connecting the yard to the coop. On sunny days Copper would prop it open so the chicks could scratch in the dirt and take in some air. The chicken wire protected the doodles from scavenging possums and fierce chicken hawks.

Copper scrubbed all the feeders and water containers and left them to dry in the sun. She would water the little birds from a Mason jar turned upside down and placed in a shallow, slant-sided glass dish. The dish had a glass crosspiece that kept the rim of the jar from touching the bottom, thus allowing small amounts of fresh water to trickle into the saucer at all times.

Next she carried a twenty-five-pound burlap bag of rolled oats that Daddy had put on the porch for her out to the coop and left it there to feed to the babies when they hatched. She felt ever so much better. As Mam was fond of saying: "Busy hands make a happy heart." Besides, Copper had never been able to carry a grudge for long.

Once the repair work was done and the cleaning finished, Copper retrieved her woven egg basket from the kitchen and went to gather the fresh eggs. She had marked the setting eggs with an *X* on the rounded end with a wax pencil so she could tell the newly laid ones from the incubators. The setting hens reminded her of the old adage "A man works from sun to sun, but a woman's work is never done." Here were the hens still producing eggs daily while also bringing new chicks to life, and there was Cock-a-Doodle high-stepping it around the farmyard, occasionally stopping to preen his long, glossy, red feathers. As far as Copper could see, Cock-a-Doodle's only duty was to serve as an alarm with his loud crowing at dawn.

Copper uttered a soft *cluck-cluck-cluck* as she went back into the henhouse. She had made pets of most of the hens, and they didn't fuss too much when she searched their nests. Most folks thought a chicken's stupidity was outranked only by that of a turkey, but that didn't bother Copper. She thought of what good mothers these chickens made as she grabbed Fanny Mae's tail feathers with her left hand, lifted her fat bottom from the nest, and felt for fresh eggs with her right.

She'd been flogged many times as a child before she learned to treat brooding hens with authority. She smiled to remember how she'd dreaded gathering eggs. She used to stand near the door and pry the hens off their nests with a long board. They'd jump down with a great squawking and flapping of wings, then run around the chicken house as if it were the Rapture and they'd been left behind, giving Copper time to raid their nests.

When Copper felt thin cracks in the marked eggs under Bertha's bottom, she was glad she'd finished cleaning the coop. Baby chicks needed clean surroundings so they wouldn't get sick, and these would be here soon. She stroked the chicken's back. "Good work, Bertha. These babies should be hatched by morning."

Copper set her basket aside when she heard Willy call, "Sissy, Sissy, come and look! Come and look!"

The boys had been minding one wayward hen and her brood while Copper prepared the house to receive them. The ornery bird had hidden her nest in the woods, and when her progeny hatched she had proudly ushered them into the barnyard, where the food was easy pickings. She had produced five downy yellow chicks with tiny yellow beaks, and somehow she'd managed to adopt a misfit too. A gangly, web-footed, big-billed duckling that would snuggle under her wings just like the chicks did when frightened.

A funny sight awaited Copper as she stepped from the gloom of the henhouse into the glare of the noontime sun. Big Momma, as Copper had dubbed the errant hen, was frantically clucking to the duckling, warning him of extreme danger as he paddled around in a mud puddle ducking his head and slinging dirty water over his back. His tiny siblings ran behind Big

Momma, first this way, then that, as she tried to persuade her strange baby to come out of the water.

"Isn't this the strangest thing you've ever seen, Sissy?" Willy laughed at the mother hen.

"It is odd, Willy, but why don't we help her by shooing her and the doodles into the chicken coop so we can feed and water them? You and Daniel can keep the duck for a pet."

"Oh, good idea. That will be great fun," Daniel replied. "We've never had a pet duck before. Let's name him Bill—okay, Willy?"

"Yeah, that's a good name for him," Willy answered. "How about Big Bill, 'cause of his big beak?"

Daniel caught the little splashing duckling and carried him to the porch as Copper and Willy directed Big Momma and her chicks into the coop. Willy sprinkled rolled oats onto the just-swept floor while Copper filled the water jar and tapped her finger against the floor to show the doodles where the food was. Soon the chicks were scratching and pecking at the oats and dipping their beaks in the water dish before throwing their fuzzy heads back to let the water run down their throats.

"I could watch them all day, couldn't you?" Copper laughed.

"Yeah, they're sure fun, Sissy. But I guess I'd better get going and pull some weeds from the garden before Daddy comes in. Me and Daniel got sidetracked by them chickens."

"Those chickens, Willy—those chickens. It seems your language gets worse instead of better the more you're corrected."

"Oh, that's what Mam says." Willy sighed. "I ought to let Daniel do all the talking. But then nobody'd ever say anything. You know that Daniel's a man of few words."

"Well, don't ever stop gabbing." Copper smoothed his wayward hair. "I would certainly miss the sound of your voice."

Late that afternoon before supper, Copper and Mam sat on the porch, Copper snapping green beans and Mam churning butter. Daddy was still at the coal bank chunking coal with Daniel Pelfrey. Copper had seen the twins run off into the woods beyond the yard earlier to look under rocks for fishing worms.

"Help me pour off some buttermilk, Copper." Mam put the dasher aside and hefted a gallon crock to her hip. "We'll have some for supper."

Suddenly a child's scream rent the air.

"What?" Mam exclaimed before the crock crashed to the floor, splattering clabber, the same deadly color as her complexion, over everything.

"Mam! Mam! Daniel's killed!" Willy shouted as he tore from the woods and collapsed, sobbing, onto the porch.

Copper pulled him to his feet. "Stop it, Willy! What's happened?"

"Sissy. Oh, Sissy–Mam–" He gulped air. "I tried to stop him, but he went up under that cliff where the snakes live. Now he's laying up there an' he's not moving, just moaning, an' his legs are a-jerking."

"Willy, you go to the coal bank and get Daddy. Run!" Copper grabbed Mam's hand and took off toward the trees.

A short time later they came upon Daniel, lying just where Willy had said. He was deathly still except for an odd spasm in his right leg. There was a bluish tint around his mouth, and he was cold to Copper's touch.

Mam sank to the ground beside him, gathered him into her arms, and began to kiss his face. "Wake up, baby," she cried. "Please wake up."

Copper knelt and examined him. She took his right foot in her hand, pushed up his pant leg, and revealed the narrow puncture wounds of a snake's fangs. Daniel could die from the snake's venom if they didn't take action soon. What was it Daddy had told her to do if she was ever bitten by a snake? She searched her mind frantically. Finally she remembered: prepare a tourniquet and cut an *X* into the wound. Could she do that? Feeling sick, she studied the ugly mark of the snake. How could she bring herself to cut her little brother's leg?

Daniel moaned and raised a feeble arm toward her before his hand fell back against the ground.

Lord, help us, she prayed before she took action.

"Mam, you need to sit behind him and hold him up against your chest," Copper urged. "Keep his head higher than his heart so the poison will travel more slowly." Copper tore a long strip of material from her petticoat and wound it around Daniel's leg above the bite, tourniquet fashion.

"I need something sharp." She glanced helplessly around her. "Do you have your sewing scissors in your pocket? Yes? Give them to me."

Mam's hand trembled as she passed the small scissors to Copper. Copper opened them and without a moment's hesitation, cut an *X* deep into Daniel's wound with one of the blades. Bending low over his leg, she sucked on the bite and spat blood, then loosened the tourniquet for a short time before she sucked and spat again.

"Laura Grace," Mam pleaded, her face ashen, "is he alive?"

Copper held her breath. He didn't look good. She'd never seen a body with that waxen color, and his head lolled around on Mam's chest. Placing her hand on Daniel's chest, she felt a wild pulse against her palm. "He's living, but his heart is racing from the poison." Her eyes met Mam's. "We can only wait for Daddy and pray. Oh, Daniel, what were you thinking?"

After minutes that seemed like hours, the heavy thud of footsteps running through the forest announced the men's arrival. Daniel Pelfrey, carrying little Daniel, ran next to Daddy all the way to the cabin, where he handed Daniel over to his father. Daddy sat with his back against the porch wall and moved Daniel into a sitting position between his legs. Copper followed, barely able to catch her breath after pushing herself to keep up with the men's long legs.

"Will," she heard Daniel Pelfrey say, "there's a doctor over at Miss Lottie Boone's. Do you want me to fetch him?"

"Might be good to have some help," Daddy agreed. "I reckon you'd better hurry, Dan."

A doctor, Copper thought. *Daddy's sending for a doctor! Is Daniel going to die?*

"Copper," Daddy told her, "go kill the fattest hen you can find. We need some unctuous flesh to draw out the poison."

Copper gasped for air and waved at Willy, who came onto the porch with Mam. "Come and help me, little brother," she urged. Willy looked like he might faint; she needed to distract him.

They hurried to the chicken yard. Copper knew she had to grab the first hen she saw, and she hoped it wouldn't be Bertha or Big Momma. Thankfully, the bird that soon picked its way across her path was not a favorite and was fat and slow . . . an easy target. "You're lucky a wily fox hasn't eaten you already," she told the hapless hen before turning to her brother. "Willy, grab the hatchet."

The log they killed chickens on was at the side of the barn under a large-leafed catalpa tree. It was the end piece of a hardwood tree trunk about twelve inches in diameter. It sat upright and two large nails, spaced the width of a chicken's neck apart, protruded from its surface. Copper laid the chicken across the log, its head hanging over the edge, its neck secured between the nails. She took the hatchet from Willy, raised it over her head, and without a blink severed the hen's neck with a quick whack.

In her haste to release the chicken's body from the log, Copper lost hold of it and watched as the headless bird staggered a few feet down the dusty lane and fell over in the dirt. Willy carried it back, holding it out from his side by the feet, leaving a trail of spattered blood. Copper quickly cut a chunk of marbled breast meat and handed it to him. "Run this to Daddy," she told him. She had to have a moment with the Lord.

"Save them chicken feet," he called over his shoulder as he tore down the path toward the cabin. "Me an' Daniel will want to play with them."

Copper watched him go and knelt in the bloodstained dirt. *Dear Lord,* she prayed, *please heal Daniel of the snakebite. Whatever would we do without him?*

She shuddered, suddenly cold even as the waning sunlight bathed her in its golden glow. She knew God could perform miracles, could heal the sick, could move mountains if He had a mind to, but she also knew that sometimes God revealed His plan for His children through pain and suffering. He did not always say yes. As Mam often said, "God is not Santy Claus."

Copper's heart jerked in crazy rhythm a moment later when she heard Mam's scream and saw one of the Pelfrey boys running toward the road. *He's dead!* she thought. *He's dead and I'm not with him.*

Desperate in her haste to join them, she cried out in frustration and pain as her feet tangled in her skirts, pitching her face-first to the ground. "Please," she whimpered. "Lord, please."

CHAPTER 21

When Will took his eyes off Daniel to look out over the yard, it seemed like the whole neighborhood had assembled here. He saw Pelfreys of every size and description, several families from church, Mailman Bramble, Mr. Smithers, Oney Barlow, and even Aunt Ida Sizemore, who hadn't moved in three months. Every eye was on Daniel and Will who still held him. Brother Isaac knelt beside them on the porch, reading Scripture from his open Bible and praying aloud.

Aunt Ida, who must have been a hundred if she was a day, worried the snuff in her upper lip with a slender frayed stick. Someone had fetched her a straight-backed chair, and she worked it like a throne. Slowly, she raised her arm and pointed a long, bony finger in Daniel's direction. "That there boy's done died, Will Brown," she croaked. "Ye don't come back once the rigor starts. Might as well set about the digging."

"No he ain't!" Willy looked fiercely in her direction. "No he ain't. Is he, Daddy?" No one missed the quaver in Willy's voice as he pleaded with his father.

Will didn't know how to answer. Daniel lay across him like a piece of timber. His face had gone completely gray. A lacy reddish froth spilled from the corner of his mouth. Then it started—with a mighty twitch and jerk, Daniel folded like the blade of a jackknife, then snapped back open.

"Lord, help us," Will murmured, his heart in his throat. "Where's that doctor?"

"Lay him down," Copper said. "Somebody get me a spoon."

John Pelfrey knelt beside Copper on the porch and handed her the spoon. "Tell me what to do," he said.

"Just hold his head while I—" Deftly she slipped the handle between Daniel's clenched teeth. "This will keep him from biting his tongue." She sat back on her heels.

"They're coming!" one of the Pelfrey boys yelled as he ran into the yard. "I seen 'em coming up the road."

John ran out to take the horses from his father and a stranger.

"See to Pard, won't you?" Will heard the man say as he dismounted. "He's worked himself into a lather, racing down the mountain."

John took the reins. "They're yonder," he directed, as if there was any doubt, "yonder on the porch."

Will watched the well-dressed stranger make his way through the crowd. "Mr. Brown?" The doctor set his black leather medical bag down and extended his hand. "I'm Simon Corbett. I hear there's been an accident."

Will shook the doctor's hand. "This young'un's been snake bit. He's in a right precarious way. We'd appreciate any help you could give us."

The doctor squatted beside Daniel and removed the fatty poultice from above the boy's right ankle. The people in the yard drew closer to the porch. There wasn't a sound to be heard, other than Aunt Ida's chair scraping across the ground. A scalpel blade flashed as Dr. Corbett ripped the seam of Daniel's overalls and did a cursory exam. Everyone could see the swollen limb as well as the red streaks spreading up the leg almost to the groin. He rummaged through his bag and retrieved his stethoscope, which he placed on Daniel's chest.

He looked at Will. "Do you know what type of snake bit your boy? I have a treatment for a rattlesnake strike, but it's potent. The side effects could make him very sick. I don't want to give that to him if it's not necessary. If, on the other hand, it was a cottonmouth moccasin, there is nothing we can do but keep him comfortable and pray for a miracle." Dr. Corbett scanned the crowd. "Did anyone see what happened?"

"His brother was with him," Will answered. "Willy, come over here and tell the doctor what you saw."

"I wish I had seen the low-down varmint that bit Daniel," Willy choked, his face screwed tight against his tears, "but the snakes had left when I got there."

"Just tell us what happened the best that you can, young man," the doctor prompted. "Tell us anything you can remember."

"It's like this." Willy leaned against Copper for support.

"Daniel would of never been in this predicament if he'd of listened to me." His words rushed out, a veritable torrent of speech. "We'd just turned over a big old rock up there under the cliff above the creek. There must of been a million fishin' worms all wriggling around. Daniel asked me, 'Don't this remind you of the camp meeting, Willy? Remember those men and the snakes? I bet I could do that.' 'Daniel,' I told him, 'you must be tetched in the head. That's even dumber than the time you thought you could walk on water an' you nearly drowned afore I throwed you that branch, an' you nearly drowned again 'cause it hit you in the head, an' I had to jump in and fish you out. Now you think you can be a snake handler? Don't you never learn, boy?' Then Daniel says to me, 'I want to be like that dancing preacher.'

"And here's the worst thing—the really bad thing," Willy told his hushed audience. "I said, 'Go on then, Daniel. Go find you a snake an' see what happens. I'll just have to go fishin' by myself while you're off gettin' snake bit.' And so he did. I was busy puttin' the worms in the coffee tin that Mam gave us when I heard him holler, 'Come and look, Willy!' But I didn't go right away 'cause I had dropped the can, an' worms were going every which way."

Willy stopped to take a deep breath, then rattled on. "All of a sudden it seemed awful quiet, seemed like even the birds hushed singing, an' I sneaked up the hill to where Daniel had gone, an' I didn't see no snakes, but I seen my brother layin' there all still-like. Just layin' there in the quiet. The air was real funny, just glowin' and smellin' real strong of cucumbers. An' the next thing I remember is seeing Sissy on the porch."

Finally Willy stopped and took a long breath, pausing as if he might have more to say. "That's all there is, Doc."

Copper grabbed Willy and exclaimed, "Cucumbers, Willy—cucumbers! Oh, how wonderful." Copper kissed the squirming Willy on his dirty cheek. "That means copperheads, right, Daddy? A copperhead's den smells like cucumbers."

"That's right," Will said, his voice a rush of relief. "Only one I ever heard of dying from a copperhead bite was that little Hawkins baby. Daniel should be old enough to survive a copperhead's bite, don't you think, Doc?"

"I think his chances are good, but—"

A jerking started in Daniel's legs and moved up his body. The spoon dropped from his mouth and clattered across the porch. His hands fisted and beat at the air.

The doctor listened with his stethoscope again. After what seemed an eternity, he took out one earpiece and asked, "Has he done this before?"

"Just the once," Will replied, "but it was a golly whopper. He folded up like a closed book a few minutes before you come."

The doctor's brow furrowed as he nodded. "Let's take your boy in the house and make him comfortable. Willy, you can bring my bag."

Will scooped Daniel up. Willy grabbed the doctor's bag, Copper hastened to open the screen door, and Grace passed out cold, hitting the porch floor with a sickening thud.

"Oh!" the forgotten audience exhaled.

"Mrs. Brown?" Dr. Corbett pulled out his pocket watch and reached for her wrist. His long fingers rested on her pulse. Next he snapped a tiny glass ampoule and waved it under her nose.

She coughed and sputtered, looking wildly about the porch. "Will?"

"Right here, darlin'," he replied from the open door where he paused with Daniel.

Grace was shaky but got to her feet, her knees wobbling dangerously. Quickly Copper slipped her arm around her waist and helped her inside and to bed. Will stood by the bedroom door, Daniel still in his arms, as the doctor took his bag from Willy and Copper lit the coal-oil lamp.

Dr. Corbett withdrew a vial of clear tincture from his kit and administered a few drops to Grace. "Valerian," he said to Will. "She's had a swooning spell. It's just the shock of everything. She'll be fine after a good night's sleep." The doctor took Daniel from Will's arms. "You stay with your wife, and I'll see to Daniel."

Copper wet a rag and placed it on her mother's pale face. "Rest, Mam. I'll watch over Daniel tonight."

Tears leaked from the corners of Grace's eyes when she grasped Copper's hand. "You'll call me if . . ."

Copper knelt for a moment at the bed. "He's going to be fine, Mam," she said as Grace's eyelids drooped. "He's going to be fine."

CHAPTER 22

Past midnight, the house was finally quiet as Copper put another pot of coffee on the stove. Brother Isaac had stayed way past bedtime, and some of the deacons from church had come to pray and anoint Daniel with oil. All the commotion had Copper so keyed up she doubted that she'd ever sleep again.

Daddy was asleep in a chair beside Mam's bed with the bedroom door ajar. Willy slept on the floor, the yellow-clawed chicken feet clutched in his hand. He refused to leave Daniel, who was propped up on the settee with a bolster. "He'll be scared if he wakes up and I'm not here," he'd pleaded. So Copper had made Willy a pallet, and he was asleep before his head hit the pillow.

The doctor was spending the night. Every so often he took

out a vial of sassafras oil and, very precisely, dropped exactly fifteen drops down Daniel's throat. Copper watched him measure the medicine. He told her it was an effectual antidote against the venom of a copperhead.

He sat at the kitchen table, his head resting on his folded arms. He'd asked for coffee just a minute before, but now his faint snores were the only noise in the house.

Copper was in a quandary. The coffee was ready, but the doctor was asleep. Should she pour a cup and wake him? It wouldn't be seemly to touch him while he was sleeping, but what if Daniel needed him? Maybe she should drop a pan—that'd make enough racket to stir him up, but then she'd wake everyone else also. She just stood there, holding an empty cup, feeling out of place in her own kitchen.

Seconds later Daniel coughed, and the doctor was instantly on his feet. He quickly took a brown suction bulb and sucked frothy sputum from Daniel's mouth.

"Bring the light closer, please," he instructed. He pulled up Daniel's eyelids and peered intently, then hung Daniel's left leg over his own arm and pecked at it with a little rubber hammer. Daniel's leg swung out and nearly hit Copper on the chin, she'd bent over so close.

Daniel whimpered and struggled to sit up.

"Good, very good. He's coming around," the doctor said.

"Shush, Daniel." Copper stroked his face. "You're all right. Go back to sleep."

"Where's Willy?" Daniel mumbled. "I want to—"

"He's right here on the floor, fast asleep." She brushed the hair from his forehead. "Rest now."

Dr. Simon Corbett sipped the strong black coffee and gazed at the scene before him of a devoted sister caring for two brothers in a self-assured way he would not have expected to find in the hills of eastern Kentucky. He looked around the room, for the first time noticing the full bookshelves. The young woman must be well-read, for she seemed intelligent and well-spoken. She was dressed a little rough–no shoes and a torn dress that obviously covered a fine figure–but she was graceful and kind. *Remarkable, just remarkable.* He slumped back in his chair and took off his glasses.

The young doctor was bone weary. He'd arrived in Troublesome only the day before from his home in Lexington, and he'd spent his time seeing to a relative in his care. Lottie Boone, an ancient, diminutive woman, was his late mother's second cousin. She was still strong of body with the heart rate of a workingman, but her mind had gone south.

Foolishly he'd promised her years before, while she was still sound, that he would never make her leave her mountain home. And now, because of that promise and because he'd pledged to his own mother that he'd see to her cousin, he trekked to the mountains twice a year to make sure the local he'd hired as a nursemaid took good care of Lottie. And she did. The log house, such as it was, was always clean, and Lottie was well nourished. She could live for years.

Simon rubbed his face and reseated his spectacles. For as long as he lived, he'd never be able to figure out why these clannish people preferred to live so far away from civilized society and chose instead these remote hollows without decent schools and medical help.

Try as he might, he couldn't keep his eyes off the young woman who kept herself busy with her brother. Had Mr. Brown called her Copper? Yes, Copper. It must be that she was named for the color of her hair, he figured, as he watched her straighten the pillow under the boy's head. Her hair was loose and hung past her shoulders; it glinted in the lamplight, streaks of gold in copper.

"Harrumph." Clearing his throat, he put his coffee down and turned to busy himself with the small apothecary he kept in his black bag. After much clinking of bottles and snapping the kit sharply closed, he examined Daniel again.

The clock struck three. "Your brother will sleep through the rest of the night, Miss Brown. Why don't you get some rest also? You must be exhausted."

"I'm fine, thank you, Dr. Corbett." She eased her brother's head up and laid it on her lap. "I'll just sit here with Daniel."

The doctor pulled out a second straight-backed chair. "Then I'll just rest my eyes for a bit." He'd barely sat down and propped his booted feet on the other chair when his shoulders slumped forward and he was asleep.

Intrigued, Copper watched the easy rise and fall of the doctor's chest. His shirt was so white it gleamed in the lamplight, and he wore a navy tie that looked like silk. He'd loosened it during the course of the night and rolled up his sleeves, but he was still the most elegant man she had ever seen. He was small compared to her burly father, maybe half a foot taller than her own five-foot-three, but she'd taken note of his wide shoulders and the muscles that rippled under his shirt when he'd shifted Daniel onto the couch. He seemed neatly put together and moved with the economy of motion she'd seen in the mountain lion that prowled the ridge, each step measured and precise. Anybody would have to notice his clothes fit like they'd been made just for him—no shirttails hanging out, no ankles showing beneath his pant legs. *Handsome, very handsome.*

She slept on and off on the settee with Daniel's head in her lap until her legs began to cramp. Finally she slid out from under him and propped his head on a pillow. She had to step over Willy, who'd rolled halfway across the kitchen floor, before she could dip herself a drink of water from the granite bucket on the washstand. She took a sip, noting that she'd need to draw some fresh water in the morning, and stared at the mirror. Even lamplight did nothing to hide the effects of the day. Daniel's blood streaked her face, and her hair had slipped out of its combs and tangled wildly past her shoulders.

She stepped back and noticed that clabber stained her apron, and the sleeve of her yellow daisy-print dress was hanging by a thread. Worse still, her dirty bare feet peeked out from under her grimy dress hem. *So this is why Mam is always after me to wear my shoes. One never knows when a handsome stranger will show up.*

Grabbing a towel and a bar of soap off the washstand, clean clothes from her bureau drawer, and some shoes from under her bed, she opened the screen door, holding her breath as it screeched, and slipped out into the muggy summer morning.

"Oh!" She took a fright. There was a body on the dark porch. Creeping closer to investigate, she found John Pelfrey sleeping under the kitchen window. She let her breath out. *It's just John.*

The dark path to the creek was lit by the full, bright moon and guided her way. She discarded her torn and dirty clothing and dived into the cool, dark water. After swimming across and back several times, she floated for a while in the refreshing pool, watching the moonlight play upon the water.

What a day. It was impossible to keep tears at bay when her mind replayed Daniel's frightful accident. The shock still squeezed her heart, though he seemed ever so much better now. Something tugged at her mind, something out of place. Of course—John sleeping under the kitchen window. What was he doing there? She lathered the soap and scrubbed her scalp, wishing she had vinegar water to rinse her hair.

The soap smelled clean as she washed away the grime of the day, like the doctor had smelled when he bent over Daniel. Her mind wandered. What was that scent exactly? Freshly ironed linen! He smelled like Daddy's Sunday shirt just after it was pressed. And had she detected a hint of lavender? Maybe his wife sprinkled his starched shirts with lavender water before she ironed them.

Wife? Copper guessed she'd better stop daydreaming and get on back to Daniel.

Rejuvenated from her bath, she towel dried her hair and ran her fingers through the tangles. Afterward, dressed and shod, she made her way back up the path to the cabin.

Dr. Corbett leaned on the porch rail with what seemed like his hundredth cup of coffee and watched as Copper walked toward him. It was all he could do to hold himself back from hurrying down the path to meet her.

He was more than a little surprised at his response to the sight of her. He was considered an eligible bachelor in Lexington and had squired his share of beautiful young ladies to dances and parties. Lately he had seen much of one such debutante: Hester Louderback, the daughter of his only sister's closest friend. Any thought he might have entertained of considering a future with Hester fell away last night in Troublesome Creek, however. He suddenly understood how passion frequently overruled good sense, for his heart determined that he must see this young lady–this mysterious Copper Brown–again.

"Are you hungry, Dr. Corbett?" Copper climbed the few steps to the porch and looked around. *Where is John? Oh, well, no matter. He must have gone home.* "I'll have biscuits on the table shortly."

"Thank you. I am suddenly ravenous." He took a deep breath and stretched. "This mountain air is as good as any tonic."

Just as Cock-a-Doodle crowed the dawning of a new day, Willy burst through the screen door and Daddy stepped out of the house, pulling his suspenders over his shoulders and dropping his shoes on the porch.

"Doc," he said, "we sure appreciate all you've done for our boy. What do I owe you?"

"Nothing . . . nothing," Doctor Corbett answered. "But if we could barter a little, I'd like to trade my knowledge for yours.

I wonder if you would allow me to go hunting with you? It's a sport I've just recently become interested in, and I must admit I'm a poor shot."

"Well, Doc, that's easily fixed." Daddy pressed two silver dollars into the young man's unwilling hand. That was his way, Copper knew. He always paid back more than he owed. She saw the smile tugging at the corners of Daddy's mouth as he spoke. "I'll be leaving at sunup come Saturday morning. You be here and I'll make a crack shot out of you by evening."

Copper couldn't figure out a way to be included. She was usually brazen, but the doctor made her feel shy somehow.

"Thank you, Mr. Brown."

"Doc, don't stand on ceremony. Call me Will."

"Then you must call me Simon," he said, thrusting his hand out for a firm shake and meeting his steady gaze. "I must say I'm impressed with your care for Daniel. You did all the right things for a snakebite."

"Most of that's due to his sister." Daddy indicated her. "She thinks fast on her feet—Copper does."

Copper blushed at Daddy's compliment in front of a stranger. Opening the screen, she let herself into the kitchen. Mam stood at the stove, frying fatback in the iron skillet. She put her arm around Mam's narrow waist and hugged her tightly. "Are you better this morning?"

"Oh, Laura Grace, yes. Yes, I am. I am so very grateful for God's rich blessing. Daniel was awake when I got up. I'm sorry I left you to care for him last night. Thank you, Daughter."

"You're welcome, but actually Dr. Corbett did everything. I just watched." Copper opened the oven door and checked on the biscuits, grateful for a new day and for the unusual warmth of her mother's words filling the kitchen.

"It was comforting to have you with him in my absence, nonetheless," Mam answered.

They laid a breakfast of thick-sliced bacon, eggs over easy, fried potatoes, sliced tomatoes, fried apples, and biscuits, along with fresh-brewed coffee. Daddy and Dr. Corbett carried the settee to the table so Daniel, his leg propped on a pillow, could eat with the family.

Willy stayed right beside him the whole time. He would not allow anyone else to fetch for his brother. Not even Mam had the heart to scold when Willy shoved the saved chicken feet in Daniel's face.

"Thanks, Willy," Daniel responded weakly. "These are grand." He took a bite of egg. "I passed my test, Willy."

Not a soul stirred.

"What test is that, Son?" Daddy finally asked.

"The serpent, Daddy. I took him up, just like the deacons at the meeting."

"But you got bit!" Willy exclaimed before anyone could stop him.

"It wasn't the snake I took up that bit me." Daniel leaned back against his pillow; a light shone from his face. "It was the one I stepped on. Poor thing—he couldn't help it."

Copper's mind swirled. She had much to think about as she hurried to the barn after breakfast, late for milking. "Why, Molly, I thought you'd be bursting," she said to the contented cow who was ruminating in the barnyard. "Who took care of you? John?"

She glanced out the window by Molly's stall, expecting to see John off in the distance walking back to the Pelfrey farm. Not spying him anywhere, she turned to her chores. "I'd best get to the springhouse and see to the milk."

She was surprised to find John in the springhouse, pouring milk into the container on top of the separator that spun the milk through a series of funnels and separated out the cream. His ears flamed red when he saw her.

"Goodness sake," Copper cried, "where'd you get to? I saw you sleeping on the porch when I went down to the creek, but you were gone when I came back. Why didn't you come in for breakfast?"

"Um . . . um . . ." he stammered and looked away. "I went home to do my milking first."

"I could have done this, John." Copper drew alongside him and leaned her elbows on the countertop where he worked. "You didn't have to stay the night."

"I wanted to be close in case you needed me." He paused to cast her a concerned glance. "How's Daniel?"

"He's much better. He ate some breakfast."

John poured the cream into a tin, tapped the lid in place, and lowered it into the spring. After that he poured the rest of the milk into a yellowware crock. "Is that man still here?"

"Dr. Corbett? No, he's gone," Copper said, wondering when he'd be back. "He left instructions for Daniel's care with me."

"Why you? Why not Miss Grace?" John stared at her hard.

"I don't know." She dropped her eyes and turned her back. "Maybe because Daddy told him I did a good job. Why does it matter?"

"I don't trust him is all," John admitted.

"Why, John—" Copper turned toward him and took the empty bucket from his hand—"you don't even know him."

John pulled away and started toward the door, then stopped and fixed her with a stare. "Just you remember, Pest. You don't know him either."

Copper stayed busy all day caring for Daniel. He continued to improve and by late afternoon was begging to leave his confinement on the settee. She carried him to the porch, where she settled him in Mam's ladder-back rocker. An overturned bucket, positioned just right, served as a prop to keep his feet up like the doctor had said to do. She was just tucking a brightly colored crazy quilt over Daniel's legs when she spied the doctor looping his horse's reins over the hitching post in the barnyard.

Carrying his black kit, he strode across the yard and climbed the steps to the porch. "I thought I'd better make rounds," he said. "You never know how these things can go."

"We thank you for coming," Copper said. "He's feeling better. Aren't you, Daniel?"

"Yes, Sissy," Daniel responded as he grabbed her hand tightly. "Are you going to hit me again, Mr. Doctor?"

Doctor Corbett knelt down and took Daniel's other hand. He glanced at Copper with a questioning look.

Willy had been watering Mam's flower garden next to the porch. Now he stopped dipping water from the rain barrel and answered the unspoken question. "Daniel says you keep a hammer in your bag, Doc," he said knowingly. "I told him you probably had to hit his knee to knock that viper's teeth out of his leg."

The doctor dropped his head. Copper knew he struggled not to laugh just as she did. Finally he opened his bag and took out the small rubber hammer he'd tested Daniel with during the night. "Come up here, Willy," he said, "and I'll show you both how to use this. May I?" he asked, taking Copper's arm in his hand.

She nodded, unable to speak. Just the touch of his hand made her whole arm tingle. He placed his fingers on either side of her elbow and tapped her lightly with the hammer. Her forearm jerked. He tapped it once again.

"There, Willy," Dr. Corbett said. "Did you see how your sister's arm jerked? That is a reflex action, and that is what I was checking when I tapped your knee last night, Daniel. I was making sure your reflexes were strong."

Willy's eyes took on a devilish look. "Hey, Doc, what'd happen if I checked Sissy's head with this here hammer?"

Copper was mortified. She gave Willy a look meant to stop him in his tracks and said, "Willy! Go finish the flowers."

"Oh, all right," he said, giving in, "but I might want to see that hammer again, Doc."

Dr. Corbett smiled. "You may borrow it anytime, Willy." He stood beside Copper as Willy trudged back to the flowers with another dipper of water. Copper didn't dare move, for he still held fast to her elbow. Somehow she didn't want him to stop.

Just then Mam stepped onto the porch, drying her hands on a small linen towel. "Doctor Corbett, it is so kind of you to come again so soon. Won't you stay for supper?"

Casually, as if he was not aware that he had held her arm all that time, Dr. Corbett let it fall and reached out to Mam. He took her hand in both of his and said, "Why, thank you, Mrs. Brown. I don't mind if I do. But tell me, have you quite recovered from your swoon?"

Copper slipped inside and left Mam to talk with the doctor. She was in another quandary. Why did the stranger's touch make her warm all over? Why did she hanker for him to touch her again? Pulling dishes from the cupboard, she began to set the table. Supper would be easy to fix, because neighbors had been bringing food by all day. She dished up the meal: a round of corn bread slathered with fresh butter, mustard greens boiled down with bacon grease, corn pudding, and rabbit fried to a tasty crisp brown. Dessert would be Mrs. Wilson's cake. Swiping a lick of caramel icing with her finger, Copper reckoned there'd never been an illness anywhere in the hollow that Mrs. Wilson's cake didn't soothe.

Brother Isaac came by on his round of sick calls and became the seventh person at the table. Willy dragged the bench in from the porch so they would have enough seating.

They all bowed their heads and clasped hands as Brother Isaac blessed the food and thanked the Lord for Daniel's life. Copper tried mightily to keep her mind on the prayer, but she was seated next to Dr. Corbett, and as luck would have it, his hand was in her own. He didn't need to hit her with a hammer to start the tingling in her arm again.

John and his father stopped by after supper, and all the men-folk settled on the porch. All the men except John—he went to milk Molly. Copper and Mam washed the dishes and tidied up the kitchen before Mam said they could hang up their aprons and join the men on the porch.

Mam took a seat on the bench beside Daddy, so Copper lifted Daniel and sat with him in Mam's rocker. He snuggled down and soon fell asleep in her arms. It was comforting to sit and listen to the men as the whip-poor-wills tuned up for their nightly serenade and the lightning bugs turned their little lanterns on and off, off and on. Willy ran wildly about the darkening yard capturing the insects in a fruit jar, rushing up now and then to show off their greenish glow. Finished with milking, John settled down on the porch floor near her feet. Copper breathed a sigh of contentment and let go of the worry that had knotted her shoulders since Willy had run screaming from the forest.

Copper learned a lot about the doctor that evening, and she never had to ask a single question. Matter of fact, she never opened her mouth, just sat and rocked Daniel. Brother Isaac took care of the questions for her—he was as good as a lawyer at getting answers from folks. And he had once gone to school in the city, so he and the stranger had something in common.

Doctor Corbett was twenty-six and had his own medical practice in Lexington. His parents were deceased, and he had one sister, Alice, who was married to a banker. He told them about his elderly cousin, and Copper thought him very kind to care so tenderly for the old soul. But the thing that set her heart to fluttering was when she learned that he was not married but a bachelor living on his own.

She took this little ray of hope and nurtured it like a cupped candle flame as she prepared herself for bed that evening. Pulling the combs from her hair, she braided a thick plait that hung halfway down her back before shimmying into her nightgown and slipping under the covers. The window by her bed was half open, and she could hear the same whip-poor-wills that had begun their song earlier in the evening; some tiny tree frogs added their peeping to the music of the night. The moon was halfway up its climb in the dark sky, and she couldn't help wondering if Dr. Corbett was looking at it now. And was he maybe thinking of her as she was thinking of him?

Simon Corbett propped his feet on Lottie Boone's porch railing and stared at the big yellow moon. What was happening to him? Try as he might, he couldn't get the feel of Copper Brown's touch from his mind. He'd held many a young woman's hand in his but never one like hers. Hers was firm, almost hard, and she kept her nails short and trimmed straight across like a workingman's.

He dropped his feet from the rail and let the legs of his tipped-back chair fall to the floor. Leaning forward with his elbows on his knees, he rested his head in his hands and tried to get a grip on himself. She was sixteen, he'd learned. *Sixteen! This cannot go on.* But his parents stole into his mind. His father had also been a doctor, and he'd captured Lilly Mae Mitchell's heart and married her at the tender age of fifteen, though he had been twelve years her senior. Simon had never known a better-suited couple than his parents, but still . . . sixteen? It happened, he knew—it was not even unusual. But he never supposed he'd be smitten by such a young girl.

He stood and stretched, chuckling softly at the wandering of his mind. He'd just met the young woman and his mind was planning a wedding? He needed to be careful. . . .

CHAPTER 23

Simon Corbett spent the next day tending to his cousin's needs.
Meeting with her nursemaid, he laid out plans for the invalid's
next six months of care. He wouldn't be back until early winter,
and he wanted to be sure everything was in order.

With the rising of the sun, his mind had cleared. The stirring
in his heart the night before was replaced by calm logic. Yes,
Copper Brown was beautiful, and yes, she was intelligent and
charming . . . but she was not the girl for him.

He ate a biscuit and a piece of ham and washed it down with
hot coffee, thankful the nurse was also a good cook. Taking an ax
from the shed, he went out to clear the scrub brush and Virginia
creeper vines that threatened to overtake the porch. His day continued in such a vein, and by late afternoon the yard was free of

bushes and weeds, and a stack of firewood lay neatly by the back door.

Wonder how the boy is doing, he thought after a quick wash in the creek. *What if he took a setback?* Maybe he should go by the Browns' and check on Daniel.

Simon stroked his cheeks. Maybe he'd shave first.

Willy saw Dr. Corbett first. Copper heard him yell from the barn, "Sissy, set another plate. Doc's back again!"

She peeked out the screen door, and indeed there he was, ambling across the yard with Willy, who swung his black doctor's bag. Thankfully, Mam had fried some extra chicken, just in case.

"Oh no, ma'am," Copper heard him say when Mam met him on the porch and asked him to supper. "I don't want to trouble you. I just came by to check on our patient."

"Nonsense," Mam replied. "You'll stay and eat. Come on in. Daniel's on the settee."

His presence filled the cabin as he knelt and pulled up Daniel's nightshirt. Copper watched him probe the wound with his long, slender fingers. "Does this hurt?" he asked as he made his way up Daniel's leg. "How about this?" Then the words they'd waited to hear: "Daniel, you're going to be just fine. Let's try walking a few steps."

Daniel slid to the edge of the settee and stood. Willy supported him on one side and Copper on the other as he took his first wobbly steps.

"Now," the doctor said, "let's see you walk by yourself."

Mam stood by the table with her hand to her mouth, and Copper held her breath as Daniel hobbled to the door and back, wincing with each step. His eyes found his mother's. "It feels funny. It feels like something's too tight . . . like my leg is drawing up."

"Hmm," the doctor said. "Hmm." He lifted Daniel and set him on the corner of the table. Taking Daniel's foot in his hand, he asked him to push as hard as he could.

"Mrs. Brown," he said finally, "Daniel's going to need a bit of work. Seems the poison has affected this long muscle." He traced upward from Daniel's ankle to his knee with one finger. "The muscle's cramping when he walks. It's causing him to limp."

"What does that mean?" Mam asked, a note of panic in her voice. Copper slipped her arm around Mam's waist. "Will my boy be crippled?"

"Oh no, my dear," he answered assuredly. "Not at all. I'll just need to teach you how to exercise this muscle to get it back to full function."

Copper lifted Daniel from the table and held him on her hip. He nestled his head against her shoulder. His little white night-shirt billowed around her waist. "Teach me, Dr. Corbett. I'll see to Daniel."

"Yes, please," Mam said, her voice still shaky. "Please show Laura Grace what to do."

"Me too," Willy piped up. "Do we get to use that rubber hammer?"

That evening Copper sat on the porch with Dr. Corbett and practiced Daniel's care while Mam and Daddy did her chores.

Over and over he showed her how to contract and release the muscles in the leg. Willy was their willing patient and Daniel watched, laughing from his chair. When she was sure of the exercises, the doctor taught her how to make and apply a poultice to draw out soreness and inflammation.

As Mam and Daddy took seats on the porch, Doctor Corbett took a hickory nut–size lump of alum and mixed it with egg whites in a tin pan. He stirred and stirred until the alum turned to jelly. Pouring the whey into a clean jar, he took the jelly and put it on a clean cloth before wrapping it around Daniel's lower leg. Copper was to wet the cloth with the whey several times a day for the next few days, making more as needed.

Afterward she watched, fascinated, as the doctor took a tortoiseshell fountain pen from his bag and dipped it in a tiny pot of ink. He wrote the directions for the alum jelly in a precise hand, waved it in the air for a moment, and presented it to her.

The combination of alum and egg whites made for a sticky mess. "Time for a washup," she said, and he followed her to the outdoor bench where they kept a basin and a bucket of water.

She took a dipperful of water and poured it over his hands as he scrubbed them with lye soap, and then he did the same for her. It seemed like a very intimate gesture somehow, sharing a towel, and she found herself wanting to lean against him as he stood beside her at the bench. When his hand accidentally touched hers, she trembled, and when her eyes met his she saw his yearning.

The spell was broken when Pard let out a long and lonesome neigh from the barnyard. "Poor old Pardner," Dr. Corbett said.

"I've been neglecting him." He hung the towel on a nail and turned to Daddy. "Mr. Brown–"

"Will," Daddy said, a sparkle in his eyes as if he knew what was coming next.

"Will–" the doctor cleared his throat–"I wonder if you'd permit Laura Grace to take a stroll with me. I was thinking of taking Pard to the creek for a drink."

"That would be fine, Doc," Daddy answered straight-out. "Just fine."

"I'm sure Willy would like a walk also," Mam interjected.

"Boy howdy, would I! Can I ride Pardner?" he called, already running across the yard. Suddenly he stopped and ran back to Daniel. "I won't be gone long, buddy, and I'll bring you something special."

⚜

"I'll bet Dr. Corbett was glad you suggested Willy go along," Will teased. "Did you see the sparks between those two? I was afraid they'd set the porch afire."

"What's wrong with the cattle trough by the barn?" Grace asked, her eyebrows raised. "Last I looked it was full of water."

"I haven't seen Copper so lit up since I gave her that shotgun for her birthday. Maybe we ought to let her take the good doctor hunting come Saturday morning. He'd be curious as a hound dog on a cold trail if he could see her flush some turkeys."

"Please, Will, don't be entertaining such a thought," Grace said. She took out her hanky and pressed it against her nose. "He is much too sophisticated for her," she huffed. "I am afraid an assignation with Dr. Corbett could only lead to distress."

"Well, darlin', any man who hurts my daughter–" he stroked his beard and started rocking–"doctor or no, will find his tail so full of buckshot, he'll be using it as a sieve."

"Please don't be coarse." She rocked harder. "Can't you just send him on his way? We can care for Daniel now."

Will faced his wife. "Grace, you surprise me. I thought it was your wish to have Copper living in the big city. Think of all the fine things she'd have if she was a doctor's wife."

"But don't you see?" Grace answered, her brows knit together. "I wanted her to find her own strength before she became someone's wife. I wanted her to have an education and an avocation. I hoped she would come to know herself before she became the same as someone else's property."

"Why, Miss Grace!" Will stopped midrock. "If marrying me made you my 'property,' then I'll have to say you're the best bottomland I ever bought."

"Will Brown! Forevermore." She cast a look at Daniel, asleep on the settee they'd dragged out to the porch. "I'm just trying to explain my feelings. I thought you would feel the same."

"Let's not go borrowing trouble." He stood and stretched. "She's only gone to the creek, not Lexington. I'm sure with Willy in attendance they won't even get to hold hands, much less jump the broom."

He picked up the water bucket and dashed lukewarm water over the porch rail. Starting down the steps with the bucket, he paused. "I'll give him this: he has a firm handshake, and he looks a man in the eye. If it's meant to be, it will be. We'll have to trust the Lord, I reckon."

"Doc, Doc . . . watch this! Watch this." Willy selected a thin, round rock and let it fly. "Hey, good one. That was three skips an' a hop. I can teach you how to do this if you want."

Copper watched as Dr. Corbett squatted beside Willy on the bank. He looked over his shoulder and gave her a wink as he threw a stone that sunk without a skip in the middle of the creek.

"Boy, Doc Simon, you've got a lot to learn. Here, you got to hold it just so an' kind of slide it off your fingers so it glides instead of plops." Willy chucked a few more stones. "Maybe if I could find some more thin ones you could do better. You wait here with Sissy, an' I'll be right back."

"Come sit beside me while we wait for Willy," Dr. Corbett said to Copper. "I've a feeling it won't be long." He spread his jacket on the grass.

Feeling strangely shy, she took the offered seat. A queer, fluttery feeling settled in her chest, and she could feel the color rising in her cheeks. She sat stiffly, nearly touching his shoulder as he leaned back, resting on his elbows.

"I hear there will be a pie supper at the church on Saturday," he offered. "Will you be going?"

"We're all going. Daddy always pays the most for Mam's pie." She kept her eyes straight ahead as if there were something fascinating on the creek bank, afraid she might see that look in his eyes again. "One year he paid a dollar fifty. Last year John Pelfrey bought mine for a quarter after Silas Parker bid fifteen cents. It's always great fun." Scooting away from him a little, she tucked her skirts firmly under her legs.

"John Pelfrey? Is he the son of the man who came to get me yesterday?"

"The very same. He said my crust was as tough as groundhog leather, but I've learned to make it flaky since then. I haven't decided what I'll bake, but I'm thinking of blueberry or maybe chocolate. . . . That's my favorite, but Mam says you shouldn't please the cook but please the guest." She stuck a stray curl behind one ear. "The hardest part's the meringue. Mam's peaks like snowcaps, but mine tends to droop." Copper was aware she was chattering on, overcome by nerves.

Dr. Corbett took her hand and turned it over, stroking her palm with his thumb, a delicate touch that sent shivers up her spine. He lingered, tracing the lines on her palm, as if it were a map and he needed direction. Copper feared this might be her undoing.

Thankfully, Willy came crashing up the creek bank, providing a welcome distraction. "Here, Doc, try these. They're smooth as buttermilk. . . . Even a girl could skip with these. Sorry, Sissy, but you're not really a girl anyway." He skimmed the surface of the water with a rock. "Sissy can do anything, Doc. Did you tell him about the time you decked the wildcat? If you do, be sure to leave out the part about the chickens under the bed. Mam's still sore about that."

"Speaking of Mam," Copper said, "it's dusky dark. We'd better get back."

"Oh, Sissy, do we have to?" Willy whined. "I was just starting to have fun."

"Come on, Willy," Dr. Corbett said. "Pard needs a rider."

"Did you remember something for Daniel?" Copper asked.

"Yeah, hold on." Willy pulled an arrowhead from his pocket. "Here's a fine one for Daniel to add to his collection. The tip's not broke or nothing."

With a hand up from Dr. Corbett, Willy mounted Pard and they headed back. The slow motion of the horse soon lulled Willy to sleep, and he slumped over the saddle horn. Dr. Corbett stopped Pard by a little copse of trees. Coming around to Copper's side, he took her hand once more. "Laura Grace . . ."

"Dr. Corbett?" she said, staring at her feet.

"Please call me Simon."

Carefully, she raised her eyes, staring at a spot just over his shoulder. "All right, if you want me to, Simon." She could hear the beat of her heart in her ears. "You have a beautiful name."

"As do you, Laura Grace."

"Most folks call me Copper," she replied shyly, unwilling to tell him how much she disliked the prissy Laura Grace.

"A nickname for a girl, but Laura Grace is a woman's name. Would you look at me?" he asked, his voice husky.

"I . . ." She dropped her eyes again. Pulling her hand away, she smoothed the front of her dress.

He leaned forward so they breathed the same air. "Are you afraid of me?"

Pard shook his head, jangling the reins, and Willy stirred.

"Yes," she whispered, "I think I am."

He tipped her chin so she had to see that fearsome look again. What did it mean? His eyes seemed to pull her in, as if that look was all there was in the world.

He only brushed her cheek with his thumb, but it was enough. She felt she'd lived the whole of her life for just that touch.

The sun was going down, the whip-poor-wills tuned up along the creek, and a dove sent out a mournful call. "Mam will be looking for us," Copper said and started forward, her hand resting against Willy in the saddle, and then, "Simon." His name felt good upon her tongue.

CHAPTER 24

Saturday came, and with it Dr. Corbett. He was early enough to take breakfast with the family before disappearing into the woods with Daddy and Willy. Daniel was content to stay behind and supervise the pie baking. Copper gave him the leftover dough, and he rolled out small crusts to fill for himself and Willy.

The kitchen was a mess, but finally Copper put her chocolate pie on the windowsill alongside Mam's lemon meringue. Her mouth watered at the sight as she cleaned up the kitchen. When she'd wiped up the last spill and scrubbed the last dish, Copper hung up her chocolate-stained apron and pulled her dress off. "Can you help me with my hair?" she called out the screen door to Mam.

As Copper bent over the outdoor wash bench, Mam poured a kettle of rainwater over her head. "Is that warm enough?" Mam asked.

"It's just right," she spluttered as water streamed over her face and shoulders. She shampooed with a bar of Mam's fine-milled rose soap, then gasped when Mam dumped a finishing rinse of cold water laced with vinegar on her hair to bring out the shine.

Finished, she sat on the porch floor, her petticoat pulled down over her knees, while Mam tugged a wide-toothed comb through her tangles. Daniel played scout, watching the woods and the road, ready to sound a warning if any man appeared.

Sitting in a spot of sun, she waited for her hair to dry. Her mind wandered back to the creek bank and the touch of Simon's thumb against her face. Why had his touch felt so different from John's?

John! His open, honest face swam before her eyes. There was no mystery there. In her mind, he looked at her accusingly. *I'm sorry. I'm sorry, and I haven't even done anything to feel sorry for.* Things were sure getting complicated.

Mam fashioned Copper's dried hair into a twist secured with pins and then pulled finger curls loose to frame her face. "Why, Daughter," she said, "you're every bit as pretty as the ladies in the fashion magazine I got in the mail last week. Now I have a small surprise."

Copper followed her into the bedroom, where Mam pulled a dress from the walnut chiffonier. "This was your mother's," she said gently. "I've saved it all these years, and I've altered it to fit the fashion. You can wear it to the pie supper tonight."

Copper sank down on the bed, the apple green linen dress draped across her lap. "My mother's?" she asked, shocked. It was unbelievable to think her mother's dress had lain tucked away in the wardrobe for years, and she never knew. "You mean your dress, Mam?"

"No, Laura Grace. This was Julie's." Mam sat down beside her with a faraway look in her eyes as she fingered the sleeve of the dress. "My mother—your grandmother—had it made for Julie to wear to a luncheon on the day of her debutante's ball." Mam's hand fell away. "Unfortunately, mother fell ill and died," she said sadly, "and we were in mourning when the time came, so Julie never got to be presented to society. I had thought you might wear this when we toured boarding schools but since—"

"Let's not talk about that now." Copper stood abruptly and held the dress in front of her, staring at her reflection in the wavy full-length mirror of the chiffonier. "Why do you never talk about her?" Laying the dress across the bed, she turned to confront Mam. "Why have you never told me about my mother?"

"The time just never seemed right, Laura Grace. It's all so very sad. . . ." She grimaced and put her fingers to her temples in a gesture Copper found all too familiar.

"It's all right, Mam. Do you need some headache powders?"

"No, no, I'll be fine. I just . . . here," Mam offered, as she pulled a pasteboard box from deep within the chiffonier. "I ordered these for you to wear with the dress."

The top fell away and revealed a pair of black patent-leather pumps. "Forevermore!" Copper exclaimed. "There're no buttons or laces. How do you keep such flimsy slippers on?"

"Try them," Mam replied.

Copper wiped her bare feet on the faded Turkish rug, then shoved them into the shoes. This was not right. She didn't like the way the pumps left the tops of her feet sticking out, and her ankles wobbled dangerously when she walked. "Mam—" Suddenly she was overwhelmed: first her mother's dress and now high-heeled shoes! Her mind was a swirl of conflicting emotions, and her throat filled with tears. "I can't wear these."

"You sound hoarse, and your face is flushed." Mam placed her cool palm on Copper's forehead. "I hope you're not getting the quinsy. Maybe I should get the tonic." She was out of the room in a flash and back with a small brown bottle and a silver tablespoon before Copper could find a place to hide.

Copper shuddered just thinking about the nasty stuff. "I'm not sick, Mam."

Mam pinched Copper's nose. "Better safe than sorry. Open up."

Copper gagged as a vile concoction of red pepper, vinegar, salt, and pulverized alum slid down her throat. She wheezed and coughed and clomped around in the hateful shoes. "Ouch," she squeaked, her throat on fire. "These don't fit, Mam."

"They will when you have stockings on," Mam said, setting the bottle on the dresser and casting a critical eye over Copper. "Walk lightly—you're not going to milk the cow."

Copper kicked off the fancy slippers and sat down on Mam's bed. "Tell me about the dances. Tell me about society."

Mam sat down beside her with a sigh. "I've been away so long, Laura Grace—it seems like another life. But when I was young, there were socials and parties nearly every week. All the ladies dressed in splendid gowns." Her eyes glittered as she continued. "We were laced into tight corsets that made for tiny waists and full bosoms, and the men wore long jackets and cravats. There was wonderful music and dancing."

Copper watched a wistful smile transform Mam's face; she could almost picture Mam young again as she went on in a dreamy way. "I wish you could have seen us, my friends and me, twirling around the dance floor, barely resting for a moment before another gentleman claimed us. We had so many suitors it was hard to keep them all straight. We had such fun."

"Sure, Mam." Copper was unable to imagine being twirled about in an uncomfortable gown and shoes that made your toes scream in protest. "That sure sounds like fun." She glanced at the dress on the bed. "I don't need a corset with this dress, do I? Seems like it'd be hard to eat pie with a corset on."

"Not one so confining as the ones we wore in my day." Mam rummaged in the chiffonier, pulled out a buckram-stiffened, front-buttoned, lightly-boned corset with laces in the back, and waved it at Copper. "Just a light foundation. A dress will not fit properly without the proper foundation."

Copper couldn't help but wonder what other torture devices Mam had in the bottom of her innocent-looking clothes closet.

Mam hung the dress on the outside of the wardrobe door. "You do need to remember your manners though, young lady–" she shook her finger at Copper–"and have only a very small piece of pie tonight. Now you should iron the linens to line the pie baskets with. I think that small piece you finished last week will be perfect. Don't you?"

Copper put the heavy sadiron on the cookstove and unrolled a dampened dresser scarf onto the padded, wooden ironing board.

She smoothed the embroidery, admiring her handiwork. Blue-birds flew among roses and daisies on each end of the piece that had taken her a month to finish. Grasping the iron with a folded tea towel, she tapped the bottom with a wet finger, watching the spit sizzle. Copper loved the smell of starch released by the heat of the iron. And seeing the stacks of crisp clothing on the kitchen table was a joy. It was like hanging out the wash—you could see the result of your labor, even if only for a little while. She finished her piece, pressed her dress and some dark green ribbon, and then ironed Mam's latest work of art, with its perfect stitches as well.

"Hey, Sissy, can I have a piece of this pie?" Willy called through the window. He stuck a dirty finger into the sugary-sweet meringue.

"Willy, you rascal! You get your hands off my pie before I crack your head." Copper ran from the kitchen brandishing a wooden spoon. She burst through the screen door and gasped in shock when she collided with Simon Corbett.

"Oh, Dr. Corbett . . . Simon," she stammered. "I didn't realize—that is, I would have put my shoes on had I known . . . I mean, I wouldn't be chasing Willy with a spoon if he had told me you were . . . oh, dear. Please excuse me. I left something burning on the stove." Copper backpedaled into the kitchen, slapping the screen door in his face, and fanned herself with the skirt of her apron.

"Laura Grace?" She could hear him from the other side of the door. "May I come in?"

"Um, just a minute." She searched frantically for her shoes. Where had she left them? They must be on the porch. She grabbed the high-heeled pumps and quickly put them on. Managing to stagger as far as the kitchen table, she put out a hand to steady herself. "Come in," she said in a tone as sophisticated as someone on the point of collapse could be.

"I only have a minute," he announced, "and I want to tell you good-bye."

"Good-bye!" She stood by the table, afraid to take a step toward him for fear of falling. "But I thought you'd come to the pie supper tonight."

"I would like to, but I've stayed longer than I intended already and I have patients who depend on me." Quickly he closed the space between them. "Please don't be upset. I'll be back late fall or early winter, before the snows get too deep."

"Oh," she said, finally able to meet his eyes without dissolving. Reaching deep to find some pride, she held her head high and said, "I'm not the least upset. My goodness, you must see to your patients." She wanted to walk away, but she couldn't very well do that in her wobbly shoes, could she? Obviously she had misread the doctor's intentions. Maybe it would be better for him to leave. Maybe then she'd be able to breathe.

"I'll look forward to seeing you come winter, Simon," she said, her voice as friendly as a dog's wag, though she was careful to let it say nothing more than "let's be friends."

"I'll see you then, Laura Grace. Take good care of Daniel." And he was out the door.

She peeked from the kitchen window as he checked Daniel's wound, tipped his hat to her mother, and shook hands with her father. Willy followed him all the way to his horse, lugging the doctor's bag. When Simon looked toward the window, she ducked behind the curtain, but she could still see the back of him as he rode off.

Her reflection stared back from the window. "Well, I am a ninny, letting a stranger turn my head." The reflection of her mouth worked in the glass, making her laugh. Thrusting the miserable shoes under the table, she took her pie from the sill and began packing her basket.

Simon Corbett wasn't going to ruin her pie supper.

What Simon was thinking as he headed his horse across Troublesome Creek startled him. He wanted her. He didn't even know her, but he wanted her. He had a vision of himself and Pard racing up Lexington's main street while she—barefoot, wild, and lovely—clung to his back. He was a foolish man, thinking a beautiful young woman like Laura Grace Brown was going to fall in love with him virtually overnight. Best to put some distance between them or he was lost. He'd have plenty of time to get his heart straight when he got home. Plenty of time to deconstruct the trap he'd laid for himself.

He leaned forward in the saddle and patted Pard's long neck. "Let's go home, old friend." He sat up straight and squared his shoulders, full of resolve. "Take me home."

"Who is this grown-up lady on my front porch?" Will asked as Copper posed for him, ready to attend the church social. His eyes teared to see her there, so similar to Julie. Yesterday his little girl . . . today a young woman, her hair dressed, held in place by tortoiseshell combs, high-heeled slippers on her feet.

"Oh, Daddy, please take this basket. I can barely walk in these shoes. How's a body supposed to get about without breaking her neck? How am I supposed to eat chocolate pie with this corset on?" She tugged at the offending garment.

"Laura Grace," Grace scolded, "do not be indelicate. A lady never mentions her undergarments. Let Willy take those shoes and scuff the soles for you. Careful, Willy, just the soles!"

"Hey, Sissy, want me to break in that corset for you too?" Willy giggled and rubbed the bottom of the shoes against the bark of the apple tree. "Do you think John Pelfrey will let me have some pie if you can't eat your piece?"

"Who says John Pelfrey will bid on my pie?"

"I do," Willy said, "'cause I know he's sweet on you."

"Yeah, Sissy," Daniel chimed in. "Me an' Willy heard him tell Silas Parker he's gonna walk you home after the pie supper an' he's gonna steal a kiss!"

"Sounds like I'd best load my shotgun," Will said. "Willy, get that box of buckshot from off the pie safe."

"That will be enough of such foolishness." Grace's stern voice cut through the teasing. "There will be no kissing, thus no need for buckshot. Will, please get everyone into the buggy."

"Okay, darlin', but there better not be another bidder for that lemon pie in your basket, and I can't promise not to steal some of your sugar tonight."

"Will! Little pitchers. Sometimes I don't know what to think of the lot of you."

"Let's go!" Willy called. "But, hey, did somebody forget something? What are me and Daniel s'posed to do for pie tonight?"

"Don't worry," Will replied. "There's sure to be an old maid there with some mincemeat left over from Christmas."

"You and Daniel will eat with Laura Grace and whoever buys her pie," Grace instructed as they assembled themselves in the buggy. "You will be excellent chaperones."

"I'm not quite sure what a chaperone is," Willy pondered, "but if it's got anything to do with eating pie, then we'll be excellent for you, Mam. That's for sure. Here, Daniel, put that sore leg up on my lap. We don't want you getting bumped. Go real slow, Daddy."

Will watched a smile spread behind Grace's gloved hand. Daniel's accident had made them both more aware of the fragility of life. God loaned children to you for only a short time. You were sure to lose them one way or another. He reached across the seat to take her other hand. *Ah, such blessings. Thank You, Lord. I'm one lucky man.*

CHAPTER 25

A festive air met the Brown family as their carriage rolled onto the church grounds. Small boys holding bugs chased squealing little girls. Old men sat under the eaves pontificating about the weather, while mothers jostled squirming babies. Young men peered into baskets pretending to size up the best-looking pies, though everyone knew it was the bakers—not the sweet treats—that really drew their interest.

Copper had quite a following as she strolled across the yard to the auctioneer's stand in her green linen dress, her new shoes kicking up puffs of dust. John Pelfrey and Henry Thomas argued over who would carry her basket.

"You might as well give it up, John," Henry sneered. "You ain't got the funds to outbid me."

"Says who?" John tugged at the basket in Copper's hands. "I got the same pay from old man Smithers for grubbing roots as you did."

"Tell me you didn't give half your pay to your ma." Henry jerked the basket his way.

"What if I did? Don't you help out your family?"

Henry stopped. "Why should I?" He rubbed a scabbed-over scratch on his jaw and glared at John. "Ma never gives me anything 'cept the back of her hand."

"For heaven's sake, you two." Copper clutched the basket to her chest. "I can carry it myself."

She was miffed that Henry thought he had any right to her pie, but she suspected he did have the funds to outbid John. Rumor was that someone had snaked under Brother Isaac's henhouse fence a couple of nights ago and stolen two fat baking hens. From the scratch on Henry's face and the jingle of coins in his pocket, Copper surmised he was the thief and had sold the chickens to get more money for tonight.

They reached the flatbed wagon. John hopped up on it, and Copper handed him the basket. He put it last in line, the place of honor.

"I can taste that chocolate now," Henry said.

"Henry, I'll bust your nose if you don't shut up."

Brother Isaac laid a hand on John's arm and shot a stern look Henry's way. "Settle down, boys. We've plenty of pies for the both of you."

"It ain't the pie, Preacher," Henry said with a laugh as he walked off. "It ain't about the pie."

The crowd hushed as Brother Isaac blessed the meal the

ladies had prepared. Everyone rushed to the sawhorse tables spread with ham, fried chicken, chicken and dumplings, all manner of vegetables, and breads still warm from the oven. They'd have supper on the grounds before the desserts were sold.

It took a few minutes to restore order as some recalcitrant big boys broke into the front of the line, only to be reprimanded by their mothers and sent to the very back. You couldn't blame them, Copper thought, for everyone wanted a piece of Ma Hawkins's fried chicken. It was the best and sure to go quickly.

Soon they all were in their proper places. The preacher was served first, followed by the men, then the women and girls with the babies and children in tow. Last were the newly humbled big boys, who teased that by the time they got to the platters nothing would be left but gizzards and necks. Joe Amos said he'd never had a piece of chicken but the neck. Copper thought that must be why he was so skinny.

Families settled together on bright quilts or tablecloths spread on the ground, trying not to spill their heaping plates, calling greetings to other folks as they ate.

Copper was having difficulty just breathing, much less eating. "Mam," she whispered, "this corset does not bend. Everything I have is pushed up under my neck! Can't I go to the outhouse and take it off?"

Mam sighed. "Mimic me. Imagine a straight line from your tailbone to the top of your head. Do not slump. Fold your legs to the side. Take tiny bites." She paused, her eyes taking Copper in. "There—isn't that better?"

Copper nibbled potato salad and nodded at Mam. No sense in arguing. She needed all her breath to keep from swooning anyway. Feeling like a stuffed goose, she glanced about the crowd of neighbors and friends, hoping against hope to spot Dr. Corbett, although he'd told her plain enough that he wouldn't be here. Surreptitiously, she tugged at the offending garment that dug into the soft flesh of her waist. What was the use of all her finery if he wouldn't see how grown-up she looked? It would all be wasted on Henry and John.

Sighing loudly, she dropped her fork onto her plate and shifted her weight from one hip to the other, seeking comfort. *This corset is nothing but torment,* she pitied herself. *Why does Mam tolerate such a thing when it's obvious that no other woman here has one on? I much prefer the look of a loose housedress covered by an apron. Then I could have two helpings of potato salad with room left for more of Aunt Emilee's spoon bread.*

When nothing was left on the serving plates, the crowd slowly filed to the auctioneer's stand. Preacher Isaac held aloft a double-crusted blackberry pie. Isaac was a good hand at auctioning. He could sell salt at a salt lick. "Shell out, folks," he boomed. "We need to swell the church coffers."

The first offering was quickly dispensed as Joe Amos bought the blackberry pie for fifteen cents.

People chuckled when Joe blushed as red as a beet as he claimed the proud baker, Jane Elizabeth Combs. Jane grinned and curtsied when Joe offered her his arm. Her red face matched Joe's when some children started the K-I-S-S-I-N-G song.

There were twenty pies in all, and the bidding went quickly.

Will paid a high price—one dollar—for the pleasure of eating Grace's pie.

A titter went through the crowd when Willy questioned, "Daddy, why don't you just give that dollar to me? There's a pie just like this one at home in the pie safe."

The bidding continued. Pastry fairly flew off the wagon, and then Silas Parker gave in to temptation and plunked down twenty-five cents for the honor of sharing a delicious-looking apple tart with Martha Miller.

That left just one pie—chocolate, with slightly droopy meringue—and just one pie baker—anything but droopy—Copper Brown.

The preacher held the pie aloft. "What am I offered for this good-looking treat?" his voice rang out in a rich singsong. "Ten cents? Fifteen? Now a quarter to John Pelfrey. . . . Thirty-five? I've got thirty-five pennies from Henry Thomas. Thirty-five . . . thirty-five, now forty . . . forty-five, fifty . . . sixty cents?"

John turned his pockets inside out, and the crowd sighed— everyone had bet on John. Brother Isaac's gavel hung in the air as he called, "Sixty once, sixty twice—"

Henry shoved his way to where Copper stood, hands on her hips, murderous that she'd suffered a stupid corset for the likes of Henry Thomas.

"Sold! Sold to—"

But before the mallet could hit the auction stand, a masculine voice rang out from the back of the crowd. "Ten dollars! I bid ten dollars!"

A collective gasp went up from the assembly. Ten dollars? That was more than a week's wages.

"Well, now," Brother Isaac said. "Ten dollars once, ten dollars twice—" his gavel slammed against the wagon bed—"sold to the man in the back!"

Surprised, Copper turned with the crowd to watch as Simon Corbett strolled to the auctioneer's stand and claimed his prize. "Sorry, young man," he said to Henry, "but this one is mine." He held out his arm to Copper and tipped his hat to Mam. "With your permission?"

"Of course, Dr. Corbett," Mam said, relief palpable on her face. "It is good to see you once again. Daniel? Willy?" she called the twins to her side. "Go with your sister."

❧

Willy grabbed the basket, and Dr. Corbett lifted Daniel into his arms and carried him to the shady site, where Copper spread a blue-and-white, double-wedding-ring quilt. The smell of cedar from the blanket chest filled the air. Between Daniel's sore leg and Copper's corset it took a bit of maneuvering, but they were soon settled under the leafy branches of a sugar maple tree, away from prying eyes.

Copper retrieved dessert plates and pressed-glass goblets from her picnic basket as Simon cut and served the pie. She poured cold sweet tea from an earthenware jug and handed out silver forks wrapped in the linen napkins she had ironed just that afternoon.

"Thank you, Simon," she said. "I fear my fancy cutlery and starched linen would have been wasted on Henry Thomas."

"I feel a little sorry for the young fellow," he replied around a forkful of meringue. "There's not a man alive who wouldn't want to be sitting where I am tonight."

"That's for sure," Daniel interjected, "'cause Sissy makes good chocolate pie. Can I have just one more piece?"

"*May* I, Daniel, *may* I. Hand me your plate, please. How about you, Willy? Want another piece?"

"I think I've got a bellyache, Sissy. I ate a bunch of them green apples from that tree yonder. Hey, Doc, can you help me out here?"

"Time will cure that stomachache, Willy. What if we save a piece for you?"

"Uh, maybe you'd better just go ahead and eat it yourself, Doc," he yelled over his shoulder as he beelined for the outhouse. "I'll probably be busy."

The clink of cutlery filled the awkward silence that descended with Willy's departure. Setting her plate aside, Copper made room for Daniel's head to rest in her lap as he stretched out on the quilt and nodded off to sleep. She and the doctor sipped their tea and watched as several boys started an impromptu ball game.

Without taking her eyes from the game, Copper asked, "Why did you come back?"

"I was halfway down the mountain," he said, "before I discovered I'd left something important behind."

Her heartbeat quickened as she slowly stroked Daniel's forehead. She gazed off across the field, and the air shimmered before her eyes. The crack of the wooden bat against the ball, the chattering of folks, the song of a mockingbird, the pinch of her corset all faded. The very world vanished. It seemed there was nothing in the churchyard save for her double-wedding-ring quilt, the doctor, Daniel, and her. "That important thing," she murmured, "did you find it?"

"Yes," he said as he closed the space between them, "I most assuredly did." He began that delicious caressing of her palm again. "With your permission, Laura Grace, I'm going to ask your father if I may call on you."

Daniel shifted his head in her lap, and she eased him off onto the quilt. She turned her face toward Simon. Her eyes took in the neatly trimmed mustache over his thin upper lip, his shiny black hair styled with a side part. It was combed off his forehead and slicked back at the sides to reveal nicely shaped ears that lay flat against his head. He was sure pretty to look at.

She answered him in a voice as soft as his own. "That will be hard when you live so far away."

"I'll work that out," he replied. "I'll get another doctor in town to help with my patients for a while. Then I'll be free to come up here every few months." His eyes met hers, and she thought she might drown in the dark depths of them. "All I know for sure," he continued, "is that I must see you again."

A signal of alarm trilled in the back of her mind. He was a stranger, and his very presence threatened her in a way she didn't understand. But his eyes held hers, and she found she couldn't turn away. What was happening to her? She should stop this now, before it was too late, but instead of protecting herself against the danger of his closeness she answered his need with her own. "I'd like that. If my daddy approves, I'd like that very much." Finally, forcing herself, she lowered her eyes and began to gather up the plates and glasses.

"I'll speak to your father in the morning," Simon said, his voice husky. Without warning, he captured her hand and pressed his lips against her inner wrist. She could feel the throb of her pulse before she jerked away.

"Whatcha doin', Doc? Sissy got chocolate on her hand?" Willy settled himself on the quilt and picked a piece of crust from the pie plate.

"Forgive me," Simon entreated immediately. "That was presumptuous."

"Don't worry, Doc Simon," Willy interjected. "Copper's not the least bit squeamish. Why, you ought to see her gut a fish. She saves the lights for me an' Daniel."

"Lights?" Simon asked.

"The lungs," Copper replied, her pulse still pounding. "They play with them."

"That's hard, Doc," Willy said, "getting the lights out without popping 'em. Like I said, Sissy's a good gutter."

With a rush, Willy's appearance caused Copper to take note of her surroundings. While she and Simon talked, getting to know each other, the evening had passed; it was near twilight. People were gathering their belongings, and she heard their calls of good-bye one to another. Thankfully no one seemed to be aware of what had transpired under their tree.

"Wake up, Daniel." Copper shook him softly. "It's time to go home."

She allowed Simon to help her to her feet—actually, it was a necessity. She thought she might never walk again. Her legs were tingly from sitting in such a ladylike position, and that corset had absolutely cut her in two. Spying Mam caught up in a group of ladies, Copper kicked off her offending slippers and tucked them in the basket with the dirty dishes.

"There–" she straightened her dress and grinned up at Simon–"that's ever so much better." If he was going to come calling, then he'd have to take her as she was.

By the time they crossed the yard, Daddy and Mam were waiting in the carriage. Willy scrambled aboard, and Simon helped her and Daniel in. "Good night," she called out with a wave as they drove off. "Good night."

With a sigh she settled back against the buggy seat, already looking forward to the morning.

The old churchyard was finally empty. A masked raccoon ventured from the woods to scavenge bits of potato salad and crumbs of bread. A quick, swirling breeze snagged a piece of greasy newsprint and tumbled it across the ground into a copse of hackberries.

John Pelfrey grabbed the paper and used it to scrub hot tears from his cheeks. He'd hidden himself away once he lost the bidding on Copper's pie, and no one had missed him. Least of all her. A noise from the underbrush caught his attention, and he jerked his head around, afraid someone had caught him crying. But it was just the raccoon scurrying away, a chicken bone clutched in its mouth.

John had spent a miserable evening watching Copper from his hideout, and when she'd let the stranger kiss her hand his heart nearly stopped. Henry Thomas and his ilk he could handle, but this was a doctor with money and stature. Had he lost her already? He scrubbed his cheeks again with the scrap of paper, stuck it in his pocket, and started down the path.

That stranger will leave, John thought as he ambled along. *And then she'll forget all about him. I know Pest, and there ain't no man can make her leave these mountains.* As for himself, he thought he'd take that job Mr. Smithers had told him about over at Torrent Falls. He'd take his horse and light out in the morning, make himself scarce for a while. By the time he came back, she'd be ready to set up housekeeping.

Feeling better, and more sure of himself, he shrugged and whistled a little tune to keep himself company on his lonely walk home.

CHAPTER 26

Copper lay in bed, unable to sleep. She pressed her wrist against her cheek, Simon's kiss still there, hot as a brand. Finally she threw back her cotton quilt and tiptoed to the porch. A faint smell of tobacco and a familiar cough told her she was not alone. "Daddy? Can't you sleep either?"

"Oh, Copper . . . it's so hot tonight." He stood with one foot propped up on the bottom rung of the porch railing. "I can't seem to settle down. What's keeping you awake?"

She leaned on the railing beside him. "So many worrying things have happened lately. I can't get my mind straightened out. I've been wanting to talk to you."

"Now's as good a time as any." He pulled two rockers together. "Sit here and tell me what's bothering you."

"First I want to ask you about the deacons and the snakes. Do you think they're right? Does it really say in the Bible to take up serpents?"

"You could look that up for yourself. Your Bible has all the answers. But, yes, it is biblical. I personally don't believe that the signs are for our time, but I do believe that God reveals Himself to different folks in different ways." He patted her leg. "Those snake handlers love the Lord in a great big way, and they are wont to prove it. I can't argue with their faith."

"Did what they do cause Daniel to get hurt? He thought he was proving his faith too, Daddy."

"Having faith doesn't protect us from harm. You know that. As the Scripture says, it rains on the just and the unjust alike. It only gives us a shield against the pain. What if Daniel had died? Could we bear such a burden without our firm conviction, without our promise of eternal life?" His rocker creaked a slow song in the still night air. "Folks who follow signs such as that don't do it to prove their faith; they do it because it is an expression of their belief. They do it to obey what they understand as God's will for their lives."

"I'll have to think on that." She rocked, staring out across the dark yard. "Did you enjoy the pie supper?" she asked finally. "Was Mam's lemon meringue as good as usual?"

"Way too good. That pie is why I can't sleep. It's not good to go to bed with such a full belly. And yourself? Did you have a good time?" He chuckled. "That ten-dollar bid stirred up some talk. People around here will have something to chaw on for a while."

"That's why *I* can't rest." Copper let out a huge sigh. "Simon wants to call on me."

He chuckled again. "I had a sense he'd want to see more of you."

"I'm so confused. In the morning he's coming to talk to you." Her rocker stopped. "What will you say?"

"I like him all right, but it's up to you whether he comes calling or not."

Copper stood and walked to the porch rail. "How can we be sweethearts when he lives so far away?" She leaned her head on her crossed arms. "When he kissed my hand, I felt filled with light. My head's still swimming. Is that what love feels like, Daddy?"

Standing, he put his arm around her shoulders. "Don't be jumping the broom before it's laid down. When he leaves, you'll either pine away or forget about him. Best to let nature take its course." He took a draw on his pipe, and she could see the embers in the bowl glowing in the dark. "What about John?"

John! Oh no. As soon as Simon showed up she'd forgotten all about him. "I don't know. I had thought . . . well, John wants us to marry and set up housekeeping. But the world doesn't stop turning when I'm with John."

"Hmm." He knocked the tobacco from his pipe. "Just you be careful, Daughter. When the world stops turning, there's a good chance a body could fall off."

Copper stifled a yawn and reached up to kiss his cheek. "Thanks, Daddy. I think I can sleep now. Good night." She paused at the screen door. "Not tonight, but soon—I want to know about my mother."

Will's heart lurched. He never wanted to think about that time again. That time when his world stopped turning, first from love and then from grief. He should have told her about her mother years ago. He'd have to tell Copper about that and also about his and Grace's decision to leave here and take the boys to the city for a while until they got their education. What a lot for Copper to take in.

A sigh led to a coughing spell. *No help for it now,* he thought when he could catch his breath again. Pouring tobacco into the bowl of his pipe, he struck a match to it. He for sure wouldn't be able to sleep now.

He and Grace had finally reached an understanding, and he'd felt a sense of peace for the first time in years. His wife had finally let him into her heart, and he was happy. He knew he'd pay a big price for that, for he'd thought he'd live out his years right here on Troublesome Creek. But it seemed worth it, especially after Daniel's accident. And really, wasn't it Grace's turn? He'd adjust to leaving . . . somehow.

But how in the world would he tell Copper?

As Jacob wrestled with God's angel at the place he christened Peniel, Dr. Simon Corbett wrestled with his conscience this long night through. He feared his own emotion, his longing. He prayed for God's guidance, and toward daybreak he felt assurance. He believed God walked with him daily, that God directed his path, and he trusted that this time the path led to the woman he would marry.

In the morning he went to Will Brown with his hat in his hand and his heart in his throat. He received Will's blessing, with a few admonishments, and a commitment of sorts from Laura Grace. They walked alone along the banks of Troublesome Creek. He made his intentions clear to her—probably in haste, but he felt he had no choice. He couldn't risk losing her.

"Are you talking about courting, Simon?" she asked, getting right to the heart of the matter.

Her directness pleased him. He'd squired his share of lovely ladies, and he detested the games they played. Obviously he'd never have to guess what Laura Grace was thinking. "I spoke to your father. He said it was up to you."

She turned away from him and busied herself picking the sweet williams that grew wild beside the creek. "Simon, there's someone else. I can't make you any promises before I talk to him."

"Forgive me," he said. "I don't mean to be presumptuous, but I can't leave until I know you will be true to me."

"True to you, Dr. Corbett?" Copper tucked a sprig of blue flower into the buttonhole of his jacket. "I hardly know you."

Taking advantage of her nearness, he caught her arms and pulled her into an embrace. They were nearly hidden under the drooping, sighing boughs of a weeping willow. He could barely hear the rush of water in the creek over the thudding of his heart. The feel of her in his arms was enough for him to savor until he returned, though only his promise to her father kept him from kissing her, for he longed to taste her sweetness.

It was Laura Grace who broke the hug, pushing gently against his chest. "You make me swoon. Look how my hand trembles."

He cupped her chin in his hand. "Does your other fellow make you feel like this?"

Copper met Simon's gaze and saw herself reflected in the passion of his dark eyes. "No," she answered, tucking her hands under her arms to stop their shaking. "No, he doesn't. But still I care for him."

Those eyes of his. They pulled her in as if she no longer had control of her own mind, her own body. Suddenly, without a thought, she stretched up and kissed him right on the mouth. It was just a little peck, really, but she tasted clover and wild strawberries, and starbursts shimmered behind her closed eyes.

Simon wrapped his arms around her and held her tightly. "Oh, my sweetheart," she heard him murmur against the top of her head.

"Hey, Sissy! Where're you hiding?" Willy yelled. "I need to tell you something." It was with some difficulty that she extricated herself from Simon's embrace just before Willy burst into their leafy hideaway. "Mam says you and Doc have had enough alone time. She says come to the porch an' have some lemonade an' chocolate cake."

Willy paused and when his innocent eyes took them in she wished a sinkhole would open and swallow her up. "Well, hey there, Doc," he chattered on, obviously unaware of her misdeed. "You look like you've been struck by lightning. Daddy says he's about to eat all that cake by his lonesome. Daniel's sad 'cause he couldn't come, but he still has that limp. Will that ever go away, Doc Corbett?"

"Let's wait until we get to the house to ask questions," Copper said, glad for Willy's interruption. She was bewildered by her behavior and at the same time wanted nothing more than to kiss Simon again. "Run ahead and ask Mam to pour the lemonade. We'll be right behind you."

As soon as Willy was out of sight, Simon gathered her up again. "What just happened here?" he asked. "You astonish me."

Copper's face blazed, and she hid it against his chest. "You aim to make me miserable." Her voice quivered, and she feared she might burst into tears.

"Oh, dear one, no."

"I shouldn't have done that." The dreaded tears streamed down her face. "You'll think I'm wanton . . . and what would Mam say?"

"There's nothing wrong with a kiss between sweethearts," he said as he gently stroked her cheek.

"But kisses are serious, Simon." She looked up at him. "Kisses are promises."

He dropped to one knee and gazed adoringly up. "Then let's make a promise. Let's promise to marry when I come back at Christmas."

"Marry?" she asked, astounded. "What about the courting?"

"Seems we don't have time for that," he answered, standing.

"But I need time, Simon. I have to sort all this out. John . . . you. I'm just not sure."

He fished in his pocket and handed her a clean white handkerchief. "Don't you see, Laura Grace? God would not have thrown us together in such an unexpected way if He didn't mean for us to be together always."

Turning away, she caught a dangling willow frond, stripped its leaves in one quick motion, and dropped them into the slow-moving creek. They twisted and turned in the water and clumped up against the bank for a moment before finally breaking free and meandering away. Her voice broke as she pleaded, "Give me some time."

"I don't know if I can." His hands on her shoulders pulled her around, and his kiss was long and slow and oh so gentle. "I'm breaking the promise I made to your father," he whispered in her ear, "but you started it."

The next kiss was hard . . . urgent. She felt as if her very bones were melting as she slumped against him. Roughly, he tangled her hair in his hands and tipped her face up to his own. "You belong to me! Say it. Say it back."

Copper felt herself give way. "I belong to you, Simon Corbett. . . ." The pledge seemed so true. "I belong to you," she whispered once again. She averted her eyes from his and begged, "Please leave now. You make me so confused—I can't think straight with you here."

"I'm going." He caressed her face and kissed her gently one last time. "But I'll be back at Christmas, and that's all the time I'm giving you."

CHAPTER 27

It was days after Simon left before Copper felt she was her true self again, days before she could think clearly. Finally her head quit swimming, and she felt she could get a hold on her emotions. When he had truly left, when Pard had cantered out of the barnyard for the last time, it was all she could do to keep herself from running down the dusty road after Simon. It was his last words to her father that stopped her. Words that chilled the very marrow in her bones. . . .

They had come back from the creek to Mam's cold lemonade and chocolate cake, Daddy's handshake for Simon and slow wink to her, Willy's infernal questions, and Daniel's puzzled look. It all felt so strange to Copper, as if they were celebrating something that might be her undoing. Simon had stayed for the longest time, past the noon hour and nearly until Molly's milking.

But before he took his leave, her family had given them a moment alone. He'd brushed her cheek with his lips and whispered, "I love you, my own," before they all trooped back out to the porch to see him off.

She'd stayed behind as Daddy walked him across the yard, his hand on Simon's shoulder. But she could hear them clear enough when Simon stopped and said, "I intend to come back for Christmas, and when I do, I'll ask you for her hand. I mean to marry your daughter, Will."

"You know, Doc," Daddy replied, "it's all up to her. It's Copper's choice—not yours."

"You'll find it's meant to be," Simon answered. "And I promise you this: Laura Grace will be happy in Lexington. I give you my word."

Now, as she stood in the garden scratching at a bunched-up hill of potatoes, those words still chilled her, though the late-summer day was hot and as dry as a moth's wing. Taking off her bonnet, she leaned against the hoe and fanned herself. Copper was glad to be alone in the weedy patch, thankful that the boys were off at the Pelfreys' and Mam was busy in the kitchen. She finally had some time to think.

The ground beneath her hoe was cracked and parched. She'd need to carry buckets of water up from the creek. Her bare toes scrunched down into the dry dirt. It took a few good whacks from her hoe to finally find some moisture. Squatting between two hills of potatoes, she reached deep into the hole she'd dug and pulled out a handful of loam. The soil was dark and rich and formed a ball when she clenched it tight, releasing the scent of promise—the promise of life and growth and hope for the morrow.

Just like the Resurrection, she mused as she let the clump fall from her grasp. Every spring when her garden renewed itself, issuing forth lush and green from dead-looking seed, she was reminded of Jesus' victory over the tomb. How could she leave this sacred place?

Over and over, she kneaded the damp ball of earth with her foot. Nothing felt better than mud between your toes while you worked the garden. Were there gardens in the city?

Swimmy-headed again, she nearly fell before she made it to the creek and lowered herself onto the bank. Cupping her hand in the water, she splashed her face and neck, then leaned back against the trunk of a sycamore tree. In a rush, Simon's words came back and made her stomach ache.

Lexington! He wanted to take her away from Troublesome Creek to live with strangers in a strange place. The thought astonished her. Why wouldn't he live here?

"Forevermore, Laura Grace," Mam had said when Copper had broached the subject with her. "That's not how things are done. Besides, he has a medical practice. Surely you wouldn't think of taking him away from his patients."

And she wouldn't. Of course she wouldn't. But how could she even think of leaving her home place? Every time she pondered the loss, she got so sad she was physically ill. And as far as she knew, there was no herb, no cure for homesickness.

Feeling a little better after the splash of cold creek water, she rested her eyes for a minute. The only thing that restored her equilibrium was the realization that kept coming back to her: she didn't have to leave. She didn't have to. The power was hers. Or it was until she thought of him, of his kiss, of his fingers caressing her cheek, and then she was in turmoil again.

Sitting up straight, she rested her arms on her bent knees. What was she to do? How could she choose between the love of a man and the love of a place? After all, she'd known Troublesome Creek much longer than she'd known Dr. Simon Corbett.

A commotion on the far bank, up the creek a ways, caught her eye. A creature of some sort was sliding through the underbrush, probably coming down for a drink. Last night at supper Daddy had warned her about a wild boar that had ruined a patch of corn. Reaching beside her, she grabbed the hoe. Why hadn't she thought to bring a gun or the slingshot? Holding her weapon at the ready, she craned her neck and waited for the thing to show itself.

Finally little hands parted bushes on the far bank, and Copper dropped her hoe in delight. "Remy!" she cried as she splashed across the creek, nearly falling into the water in her haste. "Oh, Remy!"

Remy's eyes warned her not to get too close, so Copper hugged herself in joy to keep from grabbing her little friend. "I'm so glad to see you. What are you doing here? Where have you been?"

"Ye need too many answers at once, Purty." Remy ducked her head and took a step backward.

"I'm sorry, Remy, but it makes my heart so glad to see you!"

"I seen yore buddy over to Torrent Falls," Remy said as if that answered Copper's questions. "The one that brung my ma them vittles."

"John," Copper said. "That's John Pelfrey. I wondered where he'd gone off to. But it's a long way to Torrent Falls. How did you get there?"

"My mammaw's got a mule."

"Your mammaw? Are you living with her then?"

"Ye shore are nosy, Purty."

"Sorry," Copper said again. "You look real pretty, Remy." And she did. Her white hair was plaited in intricate braids, and her face was full. Copper could tell she'd been eating regularly, and her dress was clean and actually fit. She didn't have on shoes, but then neither did Copper.

"'Purty is as purty does,' Mammaw always says."

Copper held out her hand. "Please come sit with me a spell."

Remy didn't take her hand, but she followed Copper back across the creek and sat on her heels as Copper plopped down on the bank. "Air ye spoke for now, Purty?" Remy asked in the low gravelly voice that had become so familiar.

"I swan, Remy. How do you know so much?"

"I gets around. Air ye? Air ye spoke for?"

Copper wrapped her arms around her knees. "Seems like it. I guess I am."

"Ye ain't happy 'bout it; I can tell." Remy shifted her weight and stared at Copper with her pale blue eyes.

"I'm so confused." Copper shook her head. "He wants to take me away to live in a city, and I don't want to leave Troublesome Creek. This is my home. I'm happy here."

"Onliest thing that matters is folks, Purty. Yore home ye can tote with you."

"How, Remy? Tell me how."

Remy tapped Copper's chest with her closed fist directly over her heart. Copper didn't dare breathe, afraid her friend would dart off as quick as a hummingbird if she moved. It was so rare to feel Remy's touch. "Ye carry it here, Purty. It'll be safe here."

"Hmm, I'll think on that. But what of you? You must tell me a little about yourself. And of your family . . . I'm so sorry about baby Angel."

"It's all right, I reckon." Remy began flinging little stones into the creek. "Ma cried fer the longest time."

A silence enveloped them. It seemed Remy had run out of words.

"So you're living with your grandmother?" Copper asked.

"It's real tight there . . . doors and window lights all closed up." Remy's eyes drifted as if she'd already taken her leave. "I'd druther be buried without an oak-board coffin as to live indoors." She stood and started back across the creek. "Makes me feel all stove up."

"Don't go," Copper begged. "Stay awhile."

"I got places to be. Ye can come along."

"Don't tempt me."

Remy's feet barely rippled the water as she went. When she reached the far bank, she paused to wave good-bye and raised her hand as if in blessing. "Yore place is here, Sister. Where things stay still." A bright, new, red foxtail bobbed at the seat of her dress as she disappeared once again.

Copper stood and strolled back to the garden, lost in thought. She raised her hoe and struck out at the weeds that threatened to take over the potatoes. Sister? Had Remy called her sister? A Scripture came to mind: *"There is a friend that sticketh closer than a brother."*

I could use a friend like that. I surely could.

Summer passed and ushered a long, wet fall into the mountains. Copper was miserable. At times she wished there'd never been a pie supper, that she'd never allowed that first kiss. But then she'd remember the clean, starched-laundry smell of Simon or the feel of his strong arms around her. She'd trace the outline of her lips with her finger, and a longing so intense she'd have to sit down would overtake her. She wished she'd never met him. She'd been so happy before he came, lost in her childhood.

Mam was no help. She'd just look at Copper with half a smile and give her more sewing to do. They were filling the cedar chest Daddy had made her with all manner of sheets, pillowcases, and towels. Everything had to be marked with the initial *C* so she couldn't change her mind. It drove Copper mad to have her life predicted in such a way. But then it was a *C* . . . that also stood for Copper.

Finally the weather broke. A glorious Indian summer blessed the mountains with soft sunshine and gentle breezes, and Copper was out the door as soon as she could escape Mam's chores. She went hunting nearly every morning after she finished milking. Though Willy begged to go along and Daddy would have been glad to keep her company, she went alone. She had to decide if she could actually leave this place . . . this place of her heart.

Every day she came home empty-handed save for a few late mushrooms, and once she stumbled on some ginseng. She'd take aim at a fat, nose-twitching rabbit hiding in a pile of leaves or a tail-shaking squirrel on a black-walnut limb, then not be able to squeeze off a single shot. Her mind played tricks on her, for every animal she saw she imagined a mate and children waiting at home in burrows or dens . . . a family. So she left her gun at home and took Daddy's walking stick instead.

One day she packed a wedge of corn bread and a raw turnip and settled down for her noon meal halfway up the mountain under a butternut tree. She'd just gotten comfortable, shifting about in a pile of leaves, when John Pelfrey's hound dog bounded up, demanding a share of bread.

"Hey, Faithful. Where's your master?" She stood and looked around. There he was, kneeling at the base of a hickory, cracking nuts with a rock, acting like he didn't see her. "John? Aren't you speaking?"

"Didn't know you wanted company."

"You're not company. . . . You're just John."

He dusted bits of hickory shell from his hands and looked up at her with eyes swimming in tears. "Just John?"

Flustered, she replied, "You know what I mean. You're my friend."

"Are you fixing to leave, Pest?"

Unable to bear the anguish in his voice, she didn't answer but began to gather red and gold and orange leaves. "We missed the prettiest leaves this year. It was too wet."

His hand rested on her shoulder. "I deserve an answer."

Suddenly Copper sank to her knees, shaking her head, and started to cry. "I don't know. I don't know."

John knelt in front of her and took her hands. "I'd marry you, Pest, and you could stay. You wouldn't never have to leave."

She let him hold her and cried upon his shoulder. "Oh, John. I wish it so. I wish it was you I loved."

"I love you. Ain't that enough?"

She patted his wet cheek. "No, John. No, it's not. You think you love me because I'm all you know."

"Could I kiss you, Pest?"

She closed her eyes and offered her lips, and he brushed her mouth with his own. It was sweet and gentle, just like John himself, but there was no starburst . . . no longing.

"I been wanting to do that for the longest time."

They sat side by side. She rubbed his knuckles with her thumb and thought her tears would never stop.

He put his arm around her and drew her close. "Don't be spilling all them tears."

"I can't stand to hurt you," she sobbed, her tears like a river in the crook of his neck. "I wish you didn't love me like a sweetheart. I wish we'd just stayed friends."

"It ain't the loving you that's hard. It's you not loving me." He sighed and ran his hand through his shock of yellow hair. "Don't be sad for me." He patted her arm. "I'll be all right if you're all right."

Mopping her face with her dress tail, she leaned against his shoulder. "How do I know what's the right thing to do?"

"You got to go where your heart leads you."

She got to her feet and pulled him up. "I never set out for this to happen, but I love him, John."

"Well," he said, shrugging. "Well." He chucked a few hickory nuts at a raucous jay, then reached in his overalls' pocket and pulled out a piece of smeared newsprint. He handed it to her. "Guess I'll be leaving too."

She unfolded the small square of paper and read out loud: "'Corsets made to order. You furnish the measurements and we'll make the garment. Money-back guarantee. Sophie's Fine Confinements.'" She looked up, confused. "You're going to make corsets?"

Red-faced, he snatched the paper from her and turned it over. "Tuther side, Pest." They sat back down, and he showed her a story about a sailing ship bound for the Orient. "See, it says they're taking on hands. Says they give good pay and you can see the world. Wouldn't that be something—to see the world?" He carefully folded the paper and stuck it back in his pocket. "I guess we both got big plans."

"I guess so." Copper started, then yelped as a hickory nut bounced off her head. She shaded her eyes and looked up to see a gathering of squirrels chattering maniacally and beaming hulls their way. "Ow! Ow!" She and John clasped hands and ran away, doubled over in laughter, children again . . . for a little while.

The beautiful Indian summer was gone. Winter was fast closing in. There wouldn't be many more days of comfortably wandering the woods.

One morning as Copper tied a little poke of bread and meat together, Daddy said, "Add a piece of sausage and biscuit for me, Daughter. I aim to go along."

She saw the look he exchanged with Mam, and her mouth went dry. *He's going to tell me about my mother,* she thought, and then wondered if she really wanted to know.

He led her to the creek. It was clear and running swiftly over moss-covered rocks. A sudden cold wind gusted, and she drew her shawl tightly around her arms.

"It all started here," he said, his voice suddenly gruff. "It was a flash flood that carried your mother away."

They talked and walked for miles. The sun warmed them as they went, but the wind nipped her nose and the back of her neck with its icy fingers. It was nearly over, she knew—the restless fall. The trees were spent, standing naked and proud, save for the oak that clung relentlessly to its faded beauty, like an old woman with her memories.

Her father's cough was worse and sometimes stole his breath, but he insisted on leading her up an unfamiliar holler. In the exact spot where her mother's body had been found was a little marker—a pile of stones in the shape of a cross. It was neat and clean of weeds or vines as if someone kept it up. "Daniel Pelfrey," he said, without further explanation.

They walked back down the creek and found a sunny spot to sit and eat. "I should have told you sooner," he said. "It's something I've wrestled with for a long time."

"It helps me to know. I always thought I killed her being born."

Daddy took her hand. "I'm sorry." His hand tightened and he sighed. "There's more I have to tell you, Daughter." He took off his old, shapeless, felt hat and drummed it against his knee. "I'm not sure how you'll take it."

Copper couldn't swallow; the bread turned to sawdust in her mouth. She spat it out and sipped cold black coffee from the pint jar they'd brought along, then passed it to him. "Better just tell me straight-out."

He took a swig and wiped his mouth with the back of his hand. She watched him fiddle with the jar lid. He screwed it on and off half a dozen times before it seated itself to his satisfaction. "Aggravating thing's wore out. I ought to just throw it away."

"Daddy?"

He looked out over the creek, then cleared his throat. "Your mam's set on going to Philadelphia, Copper, and I aim to go with her."

"Philadelphia! Whatever for?"

"There're schools up there she wants for the boys." He cleared his throat again, as if he choked on the words. "That friend of hers—Millicent, the one who owns that fancy school—says she'd find us a house."

"But, Daddy . . ."

He turned his strong, true gaze on her. "It's pretty much settled, Copper. Your mam fears for Daniel if we stay here. He's not sturdy like you and Willy."

Copper's face flushed as her anger flared. "How could she ask that of you? How could she dare ask you to leave here?"

"I asked it of her near seventeen years ago, Daughter."

"That's different," she sputtered.

"How so?"

"'Cause, Daddy, there's not another place like this."

"Don't I know it. But it's her turn, I figure."

Copper wondered at the tenderness that filled his voice. Could he love Mam like she loved Simon? How strange to think that that could be after all this time. "What about your work?" she asked, unable to keep the anger from her voice. "What would you do there?"

He squinted and set his hat back on his head. "She wants to teach. And me? I'll find a coal bank somewhere."

"What about me?"

"Well, honey, we figured to hog-tie you and throw you in the back of the wagon. But, now—"

"You mean Dr. Corbett?" she asked with resignation.

"It clouds things, doesn't it?"

"It sure does, Daddy. It sure clouds things."

He stood and stretched and scratched about in the dirt with his walking stick. "You don't have to marry, you know. I'm not quite ready to give you up."

"Daddy?" A thought had just occurred to her. A thought that could set her free. "What if I stayed on here . . . by myself? After you and Mam leave?"

The look he gave her held no surprise. "This hardscrabble farm is yours if you want it, but what will you do with Doc Corbett? I don't see him giving up on you very easy."

"I don't mean forever—maybe just a couple of years until I know for sure what I want. Everything's happening so fast it makes my head spin." Scattering her bread for the birds, she secured the poke around the half-empty coffee jar. "I'm afraid if I don't take my time I might live to regret it."

"Well, there's truth in that old saw 'Marry in haste, repent in leisure.' If Simon really loves you—and I trust he does—then he'll wait." He studied her face. "I've not known many folks I thought could handle any situation the good Lord throws their way as well as you, Daughter."

She stretched to kiss his cheek. "I love you, Daddy."

"I love you too, sunshine," he choked. "I love you too."

CHAPTER 28

December came with a light dusting of snow and a cutting wind so cold it rattled teeth and caused the backs of eyes to ache. Nobody ventured far without a layer of wraps, from crocheted mufflers over red noses to double stockings over numbed feet. Still, Copper couldn't resist stomping on each glass-skimmed puddle on the way to the barn, just to hear the ice crack.

Molly didn't seem to mind the weather; she was stabled at night with an extra rasher of feed. She greeted Copper with a soft *moo* when the barn door opened. Copper scratched her behind the ears, and Molly swung her head in cow contentment, hay sticking out of the corners of her mouth.

Copper leaned her head against the cow's warm side and stripped the dangling teats. The swish of milk against the side of the tin bucket was a comfort. Her heart never felt so sore, her emotions still battling within her.

Dr. Corbett was coming for Christmas. She wished he wouldn't. Her memory of their time together was beginning to fade, and she found it tolerable to think of never seeing him again. She could stay on Troublesome Creek alone after Mam and Daddy left. Handling the farm wouldn't be hard. All she'd need was one hired man. Even with John gone there were plenty of near-grown Pelfreys at hand, and Henry Thomas was always looking for money.

"How could I leave you, Molly?" she asked the sleeping cow. "How could I–?" Her voice caught on a clot of tears. She was so tired of crying. Finished, she stood.

The little milk stool tumbled over and Molly awoke. She looked at Copper with her soulful brown eyes as if to say, "I agree. How could you?"

Copper toted the half-full pail to the springhouse and poured the fresh milk into the separator. Mam wanted cream for candy and for the caramel icing she'd top her Christmas jam cake with. After pouring the blue-John into a crock, she stirred the watery milk with a ladle. *Funny thing to call milk: blue-John,* she mused. *Looks like I feel, like my blood has turned to water, like the fullness of life has been skimmed off.*

She reached into her pocket and pulled out the thick cream-colored envelope that had come in the mail just yesterday. Dr. Corbett had a beautiful hand. The ink flowed pretty as you please scripting her name, *Miss Laura Grace Brown,* across the front.

She had written him only once, every other word an inkblot,

what with Willy or Daniel interrupting her every minute and Paw-paw jostling her elbow, begging for a piece of biscuit. Besides, she didn't know what to write. Words that usually came so easily to her jumbled up on the page, but she'd carried the missive to the post office anyway, feeling like she was playing grown-up.

She smoothed the sharply creased stationery against her skirt. *"Dearest,"* she read, *"I can hardly wait until you are in my arms again. My days are bereft and my nights an agony of longing."*

She stopped to fan her face with the paper. Her resolve to live without him melted like butter in July and threw her into confusion once again. What she needed was time, more time to come to her own conclusions. She'd write him once more and ask him to wait until spring to visit, and she'd ask him to not write to her and tell him that if he did she'd leave the envelopes sealed.

She busied herself scraping the rich yellow cream into a crock. She felt better, lighter, her mind clear for the first time in months.

After Christmas, the weather turned damp and bleak. It had warmed just enough to allow a chilly rain to seep into every nook and cranny of the cabin with its persistent gray drizzle. Everything in the house felt clammy, and it was impossible to dry a wash. Days after the laundry was done, overalls and flannel shirts still hung on a line stretched across the kitchen.

Willy dragged the sled up on the porch in hopes that the rain would turn to snow. Daddy said he doubted it. He said it was the kind of weather that turned mean, causing sleet instead.

Everything felt mean to Copper, who sat at the kitchen window in her cotton slip, her hands cupped around a mug of strong, hot tea, an old quilt draped across her shoulders. The fire roared in the fireplace, but its warmth couldn't seem to make its way across the floor to where she sat, her feet drawn up under her.

"Laura Grace," Mam said around a mouthful of straight pins, "let's try this one more time."

Copper moaned but threw off her quilt and went to suffer yet another fitting. She raised her arms, and Mam settled a bodice of blue-and-green-plaid bouclé around her.

"Turn," Mam said. "Stop. There's the problem—this needs single bust darts." She pinched the material under Copper's arm. "You see how it pulls with two?"

No, Copper didn't see. She shrugged out of the garment and handed it to her mother, who ripped out the offending darts with the skill of a surgeon.

"One can't always trust the pattern," Mam instructed. "A poor fit will always show."

"Mam," Copper replied, "why are you wearying yourself so? I may not even need all these dresses you insist on sewing."

Mam settled herself at the Singer, positioned in front of a window to take advantage of the light. "On the other hand, you might. I'll not have you going off to Lexington with nothing but common clothing. Stop moping about and cut the braid for the trim. No, not that piece—it's for the jacket. Use the navy."

Copper could barely hear Mam's reply above the whirring of the sewing machine. She took up the yellow tape and measured a length of navy blue braid. The pattern showed the trim extending from underneath the arm to the hem of the walking-length skirt. Mam said walking-length was the newest style. Copper picked up the epaulets that were already finished, fashioned to make her shoulders look wider, which in turn would make her waist look slimmer. Mam had *tsk-tsk*ed to measure Copper's waist at twenty-two inches and had sighed mightily when she slipped the tape around her bust, pulling a little tighter each time.

Copper held the epaulets to her shoulders and walked to the mirror. "Well, la-di-da," she said to her reflection. "Molly will love this."

Mam stopped pedaling. "Put your quilt back on. Your father's coming up the walk with the mail."

Daddy opened the door. A draft sailed up Copper's bare legs and made her shiver.

"What's going on in here?" He peered underneath a piece of laundry. A long johns' trapdoor hung in his face, sending Willy into paroxysms of laughter. "Don't we have enough clothes hanging about without you making more, Grace?"

"Daddy? Daddy!" Daniel tried to get his father's attention.

"What's that, Son?" Daddy said from behind the union suit.

"Daddy, you've got underpants in your face."

"Nah, surely not. That wouldn't be seemly." He walked farther into the room, and the long johns came with him, stretching the line to near breaking.

"Will, if you dirty those clothes, you'll do the next wash," Mam said, her back to him, pedaling away again.

"These are dry anyway. Come here, you two rascals, and take these down. Mind the clothespins. I don't hanker whittling more."

"We could whittle them, Daddy," Willy replied. "If you'd let us have back the knives Doc Simon sent us for Christmas."

Daniel nodded.

"When I can trust you not to carve your initials on a church pew again—that's when you'll see those pocketknives, Son."

"But, Daddy, I found yours—W. B. 1848—on the back of the pulpit." Willy pulled hard on a pair of pants. The wooden pin securing one leg to the line popped off, shot straight up, and came down like a fallen arrow, straight on the bald spot atop Daddy's head.

Willy guffawed. Daniel giggled. Daddy's face turned red as he rubbed his scalp. Copper secured the quilt she wore with the errant pin, then started taking down the laundry.

"Leave that to these two ruffians," Daddy said. "They can take 'em down and fold 'em too. Here . . . I brought you something." He pulled a stack of mail from his coat pocket and handed a familiar-looking, cream-colored envelope to Copper.

She sighed and took a sip of her tea before walking to her room. The air was frigid when she opened the door, so she left it cracked and hurried to her bedside table. She pulled the drawer open and pushed aside the gift Simon had sent her for Christmas—a heart-shaped locket—then retrieved a bundle of unopened letters tied with pink ribbon. What to do, what to do? She knew if she read just one page the decision would no longer be hers to make, for Simon stirred her senses and weakened her resolve without even being present.

Between Mam and her dresses and Simon and his missives, she felt bombarded with the desires of others, and she wanted to be true to herself. Wasn't that what was ultimately the most important thing? To be true to oneself? She held the little packet of his correspondence pressed to her chest, the weight of his words like a stone on her heart.

Across the room under her brothers' bed she could see the ends of two trunks. One was hers. It was nearly full of frilly under-things, gowns, wrappers, slips, and several new dresses, not to mention shoes and hose. The other trunk was her family's, mak-ing ready for their departure to Philadelphia. If she was married they wouldn't need to wait until she turned eighteen. Copper knew Mam hoped to move and get the family settled before a new school term started in the fall. If she didn't marry, she would disappoint Mam greatly. If she did, she might disappoint herself.

Copper tapped the unopened letter against her chin thoughtfully, then put it on top of the others and secured them all with the silky pink ribbon. She took up the locket. Its fine gold chain was twisted around the basket necklace John had carved for her. She unknotted it and warmed the precious metal in her hands, then pushed the little clasp. The locket sprang open, and Simon looked out at her. She traced his dark mus-tache with one finger. He was so handsome. A tear started in the corner of her eye.

Leaning across the bed, she pulled aside the heavy curtain Mam had fashioned to keep out drafts. It was almost dusk. She'd have to hurry to get the milking done before supper. Sitting on the edge of the bed, she put on her scratchy woolen stockings. The sound of Daddy's laugh made her smile. The oven door creaked, and she smelled corn bread and brown beans, saw in her mind's eye her family gathering around the table, heads bent and hands clasped. But she didn't see herself there.

She missed them already.

✥

"Laura Grace. Laura Grace."

Copper was curled under her quilts, toasty warm in her bed. She didn't want to wake up, but Mam shook her shoulder persistently.

"What? What is it, Mam?"

"Your father's ill. Come and help me."

She struggled out of the nest of blankets, Willy and Daniel curled on either side. She hadn't even noticed when they'd snuck into her bed. *What did Mam say? Daddy's sick? Probably just that cough again.* Her long white nightdress flapped around her as she hurried to their room.

He lay back against the pillow, heaving for breath. She could hear the whistle of his lungs.

"Mam, help me set him up. He's smothering."

They wrestled him up and stuffed the pillow bolster behind his back. Copper put her ear to his chest. She could hear a gurgling and feel heat against her cheek. "I'll be right back."

She ran to her bed and reached under the mattress for the medical book she kept secreted there. The boys didn't even stir. She thumbed it as she hurried back to Daddy. "I'd guess he's got pneumonia, Mam."

Mam's hand flew to her throat. "Oh no, Laura Grace. What can we do? Who will help us?"

Copper held up her hand, palm out. "Just a minute." She turned up the lamp wick and studied a few pages. "Mam, go heat some water." She heard the clanging of the heavy iron teakettle as she knelt on the bed. "Daddy! Wake up. Can you hear me?"

He wheezed and strangled but opened his eyes. "Cop . . ." He struggled. "My remedy."

She bustled into the kitchen and pulled on her boots.

"Where are you going?" Mam asked. "What are you going to do?"

"Squeeze a lemon and measure out some molasses," Copper directed. "I'll be right back."

The clouds had lifted, and a million sparkling stars greeted her run across the barnyard. The cold, clean air seared her lungs as the wind whipped around her. She pushed the barn door open and stood for a moment, orienting herself. Where had she seen that jar? The grain box. Tucked way down inside, the little gray jug was buried in the cow's feed.

The kettle whistled on the stove and Mam was piercing the lemon with a sharp knife when Copper stepped back inside the house.

"What is that?" Mam asked. "Where did you get–?"

Copper plunked the jug on the table and pushed out the little cork with her thumb. The tang of spirits stung the air. "Corn liquor, Mam. Uncle Daniel makes a little now and then. Daddy takes it for his cough." She poured a dollop into an ironstone mug, followed by a squeeze of lemon and a tablespoon of molasses. After that, she topped it off with a measure of boiling water. "Bring the footbath in. We'll want to soak his feet to break the fever."

Mam caressed her right temple, a look of pain clouding her features.

"Mam!" Copper demanded, seeing the familiar hesitation. "Get the footbath."

"I'm sorry," Mam replied. "It's just that I can't bear sickness."

"That's all right," Copper said, taking pity. "Just help me—I know what to do." And she did. Copper had cared for every sick and injured animal that had dragged itself her way since she was a child. Not to mention caring for all the twins' various ailments. It was her gift to make people feel better.

It took both of them to hold him upright and put his feet in the hot water. His hand trembled and the medicine sloshed out. Copper steadied the mug, and he gulped a long drink. "Get a clean shirt, Mam. We've got to keep him warm and dry."

She turned her head and held her father steady, while Mam slipped the wet garment off and replaced it with the flannel gown she'd made him for Christmas.

"Okay, he's starting to sweat," Copper said a moment later. "Let's get him covered up."

They eased him back against the bolster and pulled the quilts around his shoulders.

"I'll warm a blanket," Mam said, her voice shaking.

Copper followed her into the kitchen. Mam put lumps of coal on the grate and laid a folded woolen blanket on the hearth. Rummaging in the pantry, Copper felt a cold sweat of fear break out on her forehead. When had Daddy last been sick? Seemed like just a few weeks ago. His cough was much worse than usual this winter . Had he lost weight? Finding the tin of salve they used when one of the boys had the croup, she pried it open with a butter knife. Mixing a tablespoon-size dollop of the camphor salve with a slug of kerosene, she smeared it on a piece of red flannel rag warmed by the fire.

"Here, Mam. Put this on his chest." They could hear a deep, rumbling cough from the bedroom. "I'll bring the blanket."

The salve must have helped because he slept the rest of the night. Copper's fear abated, and she grew confident that he would recover quickly. He'd probably just had a bad cold. . . .

But in the morning her father didn't get up.

"I'm just feeling a little puny," he said around a frog in his throat. "I'll be fine tomorrow."

Anxious to keep him comfortable, Copper and Mam moved the twins' narrow bed out in front of the fireplace, and he slept there wrapped in quilts and the wool blanket. He slept and slept, and every time he woke Mam fed him more of the medicine Copper had made.

Copper carried in the wood and coal to heat the house, hauled buckets of water from the well, and fed the animals. Everything in the house felt strange with Daddy laid up. It felt like someone had sucked the air out so she could hardly catch her breath.

❧

The third night was the longest. Mam was sitting up and Copper was dozing, enjoying the warmth provided by her sleeping brothers' sturdy little bodies, when Copper heard the front door slam against the wall followed by Mam's short, high scream. Copper jumped up.

Mam stood by Daddy's borrowed bed, her eyes round with fright, her Bible splayed across her chest. The door stood open; a wild icy gale howled into the room. It was the middle of winter, but still lightning flashed across the black sky and thunder shook the window glass. Daddy slept on.

Copper crossed the room and pushed the door closed against a strange fierce weight. She leaned her back against it.

"It's just the wind, Mam. The wind blew the door open." But she took the seldom-used key from where it hung on the jamb and twisted it in the lock. "There."

Mam stood by her chair, trembling. Her long, graying hair hung in a plait over her shoulder. "I thought . . . I thought . . ." She reached out her hand toward Copper.

"He's all right, Mam. See, he's just sleeping." Copper struggled to keep her own fear at bay, knowing she had to be strong enough for both of them. The last thing she needed was for Mam to get the vapors now. "Do you have any of that resting powder Dr. Corbett left for you?"

"Just a little, but I couldn't. I shouldn't leave him."

"He's breathing easy, Mam. I'll sit with him."

Copper fetched the little paper packet and mixed a drink.

Mam took it straight down, then went to sleep in Copper's bed. "Call me," she said from the doorway. "Call if he needs me."

Copper settled in the chair beside her father's bed. He didn't seem any worse, and his breathing was unlabored. She propped her feet under his covers and opened the book she'd kept hidden under her mattress for years: *Dr. Chase's Family Physician, Farrier, Bee-keeper, and Second Receipt Book*. She'd discovered it and pulled it from the bookcase one day years ago, when she was dusting. Even though Mam had fixed the whole top shelf for her with storybooks and nature studies, Copper had still reached for the forbidden shelves Mam had warned her not to touch. Her favorite had been Dr. Chase's medical book, and she had slipped it out every chance she got—until one day when Mam caught her with it and had a fit. She'd jerked it out of Copper's hands and whacked her legs good with a yardstick.

The next time Copper had dusted, there was the book in its rightful place, but with many pages missing. It was just about the worst thing Copper could think of, destroying a book. So she'd stolen it. She put another volume in its place, and Mam never missed it. Copper had slept on the lump of it from then on.

She shook her head now at the memory, then turned down the lamp and dozed awhile, Dr. Chase's writings and ramblings open on her lap.

She woke with a crick in her neck when the clock struck 3 a.m. The fire was dying down so she stoked the embers and put more chunks of coal on it, then decided to make herself a cup of tea. She'd hung the teakettle in the fireplace earlier, so it wouldn't take but a minute for the water to heat. She put some black tea leaves in a tea ball, set it in her cup, and was reaching for the kettle when Daddy started choking.

He coughed and gagged, sucking in air as if he were drowning. She rushed back to his bedside and held a rag to his mouth as he retched into it.

"Feels better," he wheezed. "Something stuck in my throat."

"Do you want some more medicine, Daddy? or something to eat? What if I make you an egg?"

"Not just yet," he said, his voice as raspy as an old saw. "Maybe just a drink."

She laid the rag beside her book on the little table they'd put by the bed and poured water into his glass. He drank it half down and handed it back to her. His eyes closed as he lay back against the pillow. "Thank you," he whispered.

She put the glass on the table, and then her heart skidded in her chest. The rag–the white rag she'd held to his mouth–was red. Bloodred. "Daddy, there's blood on this rag!"

He opened his eyes and grabbed her hand. "Our secret, Daughter." He looked at her, a level gaze of love and trust. "Don't tell your mam."

"How long?" Copper demanded. "How long has this been going on?"

"Since the spring, I recollect–but it doesn't mean anything, Copper. I'll get past this." His eyes drooped. He turned on his side, away from her, toward the heat. "I feel better." His voice was a ragged sigh. "I'll sleep now."

CHAPTER 29

The slow gray days of January continued, one day the same as the next—just cold and wind. But at least the rain had stopped. The house was dry, and the laundry no longer hung for days sucking up the heat. They washed only what was absolutely necessary and wore the same clothes until Mam couldn't stand it anymore and made everybody change.

Daddy was better. He was working again, but he'd fallen off so much that his overalls hung on his thin frame like a scarecrow picked clean of its stuffing.

One Saturday morning after breakfast he took down his gun. "I can't stand one more supper of pork," he declared. "I aim to get some squirrel. Doesn't that sound fine?"

Mam fussed, but he would not be deterred. He and Willy and Daniel set off around ten promising to be back by noon.

"Mam," Copper said as soon as they were out the door, "I'm going to take a bath. Will you wash my hair?"

"You'll catch your death." Mam sounded worried.

"I'll put some extra coal on the fire and get it nice and warm in here before I start, but I have to bathe. I can't stand myself any longer."

Copper carried the washtub in from the porch, set it in front of the fire, and filled it halfway with hot water. Full would have been nice, but the water was too hard to heat. Mam turned her back as Copper shed her clothes and climbed into the tub. *Mmm,* her whole body seemed to sigh with delight as she sank into the tub.

Mam poured warm water over her head before soaping her hair with a wonderful-smelling castile soap. "This smells like summertime. Like roses and sunshine," Copper said, closing her eyes as Mam rinsed her hair. "This is glorious. Thank you, Mam. Would you like for me to wash your hair?"

"No, I don't want to take a chill like your father did. That's all it was, don't you think, Laura Grace—just a chill?"

Copper was in a quandary. She couldn't lie, but then she wasn't a doctor with all the answers. "I hope so, Mam," she answered. Stepping out of the bath, she folded herself in a warm blanket, then sat on the hearth and let Mam comb the tangles from her hair. "I hope that's all it was."

Daddy had indeed brought home squirrel for supper. Copper's belly growled as she hurried Molly with the milking, fancying she could smell the meat Mam was frying. If she didn't get to the house soon, Mam would use the crisp brown skillet scrapings to make cream gravy and she'd miss her chance at the pot liquor. It would be so good sopped up with a piece of bread.

Molly shifted her bulky body and nearly toppled Copper off her stool. "Easy, girl," Copper soothed. She leaned her head against the cow's warm side and slowed her hands. *Swish, swish, swish,* the milk flowed. Molly relaxed. Her gentle snores filled the stall, mesmerizing.

Finally Copper was finished. She'd just reached beneath herself for the milk stool when suddenly she felt a hand upon her shoulder. "Remy? You've come back . . ." She whirled around, the little stool wobbling beneath her, and saw him. Her heart soared. She must be dreaming. "Oh, Simon. Is it really you?"

He pulled her up into an embrace. "I'm sorry," he whispered hoarsely into her ear. "I couldn't stay away. I couldn't bear it any longer."

Until that moment she'd thought she might be able to live without him. "I'm glad. I'm so very glad you're here."

"Are you?" he asked. "I was afraid your feelings toward me had changed. It seemed I'd only imagined our time together."

The light was failing in the barn. It would soon be dark, but she felt a radiance from within that was surely as bright as a cloudless June day. She pressed her cheek, warm from Molly's heat, against Simon's cold stubbly face.

His hand rasped across his jaw. "I need a shave," he apologized, "but I rode straight through. I took loan of a horse from the livery and traded him out halfway here. I was too anxious to stay overnight at a wayside inn."

She put her hands on either side of his face. "I can't believe it's you."

"Believe it," he replied. "I'm here and I want this—" He kissed her, a kiss so filled with longing that she had to hold to his arms to keep from swooning. "And I want an answer to my question."

"Ask," she said, her mind finally sure of her answer.

"Boy howdy!" Willy called from the barn door. "We saw a strange horse. That be yours, Doc?"

They took no more notice of Willy's voice than they did of the waning light or the dirty barn floor as Simon sank to one knee. He took Copper's hand in his own, kissed her palm, and asked with great sincerity, "Laura Grace Brown, will you marry me and love me and live with me for the rest of your life?"

"Do you want me to put your horse up, Doc?" Willy persisted, unnoticed still.

Copper looked down. She could barely see the man who sought her pledge. The only light around them was what spilled in from outside where Willy stood in the open door.

"Hey!" Willy barged along. "Can you stay for supper, Doc? Mam's made squirrel and gravy."

After a silent prayer for guidance, she gave him the answer he'd traveled miles and miles to receive. "Yes, Dr. Corbett, I'll marry you and love you and live with you for the rest of our lives together."

"Whoopee!" Willy danced a jig. "Sissy's getting married!" His voice faded as he ran toward the house. "Daddy! Get the firecrackers. Sissy's getting married."

Simon stood and swept her off her feet. He twirled her around and around, then set her down and threw back his head and laughed a great joyous laugh. "Thank You, Lord!" he praised. "I'm the happiest man alive."

The whole family awaited Copper and Simon on the porch. A pool of warm yellow lamplight lay on the plank floor just outside the kitchen window, and the fireplace glinted a welcome through the open door.

"Come on up here, boy." Daddy pumped Simon's hand. "I hear congratulations are in order."

"Watch out!" Willy lobbed fireworks high overhead.

Bang! Bang! Bangbangbangbang! came the retort.

"I like 'em tied together. Don't you, Daniel?"

Mam embraced Copper, and she could feel tears upon her mother's face. "Mam, don't cry."

"Tears of joy, Daughter, just tears of joy."

After supper, they lingered at the table and talked of the future. Simon wanted to marry at once. He wanted to take Copper back to Lexington with him.

"She'll not marry at sixteen, Dr. Corbett," Mam replied.

"Then March," he acquiesced. "We'll marry on her birth date, or I'm afraid we'll have to elope."

"Antelope?" Willy interrupted. "We don't have no antelopes in these parts. Do we, Daddy? Just a bunch of buffalos way over yonder near where we go sledding."

"June," Mam settled the matter, "and not one day sooner."

Simon decided to stay over for a few days. He bunked with Daniel. Daddy slept with Willy in Copper's bed, and Copper slept with Mam. What little she slept. Simon was only a room away, just across the front room. The bedroom doors they kept closed all day were open for the night to let in some heat from the banked fireplace, and she fancied she could tell his snores from her father's.

She desperately wanted to get out of bed and see if there was enough hot water left in the kettle for a cup of tea, but she didn't want to disturb anyone. And what if Simon got up? He couldn't see her in her nightdress, even if he was a doctor.

Earlier as they prepared for bed Mam had said she needed to have a little talk with Copper. She spoke of what marriage meant, all the changes that would occur, and how Copper couldn't be selfish because she would now be responsible for the happiness of someone else. Simon would always come first, she'd said, and Copper must always obey him. She talked about modesty and reverence and something from the Bible called "cleaving." And at the end, after she'd turned down the wick on the coal-oil lamp and the flame had sputtered and gone out, she patted Copper's hand and said, "He will want to sleep with you, Daughter. It won't be so bad. You must do your Christian duty."

Copper mulled that over as she lay in bed. Why was Mam so mysterious and so serious? Why was sharing a bed a duty? After all, she hadn't slept a night alone since the boys were born. Would a grown man take up much more space than two wiggling brothers? As long as Simon didn't hog the covers, she didn't think she'd mind sleeping with him.

Copper tiptoed to the window and drew back the curtain. The moon was high and full—just one wispy cloud scuttled across its surface. The round-faced man in the moon looked down on her, and she imagined she saw a wink.

She bowed her head and wished she could ask her heavenly Father all the questions that churned in her mind: *What is it like in the city? What will become of Molly and Paw-paw? Will my family be all right without me? What does* cleave *mean? Mam made it sound a little sinister . . . cleave.*

Instead, she prayed for what she knew she would receive: the grace to endure whatever lay before her.

The day before Simon was to leave, he and Copper walked along Troublesome Creek. It was frozen over, a dusting of grainy snow swirling on its glassy surface. Huge pines and cedars sighed their lonesome songs as the wind swept through their thick branches.

She asked him some of her questions, all except the sleeping and the cleaving—she couldn't quite get that out—and he did his best to reassure her. He described the home they would be sharing, and Copper liked the sound of the big porch out front and the gardens and stable out back, with a stall for Molly if she wanted to take her. Of course she did! Simon said he would send someone for the animal, but she wouldn't need to milk the cow herself—he had a man for that. Copper didn't argue, but she knew in her heart that no one would be milking her cow but her.

It was good to hear of her future home and know that Simon would do everything in his power to make her comfortable there, but one thing still burdened her heart. Gathering up all her courage, unsure that she wanted to hear what he would say, she told Simon about her daddy and the terrible red rag.

"I know," he said. "Your father told me."

She turned to him, her cheeks numb from the chill. "What does it mean, Simon? I'm so afraid for him."

Simon took her in his arms. "I'm so sorry, Laura Grace, but the cough, the blood, the shortness of breath . . . his weight loss. It's consumption, you know."

She felt herself go very still. The air in her lungs was replaced by his heavy grievous words, and she would have fallen to the cold, cold ground were it not for his support. "Why?"

"I don't have that answer, Laura Grace. Only God knows. But that mine he works . . . it's so damp all the time . . . coal dust settles in the lungs. And the tobacco he uses adds terrible insult."

She put her hands to her face and leaned her head against his chest. "Isn't there some treatment . . . some medicine?"

"Will and I talked at length when I was here last summer–"

"He told you then?"

"He's known for a while, sweetheart. I recommended a sanitarium in a different climate with dry air and no wet winters. I've seen good results with some of the patients I've sent there."

"That wouldn't be Philadelphia, would it?" she said, her voice shaking with anger.

"No. But, Laura Grace, your mother doesn't know, and he made me pledge not to tell her. You mustn't be angry with her."

"Is my father dying?"

Their wandering walk had led them back to the barn, and they stepped inside its warmth before he replied. "Oh no, sweetheart, not for a long while. But you do need to understand this won't just go away. He does need treatment."

"Where is this sanitarium?"

"It's in Texas–Sabinal Canyon. The infirmary is in one of the most beautiful places I have ever seen. The canyon has stretches of prairie and timber, knots of oak and pecan trees, and gushing mountain streams with bright, clear running waters that the locals say never run dry. The air is as pure as when God first made it. I don't think there is a better place for consumptives."

Copper walked to the little window. She could see nothing that was not barren–the lifeless trees, the heavy gray sky threatening snow and more snow, a curve of the frozen creek. "We have to talk to him, convince him to go there. I don't care what Mam wants."

Simon came up behind her and circled her with his arms. He leaned his chin into the curve of her neck. "It's his life, Laura Grace. You mustn't interfere. Your father is a very proud man, and he wants to take his family to a place of safety, a place where Grace will be happy without him, if need be."

"You can see, can't you, Simon? I can't leave him."

His heavy sigh warmed her cheek. "I will do whatever you want. Nothing matters to me, save your happiness."

"I love you, Simon Corbett." She turned toward his kiss.

"And I love you, my heart," he answered, his mouth against hers.

CHAPTER 30

After Simon left, the snow that had threatened for days fell softly, swirling like feathers from a goose-down pillow around Copper's face and leaving a fresh taste on her tongue when she paused to catch a flake. She climbed steadily up the mountain behind her house to the old cemetery. The gate creaked on rusty hinges when she shoved it open.

Funny that she'd ended up here. Giving no thought to her destination, she barely paused long enough to grab her coat and a scarf for her head before she had rushed from the house. She'd never meant to upset Mam when she found her at the stove stirring potato soup in her methodical way—clockwise, always clockwise. She thought her mam would be glad when she told her she was going to Philadelphia with them . . . to help them get settled. She and Simon would wait to marry. Why, he might even decide to bring his practice to the mountains. Then she'd have everything she wanted—him *and* Troublesome Creek.

Mam had whirled around, slinging bits of soup from her wooden spoon all over the kitchen. Her eyes flashed like struck flint when she said, "Young lady, I'll have no more of your dillydallying. Your father and I can manage perfectly well without your help. Decide for yourself, but if you don't love Dr. Corbett enough to move to Lexington for him and be a helpmeet to him, then you don't love him enough to marry him!"

That's when Copper had fled, the smell of scorched potatoes following her like a pall. She paused now, just inside the gate, to study the resting place dug for the old skeleton she'd found when she'd fallen into the hole. The grave was already sinking, pulling away from its edges as if its tenant were restless. *Perhaps,* she fancied, *the skeleton is yearning to join its fellows in the valley of dry bones, where it could be made flesh.* She stretched out her arm and quoted from Ezekiel: "'O ye dry bones, hear the word of the Lord.'"

They'd never figured out who the skeleton belonged to. Daddy had carried it home, and folks came to offer their opinion. Brother Isaac said from the heft of the leg bones it had to be a man. John Pelfrey had reckoned the skull was too large to have contained the brain of a woman. She'd socked him on the arm when he said that, and he'd chased her around the barn. . . .

John . . . just the thought of him still caused such pain. He'd been her buddy, her best friend. She missed him so much. She'd received a penny post from San Francisco with a picture of the ocean and palm trees on the front. *"Pest,"* he'd written, *"this ain't nothing like Troublesome Creek, but I sure liked the train ride. If it don't work out being a sailor, I think I'll ride the rails. That's what they call it. Riding the rails. Your friend, John Pelfrey."*

Some things hurt so much it was better not to think on them. Copper walked on. A broken tree branch lay across the narrow grave she sought. She dragged it off and removed a handful of last summer's daisies, now brown and lifeless, from the coffee-tin vase she'd put on her mother's grave. She wiped snow from the gravestone, then knelt to trace the inscription carved into the granite face:

Julia Taylor Brown: Beloved Wife and Mother
1843–1866
A rose plucked too soon

"Mama," she entreated, "what must I do?"

Silence greeted her inquiry. She glanced at the tiny depressions that marked the ground at the foot of her grandparents' graves, all that was left of her sisters and her brother, dead these many years, sinking with time back to the earth that bore the weight of them so gently.

She was so glad Daddy had brought her here back in the autumn. They'd walked the path to the creek where her mother had been taken by the flood, and on to the holler up Troublesome where Daniel Pelfrey had found the body, and then here, the cemetery where the woman who gave her life rested. Daddy had held her while she sobbed, and he told her how she'd surely saved his sanity then, how she'd been his reason for going on.

He'd said she was his gift from God. She sighed to remember how his story salved her conscience. She hadn't caused her mother's death after all.

She rested her back against the stone marker, feeling useless, like the second woman in a too-small kitchen. She thought of Simon—his strength, his kindness, the feel of his arms around her. She couldn't bear to think of her life without him.

A song came to her and she sang a line, "'Savior, like a shepherd lead us . . . ,'" then hummed a line. The melody led to a prayer. "Savior, like a shepherd lead *me*. Forgive my selfishness and show me the path You would have me take."

Copper sat perfectly still, her head bowed on her knees. Snow piled up around her shoes, and a sudden arctic gust plucked the scarf off her head and settled it around her shoulders. She stood, pulling a strand of hair from her mouth and wiping her nose against her mitten. The wind had turned bitter, and the snow stung her cheeks like nettles, like Mam's arrow-tipped volley of words had done. The sky had turned a dark pewter gray. Time to get home. Looked like a blizzard brewing.

The gravestones blurred, but she could make out her grandmother's: Mary Lee Brown. And there lay John's great-granny, just fifteen as the story went, when she married Ben Pelfrey. She patted her mother's stone.

The answer lies in history. All these women buried here left some place dear to them. My great-grandmother faced the fear of Indian attacks to settle in these mountains. Her mother sailed the vast ocean, leaving all that was familiar—even her own language—behind. My own mother and then Mam left dear comforts to come as strangers to these hills. How can I do less for the man I love?

"All right then, Dr. Simon Corbett," she vowed, as if he could hear her. "'Whither thou goest, I will go. . . . Thy people shall be my people.' Hopefully your sister, Alice, will take to me like Naomi took to Ruth." She dusted her snow-covered skirts and started off down the hill. "I've always wanted a sister."

CHAPTER 31

June 1, 1883

A day of warm sunshine and soft summer breezes filtered through pine needles and mountain laurel blossoms. Copper had been up since dawn, when Cock-a-Doodle preached his morning sermon. She felt the strength of Simon's presence so acutely it made her shiver. He was staying just a mountain away at his mother's cousin's cabin—the poor old soul had passed after a sudden decline. Mam let Simon visit, but he couldn't stay over. People might talk, now that they were officially sweethearts.

Copper didn't know what to do with herself, so she sat on the porch in a silk wrapper from her trousseau and rocked. Her cow was already gone, taken away by a man Simon had sent to fetch her. Molly bawled and bawled when he led her to the waiting wagon, twisting her heavy square head around to look at Copper, her big brown eyes rolling in fear. Copper had tried to reassure her with handfuls of sweet grain, but Molly wouldn't touch it. "I'll see you soon, pet," she'd called as the wagon left the barnyard, her voice thick with unshed tears.

It will be good to see Molly again, she thought. Her corset pinched if she slumped the slightest bit so she sat up straight, sticking her feet out to admire her silk opera pumps. They were the color of just-shucked oyster shells, and her hose matched exactly. Her freshly pressed dress hung on the chiffonier door. The leaves on the apple tree rustled when a warm zephyr blew across the yard–she should have covered her hair. Mam had dressed it in ornate ropes of copper, and she wore a narrow crown of cream-colored beaded ribbon and tiny pink rosebuds from the bush in the side yard.

Mam was in the kitchen, cautioning the boys, who wore new suits. Daddy had one too. Nobody in the family looked like themselves, but Mam said they all needed to get used to wearing nice things.

Butterflies fluttered in her belly again. She couldn't wait to see Simon.

Grace studied her daughter through the door. The rusted screen blurred her vision, or was it the prism of her tears that made Laura Grace seem just a shadow . . . as if she were already gone? Grace dug her nails into the palms of her hands. She would not cry. She would not.

Memories tiptoed to the front of her mind and played

themselves out against her shimmering eyelids. Laura Grace, a baby in her lap, playing with her pearls . . . her first steps, wobbling across the floor until she fell hard against the hearth and reached up with a little teardrop and a crooked smile for Grace to make it better . . . her delight in storms. "Again!" she'd cry when the thunder boomed and the lightning cracked, her arms around Grace's legs, her head thrown back. Just a baby, really, but not afraid. "Again!"

"Mam? Daddy's coming with the buggy," she heard Laura Grace call. "We'd better get my dress."

She reached in her pocket for her handkerchief and withdrew instead the letter that had come in the mail just yesterday. The letter postmarked Sabinal Canyon, Texas. She'd cornered Dr. Corbett when he visited in January, and he'd told her a truth she hadn't really wanted to know. Sighing, she put the envelope back. Time enough to talk to Will about a change in plans after Laura Grace was gone. A headache blossomed like a malevolent rose at the back of her head. Time enough then.

The little church in the valley of the mountains was packed with women and children as Laura Grace Brown entered on the arm of her father. The men waited outside, guns cocked and ready to fire in celebration.

An audible sigh went up from all the ladies when she walked down the short narrow aisle. She was a beautiful bride. Her dress was the prettiest thing they'd ever seen, the color of the richest cream, all lace at the top, made of silk so soft every hand reached out to touch it. The back of her skirt had a rounded bustle and a short train that whispered as she walked. In her gloved hands she carried a bouquet of white service berries and full-blown pink roses atop a small black Bible. Long streamers of beaded ribbon, nearly reaching the floor, fell from the flowers.

The stranger she was marrying was dressed like a judge in a gray serge, long-jacketed suit that nipped in at the waist. His shoes were as shiny as a lump of wet coal, and he dabbed at his eyes with one dove-gray-gloved finger as she came toward him. One of the little Brown twins held his top hat, and the other stood there by the preacher with a little silk pillow that held Copper's ring.

Will was hardly recognizable. He'd clipped his full bushy beard so close, the shape of his chin was visible for the first time anyone could remember. Some sitting there remembered when it had turned white overnight and shed a tear for that sad day. It sure wouldn't be the same on Troublesome now that Will's wife was taking him away. She was a fey one, that Grace Brown.

Brother Isaac stepped before them, grinning from ear to ear. Like everyone else, he'd always been partial to Copper. Her groom took her hand and kissed the back of her glove. She blushed the color of her flowers. Oh, they made a handsome couple.

Before the watching crowd could catch its breath, Copper followed her groom in pledging her troth. They could have heard a leaf twirl in the wind, so quiet was it in the church when she followed Brother Isaac's words: "I, Laura Grace Brown, take you, Simon Alexander Corbett, to be my husband. I will honor you and obey you, cherish you and love you until death do us part."

Then they were pronounced, and the doctor took her in his arms and kissed her full on the mouth before them all, kissed her as if he'd been waiting an awfully long time. Every woman commenced fanning herself with the pasteboard fans provided new just for the ceremony.

The men shot their guns into the air in celebration as the new husband and wife ran through the church door. Copper stopped long enough to cut a length of ribbon from her bouquet for every little girl in the crowd. Then she gave her flowers to Emilee Pelfrey, who would see that they were placed on her mother's grave.

Dr. Corbett pumped Will's hand, then swept Copper off her feet and carried her to the waiting surrey.

"Hurray! Hurray!" the crowd sang out amid the gunfire as the carriage pulled away.

"Wait! Wait!" they heard Copper call. Then the carriage stopped and she was out the door and running to her stepmother, seizing her with a fierce embrace before running back to the surrey again.

Cheers changed to laughter as they all looked at the back window of the buggy and saw Paw-paw settle his old-dog self as upright as a man between the couple, his stiff leg like a lover's embrace behind the bride's neck.

Copper leaned out the window as far as she dared, waving until her friends and family faded from view. Tears dimmed her vision, but a flash of red on the ridge high above the road caught her eye, and she fancied she saw a slight figure running there, keeping pace with the buggy.

Making a fist, she tapped her chest in the place directly over her heart and kept her eyes on the ridge until Simon flicked the reins and the horse pulled away, away from the swiftly flowing water of Troublesome Creek.

❧ About the Author ❧

A retired registered nurse of twenty-five years, Jan Watson specialized in the care of newborns and their mothers. A charter member of Southern Acres Christian Church, she lives in Lexington, Kentucky. Jan has three grown sons.

Always a late bloomer, she didn't begin to write until her husband bought her a word processor for Christmas seven years ago. Challenged to see writing as a ministry at a writer's conference in 2001, Jan began to take her stories seriously and so *Troublesome Creek* was born.

Jan's hobbies are reading, antiquing, and taking long walks with her Jack Russell terrier, Maggie.

She hopes to bring readers more of Copper Brown's adventures in the future.

You may contact Jan by writing to her in care of Tyndale House Author Relations, P.O. Box 80, Wheaton, IL 60189; or visit her Web site at www.janwatson.net.